BLOOD AND WRATH

Grim Grave

Gravefiction Publishing

I want to dedicate this book to my dear friends Eliza and MKD. I am so grateful to have the two of you in my life. This world and this story wouldn't exist without the two of you. Thnk You...

CONTENTS

Vegence only begets more sorrow...

GRIM GRAVE

KEY LOCATIONS

Vostaylia(Vo-Stay-Lee-ah) : Country where the Vostaylians live. Known for often having a cold climate and red trees that cover the land.

Wescreas (Wes-cre-es): The country of the Wescreans. A lush land of greenery. Beautiful grasslands and long barren roads.

Fodmery(Fod-Mer-e): The capital of Wescreas where the ruling king and their family lives. Mostly a place with nobles, warriors and a few working commoners.

Scarstone Mountain: A valley of mountains that separate Wescreas and Vostaylia.

THE BEGINNING

The sound of metal against metal echoed loudly. The smell of ash quickly filled the room.

Vlatka's eyes shot open as she sat up to find herself alone in bed. Her eyes scanned the room to find her lover. It took no time to spot him—locked in combat with a man clad in dark-colored armor.

The warrior wore armor in a dark gray color scheme with a red cloak attached to it. Vlatka knew where this warrior hailed from. He was a Sentinel, the name given to the warriors of her country. She had no doubt in her mind who was attacking them.

The Crimson Sentinels of Vostaylia had found them.

Her lover and the Sentinel were swinging their weapons with a speed that left Vlatka frozen in awe. Then she noticed two other Sentinels in the room—but they had already been killed.

Jorah. That was his name. The man she had come to love. From the moment they met, she had come to know he was steadfast in protecting the things he cared about.

His people were known to be herbalists, and they avoided killing others. Seeing him forced to kill bothered her deeply, especially because she had no idea how it affected him mentally. For the last few years, he had been forced to fight—to protect her and his people.

She watched as Jorah took a deep breath and stepped away from the Sentinel. Once he had space, he swung his sword. It made no physical contact with the enemy, but Vlatka was aware of what he had done. From spending time with his people, she had learned they dabbled in spiritual affairs.

Such practices allowed them to use their life force to affect the veil between the living and the spiritual. The Sentinel took a step forward and dropped his sword. Vlatka watched as a deep cut appeared on his body, stretching from his left shoulder to his right hip. A river of red drenched the wooden floor as the Sentinel collapsed to the ground.

Jorah stood silently, holding his sword, blood dripping from it. His sword didn't resemble anything like those the Sentinels used. It had a slight curve and gradually tapered to a sharp, narrow tip. She saw no guard on it, but carvings were inscribed along the blade.

She stood in awe at what she had just witnessed. Jorah had told her about spiritual energy—it was the product of manipulating one's life force. Near-death experiences or contact with a spirit could force one to unlock this sixth sense, known as spiritual awareness. Vlatka often wondered if she would ever reach such supernatural growth. Although, in human society, things like this were considered sorcery and condemned.

When Vlatka was young, she would hear stories of people claiming they could commune with the dead. Everyone would brush them off as scammers trying to profit off people's grief. She never expected the spiritual world to be real—at least not in a way that the living could interact with, unless they were deeply connected to it.

Jorah had told her his people had developed such a strong connection because of the tragedy that destroyed their home. Something that could take other people years to master had been bestowed upon many of them. His people were known as Hiorians, and they came from a place called Hioria.

What Vlatka saw just now was what Jorah called a ghost slash. From what she understood, some people could harness their life force to create spiritual energy. This energy could be used to affect both the spiritual and the living realm. Attacks that couldn't be seen were terrifying.

"What is happening?" Vlatka finally shouted.

Jorah, winded, started walking toward Vlatka. He still

gripped his sword tightly as he placed a hand on her shoulder.

"We must run! Your people have found us—and somehow gained da help of—"

Before he could finish, a loud sound invaded Vlatka's ears. Wings flapping. A screech so loud it pierced her soul. A chill crept down her spine, and the hairs on her neck stood on end.

Before she could react, the ceiling was ripped open.

She looked up to see a creature with eyes black as night. It had a large set of bat-like wings and claw-like feet. This was what people had come to call a vampyr.

Vlatka had heard stories as a child—about a man who had heard whispers from a spirit trapped in the spiritual world. The spirit desired to be freed, and the man had become so fascinated that he formed a cult. This cult helped him conduct a ritual where he sacrificed himself in hopes of summoning the spirit.

Instead, it was believed he returned from the other side as a monster. Then he began to turn others into what he had become. Now their land was plagued with these monstrosities, practically invincible. Being bitten by one often proved to be a death sentence—even if the victim survived the attack.

The creature before Vlatka now stared at her and screeched loudly. The sound shattered every pane of glass in the room. Not only that, but Vlatka could feel her body vibrate from the ominous sound.

Then the creature broke all the way through the ceiling. Jorah pushed Vlatka toward the wall. He held up his sword, ready to protect her. The creature lunged as Jorah swung his sword downward. Despite its size, the vampyr was agile.

It evaded Jorah's attack and shoved him aside. The vampyr approached Vlatka, staring at her with its midnight eyes. It was like staring into an abyss—terrifying and endless. She instinctively held her stomach to protect her baby.

Jorah tackled the vampyr and pulled it away from her. The two struggled as the vampyr tried to flap its wings and fly out of the building. Jorah managed to plunge a shard of glass he had picked up into its neck. It let out a loud screech as it lifted him into the air.

Vlatka stumbled over to Jorah, but it was too late. The creature carried him into the sky.

She quickly rushed over to Jorah's fur coat, still hanging on a hook in the corner of the room. Wrapping it around herself, Vlatka rushed outside, hoping to get a better view of what was happening above. When she stepped outside, she saw the battle raging on.

The field was littered with bodies of Hiorian children and women. The Hiorian men and women still able to fight were overpowering the Sentinels. Unfortunately, cannons were being fired—taking the Hiorians down with ease. She also saw more vampyrs flying overhead.

Why did this have to happen now? Why did they pursue the Hiorians so far from their homeland? It made no sense—until Vlatka began to wonder if it was because of her. Did they find out she was still alive and living among them? If so, who told them where she was?

So many questions made her head spin. And then—the horror continued. A loud thud landed on the roof of her small shack. Vlatka turned to see the vampyr and Jorah rolling down, crashing into the snow, still fighting.

The vampyr dug its fangs deep into Jorah's neck. He cried out in pain.

Vlatka screamed.

She tried to rush over to help, but he glared at her. Vlatka froze as she watched Jorah plunge his sword into the creature's neck. She saw his eyes glow. He gritted his teeth and dropped to one knee. The vampyr still had its mouth latched onto his throat.

A burst of blood erupted from the vampyr's neck as its body slowly pulled away from its head.

Jorah dropped his sword, breathing heavily. He tore the vampyr's head from his shoulder and threw it aside.

Vlatka stumbled over to him and caught him in her arms.

His face had become pale. His skin was cold. Slowly, Vlatka's eyes welled with tears as she caressed his face. She saw the light fading from his eyes.

"You must stand so we can flee," Vlatka whimpered.

"I am sorry... I shan't be able..."

The light had faded from his eyes as he let go of his sword. Vlatka began to wail as she held him in her arms. His body had quickly grown cold. The pain in her chest was unbearable as she held him tightly.

The sound of boots crunching the snowy surface of the ground caused her to look around. She saw three Sentinels approaching. They all had their swords drawn and pointed at her. Another approached with a banner that bore a sword with a winged serpent wrapped around it. This was the banner of the Dracul family.

She heard the men begin to chuckle underneath their helmets. Vlatka could feel her heart pounding as her blood began to boil. Despite the cold, she felt extremely hot as rage overtook her. She gently laid the lifeless body of her lover in the snow.

She picked up his sword and held it in front of her. Growing up, her father had kept her away from weapons and battle. After his death—and getting to know Jorah—she began to learn how to fight, with both a sword and hand-to-hand.

The Sentinels' chuckling became full-out laughter as Vlatka stared at them with menacing eyes. She knew it was because she was with child. Not only that, but her child could be born at any day. Her body ached and her feet were freezing.

Before anything could take place, she saw a group of people walking toward her. One was a man wearing a cloak dyed in the royal color of the crown. Clearly, someone had taken the throne after killing her father and mother. It was likely they were trying to kill Vlatka to ensure no heir of her father's remained alive.

She couldn't see his face, as the helmet he wore concealed it. One of the king's guards was the only person she could think of. If it was one of them, then she would make sure they were punished accordingly for their betrayal.

Behind the masked king were a group of people wearing purple robes with a symbol on the left side. The symbol appeared to be wings with a set of eyes and a dark cloud surrounding it. They were the Acolytes of Vetala.

Stepping from behind all of them was a man that surprised Vlatka. A tall, slender man with pointed ears stared down at her. His brown skin and light brown hair made it clear what he was: a Hiorian—one thought to have died.

This man's name was Jiya Ashspell. He was the head of a family that had mostly been wiped out during a battle with the vampyrs. Vlatka couldn't understand how he was alive—or why he was with the enemies of his people.

"It is a shame Jorah died before I got to see him again," Jiya said, pretending to sound disheartened.

"How are you alive, and why are you with them?" Vlatka asked loudly.

"Hiorians can endure a great deal of sufferin'. Well... most of dem can."

Jiya's eyes were transfixed on Jorah's lifeless body. Vlatka took a step forward, but the Sentinels moved as if to block her. Jiya quickly stepped forward and gestured for them to lower their weapons.

The area was illuminated by the bright flames engulfing the little village the Hiorians had built. She couldn't believe this was happening. Then she began to blame herself. If she had died with her family, would all of this have been prevented?

Jiya walked over to Vlatka, now standing only a foot away. She lunged at him and swung the sword. Instead of evading, he caught the blade with his bare hand. Vlatka's eyes widened in horror—she couldn't believe what he had done.

"When we arrived here from our homeland, the chosen elders of our families were selected. My family did not choose me, but instead my brudda," Jiya explained.

Vlatka hardly paid attention to his words—still stunned by his ability to stop her sword strike with his hand. As he stood before her, he felt like a giant. His presence seemed to take up all the air around her.

"Jorah's papa, A'Jorah, was one of da elders. I told him and my brudda it would be unwise to try and form a relationship wit you humans, but they did not listen!" Jiya exclaimed.

Vlatka's sword snapped in half, and she stumbled forward. Jiya stepped aside as she fell to the ground. She cried out in pain, grabbing at her stomach. The cold air made her shiver as she placed her hands on the ground to push herself up.

"I still cannot fathom what has behooved you to ally with the humans who betrayed you!"

"They are allied wit *me!*"

"What of thy mate? This is her family you are slaying!" Vlatka exclaimed.

The rage and conviction in Jiya's eyes wavered briefly. Vlatka had hoped he might come to his senses. But sadly, that rage quickly returned.

"She abandoned me. I was left for dead! My family burned and was slaughtered!"

"Then why do the same to thy own people? To the family of the woman you loved?"

Jiya stood silently for a few seconds. "I will do anythin' to save my people. Even if it means I have to destroy dem."

His words were as cold as the frosty winds that lashed Vlatka's face. She stared up at him in disbelief, unable to comprehend what he meant. Then she looked around and saw figures emerging from the forest—their eyes glowing a pale green.

"I discovered a means to summon da dead back to their bodies. I call these people... revenants."

"Why not use them to destroy Vostaylia and the humans living there?"

"I was shunned by my own people for not agreein' wit da leaders. Then, after my conflict wit A'Jorah—and wit my own brudda—I got cast out completely."

Jiya knelt beside Vlatka as she remained on the ground. She

could see the rage in his eyes. Even when she had first met him, he always seemed angry. He had always been reluctant to interact with her people.

She even recalled him berating Jorah for spending time with her. It had always been clear that he didn't trust humans. As much as she didn't want to admit it, she couldn't deny that she understood him.

"Also... Jorah is da reason my daughta is dead."

"Preposterous!"

"She loved him, but his gaze never glimpsed her. Her mama told me she saw da two of you together, and it broke her. My sweet lil girl... killed herself."

"I am truly sorry, Jiya. But that doesn't mean you should betray your people."

"In due time, I'm sure dey'll understand why it must be dis way."

Jiya stood tall over Vlatka and waved his hand. As he turned away, a blur passed her.

A tall figure lunged at Jiya. He stumbled back in surprise as a knife cut across his face.

Standing before Vlatka was Jorah.

Blood poured from the wound on his neck. Vlatka could hear his ragged breathing as he stood his ground. As she struggled to her feet, her nightmare became worse.

Jiya roared in a fit of rage as he rammed a sword into Jorah's stomach. Jorah stumbled back but held onto Jiya. They struggled for a moment before Jorah dropped to one knee.

"Till our next full moon... my love..."

Jorah's eyes met Vlatka's as the light faded permanently from them. Jiya pulled the sword from his body and stepped back. Vlatka cried out as she rushed to catch Jorah's falling body.

Jiya turned away as the Sentinels rushed her. They grabbed her and tore her from her lover. She roared in fury, struggling to get free. But being on the verge of giving birth, she had no strength left. Her attempts to bite and scratch were useless against their armor.

"To see you survive such a perfidious night, 'tis forsooth a blessing, Princess," said the man Vlatka assumed to be the new king.

He removed his helmet, revealing dark, luscious hair falling around his face. His dark brown eyes stared at her with triumph.

Vlatka recognized him instantly—from her father's kingsguard.

Sorin Dracul. Her father's brother. A man he adored and trusted with his life.

Seeing him now infuriated her. He had betrayed his own blood. Sworn an oath of loyalty—and broken it.

"'Tis you who slew my parents?" she asked, easily slipping back into her native tongue.

Sorin smiled as the Sentinels forced her to her knees. Her teeth rattled as the cold began to consume her. Sorin leaned close so they were eye to eye.

"I had forewarned him that such a day would come," Sorin said smugly.

"Why did you betray my father?"

"A time to avouch for the crown had presented itself before me."

Vlatka spat in his face, and the grin disappeared. He stood upright and struck her across the face with the back of his hand. Her skin split where something sharp on his gauntlet had cut her.

"You should be beholden to me. I could offer you to my Sentinels. Alas, Sir Jiya has proposed something more vital."

Sorin gestured to the hooded men to approach. Vlatka felt goosebumps rise—not from the cold, but from fear.

She knew what was being planned.

And she didn't like it at all.

*

A few hours passed before Vlatka found herself at a tower. She was chained and being dragged toward it. People were everywhere, watching her as she was taken. Her toes and fingers were numb as she struggled to walk.

Outside the tower stood a large stake driven into the ground. Symbols were etched into the snow around it, forming a wide circle. They were going to use her for their ritual.

The hooded figures placed her beside the stake and brought more silver chains to bind her to it. As she struggled to break free, another hooded figure approached, carrying a bowl filled with liquid. This one had long, dark brown hair and, from what Vlatka could see, feminine features.

Two of the hooded figures held Vlatka's head still as she screamed and thrashed, trying to get away. The woman forced the bowl to Vlatka's lips. A red liquid slipped into her mouth. She coughed, trying to turn away, but they forced the black substance down her throat.

A metallic taste lingered as they finally stepped back. Vlatka gasped for air, tears streaming down her cheeks. Then the others began pouring what she feared was blood over her. They bathed her in it until she thought she might drown.

She couldn't understand why these people would summon something that would likely kill them all. And to subject one of their own to this? It was unforgivable.

"Lay these words to your heart! What you desire to bring upon us from the other side by killing me will not come to pass. Only wrath will be bestowed upon you—and it will be mine! I will burn this world asunder! Pray to the spirit you worship, for when I return, I'll send all of ye to meet him!" Vlatka's voice echoed through the night.

The woman with the hood stepped forward and removed it, revealing a strikingly beautiful face—she appeared only a few years older than Vlatka. Other robed figures began placing wood around the stake. She also saw them scattering powders and herbs.

The woman was handed a torch and stepped closer.

As Vlatka's vision blurred, she thought she saw a figure

in the distance—someone with a hood and a lantern. This strange figure had an aura about them that made Vlatka wonder who they could possibly be. How were they connected to these people?

What exactly was she seeing? She couldn't be sure. The figure slowly vanished. A part of her hoped it was someone coming to rescue her from this nightmare.

But saving the damsel in distress was for fairy tales.

Vlatka returned her attention to the woman before her.

"Then take heed of my name, if you think a gainrising is possible. My name is Roxana Toma."

The name made it clear—Roxana was from Vostaylia. Knowing that only fueled Vlatka's rage.

Roxana tossed the torch onto the wood. Slowly, flames began to rise around Vlatka. The blazing heat began eating at her skin, but she did not scream. Her eyes remained locked on Roxana, filled with the desire to kill her.

Her spirit would not rest until she had the chance to take revenge on those who destroyed her home, killed her family, and massacred her lover's people.

Even death would not be enough to keep her from vengeance.

CHAPTER 1

The trees whispered as the wind blew through the forest. A soft drizzle of rain was falling from the night sky. Gentle moonlight gave the forest some illumination in the dark.

A wanderer stumbled silently through the trees. They had no real direction, only that they were on a path of darkness. They stopped when they came across a figure kneeling. He had swords in his back and was surrounded by a pool of blood being washed away by the drizzling rain.

The dead man had pointed ears and brown locks. The wanderer also noticed his brown skin—it made it clear he was a Hiorian. The wanderer stared at the swords in the man's back. It only took a glance to recognize the craftsmanship of the weapons. They were from a country known as Wescreas.

The figure knelt beside the Hiorian as her soaked, raven-colored hair covered her face. She examined the man before standing back up. He was dead, and the smell of blood was becoming overwhelming. She needed to keep moving.

"Things have certainly gotten worse over the years," she muttered to herself.

As she trudged further through the forest, she found more bodies littering the floor. Hiorians as well as armored men. She saw a flag staked into the ground with a symbol on it—a shield with a horse. The wanderer knew this symbol belonged to the royal family of Jacquard. She was amused to see they still ruled in Wescreas.

The warriors of this country called themselves Chevaliers. V recalled them being known for their skill in combat while on horseback. Their swords were often longer, and some wielded weapons known as rapiers. The Wescreans' style had always focused on speed and lethality.

Unlike the Sentinels of Vostaylia, the Chevaliers didn't wear heavy armor. The Sentinels weren't as fast, but their armor allowed them to withstand great punishment. The Vostaylians, however, were superior in archery and close combat.

As she stood motionless, her ears picked up something faint —a sound like a heartbeat, but it was growing quieter. She looked among the bodies and walked slowly.

It didn't take long to find a woman leaning against a tree, bleeding from a stomach wound. Her brown skin was losing its warmth. Her thick hair, styled into locks that swept to the left side, was dripping wet.

As V stood over her, she noticed twin blades at her sides. They were fairly short, with curved ends. The wanderer couldn't make out what material they were made from, but the blades seemed well-suited for cleaving enemies and blocking attacks.

The woman's silvery eyes looked up at the wanderer. V was surprised to see no fear in them. Instead, the woman smiled and slowly shook her head.

"I had hoped to meet a Soulseer, but instead I am greeted by a cursed spirit," the Hiorian woman choked.

The raven-haired wanderer knelt beside the wounded warrior. Her sapphire-blue eyes focused attentively on her. She listened—the heartbeat was fading. It wouldn't be long now. The fact she was still alive was a testament to her people's durability.

"What is thy name?"

The Hiorian woman seemed confused and stared in silence. "You have a strange accent compared to da Wescreans."

"I come from a country beyond those mountains."

V gestured in the direction she had come from. Odessa's silvery eyes followed the motion, then nodded slowly.

"Well... I am Odessa," she finally answered.

V looked around the area, trying to understand how this battle unfolded. Most of the dead bodies were Hiorians.

"What happened to your people, Odessa?"

Odessa struggled to explain the situation in Wescreas. A war had broken out after the king fell. His son and daughter had begun to lead a rebellion to reclaim the throne.

Then she explained that her family had come here to meet the prince at a tower not far from where they were. A general had led a group of men to escort Odessa and her people—but instead, they were led into an ambush.

Odessa began to cough up blood once she finished. The smell of blood slightly intoxicated the wanderer. She covered her nose as she stared at Odessa with sadness.

"'Tis apparent you are going to die."

"I know."

"I spent years trying to control this affliction, so when I set out on my quest, I wouldn't be consumed by the thirst. I detest the idea... but I can maybe give you a chance to remain in this world."

Odessa stared silently at the raven-haired woman. V wasn't sure if she would accept—but didn't see the harm in offering a chance at revenge.

"I was raised to kill cursed spirits, not become one," Odessa scoffed.

"I never wanted this either. But it happened. My goal is to use the power I've gained to destroy my enemies."

"Who are you?"

The raven-haired woman lowered her gaze. She no longer knew who she was. Her name meant nothing anymore—because that person had died two decades ago. What she had become now was something else entirely.

"Just call me V," she answered.

Odessa furrowed her brow as she stared at V. The two remained silent for a moment, and Odessa seemed to be drifting off. V figured she'd stay with her until she took her final rest.

"How does it work?" Odessa mumbled.

"Pardon?"

"How do I become like you?"

Odessa glared at V. The question was unexpected, and V had no real answer. She took a moment, then raised her arm and pulled back her sleeve to reveal her pale wrist. She opened her mouth, revealing sharp fangs, and bit into her wrist before pulling away.

It surprised her to see a black substance dripping from her wrist into the ground. V looked at Odessa with concern.

"Take heed of my warning... If you choose to accept my offering, there is no turning back."

"I want to avenge da lost lives of my people—at da hands of da traitorous Hiorian dat is livin' comfortably in Fodmery," Odessa said angrily.

V's eyes widened as a memory flashed before her. She felt her slumbering rage stir. As quickly as it came, it faded. Now, they had a common enemy that needed to be killed.

"Henceforth, you will struggle with the same thing I do every night. The sun will be your enemy, and—"

"I understand."

Odessa's words were final. V couldn't talk her out of it. She nodded and held out her wrist. As Odessa pressed her mouth to it, V leaned closer and bit gently into her neck, drinking the blood that seeped out.

Odessa's heartbeat grew quiet as her body went limp. V pulled away and looked at her.

What had she done?

She had hoped to give Odessa power—but instead, she might have killed her.

V slowly stood, still staring at the lifeless body. She had hoped to gain a companion in her crusade for revenge. Her desire for a comrade made her realize how selfish she had been.

The Hiorian Odessa spoke of was someone V wanted to kill. He would be the first on her list. But it would be difficult—he had the Tome of Eneida.

As V turned to walk away, she thought she noticed something. Her eyes remained fixed on Odessa. She could've sworn she moved—but there was no further sign of life. Likely involuntary, V assumed. She sighed and turned to leave.

She had only taken a few steps when she felt the atmosphere change.

What she had become allowed her to sense the souls of others. She could also feel when someone channeled spiritual energy.

V turned—and saw Odessa rising from the ground.

Odessa's silvery eyes had changed to a sapphire blue, just like V's. The whites of her eyes had turned a sickly yellow. V heard no heartbeat.

She was now walking the same border V walked.

Odessa looked dazed and confused. She touched the wound on her stomach, which V assumed had healed. One of the gifts of becoming a creature of the night—rapid healing, and the strength of a hundred men.

"My misdoubts were wrong... it worked," V said, faintly grinning.

Odessa clutched her head, clearly in pain. Then she hunched over and vomited red.

V rushed to her in horror as she collapsed.

"Why is everything so loud?" Odessa whined.

"It takes time to adjust," V said softly, kneeling beside her. "But I will help you through it all."

"There are so many smells dat I never sensed before."

"Yes. Your senses are much stronger than your past self, dear."

Odessa rested on the ground as she wiped her stained lips. V stared at the Hiorian's beautiful face. Her long, rope-like tangles were soaked from the rain. A sense of regret overwhelmed V. She had turned a beautiful soul into a monster like herself.

Her selfish ambition had made her quick to act. She wondered if Odessa would manage—or lose herself. V had spent the last fifteen years trying to get her mind under control. She spent that time trying to hone her skills and overcome the temptation of the thirst.

"Odessa."

"Aye?"

"The road ahead is a long and treacherous one that neither of us may survive. Not only that, but you will struggle with the thirst. 'Tis to my understanding that blood makes us stronger... but it also leads to madness," V warned.

"You seem to have your mind."

"This is not a game, child!" V said sternly.

"What have I truly become?"

V stared at her hands and began to wonder the same thing. Then she remembered the vow she made before her demise. It was the only explanation she could come up with. Her will to seek revenge had been stronger than the ancient spirit the Acolytes had tried to summon.

"I don't know... but I had been burned as a sacrifice for a ritual by the Acolytes," V concluded.

"I have heard of them... Why are you not a vampyr?"

"I am uncertain..."

As she continued to think, she recalled seeing a strange figure. Was it possible that the person she saw had something to do with what she'd become? V figured it no longer mattered. She was no longer human. The princess she had once been had died years ago.

"Shall we go to Fodmery?"

V looked at Odessa, who had a look of ferocity in her eyes. This young woman was truly a warrior. She wanted to go to battle at once. Odessa picked up her blades off the ground. V stared at her, still in disbelief of the woman's tenacity.

Fodmery was the capital of Wescreas—and likely where the traitorous Hiorian now stayed. Unfortunately, V didn't have any combat skills, so she needed to plan. Being tactical about her revenge seemed necessary.

"Mayhaps I should build an army. But I will not make others become what I am. You were the only exception," V said softly.

"My people are still alive and still at war trying to slay da Hiorian ruling Wescreas," Odessa said.

V turned toward her, surprised. "Ruling?"

"He is da usurper. Da Wescreans carried da banner of their former king to fool us," Odessa explained.

V finally began to understand the situation better. And it was more complicated than she'd thought. The Hiorian would be resting in the castle located in the city of Fodmery. The capital.

"Do you truly believe thy people will allow us to fight alongside them?"

"It is doubtful."

"Then I shall focus on helping you soothe your urges. It would be a shame if you ended up harming them," V decided.

Odessa nodded as she got to her feet. She looked around, and the sadness started to set in. V began to wonder if she really should have turned this woman. Odessa appeared to be young and likely had a long life ahead of her. Hiorians lived much longer than humans.

"Do you have family? Anyone you were close with?"

"My mama is back at da stronghold, but my father and lil brudda are here wit me."

Odessa began to look around at the dead corpses scattered in the area. V trailed behind her as she stumbled in search of her loved ones. This was clearly the wrong choice. V should've allowed Odessa to die so she could cross to the other side. Her father and brother would be waiting for her.

"I don't hear any other heartbeats... besides the animals," V muttered.

"How do you know da difference?" Odessa looked over her shoulder as she knelt beside a dead Hiorian.

"People have louder heartbeats than animals. I spent enough time honing my skills to know these things."

V walked over to a Wescrean chevalier's corpse. She pulled off his helmet to see his short copper-red hair. His green eyes were void of life. The hair and eyes were common in Wescreas —most of the people had different shades of reddish hair.

The trip to Fodmery would take approximately two weeks on foot from where they were. V and Odessa were currently in the Ivy Forest. If she had to guess, the Chevaliers had been headed to a fortress nearby.

That meant if there were any survivors, they'd still be close. V decided she wanted to send a message at once. She stood upright and looked around for Odessa. It didn't take long to find her.

Odessa was kneeling with someone in her arms. Her cheeks were streaked with a dark substance trickling from her eyes. V rushed over and knelt beside her. In her arms was a young Hiorian male. He had a deep scar across his chest. His face had been disfigured.

"Dis is my lil brudda, Omari," Odessa sniffled.

"I'm sorry. Shall we put his body to rest?" V asked.

Odessa looked at her and nodded. V understood her new friend would need to process her grief. Being born anew made emotions much stronger than before. Everything was intensified now.

After burying Odessa's brother, they found her father. He was the man V had stumbled across earlier—the one kneeling, swords in his back. Odessa decided not to bury him but leave him where he was. She placed a few stones she found nearby around him. V also watched as Odessa gathered flowers and placed them at his feet.

"I am certain the Wescreans are not far from here. We can attack them before they get to Fodmery," V said softly.

The spiritual aura coming from Odessa made it clear she wanted to fight. Her eyes were fierce as she looked at V. This would be the perfect opportunity to show Odessa how to make use of her new abilities.

The biggest challenge would be keeping her from intoxicating herself with the blood of her enemies.

V began moving, searching for tracks. Most had been washed away in the mud. Then she remembered: Hiorians had a tracking ability they called **soul sense**. By using their spiritual awareness, they could sense the souls of others—and even determine if someone was possessed or dangerous.

V looked over at Odessa, who appeared lost in thought.

"Odessa?"

Odessa snapped out of her daze and looked over at V. There was an emptiness in her eyes that V hadn't noticed until now.

"What is it?" Odessa asked.

"Do you know how to sense if other souls are nearby?"

"Never learned how to do dat. My pa told me dat nature lives inside da veil dat separates da living and da dead. To sense tings around us, we must connect to da land itself."

"Then try it."

Odessa stood still, staring at V. Finally, she nodded and knelt, placing her hand in the dirt. V watched as she closed her eyes and began taking deep breaths. Pale green waves began to ripple around her, wrapping like a veil.

"There are spirits nearby," Odessa said.

"Try to sense anyone living. That's how we'll find the rest of the Chevaliers that left the area," V advised.

"I never thought dat I could do something like dis."

"That's because you've fully bathed in the world of spirits. Your spiritual awareness has doubled."

Odessa nodded and continued to focus. After a minute of silence, she opened her eyes. Without a word, she took off running. V watched, perplexed, before she took off after her. Odessa moved so fast she became a blur. V wasn't going to let her get too far ahead, so she picked up her pace. With ease, she caught up and ran beside her.

Odessa then suddenly stopped in her tracks. V stared at her, confused, until she began to hear it—the heartbeats of at least thirty men. They were not far from where she stood. As she listened, she saw the look in Odessa's eyes. It was a look of blood rage as her fangs showed.

V grabbed her arm firmly and pulled her close. Their noses nearly touched as V stared deep into Odessa's eyes. She had to rein her in before she lost control. Once she tasted blood, she would be lost. V had to make sure she trained this woman properly. In time, she would have to drink blood to maintain her power, but for now, she needed to strengthen her mind.

"Do not drink their blood," V ordered.

The blind rage in Odessa's eyes faded. It was like she'd been hypnotized. She nodded her head. V glared at her for a moment before letting her go. She didn't know what had just happened, but Odessa had become calm—and that was all that mattered.

V then lowered herself and began to stalk in the shadows. She could hear the men up ahead laughing and joking. From what she could gather, they were talking about how they fooled the Hiorians. She also heard them mention that revenants had aided in their victory.

V remembered what she had been told about revenants. Unlike vampyrs, they didn't thirst for blood, and there was no ritual that summoned them to the world of the living. V herself didn't seem to be a vampyr either. She had become something similar—but different entirely.

Over the years, she had researched the beings known as revenants. Jiya had introduced her to them. From what she'd seen, they were spirits drawn back to their bodies by an unknown force. When they returned, they were capable of incredible strength and speed—sometimes even supernatural powers. Each one was unique.

V listened as she hid behind a tree. A chevalier stood just four feet away. She heard him mention that most of the vampyrs had migrated away from Wescreas. His voice made it clear he was relieved.

He even said he was grateful that the Hiorian known as Jiya had taken residence in Wescreas. His army of revenants kept the Sentinels of Vostaylia from invading. The capital of Vostaylia was nearly a month's travel from the capital of Wescreas—but that never stopped a king hungry for power.

As V moved between the trees, she continued listening to their conversation. Odessa moved to a tree not far from her. Just then, a breeze picked up and a strange chill filled the air. Odessa moved closer.

"Why did it get so frigid so suddenly?"

V sensed something nearby and grabbed Odessa's hand. The presence was faint, but definitely there. As she looked around, she spotted it—a few feet away from a chevalier sitting by a tree. A giant figure in the shadows. The campfire the chevaliers had set up began to flicker, struggling to stay lit.

The chevaliers jumped to their feet and grabbed their weapons. V was impressed—they at least had enough sense to know danger when it approached.

A loud screech tore through the air, knocking several chevaliers to the ground. The dark shadow lunged from its hiding place.

V saw the large wings spread wide—it was some sort of winged beast. What fascinated her was the subtle sound it made when flapping. The creature used its talons to tear through a chevalier's armor. His stomach ripped open, and his guts spilled to the ground.

The others screamed in horror and fled.

What was this creature? And where had it come from?

V wondered if she could get it to be her ally. It would be the perfect addition to her future army.

"What is that thing?" V asked, glancing at Odessa.

Odessa stood motionless, her hands trembling. She was clearly frozen with fear. Even though they were undead, it was uncertain if they were as powerful as this creature. As it attacked, its spiritual presence grew stronger.

V stepped forward and approached while it slaughtered the chevaliers. Compared to her, it was huge—walking now on four legs. She stood by the fire, noticing one chevalier on the ground pretending to be dead.

V scoffed and snatched him off the ground. His eyes shot open in terror. He looked around at his dying comrades and tried to pry himself free. V scratched his face, drawing blood. He screamed, punching her in the face.

His strikes were barely felt. V raised her free hand and began channeling her spirit energy. As she stared at the chevalier, she thought about his blood—and, to both their surprise, it responded.

Blood from his wound began to lift into the air.

A faint vapor formed around her hand, drawing the blood. It spiraled together into a ball in her palm. She infused it with spiritual energy and hurled it at another chevalier who was fleeing.

The ball zipped through the air and struck him in the back. It tore through his body like a cannonball and exploded. Blood scattered everywhere.

V stared, amazed. The chevalier in her grasp began to lose consciousness. She figured it was from blood loss. She tossed him aside and turned back to the winged beast.

It was staring at her.

Its pale face bore a crown of gray feathers, and its yellow eyes glowed. An owl-like creature—this was the closest description she could come up with.

She didn't move an inch. It was clear this creature couldn't be tamed. It was an apex predator. And she was its prey.

V didn't like that thought. She took a step forward.

The winged beast spread its wings—and the air began to freeze.

Its spiritual energy was manifesting as a freezing power. Fascinating.

V raised her hand and focused. A spark flickered—and a ghostly flame appeared. She didn't want to kill it... but she wouldn't risk Odessa's safety.

"Forgive me. But if you won't play nicely... I'll have to kill you," V said coldly.

She had never used this power before. With the battle to come, she needed to hone every ability she'd gained. This was her chance to see how powerful she'd become.

The creature let out another screech. Debris scattered.

V sighed and lunged forward. Despite its size, the creature moved swiftly. It leapt away and began to fly. V chased it, leaping into the air and grabbing hold of one of its legs.

It ascended into the sky.

V realized this might have been foolish. There was no guarantee she'd survive the fall. But she didn't care. The ghostly flame engulfed the creature—and it began to shriek.

This wasn't a natural flame. It didn't burn flesh—it burned the soul.

As it began to descend, feathers fell from its wings. V noticed its body shriveling.

The thick greenery of the trees grew closer as they fell. Still holding its leg, V finally let go as it began to fall faster.

As she plummeted, V slowly closed her eyes.

She didn't know how bad the impact would be.

But she needed to test her limits.

And with that in mind... she could only hope to survive.

CHAPTER 2

The forest floor was wet and muddy as V lay there. Her hair clumped up with mud and her clothes were soaked. Her body screamed from the pain of her fall. Rain rolled down her face as she stared up at the night sky. She howled in pain as she popped bones back into their proper place.

She struggled to sit up as she felt her wounds beginning to heal. V looked around and saw the winged creature resting on fallen trees not far from her. Staggering to her feet, a jolt of pain shot up her knees. They buckled beneath her weight and brought her back down. A fall like that would have killed an ordinary woman—but she was far from that now.

She let out deep, ragged breaths as she struggled to rise again. To no avail. She couldn't muster the strength to stand just yet.

Odessa found her and rushed to her side. As she knelt beside V, she kept her eyes on the motionless creature.

"Do you know what that thing is?" V asked.

"A strix," Odessa shuddered, helping V to her feet.

V stared at the lifeless creature with wonder in her eyes. She knew there was a world of strange things that humans couldn't explain. What she had become wasn't easily explained. And now, she had encountered a fearsome beast that could likely terrorize an entire village if unprepared for its attack.

"I hath never heard or seen such a thing," V said, staggering toward the body of the creature.

"They are lone creatures and represent an ill omen when encountered."

V glanced at Odessa, who slowly approached the creature.

She took a moment to examine the body with great fascination —but also caution. After a few seconds, she began plucking some of the creature's feathers. It was an odd thing to see her do.

"What are you doing?"

"My people have long used their feathers as ingredients for potions."

Odessa placed the feathers in the pouch attached to her belt. V recalled learning a few potions the Hiorians would craft using herbs and other natural elements. Reflecting on the past only intensified the emptiness she felt. Her heart no longer beat—but her chest still often ached.

"We must scurry on if we wish to find shelter before first light."

Odessa stood upright and looked around at the destruction caused by the creature's fall from the sky. V also took note of the damage. It made her wonder what other things she would come to face on this journey for revenge.

When she was little, she recalled hearing stories of giants living in the Scarstone Mountains. Vostaylia was a country surrounded mostly by mountains and forests. The possibility of those childhood tales being true now didn't seem so far-fetched.

In the shadows, many things were hidden from human eyes. It came as no surprise—humans were a self-centered race that only thought of their own existence. A strange thought for V to have, considering she had once been human herself.

V and Odessa began walking in the direction the Wescreans had gone. It would be dangerous, but they might find the stronghold and overtake it. That would give them a base—one they could eventually use to build their army.

As they trudged silently through the forest, V began to pay attention to the environment. The Ivy Forest was small and damp from the rain. The canopy above let in just enough light from the sky to shine down on the thriving plant life. There was a mismatch of flowers scattered across the green scenery.

A clamor of sounds filled V's ears. Most came from vermin scurrying along the forest floor. Overhead, she saw shadows cross the canopy. She barely caught a glimpse of the flying creatures, but everything around her created an ambience of peace.

For the past two decades, she had known no peace.

For a moment, she forgot all about the blood she was going to have to shed. She didn't just want to kill those who wronged *her*, but also those who had wronged the Hiorians. Her crusade of vengeance went beyond her own pain. That was how she felt —and nothing would stop her from completing her goal.

"What is your reason for revenge?"

"Many reasons," V said softly.

She hardly wanted to talk about the past. The memories brought nothing but pain and frustration. The betrayals. The constant suffering of innocent people. She remembered how the Wescreans had killed her cousin, who was nothing more than a scholar. All he wanted to do was study and learn about other cultures.

What made his death worse was that even his own men had played a role in it. They returned home unscathed. She only knew this because her mother had overheard their conversation. When the truth broke, those men were executed.

"Do you think you can build an army?"

"I don't know if we'll succeed. Turning people is not what I want to do—I despise what I've become."

"Then what made you choose to turn me?" Odessa asked.

The question caught her off guard. They hadn't spoken about it since the moment it happened. V had hardly thought it through. She didn't know why she chose to turn Odessa. And now, she was beginning to regret burdening her with this curse.

Incredible power had been bestowed upon her—but it came at a cost. She couldn't walk in the sunlight without burning. At least, that's what it felt like the one time she tried.

She hadn't tried again since.

Her appetite for her homeland's delicacies had faded too. Her body didn't seem to digest food the same way anymore—if at all.

The body, she had come to understand, represented an aspect of one's life force. Vampyrs craved blood, which she learned was tied to that very aspect. She suffered a similar affliction—requiring the same sustenance.

She had been taught that three aspects made up the body: blood, flesh, and bone. V assumed there were creatures who fed on the other aspects as their source of nourishment.

The body, mind, and soul made up a person's life force. These things made a person *alive*. But the soul was what made them who they were. Destroying the soul, she believed, would reduce a person to a husk—one that would eventually die.

At least, that was what she had gathered from the texts she'd studied over the years.

She had learned many things. She spent much of her time jotting down notes and sketching diagrams in a journal. Even still, she knew there was much more to learn before she could truly grow.

"I had misgivings about letting you die. But also... I mayhaps was a little selfish."

V didn't know if that was a good enough answer. She could only hope Odessa would accept it and not hate her for it.

Odessa said nothing more as they continued walking in silence.

V began to smell blood as they emerged from the forest. She grabbed Odessa by the arm. Her head turned toward her sharply, eyes intense.

No matter what, she needed to make sure Odessa didn't drink the blood of a human.

V believed that if they drank human blood, they would potentially inherit their traits. She hypothesized that it would corrupt them—and they would lose their identity. Madness, in her mind, would eventually consume them.

If they drank the blood of animals, they would think less like a person and more like a predator. They would lose the sense of right and wrong. Every action would be driven by instinct.

Neither fate sounded appealing.

And V was determined to steer them far from either.

"I assume I smell blood right now," Odessa muttered.

"Yes, and as intoxicating as it might seem, you must control the urge."

"Will we not grow weaker if we avoid feedin'?"

V couldn't deny that fact—she'd been feeling fatigued for quite a while. She didn't want to admit it now, but using the spirit flame had drained her of her own life force. It was a powerful spiritual ability, but it came at a cost.

"Much needed rest works just as fine to gather your strength."

V lied, but hoped her newfound comrade would believe it. She couldn't keep up the charade much longer. Rest was needed—and she needed it immediately.

As they emerged from the forest, V took notice of Odessa's hand. It was trembling uncontrollably, and V knew what it meant. Odessa was thirsty, and her body was tempting her to hunt.

A few feet ahead of them was a river, and the forest continued on the other side. The river whispered as the water wound its way through the land, splashing against small stones resting in its current. Melodic murmurs came from the flow, and V stared in awe.

Then she noticed something on the other side.

Lying near the river was a person with a sword in their chest —a chevalier from Wescreas who no longer breathed. V knew this because she heard no heartbeat. Her eyes, sharpened by her curse, allowed her to see the other side more clearly.

Standing by the body was the phantom of the chevalier. He seemed lost and grief-stricken. As V stared at the spirit, she felt something grab her hand. She looked down to see Odessa reaching out—trying to overcome the thirst.

"Over da years, some of my people started namin' different

types of spirits," Odessa said.

"I am aware."

"Dat spirit's a phantom. They roam da place they died. He'll be stuck here till a Soulseer comes for him."

V looked at Odessa with a hint of curiosity. She recalled the mention of a Soulseer earlier but had thought nothing of it. Now her interest was piqued. She wanted to know more—about the Hiorians' beliefs, about whether they had a religion, about the unknown.

"What is this Soulseer you speak of?"

"Soulseers are beings dat come to collect da souls of da dead and guide them to da Spirit World. They also destroy spirits too powerful for somethin' called an exorcist."

V furrowed her brow. She had much to learn.

"Exorcists?"

"It's da name given to people who hunt spirits," Odessa shrugged.

"I have heard whispers of such people when I was young," V recalled.

"I was but an herbalist—I wasn't taught to fight evil spirits," Odessa scoffed.

V reflected on the past. She remembered hearing that word —*herbalist*—when she first crossed paths with the Hiorian people. Their medicines, made from herbs and natural elements, had saved many of her people during a fever outbreak. The memory intrigued her.

"Now you've been benighted into a spirit that may be scorned by thy people."

Odessa frowned, staring off into the distance. V saw the regret in her eyes. It filled her with remorse—for bestowing such a fate on someone so young.

V thought back to her return from the other side. She remembered searching for Jiya's body and finding that he had been buried somewhere sacred. The saddest part was that he had died in a land he could never call home.

"I've noticed you get lost in thought often," Odessa said.

V scoffed and marched forward. She hesitated at the edge of the running water. Something in her rebelled at the thought of crossing. Then she reminded herself—she was no longer the human she once was.

She bent her knees and flexed her muscles. With a single leap, she soared through the air and landed effortlessly on the other side.

Once across, she turned to see Odessa standing frozen at the river's edge.

V waited patiently. Odessa finally lunged forward, but she fell short and landed just shy of the bank. V lunged out and caught her hand before the current could drag her away.

As V grabbed her, she saw a faint green ripple separate from Odessa and get pulled into the water. She pulled Odessa to safety, and they both collapsed on the ground.

Odessa was distraught, her breathing shaky. Something was clearly wrong.

"What's the matter with you?"

"I nearly drowned twice when I was young. I've been scared of running water ever since," she said flatly.

V raised an eyebrow. "You can't swim?"

"My elder brudda tried to teach me, but I was too afraid."

Odessa sat silently, clearly thinking of her family. V couldn't help but feel sorrow too—they'd both lost people they loved at the hands of humans. At least Odessa's mother was likely still alive. But would Odessa even dare to seek her out?

As time passed, her thirst would only grow.

V needed to keep watch. Odessa had strength, but strength could be corrupted. She couldn't risk her new companion becoming a liability in her crusade. Good intentions wouldn't stop a fall to darkness.

"I shall carry dis curse with you till I have slain Jiya Ashspell —and another Hiorian who joined him. After dat, I must ask dat you kill me... so I can hopefully see my pa and bruddas again," Odessa said suddenly.

V stared at her, speechless. The request came out of nowhere

—but her tone was final. Her expression, unchanging.

"I give you my word," V said quietly.

She stood and looked to the sky. They needed to find shelter before the night ended. The chevaliers were headed this way—there had to be a fortress nearby.

V pushed forward into the forest, Odessa at her heels.

The smell of blood grew stronger. Rain and mud made it hard to track the scent's origin—but people had clearly died here.

After walking five minutes, V found another body. She knelt and turned it over—another chevalier. His chest armor had been torn open, and there was a large hole where his heart should have been.

He had been heading in the direction they'd just come from. Reinforcements? And if so, what had killed them?

She found another—cut in half at the waist.

Then one more—beheaded.

The slaughter was too brutal to have been done by Hiorians alone.

"Do you have any idea what did this?" V asked.

Odessa was staring dazedly at a man leaning against a tree. Her eyes were glassy, and her lips parted slightly.

V rushed over and grabbed her firmly. Odessa snapped out of it, blinking.

"Do not be overcome by it!" V snapped.

Odessa trembled and nodded. V pulled her forward, marching ahead. She had to find shelter—this corpse-filled forest was too dangerous. The deeper they went, the more bodies they found.

V began to feel something—something *lurking*. No heartbeat. No sound. But the presence was undeniable.

It was madness—fueled by spiritual energy.

Odessa drew her blades, eyes scanning the trees.

V and Odessa moved with caution, readying themselves.

Then V heard something—a sound that twisted her face in disgust.

Flesh and bone being crushed.

Up ahead, bushes blocked the view. She readied herself. But just before she stepped forward, the sound stopped.

She froze.

Footsteps.

V leapt back.

Lunging through the bushes came a tall man clad in armor. His eyes glowed green, and blackish-green smoke clung to him like a cloak. A large, freshly stitched scar ran across his face. His long strawberry-blonde hair was a tangled mess, and his face was void of emotion.

His skin was pale and dusty. No warmth. A dead man, still moving—an offense to the laws of nature.

V braced herself.

He wasn't like her. His curse was different.

Then she noticed a mark carved into his forehead—peculiar, but there was no time to ponder it.

Odessa lunged forward, letting out a loud battle cry.

The armored man locked eyes with her and raised the large object in his hand.

With frightening ease, he swung it downward—trying to smash her skull.

V watched as Odessa narrowly dodged. The hammer slammed into the earth, and V could swear she felt the ground quake.

Odessa began to channel her spiritual energy. Waves rippled around her. She swung her blade, aiming at the warrior's chest. A green wave of energy shot forward. The man dodged—but it hit a tree behind him.

For a moment, nothing happened.

Then the tree groaned—and began to fall.

V stepped back, watching in awe.

Before her transformation, she could never have seen something like this.

Her father had called the Hiorians' gifts *sorcery*.

But this wasn't evil.

It was art.

Spiritual arts—the manipulation of life force to affect both realms. It required not just strength, but creativity.

Odessa continued her assault—cleaving, hacking. The warrior evaded with skill. V heard him grunt in frustration.

She stood back, unsure if she should intervene.

Would helping disrupt Odessa's rhythm—and give the warrior the upper hand?

Not only that, but she was still weak from the fall and from using the spiritual flame. Avoiding blood consumption made her recovery time longer than normal. Odessa had just begun her vampiric life, so she had greater strength.

The warrior shouted as he managed to grab Odessa's arm. Her eyes widened as she clearly hadn't expected this. With the other hand, he lifted up his battle hammer with little effort. V realized she had to act now, or Odessa would be crushed. She lunged forward and lowered her shoulder.

She rammed into the warrior, knocking him off his feet. He dropped his hammer and rolled across the muddy terrain. V glanced over at Odessa before she turned back toward the warrior.

"What's going on with him?" V asked.

"Dis is Jiya's doin'. He is a revenant, but made in a different way so he can be stronger," Odessa said flatly.

V began to think for a moment and then remembered that phrase from years ago. It sent chills down her body as she recalled that fateful night once again. She gritted her teeth as she thought about the past.

V looked up to see Odessa staring at her with a suspicious gaze. The armored warrior shouted as he rushed forward. V ran to the right as she began to channel spiritual energy. She could smell the blood nearby and felt she should try using it to aid in the fight.

Blood was a type of life force, and she had learned she could draw it to her with the use of spiritual energy. As Odessa and the warrior fought, V continued to draw the blood in the area to her. The blood clumped together and thickened until it became a solid.

V shaped the blood into what she desired. It took a few seconds, but the clump of blood became a blade. This night had been a good one, for she had been able to test her strength. V rushed over to aid Odessa. The warrior's throat was cut open by Odessa, but there was no blood.

He merely smiled as he pulled his arm back and lunged toward her. Odessa was struck in the chest by his fist. A large gust of wind cut through the air as she was knocked back. V's eyes widened in horror as memories of her past flooded her mind.

It sent her into a blood rage, causing her to rush the warrior and begin slashing away with the blade of blood. The blade tore the warrior as if it were made of metal. With so much iron in the blood, it was possible to mistake it for a real sword.

The armor the warrior wore was being torn apart by the slashes. Still, as V cut away, blood did not appear from his wounds. He stumbled back as she began to overpower him. V's breath became ragged as she swung wildly. The warrior merely smiled as he collapsed to the ground.

Once on the ground, V began to stab him repeatedly. She aimed for his heart and, without remorse, continued her attack. When it became clear the revenant still wouldn't stop laughing, she could think to do only one thing.

She moved to the side of his head and raised the weapon high above her head. Letting out a loud scream, she swung the sword down. The blade cut through the revenant's throat. His laughter then slowly faded. V stared at him as she breathed raggedly.

She threw the blade of blood to the ground and looked around the area, her eyes darting left to right in search of Odessa. Then she saw her comrade on the ground by a tree. She rushed over to her and knelt beside her.

Odessa groaned in pain as V rolled her over. Her sapphire blue eyes stared up at V in pain. A sense of relief overcame V. She had no idea what came over her when she saw Odessa get hit. All that mattered was that Odessa could survive such attacks, despite the pain.

"Let's get going before we get caught by the sun," V said softly.

Odessa nodded as she struggled to her feet. The fight with the revenant made it clear things wouldn't be easy. Unlike them, the revenant seemed to not feel pain and was much more violent. Although, he didn't seem to use spiritual energy for what Odessa called spiritual arts. Instead, he was a mere brute of pure strength.

V wondered if all revenants were like this. If so, then it may be possible to muster up a plan to deal with them. The problem would occur if they were unique and capable of doing different things. V believed she had much to learn and needed to get stronger. The battle ahead was proving to be much more complicated.

CHAPTER 3

It took two more hours of trudging aimlessly through the forest before V and Odessa found themselves outside a stronghold. Next to the stronghold was another river. What they found there were six revenants that had slaughtered the Wescrean chevaliers.

V and Odessa battled them until the sun nearly peaked before defeating them. It had been a gruesome slugfest that left V wounded. She hid her pain from Odessa in order to keep her from worrying. V ordered Odessa inside the stronghold while she gathered the bodies of the revenants and some of the chevaliers.

Some of the chevaliers she saw on the ground had already been there when she arrived. They wore cloaks that were a slightly different color than the others. She assumed they had been part of the prince and princess's forces.

Once they were in a pile, she grabbed a torch from inside the building. She set the bodies ablaze, hoping to keep them from rising again. The revenants were a mystery, and she didn't want to take any chances with them outside the stronghold. Odessa needed the rest, and V needed to plan the next move.

V rushed to the gate and grabbed the chained pulley that controlled the doors. She began to pull it hurriedly so she could get inside before the sun's gaze reached her. The doors creaked and churned as they slowly began to close. Once it was shut, she took a brief look around. As far as she could tell, they were safe for the moment.

As the sun's rays spread across the land, V could feel her skin begin to burn. She rushed inside the large doors to the tower. V pushed them open and quickly slammed them shut as just a few seconds of light burned the skin on her face.

She now found herself staring down a hallway with torches lining the walls. The hall had a few doors on either side of it. Further down was a staircase that led to the upper levels and the watchtower.

A faint draft filled the air, which V noticed immediately. She slowly made her way down the hall, wondering where Odessa had gone. It didn't take long to find her—V could sense her presence. Odessa had gone into the third room on the right.

She sat silently in a chair, appearing lost in thought as she bit her nails. V stared at her worriedly, continuing to wonder if she had made a mistake. Odessa didn't deserve to be cursed the way V had been. It was far too cruel, and V had subjected this young woman to the same fate.

"How old are you, Odessa?"

Odessa appeared startled as she jerked her head up to look at V. She took a moment to gather her thoughts before answering. "I am twenty-two. Why?"

"Just curious."

"How old are you?"

Odessa's eyes stared at V with deep curiosity. V sometimes forgot how long it had been since everything happened. Time had passed by without her noticing. Not only that, but she didn't even remember how she looked—mainly because she had lost the ability to see her reflection. It likely had something to do with being a cursed spirit.

"I believe I am thirty-nine."

Odessa looked shocked as she looked V up and down. This made V a bit uncomfortable—she felt self-conscious. How did she look to Odessa? She hadn't thought about her appearance in a long time, but now she had someone who would be beside her often.

"But you look my age," Odessa remarked.

V realized her appearance remained the same as when she had been cursed by the Acolytes. The thought of them made her remember the woman who threw the torch at her feet. She wanted to get revenge on her—after defeating Jiya and destroying Wescreas.

With Jiya having already caused so much damage to Wescreas, their country would fall into ruin if he died. Thinking about this made V even more eager to fight. Although, that would have to wait until she built her own fleet. Even if it didn't turn out to be a large army, if they were strong and reliable, things could work.

"How do you know Jiya?"

V looked up at Odessa, surprised by the question. Her past life had become a ghost that haunted her. It was part of the reason why she needed revenge. She hoped the haunting would end once her enemies were dead.

"He's the reason my lover and his family were killed."

"At least two Hiorian families no longer exist because of him."

Odessa had a look of pure hatred in her eyes. V watched as her ally dug her nails into the palms of her hands. Droplets of red fell to the ground as she stared off into space.

"My lover had been a part of the Craft family," V mumbled.

Odessa's expression then suddenly changed. "There are still members of that family alive, if I believe."

V had a brief memory cross her mind. It put a soft smile on her face as she thought of them. She had worried they wouldn't survive, but Odessa's words gave her hope and relief. Deep down, she wanted to see them—but she knew it would be best to stay away. All that mattered was that her lover's family would live on.

"I know."

Odessa eyed her suspiciously for a moment. Then she pointed across the room. V looked over in that direction to see a table. It was covered in papers, but what caught her eye was the map spread across it. V rushed over in disbelief. Having a map would help tremendously in planning their next move.

She stood over the map, examining it with great care. Wooden pieces had been finely carved with designs. The map showed Wescreas and many of its most important locations. There were rivers listed, as well as the forest they had recently left.

One of the wooden pieces had been placed by a fortress called Skyreach Tower. V acknowledged its location from the forest and assumed it to be where they currently were. She placed her finger on the map, searching for Fodmery.

It was north of their current base and seemed farther than she expected. Why build a fortress so far out in a forest? From what she saw outside, many trees had been cut down to extend the field of view. Still, it felt out of place.

V then assumed maybe it had been built to monitor Hiorian activity. Hiorians had grown accustomed to building their homes in forests, away from humans. That had been their way ever since they were attacked so often.

As she examined the map more, she saw another stronghold established before even reaching Fodmery. It was called the Fortress of Leon the Vile. V believed Leon to be the overseer of this fortress. That meant, to get to Jiya, she needed to kill Leon first.

As she continued scanning the map, she saw a fortress to the northeast of Skyreach Tower. Its location placed it near the Scarstone Mountains and far from Fodmery. This stronghold bore the name Judith's Keep.

North of Judith's Keep appeared to be a town called Stawford. These were clearly important locations outside of Fodmery. V believed the best plan would be to claim the two strongholds, then maybe take the city of Stawford before invading Fodmery.

Taking a stronghold would give them a place to hold position until they recovered and replenished strength. They could do this twice before going to Fodmery. Taking the town of Stawford would allow them to steal any supplies the strongholds lacked.

Revenge had no real expiration date as long as the enemy lived. This would take time to pull off, but V felt it could be done. The only problem was building her army. She also realized she needed a weapon.

V turned away from the table and headed out of the room. An armory had to be in the tower. The chevaliers couldn't be stationed here without a supply of weapons. The room directly across from the one V had left was filled with gold, silver, and valuables.

She sighed as she pulled the door shut. V checked every room in search of the armory. To no avail. Now she found herself at the staircase leading up. A beam of sunlight shone down, causing V to hesitate. She could see the stairs spiraled up toward the top.

There would be no way for her to ascend the tower at the moment. V turned back and wondered if one of the other buildings held the armory. Unfortunately, she would have to wait until sunset to find out.

Odessa emerged from the room with a look of curiosity on her face. V stopped in the middle of the hall as they stared at each other. Neither said anything for a moment. V wondered what Odessa had on her mind.

"What if we cannot build an army?"

V had been thinking about that since she arrived. She had wandered for many nights, hiding in caves, wondering if she'd ever accomplish her goal. As easy as turning people could be, it wasn't what she wanted. She wanted to strike fear into her enemies as she killed them. Still, she didn't want to become the monster they believed her to be.

"I thought of it."

"With the power you have, you could easily gain one along the way. You could have a horde of cursed spirits by the time we make it to Fodmery."

Odessa took a step toward V. V didn't understand why she had suddenly started thinking like this. And yet... she wasn't wrong. Still, V couldn't subject more people to this life. She had no desire to turn humans.

"Power like this awakens the worst in good people... and

makes the worst of man more dangerous."

"That does not answer why you are hesitant when you desire revenge. Revenge don't come to those who try to hold on to their morals. It comes to those willing to step down from that sense of righteousness."

It had only been a few hours since Odessa had been turned. Could she already be corrupted? Was there a darker side in her that V had unintentionally awakened? These questions now filled V with worry—her young friend seemed different than she had earlier.

"I admit that I was selfish when I offered to turn you. That was wrong of me, and I regret it."

"My soul would not have rested anyway. Not when I know Jiya and other traitorous Hiorians are sitting in the castle of Wescreas."

"Then if I let you be... maybe you'd have returned as a revenant."

"That is an uncertainty."

"There was no certainty I would have been successful in making you like me either."

Odessa's frustration could be heard in her voice. V understood her pain and grieved with her. She wanted to kill Jiya— but now, she also wanted to make sure Odessa didn't lose her way. This meant V had to keep her own mind clear. It had already become a difficult endeavor, but now it would be ten times harder.

"I'd like to hold our position here for three days."

Odessa looked at V with a furrowed brow. "Why?"

"Either your people will show up, or the Wescreans from the Fortress of Leon the Vile will appear."

"With just the two of us, the Hiorians will kill us for sure. Besides, we barely managed to beat those revenants."

"My hope is that if the Hiorians get here, we may be able to convince them to help us. But you'll need to be kept away for a while."

"Kept away for what?"

"You are struggling with the thirst, Odessa—and it hasn't even been a full day since I turned you."

V placed her hands on Odessa's shoulders. She stared at her with worry, like a mother might. Maybe, because she never got the chance to be a mother, that was why she wanted to save Odessa.

"If you lost yourself and bit one of your family members, you'd likely never be able to forgive yourself."

"I know."

Odessa lowered her head, appearing to lose herself in thought. The world was changing—and with all the spirits and strange creatures emerging from the shadows, it would only get worse. V only hoped the Hiorians would survive the ages to come. From what she could tell, they already had a much smaller population compared to humans.

"Is it really possible to go such a long time without drinking blood?"

"No..."

Odessa looked up at V, wide-eyed. She took a step back, horrified. V couldn't hide the truth from her anymore. The truth was—when she had first turned, she had killed many humans and animals in a frenzy.

It had driven her into a brief madness, forcing her to hide from the world. She took refuge in a cave as she struggled to maintain her sanity. The longer she starved herself, the clearer her mind became. Unfortunately, being cursed meant she could never escape the thirst. As long as she desired revenge, she had a will to live.

"It's been three months since I last fed."

"I thought you said drinking blood leads to madness. You made it seem like I could do this without feeding!"

"It does—but there is a way to maintain a balance," V explained. "And I never specifically said we could go without. I told you to control your urges while we were in that forest."

Odessa stared at V in disbelief, then her face twisted with disgust. V sighed, realizing she should've been more transparent. Now, there would likely be a sense of distrust between them. She didn't want that. She wanted Odessa to believe in her—but by the look on her face, V feared everything was about to fall apart.

"I will not drink the blood of a human or my own people!" Odessa proclaimed.

"I would never subject you to such a thing."

Odessa only stared at her in silence. V wished she knew what was going through her underling's mind. The tension between them was heavy, difficult to shake. If V said the wrong thing, she could lose Odessa as an ally. She had to be careful— no more misunderstandings.

Odessa closed her eyes and exhaled deeply. "There is no going back now. You said so yourself."

The pressure V had felt eased slightly. Odessa still seemed upset, but not as much as before. V was grateful she was still by her side—or at least, she hoped so.

"Again, I am truly sorry," V said sincerely.

"I made the choice. I knew there'd be a price. Besides, you've dealt with this curse longer than I have, so I shan't complain."

"Let's try to get some rest. We'll talk more later."

Odessa nodded. V turned and headed to one of the rooms, hoping to find a place to rest. She sensed that when night came, it would be time to train for the battles ahead. Her combat skills needed sharpening—Jiya Ashspell would not be an easy foe.

*

The night came and blanketed the sky. Rain poured down from above much harder than the night from before. V stood outside on the wall looking out into the forest. Her hair was soaked, heavy with damp strands clinging to her face and shoulders. Water dripped from the ends, splashing onto the already saturated stone.

She raised the sword she had found in the armory—something she believed befitting a general—and began practicing simple slashing motions. As she moved along the wall, swinging the blade, she heard footsteps.

She turned to see Odessa approaching silently, twin daggers at her sides and a stern look on her face. Her locks were drenched, clinging to her cheeks and obscuring her expression. As V examined her, she noticed strange scars on Odessa's arms—something she hadn't seen before.

What had happened to her?

V wanted to ask, but it felt too personal. Now wasn't the time. She shook the thought away and focused on the moment.

"If I'm being truthful, I do not see you as a warrior," Odessa said.

A faint grin formed on V's face. Odessa's observation was accurate. V had never fought in a real battle. She hadn't seen war firsthand, though she knew what it could do to people. Her path had been different—her father raised her on books, more scholar than soldier.

"You'd be correct."

V leapt from the wall, descending like a ghost. She landed softly on the muddy ground, facing Odessa, who raised her blades.

"Then I suppose, until someone arrives, we'll train—and you'll teach me more about being... what we are."

V raised her sword, assuming a stance taught to her by her lover. Odessa's eyes widened.

"You appear to have learned something from the Craft family."

Odessa rushed her, daggers flashing. Her strikes were sharp and precise. V sidestepped, parrying with her sword, but Odessa didn't falter. She kept attacking, each slash faster than the last.

V gritted her teeth, planting her left foot and raising her sword at an angle to block. She pushed forward, knocking Odessa slightly off balance. As Odessa stumbled back, V lifted her sword and swung downward.

But Odessa parried with a twist of her wrist, spinning on her heel and redirecting V's momentum to the side.

V tried to recover, but cold steel kissed her neck. Odessa's blade had cut her skin. She pulled away, leaving a shallow mark.

V sighed in frustration. She'd been bested easily.

Odessa smiled, triumphant. Their duel had barely lasted a minute. V stepped back, resetting her stance, waiting for Odessa to say "try again." She wanted to keep practicing—she needed to.

"The Craft family are skilled fighters, but they fight with too much honor," Odessa said. "Honor doesn't win wars, at least not from what my sistah taught me."

"You have a sister too?"

"Yes. She's older than me. Did a lot of traveling across dis land before sailing west."

"How old was your sister?"

"About your age."

V blinked, stunned. Could she have met Odessa's sister before? It was possible—but during her time in Vostaylia, she'd only encountered four Hiorian families. None of them were from the Hollow family.

"She sailed west? But there's nothing out there but sea."

"She believed there were places far from humans—or at least the violent ones."

A flicker of sadness crossed Odessa's face. V found she liked talking to her, and hoped they'd share more moments like this. Though they'd only met the day before, something in her stirred—maternal instincts, perhaps.

One of the selfish reasons she hadn't let Odessa die was that she'd never had the chance to be a mother. That dream had been stolen from her by the acolytes—and by the one they followed.

"I'm telling you about myself," Odessa said, "but I still know so little about you."

"What do you want to know?"

"Where are you from? You don't look like the Wescreans."

The Wescreans typically had strawberry-blonde or reddish-brown hair. Their eyes were green or hazel, their skin fair or bisque-toned. In contrast, the Vostaylians had fawn or rosy complexions, brown shades of hair, and light brown eyes.

"I'm from Vostaylia—a country nestled in the Scarstone Mountains, east of here."

"You said you want to attack that country too?"

"Yes. More specifically, I want to kill the king."

"Sadly, I cannot follow you on dat journey."

"I know. But I'm grateful you're with me on this one, at least."

Odessa nodded as a moment of silence filled the air. A slight wind blew in from the forest as she raised her daggers once more.

Combat training again, V realized. She raised her sword, ready to fight.

Neither of them moved as they stared at each other with deadly intent. Odessa increased her spiritual presence to show her power. V did the same, noticing a cloud of smoke forming around her.

She didn't know what this strange mist represented, but she saw it appearing around Odessa too—less noticeable, but still there. Did it have something to do with their curse?

She couldn't help but wonder, but the thought faded—she needed to focus.

Odessa stepped forward—and vanished.

At least, at first glance, it seemed that way. In reality, she moved at a speed the normal eye couldn't catch. Fortunately, V didn't have normal eyes and spotted the movement.

She managed to block a hacking motion from the dagger in Odessa's right hand. V leapt away before the second blade could come down. As her feet brushed the dirt, she felt herself gliding forward. She had no idea what was happening, but went with it.

Steel clashed, creating sparks and a rumble. Odessa smiled, her eyes widening into a deranged glare. She began to swing her daggers at insane speed.

V now found herself being forced back, struggling to parry the attacks.

She had to find a moment to strike.

Suddenly, Odessa halted and stepped back a few feet. V blinked, confused, but took the opportunity to attack. Odessa then dropped her posture and lunged forward.

The length of V's blade wouldn't allow her to deliver a good blow from this angle. She had to keep Odessa from getting too close.

V leapt into the air as Odessa struck. As Odessa looked up, V was already gone from that position in the sky. She had landed behind her, sword aimed at the back of her underling's head.

A small chuckle escaped Odessa's lips.

"If you use your spirit energy to boost your movements, we just might have a chance."

"Don't patronize me. I know you weren't trying, little one."

Odessa turned as V slowly lowered her sword.

"Da more we practice,Da more I shall expend my energy. For now, I just want you to get comfortable fightin'."

"I suppose that makes sense."

"I'd like to take a break and talk more about your past. You seem like you don't want to—but if you're willin', I'd like to know you more," Odessa said.

V remained silent as she considered the request. She hardly thought about her past—aside from her lover, nothing else had surfaced in a long time. Not even her father or mother crossed her mind much.

"If you're going to fight alongside me, it's only fair you know who I am."

V made her way toward the tower to get out of the rain. She heard Odessa trailing behind her. This tower would be their home for the next few days, so V wanted to try and get comfortable.

Soon, more death would plague this place.

That, unfortunately, was inevitable.

CHAPTER 4

Act 1: Odessa's Isolation Pt. 1

The patter of rain continued to fall as Odessa stood across from V. She stared at the mysterious woman who had made her a fledgling. Odessa thought this woman to be mysterious and wanted to know more about her.

She could tell V had some training from the Hiorians. Learning that V had been close to someone from the Craft family gave her an idea of her skill. Although, it was clear she hadn't had enough training to truly master their fighting style.

"I would like to take a break and talk more about your past. You do not seem like you want to, but if you willin', I would like to know you more," Odessa said.

V remained silent as her gaze wandered. Odessa assumed she was taking a moment to think. She could sense that V had things she wanted to forget or bury away in the past. She understood if the woman before her chose not to say anything. Still, she hoped to learn more about who she was fighting alongside.

"If you're going to fight alongside me, it's only fair you know who I am," V replied in an angelic voice.

Odessa stood there watching V make her way to the tower. She couldn't help but admire the way her new ally spoke. It seemed strange—her voice was beautiful and calming. Even when they first met, Odessa hadn't sensed any hostility in it. When V spoke to her, it had almost felt... motherly.

Quickly, Odessa shook off the thought and took a moment to herself. She looked up toward the sky. Not far from where she stood, she could see a flock of black birds in the distance.

She was still adjusting to how her body now functioned. Her

hearing had improved to a supernatural degree. Her sense of smell allowed her to breathe in all the scents around her. The heightened awareness helped her distinguish even the subtlest smells in the area.

Odessa held out her hand and let the rain fall into her palm. Strangely, it felt like her soul could feel the wetness and the cold wind. Maybe it was just her imagination, but she couldn't deny the fascination she had begun to feel.

Sadly, she knew what she had become was something her family would despise. The dead and the living were not meant to connect in this way. No one should walk the line between worlds. Odessa closed her hand, understanding the severity of breaking the natural order.

With an exasperated breath, she turned and headed toward the tower. It would be their home for the next few days, so it seemed wise to get well acquainted with it. She knew the days to come would certainly be filled with death.

For now, she merely wanted to sit down and rest.

She entered the tower and could smell the damp air. The door rattled as she opened and closed it. She made her way down the long hall and saw V standing near the staircase. V's strange blue eyes met hers as she approached.

"You said you would like to know more about my past... so, what do you wish to know?"

Odessa stood there for a moment, pondering what to ask first. There were many things she could ask, but also some she felt it wise to wait on—at least until she better understood the person before her. She didn't know how long this quest for revenge would take, but she accepted that she would be walking it beside this mysterious woman.

"Do you have siblins?" Odessa asked.

V seemed caught off guard by the question. Odessa assumed she'd been expecting something more complex. This was just a way to test the waters—to see what kinds of questions she could ask right now. Slowly, V scratched her eyebrow, seemingly pondering her answer.

This puzzled Odessa. The question only needed a yes or no. What could possibly make her think so hard?

"In the legal sense, no. But my father was believed to have had an affair with a woman my uncle took for a wife. No one knows for sure whether she is my uncle's daughter... or my father's."

Odessa stared at V in disbelief. She hadn't expected such a complex answer. Not only that, but the question seemed to cause V to fall into reflection again. She always seemed to brood whenever there was a moment of peace. If no one tried to pull her out of it, Odessa feared she would stay in that state forever.

"Oh... forgive me if dat question was too much."

A gentle smile crept onto V's face.

"'Tis quite alright. You told me about your siblings, so 'tis only fair you know mine."

Odessa nodded slowly, thinking about what else she wanted to know. Then a question came to her.

"Is there a name for what we are?"

A silence filled the room as Odessa watched V's brooding expression return. The most noticeable sound was the faint breeze whispering in her ear as it blew by.

"I cannot be certain," V finally said. "We have a thirst for blood like vampyrs but are akin to those revenants—or whatever Jiya calls them."

Odessa stood in silence, pondering the answer. She saw herself as a spirit possessing her former body. That was the only way she could make sense of it. And the sustenance her body now required to remain strong... it was revolting. But she had accepted it out of desperation.

There was a man beside Jiya she wanted to kill. Her soul wouldn't rest until she punished him for all he did—not just for the pain he caused her people, but for betraying her... and breaking her heart.

As her thoughts overtook her, she realized her body was trembling.

V's hand rested on her shoulder, drawing her gaze. V's eyes held a look of concern. Odessa stared at her, wondering if that look was genuine.

"What troubles you, little one?" V asked.

Odessa didn't know what to say. This woman intrigued her —so many sides revealed in such a short time. And now she showed a tenderness Odessa had only ever seen in her mother.

As she thought of her mother, a deep sadness welled up inside her. Why were her emotions so intense? V had warned her that things would be different now—walking the line between worlds.

"If my mama sees me dis way... she will disown me."

Odessa's shoulders slouched as she stared at her dirty hands. As much as she wanted revenge, she still longed for her mother's love. Would that love be worth losing over revenge?

"A mother's love is something that cannot be easily lost. I doubt she would disown you for this—especially if I am to blame."

Odessa stared at V, at a loss for words. Then she shook her head and took a step back.

"You are not to blame for dis."

"I am the one who offered it to you," V sighed.

A look of shame crossed her face. Odessa could see it clearly now—behind this woman's eyes were regrets. She didn't know V's full story, but she sensed that this woman had a kind heart. And that something in her past had broken it.

"I made da choice to become dis ting dat I am now," Odessa said, her gaze sharp. "My mama ain't raise me to blame others for my own doin'."

"I saw the fire burning in thine eyes and got taken by it," V confessed. "My desire for revenge made me impulsive."

"I see you carry much burden. Do not make me one of them."

V seemed surprised by Odessa's words. Then she nodded slowly, accepting them. A quiet moment passed before V began ascending the steps of the tower. She was likely headed to the watch level.

Odessa stood there for a beat, then followed.

"What were your parents like?" she asked.

V glanced over her shoulder as she continued up the staircase.

"My mother was kind. She loved helping the less fortunate. My father was a warrior and a brilliant leader. He could be fearsome—people feared him—but he was also honorable."

Odessa took it in as they climbed. A faint sense of intrigue settled over her. She could tell their journey ahead would be grand. Though taking lives in the way she now could didn't sit right with her.

She felt at least ten times stronger than before. Her body could move faster than the humans they would likely face could comprehend. War wasn't something she had ever known.

She knew little about her people's homeland.

From her father's stories, they were a culture that prided themselves on love and understanding. They had their quarrels, sure—but they didn't kill one another.

That was hard to imagine in these lands. All she'd seen was bloodshed and war. And now her own people were at war with one of their own.

It still baffled her.

All she knew was that she couldn't forgive the traitor who had chosen to use dark spiritual forces for such nefarious reasons.

From what she remembered, he came to their newly founded settlement offering a new home—by conquering Wescreas.

He wanted to enslave and kill humans the way they had done to their people.

Odessa couldn't even begin to understand his mindset. Everything he did went against the values and beliefs of their people.

"Was Jiya always like dis?" Odessa blurted out.

She hadn't even meant for the question to escape her lips.

It had been a random thought she'd wondered about. Some of the older people of her race often spoke highly of him, and how his turn had surprised them years ago. She even remembered some of the older Hiorians saying they thought he was dead.

"I remember his desire to ensure the safety of his people. He was always uptight when his people chose to help my country. Not only that, but he didn't take kindly to me..."

V grew silent as they finally reached the top of the tower.

Odessa looked out and saw that they could see far from where they stood. A line of trees stretched for miles, and wide fields of greenery filled the horizon. To her left stood a vast range of mountains. They looked like a wall separating this country from what she assumed was another.

The land was beautiful, but she could feel the atmosphere shifting.

Maybe it had something to do with her returning from the dead. She wasn't certain, but she knew something wasn't right in the land anymore.

Could all of this truly be because of Jiya?

She had no way of knowing for sure—but she knew that if he wasn't stopped, the rest of their people would suffer. Even if he was defeated, would the humans truly accept her people?

"I fear da end of this journey," Odessa admitted.

"What do you mean?"

"Growin' up around here was hard because da humans were wary of us. I heard them call my mama a witch. Our belief in da spirit world, our desire to understand da spiritual energy in da world—they called it sorcery."

"Some people fear what their feeble minds cannot comprehend. That fear often turns into hate... or labels like 'evil' and 'sorcery,'" V said, a hint of frustration in her voice. "No matter what happens in the end... your people will live. You have my word on that."

V's words were fierce and certain. Odessa could see the woman had no doubt about what she'd said.

When they first met, everything in her told her to be cautious.

But now, she couldn't help the feeling growing inside her—a feeling that maybe, just maybe, she could trust this woman.

CHAPTER 5

Three days passed, and during that time, V trained diligently to improve her sword-fighting skills. Odessa had been relentless in their sparring, which forced V to use her mind more than just pure strength.

V enjoyed this time with Odessa. They had grown close in a short span.

Another thing V began doing was writing more in the tower. She wrote and sketched what she learned from Odessa. She continued to write down everything she learned about the Hiorians and even drew a picture of the strix she had encountered. Her scholarly past made her feel this was imperative.

V also spent time helping Odessa control herself around the smell of blood. It had been difficult, but Odessa had begun to show restraint. They reluctantly drank the blood of a deer to regain their strength. V hoped it would sustain Odessa for a few days.

Now they sat silently in the fortress, awaiting whatever might come.

V didn't know if anyone would show up, but she had to plan. The Wescreans had reason to return if they discovered the tower had been sieged. As for the Hiorians, they would surely come to retaliate.

As V contemplated the situation, she realized she needed eyes in the Fodmery. If she could find a way to monitor movements while preparing her defenses, it would greatly aid her crusade.

With the spiritual powers she now possessed, there had to be a way to do something akin to spying from the shadows. But what could her powers actually do to assist with that?

Odessa entered the room with a look of deep thought on her face. V watched as she marched over to the table where the map rested. For a moment, V said nothing, simply observing her underling as she studied the layout.

"What are you doing?"

"Tryin' to figure out where we should go next."

V sat in silence, watching Odessa trace something on the map with her finger. She must've had an idea—or perhaps she was simply tired of waiting.

She placed her finger on a spot.

"The keep. We must go to da keep."

V slowly stood and walked over to where Odessa stood. She looked down to see her pointing at Judith's Keep. V had no idea why Odessa would suggest that and looked at her with a furrowed brow.

"I do not understand."

"Dis is da daughta of da king. Maybe she can help us."

V stared off into space. Would the daughter be of any use if her brother had already been defeated? She didn't know the family dynamics, but she did know that Wescreas, like her own country, didn't typically have female warriors.

"Would she be of any help?"

Odessa looked at V, confused. It seemed she hadn't expected that question. Maybe she had thought V would be overjoyed—but she wasn't.

"I am certain she has warriors. Her brudda had been da leader. But if he is dead, then we find her."

V took this in. It might be worth a shot. Building up Judith's forces could help end the war. And if the Hiorians showed up, perhaps she could convince them to follow her to the keep.

"We will set course to venture there soon."

Relief washed over Odessa's face, and she nodded. V, meanwhile, began thinking again about the "spiritual arts" Odessa had mentioned. She needed to learn what she was truly capable of. It was the only way she could grow strong enough to be a real threat to Jiya.

"Can I inquire something, Odessa?"

Odessa stopped tracing the map and straightened. She turned with a look of intrigue.

"Of course."

"What can you do—and not do—with the power to perform spiritual arts?"

"You cannot alter time."

A look of sadness spread across Odessa's face. V felt sorrow stir within her as well. She hadn't thought about changing the past, but if she could... things would be different.

"As for other tings—we are different from da livin'. What we can do may differ from what da livin' users of spiritual arts can do."

"Is there a way we could maybe see what's happening in other places?"

"Aye."

A spark of hope formed across V's face as she leaned forward in her chair. The wood creaked beneath her weight. She had doubted the possibility, but if there were a way, she had to know.

"My mama used to use da water to see if my sistah lived."

"How does that work?"

"She pours her spiritual energy into a body of water and asks da water spirit to show her where she is. If my sister is near water, she will be seen."

"A water spirit?"

Odessa placed a hand on the scars on her right arm.
"It's somethin' my mama believes. I do not know if there is an actual water spirit. Although... da Spirit World is a mystery to da livin'." She shrugged.

"So what happens if the water doesn't show you where someone is?"

"Then you are left to wonder if they are alive."

Odessa's expression grew grim. V watched her silently, unsure what to say. It became clear that much of Odessa's immediate family had likely been lost.

"Is there any other way to see what's happening in other areas?"

"My mama also knew how to have her soul leave her body—so she could become a roamin' spirit."

"That's also possible?"

"Aye. Many tings are possible, but it is very dangerous. Both your soul and body are vulnerable to attack if separated too long. Also... you cannot stray too far from your body."

V sat in silence, processing the new information. Everything she was learning needed to be written down. It could be useful in the future.

Her eyes widened as she suddenly jumped to her feet. This had been the thing she needed to hear.

Odessa started to speak—but then froze.

V sensed it too. Heartbeats nearby. She could tell they were a mix of animals and people. Judging by the speed of the footfalls, they were running.

Someone was running away.

Then came the howls—sharp and unnatural—cutting through the walls. V had never heard anything like them. Her curiosity piqued. She rushed toward the door, Odessa at her heels.

V grabbed her sword, propped next to the door, and they didn't hesitate. Together, they stepped out into the night.

The chill hit them instantly. In the distance, they heard it—the clash of metal on metal. And then those same eerie howls again.

V glanced at Odessa before leaping onto the fortress wall, hoping for a better vantage point—but she still saw nothing. They were still in the forest, V assumed.

She moved swiftly in the direction of the battle, sword in hand. She glided across the ground, glancing once over her shoulder to see Odessa sprinting behind her. V finally came to a halt and ducked behind a tree.

Her eyes widened.

Three large figures were surrounding a fourth—also massive. Around them were great beasts cloaked in dark blue fire. Wolves. Enormous, wolf-like creatures.

The area resembled a battlefield. Trees knocked over. Debris everywhere. V stared at the back of the warrior before her—she was huge. Compared to V, she was a giant.

She moved through the chaos with a large hammer in hand. V got a better look: her arms appeared sculpted from stone, her strong thighs flexing with every swing. Her skin was gray— clearly not human. Her long black hair flowed like waves in the wind, reminding V of the sea.

She wore fur clothing from animals. Strangely, none of them —warrior or attackers—wore shoes. V found that odd.

Odessa stepped beside her, also in awe.

"Do you know what they are?" V whispered.

Odessa shook her head slowly, eyes locked on the fight.

V sighed and returned her focus. These strange people were arguing while fighting. What stood out most was that they spoke the Vostaylian language—though with a less fluent, older cadence.

"Yama! Ye must accept thy destiny!" bellowed a large, bearded man.

His light blue eyes locked on the woman he called Yama. V studied him—his muscles sculpted like stone, skin covered in scars and tribal ink.

But suddenly, his gaze shifted.

He pointed his spear directly at them.

V tensed. Had he sensed them?

"The air and the land speaks of thy presence! Come forth from the shadows so I may face thee!"

V started to move, but Odessa placed a hand on her arm— and stepped out of the shadows. She approached cautiously. The giants stared, confused.

"Doth ye know what she be, Woeton?" asked another giant.

"She be a changed one," replied the bearded man—Woeton. He now stared directly at Odessa.

"You are a blight upon the soil!"

V glanced down and saw that she was hovering.

When had that started?

She realized then—they hadn't sensed her. Only Odessa.

The wolves began circling her, ready to pounce.

"What is thy purpose here?" Woeton demanded.

Odessa stayed silent, staring at them.

Their accent was thick. Maybe she didn't understand them.

V stepped out from the shadows, standing behind Odessa.

Woeton and the other giant raised their weapons and took two steps back, glancing at each other.

V looked to Yama.

She was watching them in confusion.

"'Tis another one!"

"I know," Woeton snarled.

"What is a changed one?"

All three of the gray-skins went wide-eyed. They looked at each other, then back at V. She assumed they hadn't expected her to speak in an accent similar to their own.

"The tales were true... Such vile things do exist," Woeton scowled.

V stared at him for a moment.

"Once upon a time, I had been human. Alas, now, as you say, I have been changed... Something I detest," she said with clear dissatisfaction.

"Now, what exactly are ye people, and why attack thine own?"

"I am Woeton of the Scarstone tribe. Thy humans once hailed us as gray-skins," Woeton explained.

"Why attack one of thine own?"

"Twelve cycles ago, our tribe leader gave counsel to begin making sacrifices to Sifadi."

V stared, unsure of what he meant. She glanced at Odessa and leaned to whisper in her ear, "Have you heard the name Sifadi?"

Odessa looked uncertain, then shook her head. V guessed the name must be a deity—perhaps a spirit of the land, given how often they referenced the soil being tainted by her presence.

"What is Sifadi?"

Woeton frowned and spread his hands apart, pointing in different directions and to the ground.

"She is the land beneath thy feet, the trees, and the mountains all around ye."

"Why does she need to be sacrificed to?"

"'Tis our way. Every three cycles, a sacrifice is made," Woeton said gruffly.

"This cycle has called upon Yama! She fled instead of facing her fate!" Yonten exclaimed, cutting a look toward the grayskin named Yama.

"'Tis not our way! Why would Sifadi desire death in her name? Such travesty goes against thy teachings!" Yama shouted in a croaky, angry tone.

"Since we began this, those winged beasts hath not plagued our lands, hath they?" Woeton countered.

Yama fell silent and lowered her head. V quickly realized they were referring to vampyrs. If those creatures could harm even these powerful warriors, it made them all the more terrifying. And now, V herself had become something like them.

"Thy mother, sister, and father all hath done their part. Now 'tis thy turn to take responsibility."

"Silence, Yonten! Ye hath no place to speak of such things!" Yama frowned.

"Ye of all people should hath shame for this... I thought we were family!"

Yonten was about to speak when Woeton grabbed him.

V sensed there was more to this story. Why would their leader suddenly resort to sacrificing his people if he hadn't done so before?

"'Tis honor in thine ordeal. Tending to the land is our way. If this is the new way, then it should be accepted," Woeton said sternly.

"Please, bethink the chief's ways before his daughter's taking! Me thinks a change withered into him, for he has been ill.

The land writhes in pain when he walks."

"Do not speak such vile words about the chief, Yama! Ye've done it for far too long, and I will not stand for it any longer!" Yonten shouted.

He rushed toward Yama with his spear. V lunged forward, stepping between them. She grabbed the tip of the spear and planted her feet firmly. With effort, she lifted the weapon, pulling Yonten from the ground.

His large body flailed through the air as she held the spear. Even V still found herself surprised by her immense strength. She glanced at Yama, who stood dumbfounded.

"Woeton called you a changed one... Do ye know what it means?" Yama asked warily.

"I am a benighted spirit. And before I can take my final rest, there are a few people I must slay."

"Such a proclamation will not be accepted by me. You will be slain by my hand if I must!"

V turned to see Woeton towering over her, his eyes filled with a ferocity that would have frightened most. But V was no longer most. Her spiritual presence surged, forcing Woeton to step back. He could feel her power—and that made her more dangerous to him.

"No one is truly innocent. Especially not the people I plan to slay."

V turned away from Woeton and approached Yama, who raised her hammer defensively.

V lifted her hands, signaling she meant no harm.

She believed these strong people could be useful.

"What do ye want?" Yama asked.

"I need an army to defeat a city of the undead."

She wasn't lying. If Jiya still had that cursed book, he'd be surrounded by revenants—creatures far more useful than the living chevaliers. And if her presence tainted the land, surely the revenants would too.

"The land's unrest would appeareth to be an affliction caused by this scourge upon her belly," Woeton concluded.

"I think thy situation is much more complicated than that, sir Woeton."

V glanced over her shoulder. Woeton stood a few feet away, stroking his beard. Yonten came stumbling over, visibly shaken. V tossed him his spear, which he caught with a deep gaze of suspicion.

"What do you speaketh of?" Yama asked.

"The sacrifices your tribe leader chooses are all from thy family—no one else. That tells me he hath a personal begrudgery with thy kin."

Yama furrowed her thick brow and stared into the distance. It was clear she had no idea why her family was targeted. V assumed the answer lay with one of Yama's parents.

"Our chief is above such a thing."

V looked at Woeton, who now stared back blankly. She could hear his heart beating faster.

Could he be hiding something?

"You said his daughter had been taken. Who exactly took her, and how were Yama's parents involved?"

Woeton and Yonten exchanged a glance. They clearly knew something. V didn't want to assume too much—but her suspicions deepened.

"To see the lower lands he went, taking his daughter. Ambushed they were, by purple hoods."

V's eyes widened, and her blood boiled.
The Acolytes.

Could they really have had a hand in this too? How much power had they gained?

"Did the purple cloaks come with the winged beast?" Yama asked.

"Yes."

"Still, such a thing eludes me—why 'tis my family that is punished."

"Alas, Khangdro was his guardian."

Woeton slapped Yonten across the back of the head, sending him face-first into the dirt. The look of regret on Woeton's chiseled face could not be hidden.

"A good man, that he was."

"Blasphemy! Ye murdered me dad, and ye dare speak his name with such grace!"

Yama lunged, dirt and mud flying.

V sidestepped but reached out to grab the hammer. As she did, a veil of green energy wrapped around her arm and extended like a phantom hand.

It caught the hammer mid-swing—stopping Yama cold.

Everyone froze, dumbfounded.

V couldn't understand how she'd done it...

But she knew—she had just discovered another spiritual power.

"How did ye stop her without touching anything?" Yonten asked.

"What sort of sorcery is this?"

They couldn't see spiritual energy—but perhaps they could feel it through the land. This intrigued V. Her ghost hand yanked the hammer, forcing Yama back a few steps.

"There is a fortress not far from here. Have thy chief meet me there," V requested.

"The lowlands are forbidden to him now..." Yonten said.

"He will come if I have his sacrifice as a hostage."

Yama stared at her, confused.

V wanted to help them—but to do that, she had to understand what had truly changed the chief.

"Do ye truly believe I will accompany thee?" Yama asked in a singsong tone.

V looked at her, then to Woeton. She sighed and turned away with a shrug.

"You can accept the ending of thy family's tale—or choose to live for their sake."

She walked over to where Odessa sat leaning against a tree. Beside her, one of the wolf-like creatures rested, enjoying her touch. Somehow, Odessa had made it a companion. The others still prowled the area.

"We are going back."

Odessa staggered to her feet and nodded.

"You all were talking gibberish for da last five minutes. I could barely follow what they were sayin'."

"Their chief changed years ago after losing his daughter. He became ill... and began ordering sacrifices to appease this Sifadi character."

Odessa looked curious. As they moved through the forest, V could tell her underling was deep in thought.

"If he changed when becoming ill and started doing things he'd never done before... then he could be corrupted."

"Corrupted?"

"I was young, but I remember something happened to a friend when she lost her family. She started acting strange... I never understood why—until her eyes turned black."

Odessa stopped, staring off into space. V could sense the trauma in her.

"She killed a few people before da older Hiorians had to put her to rest. My mama told me she had been consumed by a spirit called a specter."

"Your people have such a way with naming things," V mumbled.

She couldn't imagine the horror of seeing a friend turn into something unrecognizable. It reminded her of the strange events that had begun unfolding over the years.

"Although... their situation could simply be that da loss of his child drove him mad." Odessa sighed.

She shrugged and kept walking. V paused, deep in thought—until something brushed past her.

She turned. Yama was following the wolf-like creature that had bonded with Odessa.

"I have misgivings. The chief mayhaps not come to find me."

"You said when he walks upon the soil, it writhes in pain. What does that mean?"

"I hath seen him cough up black goo. The soil withers from it. And sometimes... his eyes turn black as night."

V stared in disbelief.

Odessa had been right.

The chief was likely corrupted by a specter.

V looked at Odessa walking ahead. She could see spiritual energy emanating from her—dark and turbulent. But when she looked at Yama, her aura was bright.

"May he appear before us... so that we can help him."

V's words carried doubt. She didn't yet know everything about the spirit world.

But having Odessa at her side changed things.

Or so she hoped.

For the road ahead was filled with the supernatural.

CHAPTER 6

Odessa's Isolation pt. 2

Another three days passed and no one had arrived at the tower. This made Odessa concerned as she had begun to feel that time was being wasted here. She and V sparred periodically so that they could practice using their supernatural abilities along with normal combat skills.

Odessa had already accepted that V wasn't truly a fighter. What made her dangerous was her powers which she tried not to rely on much. Although Odessa felt if they were to get anywhere in the coming battles, V would have to use the powers she seemed to be desperate to cast aside.

While they were here waiting to see if the people V called gray skins to show up Odessa listened to the conversations she had with the young gray skin staying with them. Odessa didn't care too much to listen in on the conversations.

Odessa understood that V had a fondness for her people and actually wanted to connect with them. Seeing how she now was trying to connect with Yama made that all the more clear. This had been something Odessa found unfamiliar, because other humans never cared about other cultures—at least, this was what she had often noticed. Taking the time to learn the ways of Yama's people and how they operated—this became something Odessa actually liked about V.

She recalled her uncle traveling to a place called Vostaylia. That was where he learned that the common tongue of the people in this land varied by country. She remembered him saying the Vostaylians spoke in a serious manner most of the time. Her younger brother had learned how to sound like a Vostaylian. It amused her when he started to speak slowly and sternly, using words she had never heard of.

As she sat there thinking about her brother, she realized that he would have been eighteen today. How disheartening to know that he had to go to battle a few days before the night of his birth—a night he wouldn't get to see because of the humans.

Odessa gritted her teeth as a quick jolt of rage welled up within her. These bursts of emotion she had been having since returning from death were overwhelming. It made her head spin as she tried to keep her mind under control. Not only that, but the heartbeat of the young gray-skin stirred something ominous within Odessa. It was something that frightened her.

She had no desire to harm this young woman, who she had actually taken a liking to. Despite not understanding everything she said, she grew to like her. The gray-skin had become a friend she felt safe with. From what she could gather, Yama was at least a few years younger than her.

She assumed she was likely around the same age as her brother Omari. She understood that Yama was in danger, which had been the reason she fled from her home. Not only that, but Odessa had noticed the various tones in her voice— how it would go from a singsong tone to a croaky one when she got upset.

Now they were waiting to see if the other gray-skins would return. They were also waiting for the possible arrival of either the Hiorians or Jiya's human army. If it were the latter, they would be in for a serious battle—a battle that Odessa felt unsure they could handle. Even though she could feel that she was stronger now, she didn't know how that would hold up against an army of armed men.

As Odessa sat silently, watching V and Yama talk, she grew bored. Not only that, but fighting off the thirst was a grueling task. She despised that fact. Sometimes looking at Yama reminded her of how she felt after catching fish on her boating trips with her father. It caused her to divert her gaze from Yama whenever they were close to each other.

Odessa got up and went outside. The sun had just recently disappeared, so it seemed safe. She wanted some air to clear her mind. The sound of crickets in the distance was a nice ambience, as well as the chill breeze in the air.

She looked around the area, taking in the tower's surroundings. There was an area on the far left where she saw what looked like targets for archery practice. It got her thinking, so she began to search around. She wanted to try practicing, since it had been a long while.

After scouring the area, she found a bow and some arrows. The bow seemed a bit worn, but she figured if she tended to it, she could improve it. She spent a few minutes readjusting the bowstring and making sure there was enough tension.

Once ready, she walked over to a spot at least twenty feet from the targets. She stared at the target straight ahead for a moment. While standing there, she took note of the wind's direction. This would help her get a better feel for how she should aim.

After taking a few deep breaths, she raised the bow and nocked an arrow. She pulled the string back gently. The tension in the string made the muscles in her arm and shoulder blade flex. As she aimed the arrow, she began to feel the spiritual energy within her—and around her.

She let her spiritual energy flow into her fingers, then into the bow. Her eyes noticed the rippling green aura forming around the arrow. It reminded her of water because of how fluid the phenomenon appeared. Placing spiritual energy into things meant giving them powers beyond their natural capabilities.

When she let go of the string, the arrow shot forward. It whizzed through the air, and instead of simply hitting the target, it tore through it completely. To her surprise, the arrow kept going until it hit the wall behind the target, shaking the tower.

One thing about spiritual arts that humans never understood was that they used their own life force to create them.

Growing up and trying to master the art, her father had always urged her to pace herself.

Trying to use spiritual arts at an unnatural level in a single situation could kill someone. Odessa only knew this because her father's friend had died that way. He fought with everything he had in a battle against Jiya. Hearing about his death had broken her father—and saddened her deeply.

As Odessa stood there silently, staring at the hole in the target, she began to wonder. How did Jiya even come across the book that raised the dead? She had always wondered and never figured it out. No one around her knew either. All she knew was that the book he possessed was part of what made him so dangerous.

Now she began to question herself—because in a way, she had done the same thing. She had obtained power from something dark and could feel it changing her. Her heart no longer beat, and she felt no breath in her lungs. The fact that she could no longer see the sunrise without burning saddened her.

She had loved watching the sunrise with her brother and mother. The changing colors of the sky fascinated her as the sun's rays stretched across the land. It reminded her of the way she would stretch her limbs in different directions when getting out of bed in the morning.

That was the only comparison she could think of as she remembered the sunrise. Her thoughts continued to drift to memories of the past. She recalled her time with her older brother when he taught her how to hunt. Some Hiorian families practiced with a specific type of weapon.

Her father's family specialized in archery and were known for raising the best hunters. On the other hand, her mother's family excelled at fighting with spears. These weapons of choice had been shared between the two families once they united.

Her eldest brother was the best archer among their siblings. She missed him dearly and wished she knew what had happened to him on that last hunting trip. That mystery haunted her. He had promised to come back and take her with him on the next trip.

He had gone with a group of his friends. One of them had been someone her father paired her with. The older Hiorians had arranged pairings for the young to keep the Hiorian bloodline alive. Sometimes she didn't understand the rush to form relationships—her father had been over a century old before he was killed.

In appearance, he didn't look like a young man, but he was still incredibly fit. From what she heard from the Wescreans, they always assumed he was around forty or fifty—though she knew that was them trying to estimate his age by their own standards.

Odessa hadn't wanted a mate to be arranged for her, but she hadn't protested because she loved her father. She didn't believe he would pair her with someone who would hurt her. Sadly, she had been completely wrong about that.

His name was Zahur Silvercloud. His family were warriors who fought with daggers. They also made potions from ingredients found in the land to create smoke. The family would use that billow of smoke to confuse prey. Now, they were being forced to use it in battles against humans and revenants.

Zahur had been the one who gifted her the daggers she now fought with. She hated him for many reasons—but mainly because he had stopped her from killing Jiya. Whether she would have succeeded was a mystery. As she thought of him, she began rubbing her fingers along the scars on her arm.

One thing she remembered was that he had said she didn't have the true will to kill. Looking back on that day, he was right. When she had to cut down a Wescrean warrior, she always hesitated. She hated the sight of blood. Now, she had become something that thrived on it—and it disgusted her.

She had to remind herself it was all so that she could one day punish Zahur for betraying his family—and her. Not only that, but he had called her family cowards and even spoke ill of her elder brother. He had never been a gentle person toward her.

Nothing would ever be able to redeem his character in her eyes. Soon, she would show him who the true coward had been all along. As she thought about him, she began to wonder if she could potentially see what he was doing.

Unlike her mother, she wasn't as skilled at doing the thing her people sometimes called dowsing. She looked around the area and found a puddle. Slowly, she approached it and stood there for a moment. As she stared at the puddle, she could see her reflection.

Although, it was more shadowy and obscured, preventing her from clearly seeing her face. She recalled V hinting that she didn't know what she looked like anymore. Could this have been why—or was it completely different for her? There were still too many questions about what Odessa had become.

V didn't have the answers, because she didn't know either. Their journey was also one of finding themselves again—or who they were meant to be in this new life, if she could even call it that. They were both experiencing the change, but V had been going through it longer.

Odessa knew she had to remain strong and try her best to hold onto her family's ideals and teachings. Although, it would be a task she likely would fail. As she continued to stare into the puddle, she pondered whether she should even try to see Zahur. Maybe she should see her mother instead.

Using the skill of dowsing to find her mother would likely cause her to feel more guilt for the path she'd chosen. If she decided to search for Zahur, then maybe she could convince herself that her decision to accept the dark power from V had been justified.

The path of revenge wasn't something that could be followed while clinging to beliefs. Such a journey would force a person to go against everything they knew. Usually, people fell to corruption and became the very thing they despised. Odessa understood that—but she didn't plan to stay in the world long enough to become the monster Jiya had turned into.

Once she took care of him and Zahur, then she could rest in

peace. She only hoped that wherever her father and brothers ended up, they would forgive her and welcome her into paradise. If the spirit world had a paradise, she truly hoped she would be able to meet them there.

Slowly, Odessa let out a deep breath as she knelt next to the puddle. She set the bow down beside her and placed her finger over the water. Her mind was made up—she would try to use the spiritual art of dowsing to locate her desired person. A gentle tap of the puddle caused a ripple that obscured her already blurred reflection even more.

Slowly, the water rippled as something seemed to happen. Odessa leaned in closer, hoping to see the location—or the person—she sought...

CHAPTER 7

Another week passed since V and Odessa met Yama. Since then, V had spent time training and asking Yama questions. She wanted to learn about the gray-skins the way she had learned about the Hiorians.

Everything Yama told her, she wrote down in her journal. This journal had become her codex of knowledge on the supernatural world. Everything she had learned about what she herself had become was recorded in it. Everything she had gathered over the years had been jotted down. She didn't know why, but she felt it would be of use to someone in the future.

What she learned about the gray-skins was that their tribe lived high in the Scarstone Mountains. They were great hunters and knew much about the land. Her people studied the different plants that grew. They could tell when the seasons would change. Sometimes they could even sense danger to come, like earthquakes or great storms.

As V stood outside on the wall, she stared at the mountains in the distance. The fact that a race of people had lived there without her own people knowing fascinated her. Yama said the gray-skins always tried to avoid humans. She explained how her people watched everything humans did to one another from above.

V didn't blame them for not wanting to interact with humans. Even though she had been one herself, she couldn't deny the atrocities committed by her kind. She even thought about the things her own father had done. And what she now planned to do would be just as horrible.

Odessa and Yama didn't speak the same language, so V had to act as translator. Despite that, it appeared they had grown quite accustomed to one another. As V stood on the wall, she watched Yama and Odessa training together. Even though Yama had said her people weren't warriors, she did possess good combat skills.

V hoped that maybe there would be a way to get Yama—and maybe some of her people—to join the crusade. If she had these strong warriors with her, she could no doubt defeat Jiya's army. For now, she needed to help Yama. That would likely earn their support.

"Three nights ye hath sat upon the wall all for naught."

V looked over her shoulder to see Yama staring up at her. If the chief held a personal grudge against the family, then he would, without a doubt, show up. V believed this whole-heartedly and expected him to arrive soon.

As she continued to wonder when they would come, another thought crossed her mind. Why hadn't the Wescreans—or even the Hiorians—shown up? This made her anxious, as she felt something horrible might happen. She didn't want to rush building her forces, but she needed to be prepared for any attack.

"Something approaches us!"

V snapped her head back to see Yama kneeling on the ground, her hand pressed into the dirt. A second passed before V heard it too—the sound of a hundred heartbeats, belonging to both animals and people. From the direction of the noise, she knew they were coming from the north.

V turned and moved along the wall to get a better view. Once she reached the other side, she saw torches and men riding on mounts. She recognized the banner of the shield and horse. Their armor bore turquoise and white accents. At the forefront rode a large man on a black horse.

A shroud of spiritual energy cloaked around him, and his eyes glowed. V scoffed as she realized he had to be a revenant. The chevaliers riding behind him were revenants as well. V drew her sword, preparing for battle.

"We cannot let them take back this tower!" she exclaimed.

Without another word, V leapt off the wall into the swarm of chevaliers below. She moved swiftly, snaking through the crowd of men, swinging her sword. Red splattered everywhere as she cut her way forward, eyes locked on the large chevalier on the black horse. His sword glowed with spiritual energy.

His face was obscured by a horned mask. She could feel power from him unlike any she'd faced before. Jiya made his generals revenants under his control. The humans who followed him did so under the leadership of the undead.

This would be her first real battle—and it would determine her future. How far would she be able to make it before someone managed to defeat her? These thoughts crossed her mind as she evaded attacks.

The chevaliers surrounding her took a few steps back and raised their shields. A whizzing sound tore through the air, and she looked up. A volley of arrows rained down. Her movements were agile as she swayed side to side to avoid them.

When the arrows stopped, a heavy rumble nearly knocked her over. She turned to see Yama slamming her hammer into the ground. The force was so powerful that rubble exploded from the soil, sending chevaliers flying.

The revenant chevaliers rushed Yama, but she had no trouble overpowering them. V looked for Odessa and spotted her on the wall, firing arrows at the chevaliers trying to climb up.

"Cover the back gate, Odessa!" V ordered.

Odessa stiffened for a moment before nodding and moving along the wall, still firing arrows to slow the enemy's advance. V pushed forward, hoping to end the battle by defeating their general.

She was saving all her spiritual power for him. The chevaliers rushing her were cut down by pure strength. They were nothing to her now. Pools of crimson soaked the ground beneath her feet as she made her way toward the black horse.

The general climbed down as his chevaliers rushed to his side. He raised his greatsword toward V. It was much larger than hers—and cloaked in spiritual energy. She knew his attacks would be devastating.

"I had been told it was only two of ya that attacked this tower. Now I see my messenger had not a titter of wit. He said he encountered two—but I see three," the chevalier said in his Wescrean tongue, his voice deep.

"I take it you are Leon the Vile."

"Ja! Ya have heard of me then?"

The way Wescreans spoke was fast and sometimes incoherent. Some were long-winded, giving speeches rather than simple answers. Leon spoke quickly, but V didn't get the impression he'd talk much.

"I haven't a baldy notion who ya are," V answered, mocking his accent.

"Ya appear to be from Vostaylia. With that said, ya should know my name—for I've defeated many of the red cloaks," Leon boasted.

"Yet, you're now dead and under the control of that vile Hiorian, Jiya."

Leon fell silent, then waved his hand. In a moment, his men surrounded V. She ignored them, eyes locked on Leon the Vile. The chevaliers hesitated, then lunged at her. She evaded with ease.

She struck at the weak points in their armor—small wounds that bled freely. She did this instead of killing them instantly, to make a point. They were beneath her.

Leon continued to watch, sword still at his side. Vibrant green waves swirled around it. Once the chevaliers fell, only Leon remained.

"Ya swordsmanship is meager at best. It's clear ya no longer human, but ya don't seem to be a revenant either."

V curled her lip, revealing her fangs. She lunged, swinging wildly. Leon stepped back, raising his sword to block. The impact sent a powerful gust of wind between them. Their swords clashed, igniting sparks.

V thought she could overpower him—but the power in his

sword weakened her strikes. He began swinging faster. She could track him with her eyes, but her body couldn't keep up. She barely evaded a slash, escaping with a cut to her arm.

Black blood oozed from the wound. Her skin burned. She hissed in pain as she blocked another strike. She tried to close the distance, but Leon struck her jaw with his left hand. She stumbled, losing her balance.

He swung his sword, pouring spiritual energy into it. The force was overwhelming—like being caught in a current. She was flung into the forest, crashing through trees.

She finally landed in the dirt, rolling down a small hill before coming to a stop. Gasping in pain, she rolled onto her side. One thing remained clear: she could still feel pain. She could endure greater injuries—but it still hurt.

As she staggered to her feet, her muscles screamed. Leon was truly dangerous. If this was just the beginning, her crusade would not be easy. She had a long way to go—and needed more strength and allies.

She noticed her wound hadn't healed. That worried her. She always healed. Something about Leon's power disrupted that.

V gritted her teeth, bent her knees, and pushed off the ground. She moved fast, flowing spiritual energy into her sword to make her next strike stronger.

Trees blurred as she darted past them. Her eyes scanned for roots, limbs, anything that might trip her. Moonlight filtered faintly through the canopy above.

V burst from the trees to see Leon by his horse, waiting. She wanted to show him the wrath she planned to use to destroy Wescreas. She leapt high into the air, sword raised.

Leon looked up as she descended. She brought the blade down hard, a wave of energy blasting through the earth. Leon sidestepped, but the force knocked him off his feet. His body rolled across the field, and he dropped his sword.

V stood with her sword lowered, staring at the ground split by her strike—nearly a hundred feet long. It amazed her. But it also disappointed her. It still wasn't enough.

She saw Leon stagger to his feet. He retrieved his sword. V rushed at him, aiming to take off his head—but he knocked her sword off-course with his left hand and struck her across the face with his right.

Her head snapped to the side, her body thrown with it. She rolled across the ground but landed on her feet. She looked around, spotting Yama still fighting—but now only with her fists. She used brute force, but it wasn't enough to kill.

V wondered if she even intended to kill. If so, she'd have kept using her hammer. Most of the chevaliers were still alive, being dragged away. They needed to be dead—so they couldn't recover.

Arrows flew at Yama, but she swatted them aside like insects. V, showing no mercy, rushed the nearest archers. A few swings of her sword painted the ground red.

Then she turned back toward Leon—he had his sword again. He sprinted toward Yama.

V had no intention of letting her die. She chased him, hoping to intercept before he struck.

Yama saw Leon and braced herself. He swung at her head. V arrived just in time to block it—but the force of the blow knocked her backward into Yama.

They both hit the ground, now looking up at him.

"It's been a while since I've seen another one of these gray-skins," Leon mused.

V glanced at Yama, who looked at Leon with a frustrated expression. Yama didn't speak Wescrean, so she had no idea what Leon had just said. V quickly got to her feet and took her fighting stance again. She gripped the hilt of her sword with both hands. Defeating Leon meant his chevaliers would hopefully retreat.

"What is the meaning of what you say?" V asked.

Leon gestured to Yama with his sword. "The Acolytes had one as a prisoner a few years ago."

V briefly glanced at her comrade, realizing Leon was speaking about the chief's daughter. Could it be possible that maybe they had a chance to save her? Although, it would require finding the Acolytes.

"Where are the Acolytes?"

"Not sure, and I truly don't care. They're beneath me—worthless people who worship false idols."

Leon raised his sword, preparing to battle. V needed to ask more questions, but it was clear he was done talking. She inched forward, preparing for the next attack. Before Leon could move, one of his chevaliers ran past him, screaming in panic.

Leon's attention turned to the fleeing chevalier—and V saw her chance.

She raised her sword close to her head, aiming for Leon's neck. The blade was nearly there before he leaned in the direction of her swing. V heard bones cracking as Leon narrowly slipped away.

She looked perplexed, wondering how he had managed to evade when her sword had been so close. Then, instead of countering, Leon threw his sword at the fleeing chevalier. It struck him in the back. The chevalier cried out in pain and collapsed to his knees.

V looked around. Leon still had a great number of chevaliers standing. Most of them now surrounded her and Yama. The others were still trying to get through the gate. Odessa continued to rain arrows down on them. V could smell the blood all around.

She held out her hand and channeled her spiritual energy. Her plan was to draw in all the blood and manipulate it for an attack. Droplets of red began to float into the air, swirling toward her. The blood spiraled into a ball, growing larger the more she gathered.

After a minute, a massive sphere of blood floated high above them. V glanced at Yama and gestured for her to stand.

Without hesitation, Yama rose to her feet.

"Run," V ordered.

Yama stared at her, confused. V gestured away from the

sphere. After a second, Yama nodded and charged forward, bulldozing through the chevaliers. V then turned her attention back to Leon.

"Ya gathered all the blood that's been shed into a sphere. Don't tell me ya plan to make it rain on us."

"I have the power to control the temperature of the blood."

V tightened her fist, still raised. The sphere exploded, causing red rain to fall from the sky. The chevaliers stared upward —until they realized the drops were hot.

Scalding hot.

The blood began to melt armor and sear exposed flesh. Screams of pain filled the air as the soldiers scattered.

Leon calmly walked to retrieve his sword, unfazed by the boiling blood. V didn't like this. She had drained herself, and yet her enemy seemed completely unaffected.

"I no longer feel pain—unlike these living wankers!" Leon shouted.

A chevalier ran past him, and Leon swung his sword. V's eyes widened as the chevalier's head rolled across the dirt. Blood coated Leon's armor as he faced her again. Why would he cut down his own? Was this how he earned his name?

Leon approached, and V's body felt heavy. She had drained too much power with her last attack. The lack of blood made it hard to fight for long. Still, she believed she could beat him— somehow.

"I still haven't figured out what kind of undead creature ya are. Right now, I'm gutted to see how weak ya turned out to be. When Sir Charles came rushing to my fortress, he described ya as a monster."

V hadn't realized anyone escaped the tower when she took it. That explained why they'd arrived with so many. What didn't make sense was why it had taken so long.

"'Tis only a drop of what I can do!" V exclaimed.

It was a bluff. She had nothing left in her arsenal. Her body was drained. Drinking blood was how vampyrs replenished their life force. The longer she denied it, the more the thirst grew—and the more blood she'd need to recover.

"Ya've run yourself dry doin' that spectacle with the blood."

Leon read her like a book. There was no surprising him now. She raised her sword, bracing for his next attack—when a loud horn sounded through the air. She looked around to see some chevaliers climbing onto their horses. One blew a horn, still pressed to his lips.

After a moment, the chevaliers began marching back the way they had come. V looked around to see the remaining ones dragging their wounded away. Relief washed over her. This meant she could recover.

"What are ya prats doing?! I didn't request a retreat!" Leon roared.

He grabbed a fleeing chevalier and cut him down. V watched as Leon spiraled into a frenzy, slaughtering his own men. He was mad—unhinged. Maybe that was why he died in the first place.

Finally, Leon looked around, then marched to his horse. He pointed his sword at V.

"Cheerio, then! We shall meet again, mon cher. But next time —I'll leave with ya head!"

He yanked the reins, and the horse took off into the distance. V watched as he and his men disappeared. She lowered her sword and collapsed to her knees. Her vision spun. She fell onto her back.

This fight made it clear she had a long way to go. The journey ahead wouldn't be easy. The battles would only grow harder. She needed to become stronger. But was she willing to dive deeper into the dark?

V slowly closed her eyes and drifted off into a deep sleep.

*

The moonlight's faint glow stirred V awake. She sat up, realizing she was still in the field where the battle had taken place. The smell of blood filled her nostrils. Its intoxicating aroma tempted her as she looked around.

Odessa was dragging corpses into a pile. A white substance

was scattered around them.

Her time with the Hiorians had taught her much. Sometimes, they placed salt around the dead to purify their souls before burning the bodies. They often did this for people who had been cruel in life—to keep them from coming back as corrupted spirits.

V looked to see Yama standing nearby, holding a torch. Beside her sat the wolf-like creature that had grown fond of Odessa. V couldn't help but wonder how long she'd been asleep. Slowly, she staggered to her feet. Her muscles ached as she stumbled forward. The cut from Leon's sword still hadn't fully healed.

Yama noticed her and began walking over. She actually looked... concerned. That amused V slightly—this stranger showing her compassion.

"Are ye alright?" Yama asked.

"How long hath I been slumbering?"

"Good, you are awake!" Odessa shouted as she threw a dead body onto the pile of corpses.

As V watched Odessa, she noticed something that concerned her. Odessa's hands were trembling as she approached another dead chevalier. She still struggled with the thirst and was clearly doing her best not to be consumed by it.

"Odessa, that is quite enough. Go get cleaned up," V said softly.

"I am fine. We need to ensure none of these people come back."

"It can wait. Now go and get yourself cleaned up," V ordered.

Odessa stiffened and stopped moving. She dropped the body she had started to lift from the ground. Her hands were covered in blood, and she stared at them in a trance. V rushed over and grabbed her by the shoulders.

"Don't."

"Ye be putting a flame to these bodies?"

V glanced over her shoulder to see Yama picking up two corpses. She nodded as she watched Yama throw them onto the pile. V thanked her, then led Odessa toward the gate into the tower.

Once inside, V led Odessa to a large bucket where they had been collecting rainwater. She forced Odessa's hands into the water and urged her to wipe the blood off as best she could.

"You act like a mama," Odessa mumbled.

V paused and looked at her. She hadn't realized how she had been acting. Unfortunately, she couldn't help it. Odessa was the closest thing she had to caring for a daughter.

"I am sorry."

"No... it is fine. It makes me wonder about you more," Odessa said sincerely.

A faint smile formed on V's lips. She lowered her head as she began to wonder what it would've been like to raise a daughter. On instinct, she held her stomach, recalling her past life. Her dead heart ached for her family.

"Did you have a daughta?"

"I did not have the pleasure to raise her," V sighed.

A silence filled the air as she stared off into the distance. The silence was short-lived as Yama entered the fortress. V watched her close the gate behind her. The smell of burning flesh filled the atmosphere. It smelled horrible, likely due to the things the Wescreans ate.

"You didn't kill any of them."

V turned to Yama, who had crossed her arms. She wiped the dirt off her hands with an impassive look on her face. It made it hard for V to know what the giant was thinking.

"Life is precious, and I shall not take it," Yama finally said.

V thought long and hard on that statement. Years ago, she couldn't have fathomed hurting anyone. Now, she hardly gave it a second thought. She wouldn't deny that she had become a killer—though she hadn't chosen this as her destiny.

"What if 'tis possible thy chief's daughter might yet live?"

Yama's eyes widened, a quizzical look forming on her face. From what Leon had said, it was possible the Acolytes still had her. Although the likelihood seemed slim, V realized the girl could have been used in another ritual.

If that were the case, Yama could consider the chief's daughter as good as dead. Everything pointed to uncertainty, but for now, V believed she could offer Yama hope. If there was a chance the daughter lived, then maybe the tribe chief wouldn't sacrifice Yama.

"Are ye certain she lives?"

"No, but from what that undead chevalier said, 'tis possible a cult has her."

Yama furrowed her brow and tilted her head. "'Tis a cult that took her, ye say? What that be?"

"Those purple cloaks Woeton spoke of."

"What would they want with Tora?"

"So that be her name?" V asked. Yama nodded. "It sounds different compared to you and those other two."

"From the north is where her mother comes. A tribe foreign to our own."

V took a moment to ponder this. "Well, they may have taken her to sacrifice her to Vetala."

"Then why paint a picture of hope before me if thy words bear no fruit?" Yama asked.

"That man I fought said he saw her—so 'tis possible she may yet live. Maybe they kept her alive to study her."

"The chief searched for answers from Sifadi. I doth not believe he obtained any consolation of hope for his daughter," Yama frowned.

"How does she communicate to your people?"

"Sometimes rocks fall from the mountain. Sometimes flowers that hath not been seen in ages appear. She speaks in many ways."

V took a second to process this. Yama's people were a peculiar bunch. They fascinated her and sparked a desire to know more. She had learned much about the Hiorians—now she was learning of another race that lived quietly in the world.

"Well, I would still like to try and find out what happened to her. Maybe it will give thy chief closure."

"Why help us?"

"'Tis balance that I hath been taught maintains the world. For all the wrong I hath done—and will do—some good must make up for it."

Yama took a moment to ponder her words. Finally, she nodded to indicate she understood. V hoped this conversation brought some level of understanding between them. The fact Yama had fought alongside her showed that she, at the very least, slightly trusted her.

"We need to prepare. We will not survive da next attack," Odessa suddenly said.

V had almost forgotten she was beside her. She felt a twinge of guilt, though Odessa didn't seem bothered.

"You are right. And I need to get stronger so I can defeat Leon the Vile."

As the trio stood beneath the faint moonlight, the wind began to blow. The wolf-like creature began acting strangely —and so did Yama. In the distance, strange howls echoed through the forest.

The gray-skins were on their way to the tower after all.

V only hoped they could have a cordial conversation... without violence.

CHAPTER 8

Odessa's Isolation Pt. 3

The battle had ended, but it didn't feel like a victory. Bodies were scattered everywhere, and Odessa felt drained. She had climbed down off the wall onto the corpses that lay on the ground—arrows sticking through the armor of these unfortunate warriors.

A field of bodies littered the area, with blood pooling into the muddy ground. Blue flames were slowly fading from the corpses of what she assumed had been revenants. This was the path she chose, and she had to walk it now. The journey would have many more nights like this.

These sad warriors were no match for her as she stared down at the dead beneath her feet. Still, it pained her to see so much death—death that had occurred at her hand. A sense of shame weighed on her slightly. She had to remind herself that these people saw her as nothing more than something to be feared and destroyed.

Even before being turned, they had shunned her people and looked at her with disgust. A part of her faintly relished punishing them for mistreating her kind. Her face twisted with disdain at the thoughts she was having.

Two hours had passed since the battle. She had begun putting the corpses into a pile. V had fought so earnestly that she had worn herself out. Not far from her, she saw V lying on the ground with her eyes shut. Even in what she assumed was sleep, V seemed bothered by something.

Odessa stood silently, surrounded by the overwhelming smell of what she assumed was blood. It left a metallic taste in her mouth as she bent down to pick up a dead body.

She hoisted the fallen warrior over her shoulder and turned around. As she marched toward the pile she had been building, she did her best to ignore the smell. When she reached the pile, she noticed V had finally woken up. That surprised her—just a second ago, she hadn't moved.

"Good, you are awake!" Odessa shouted as she threw the dead body onto the pile of corpses.

Odessa noticed her hands were trembling as she approached another dead chevalier. She still struggled with the thirst, but she did her best not to be consumed by it. She had to remain strong—not drink the blood all around her.

"Odessa, that's quite enough. Go get cleaned up."

Odessa heard V say it in a soft tone—one filled with concern —but she didn't want V to think she couldn't remain in control. She feared V would be disappointed if she failed to overcome the thirst.

"I am fine. We need to ensure none of these people come back."

Odessa didn't know how Jiya's dark spiritual power worked. All she knew was that burning the bodies of the dead within a circle of salt purified their souls. At least, that's what her father had taught her and her siblings.

"It can wait. Now go and get yourself cleaned up," V ordered.

Odessa stiffened and stopped moving. Sometimes, when V gave her an order, a strange force took over her. No matter what she did, it was as if she couldn't ignore V's direct command.

It frightened her—because in those moments, she had no control over herself. She dropped the body she had started to lift. That's when she finally noticed the blood. Her hands were covered in it, and she stared at them in a trance.

"Don't!"

A voice yelled as someone grabbed her. Whoever it was shook her a few times. Still, she felt stuck in that trance-like state. Yama's voice rang out in her own tongue—something that sounded like a question.

Odessa heard V's voice before she felt herself being pulled along, led toward the gate into the tower. Once inside, V brought her to a large bucket where they had been collecting rainwater.

Odessa didn't resist as she felt the hands of the woman who had given her this curse. V forced her hands into the water, clearly trying to wash the blood away.

Odessa began to notice the motherly nature V had started to show. It felt strange—but she appreciated it. This woman cared about her.

"You act like a mama," Odessa mumbled.

This gave V pause as she looked at her. It was something Odessa had meant to keep to herself, but it slipped out. She meant no harm by it—but saw that it bothered V. A look of shame crossed V's face as she stepped back.

"I am sorry."

Odessa's eyes widened. She hadn't meant to hurt her feelings. She'd grown to care for V in such a short time. She respected her—and wanted to be a good friend.

"No... it is fine. It makes me wonder about you more," Odessa said, trying to show her sincerity.

A faint smile formed on V's lips. She lowered her head. There was a brief silence before Odessa noticed something—V gently held her stomach.

"Did you have a daughta?"

She wasn't sure if she should ask—but she was curious. V had implied she had selfish reasons for offering to save Odessa. Judging by the way she often acted, Odessa believed that had been the reason. Before becoming whatever they were, V had been a mother.

A look of sadness appeared on V's face. It was disheartening. Odessa stood there quietly, waiting for an answer.

"I did not have the pleasure of raising her," V sighed.

A silence filled the air again as V stared off into the distance. The quiet was short-lived as Yama entered the fortress. Odessa watched her close the gate behind her. The smell of burning flesh filled the air.

It was grotesque. Odessa had to pinch her nose. Her enhanced sense of smell didn't help at all. She could still taste the foul stench. One thing she never liked about the Wescreans was their tendency to wear strong perfume to mask their odor.

Her mother used to berate her when she made comments about their smell in public. Smelling their corpses was no better—it was just as bad.

As she stood there holding her nose, she heard V speak to Yama. Yama turned and wiped the dirt from her hands. Her face was impassive.

"Life is precious. I shall not take it."

Odessa wasn't sure if she heard her right—but that's what it sounded like. Despite her supernatural hearing, she couldn't always make out words due to Yama's thick accent.

A brief pause followed before V spoke again. "What if 'tis possible thy chief's daughter may yet live?"

Yama's eyes widened in disbelief. "Are ye certain she lives?"

"No, but from what that undead chevalier said, 'tis possible a cult has her."

Yama furrowed her brow and tilted her head. She asked another question, it seemed, but Odessa didn't pay close attention. They continued going back and forth, and Odessa merely stood there like a lost pup. She felt a flicker of annoyance. Was it jealousy? No—it couldn't possibly be.

"What would they want with Tora?" Yama asked in her singsong voice. The name didn't sound like it came from the same place as Yama. Then she explained—Tora's mother came from a northern tribe, foreign to their own.

As Odessa stood in silence, her ears picked up a sound in the distance. Heartbeats—louder than the faint ones she had been tuning out. From what V told her, the louder heartbeats usually belonged to people.

"We need to prepare. We will not survive da next attack," Odessa blurted out.

"You're right. And I need to get stronger so I can defeat Leon the Vile."

As the trio stood underneath the faint moonlight, the wind began to blow. The wolf-like creature began to act strangely —and so did Yama. In the distance, strange howls echoed through the forest.

Odessa understood what this meant. The gray-skins were on their way to the tower after all. She didn't know whether they were coming with ill intent, but she was prepared to fight. She wouldn't let any harm come to V—or even Yama, for that matter.

Regardless of whether the gray-skins were Yama's people, Odessa would cut them down. From what V had explained, they were trying to use the girl to appease a deity they believed in. Odessa had no desire to infringe on anyone's beliefs, but this didn't sit well with her at all. With that in mind, she would stand firm—even if it meant standing between her people.

Like V, Yama didn't seem like a warrior, but she could fight. That much had been proven tonight in the battle to hold the tower. Though she fought with great ferocity, she hadn't killed anyone. The revenants were the only ones she'd been even re-motely brutal toward. Even then, Odessa had to shoot them down—or V had to cut them down—to keep them from getting back up.

"These people are not to be harmed, Odessa."

V's soft tone carried a sternness that made Odessa tense up. She looked over at her to see the serious look in her eyes. Then, without another word, V walked over to the ladder propped against the wall. She climbed up to stand watch and wait until the gray-skins arrived at the gates.

Odessa began to wonder—could V read her mind? Not that it was impossible. Could it be? How else had she known Odessa had been prepared to fight them, if needed? A chill crept across her skin as she stared at V's back. The woman was shorter than her—but she boasted a presence that felt ginormous.

CHAPTER 9

V stood on the wall, staring out at the forest. She was waiting for the arrival of the gray-skins and their chief. They were extremely close—she could hear their hearts beating. She could also hear their footsteps as they trudged through the forest.

She stood there patiently for nearly twenty minutes before they emerged. Woeton and Yonten were at the head of the group. Behind them were six wolf-like creatures. Bringing up the rear were three other gray-skins.

The one who stood out to V was the one holding a staff. He wore clothes with unique patterns in blue, made of fur and some other material V couldn't quite identify. She saw dark circles under his eyes and his long black hair was disheveled.

A strange cloud surrounded him, which made V suspicious. She watched him cough up black residue—something that reminded her of what had replaced her own blood. Could this be the chief Yama had spoken of? Compared to the others, he was the tallest. The closer he got, the stronger his spiritual aura felt. He carried great power.

"Such a foul stench. What doth ye set ablaze?" Woeton asked as he approached the gate.

"We had a problem arrive a little before ye, but 'tis been dealt with—for now," V answered.

Yonten stepped up beside Woeton with a serious look on his face. "Are ye going to let us in, changed one?"

Woeton elbowed him hard in the ribs. V stared at Yonten in annoyance. She despised the phrase they used to describe her. Unlike Woeton, Yonten lacked manners.

"I loathe thee," V mouthed.

Yonten merely scoffed and looked away. The large gray-skin pushed his way to the front of the group. His eyes were blue like the morning sky. It had been so long since V had seen the sky during the day. This seemed to be the closest she'd get again.

"Yama, the soil beneath thy feet betrays thee!"

His booming voice echoed through the air. The wind became but a whisper beneath the weight of his presence. He spoke like a leader—and carried the presence of one.

V glanced over her shoulder to see Yama standing silently, arms crossed. Odessa was kneeling next to the wolf. V hoped no one would try to take Yama by force. She needed to be certain.

"I cannot force her to see you, but I will say that I can see what made her question thy motives for the sacrifices."

The two gray-skins in the far back began whispering to each other. Woeton and Yonten looked at each other, then at the chief. The chief stared at V with unwavering eyes.

"Honor awaits her in the village. A duty she should be grateful for."

As V stared at him in silence, Odessa climbed up onto the wall. She stared down at the gray-skins and the wolves for a brief moment, then leaned close to V.

"He is bewitched by a specter, and I see lil hope in saving him."

V looked at Odessa with concern in her eyes. If they couldn't save the chief, then this was all for nothing. Yama would be forced to run forever. If she returned, they'd sacrifice her—and her family would no longer exist in this world.

The chief coughed, an insidious sound. "What doth that thing whisper to ye?"

V glared at him as her blood began to boil. She didn't like the insult he had just made. The way he spoke made it clear he saw Odessa as less than human.

"That thing you refer to is my fledgling—and she is a Hiorian. I shall not tolerate thy insults of her," V said coldly.

The chief narrowed his gaze and remained silent for a moment. "What say she speak to thee?" he demanded.

V's face twisted with annoyance. Yama had been right about him. His words were far from gentle. Talking to him irritated her greatly.

"She says you are benighted by a spirit known as a specter."

"How can she know this?"

"Your people can feel disturbances in the land—and perhaps in the body. As for her and I—we can see between the veil of the living and the spirit."

V noticed the perplexed expressions on Woeton's and Yonten's faces. She returned her gaze to the chief. He wore a grim look. The dark cloud surrounding him began to shift. Something was stirring inside him—and it concerned V.

"Ye must release Yama from thy clutches and hand her to her people," he ordered.

"She's not my prisoner. And you are in no position to make threats to me," V said in the most menacing tone she could muster.

The chief didn't seem to like her response. He clenched his staff tightly. V didn't know what the outcome of this meeting would be. Could they even remove the spirit possessing this gray-skin?

"Thy presence as a changed one defiles the body of our deity —and stifles our efforts to make offerings to appease her!"

V threw her hands in the air in disbelief. Why did so many people want to sacrifice innocent lives to beings they couldn't see or interact with?

"What if I told you there's a chance your daughter still lives?"

The chief stiffened. His eyes slowly widened, and his mouth dropped open—but no sound came out. The cloud surrounding him quivered and shrank slightly. He began a coughing fit, hacking up more black goo.

Woeton, Yonten, and the other two gray-skins looked just as confused. What she'd said could be a lie—but if the daughter still lived, it was worth knowing.

"Sifadi would hath given a sign that she still lived," said the female gray-skin.

V watched her step forward. She was slightly taller and more muscular than Yama, with long hair pulled back into a braided ponytail. A large scar ran across her face—clearly inflicted by some kind of beast. It made V wonder what creatures lived in the mountains beyond the vampyrs.

"'Tis not a certainty, but I believe it's worth looking into. Even if she's not alive, at least you'll gain closure."

"After so many cycles... she may be lost," the gray-skin said in a raspy voice.

"She may be with the people who took her. I plan to find out where they are. Doubtful they've seen anything like her—so they may be studying her."

The chief stared at V with suspicion. "Why help us?"

"I would want to know the fate of my children as well."

As V said this, she began to ponder what life her children could have had. If she'd been able to raise her little ones— would she have been a good mother?

"So ye hath known such loss as well?" the chief asked.

His tone changed. His gaze softened, and he lowered his head. The cloud around him distorted. He seemed to be fighting for control. Woeton and Yonten glanced at him, both visibly concerned.

"My situation is much more complicated."

V stared off into the distance, feeling a longing for something she couldn't have. The family she wanted with her lover had been stolen. Her mate was killed. She had been turned into a monster. The least she could do now was deal with the Acolytes—so no one else would lose everything.

Her list of enemies was growing—but she remained steadfast. She would rid the world of all of them. They would not die of old age or illness. They would all meet her wrath.

"What doth ye pursue?" Yonten suddenly asked.

"For now? I want to save your chief's soul."

All of the chief's people looked at him with worry. They had clearly suspected something was wrong—but they'd tried to ignore it. That had led to the chief killing a family of his own people.

"Save my soul? How doth ye plan such a thing?" the chief asked.

V looked over at Odessa. She hadn't even thought to ask if Odessa could do anything about this. If she couldn't, things would go very badly.

"Can you get the specter out of him?"

"I am not an exorcist, V."

V looked at Odessa with concern. She had hoped Odessa might know a way—one that wouldn't require doing what her people had done to her friend.

"There has to be something other than... that," V emphasized.

Odessa took a deep breath and looked at her with determination. "We have most of da tings here dat can affect da spirit. Though... I do not know how well it will work since I am a cursed spirit."

"What happens if you cannot?"

Odessa's expression turned gloomy. "I do not know. He does not appear as corrupted as how my friend became."

V stared down at the gray-skins with doubt. This had to work—if they agreed to it. If not, the consequences would be dire.

"Her people have spent years learning how to cleanse souls. If you're willing to let her practice what she hath been taught— I shall grant you entry."

The gray-skins spoke amongst themselves for several minutes. V waited patiently, wondering what their answer would be. She overheard the woman whispering that she truly did worry about the chief. V also learned that he had killed others years ago—people who had spoken out against the sacrifices.

Hearing this was an eye-opener. Woeton, unfortunately,

kept trying to make excuses. V disliked that about him—but he wasn't as bad as Yonten. Still, she could see the doubts in all of them. They clung to their beliefs—and their leader—even as things crumbled.

"A price must be paid. So what shall it be?" the chief finally spoke.

"Either the thing possessing thee is removed—or you die."

The gray-skins all stared up at V in horror. Being forced to give a definitive answer frustrated her. But this was the world she now knew.

"If ye give me thy word that ye shall help us learn what happened to my child—then I agree to this," the chief said.

"You have my word." V bowed her head.

"Rejoice, my people—for Sifadi has dawned a glimpse of hope upon us! In this moment, I feel some sense of clarity," the chief said, his voice regretful and heartfelt.

They had to hurry with the exorcism before the chief lost control again. If the specter took over, he might command his people to attack. V had no desire to harm them. They seemed kind-hearted—but like all people, they had their problems.

"Then let us hurry—before the morning comes."

V glanced up at the sky. Time was running short. She and Odessa would be imprisoned in the tower once the sun rose. She gestured over her shoulder for Yama to open the gate. The thought of an exorcism both frightened and fascinated her.

Soon, she would learn just how troublesome it could be.

*

Things were off to a rough start as Odessa made her preparations. When she had requested for the chief to be tied up, his people were unhappy. Being the translator between these two races both fascinated and worried V at the same time.

The gray-skins didn't like the idea of restraining their leader, but when Odessa had someone place a silver necklace around his neck, they understood. His howls of pain were unnatural. His eyes began to glow a pale green, and his veins bulged, appearing black.

V had never witnessed a possession—or even an attempt at an exorcism. Odessa had drawn a ring of salt around the chief. She also had a pile of dirt covering his feet. Like the gray-skins, Hiorians believed the land was connected to the aspect of life. Placing the chief's feet in the dirt during the ritual was a way to reconnect him to the world of the living.

Another strange item Odessa had brought was an urn-like object. In her bag, she kept a significant number of tools. What fascinated V the most was that Odessa had made some kind of potion. One of the ingredients was the feathers she had collected from the strix. Once she had brewed it to her liking, she forced the chief to drink it.

V realized this had been the reason for the chains. After ingesting the potion, the chief began to convulse wildly. A surge of spiritual energy erupted from his body. The gray-skins rushed to unbind him, but Odessa stepped in their way. V had to explain that the chief understood the severity of the process and had agreed willingly.

The only person not inside the tower was Yama. She remained outside, which concerned V—though she understood why. The chief had ordered the death of her family, even if it had been in the name of sacrifice for their beliefs. V also understood that it hadn't been entirely the chief who made those demands.

"'Tis torture that takes place before me!" Yonten complained.

V glared at him until he noticed her gaze. His expression softened, and he fell silent. She hoped he would remain that way until the process was over. The ritual could take hours— perhaps even days. And since Odessa wasn't sure she could do it successfully, there was no telling what the outcome might be.

V decided to step outside for a bit of fresh air. The atmosphere inside the tower had begun to make her skin crawl. Woeton accompanied her. Neither of them uttered a word as they stood out in the open. V stared at Yama, who sat on the wall looking out into the distance.

"As a guardian of our village, I carry shame for not speaking out on the chief's request," Woeton whispered.

V didn't look at him as she continued watching Yama. She had grown a soft spot for the lost. Maybe it reminded her of how lost she had once been. Helping people like Yama and Odessa kept her sanity. Without them, the darkness would consume her soul. Her sense of humanity would be lost.

"I am not going to counsel you to apologize to her." V folded her arms across her chest. "But you suspected something to be amiss from the beginning and chose to turn a blind eye."

"The chief is our shepherd and guides us through the pastures of this life. 'Tis uncanny to speak against his wishes."

"What about when he had you all slay the people who spoke against the sacrifices?" V glanced at Woeton and saw a startled look on his face.

He parted his lips to speak but quickly lowered his head. The look of shame remained ever-present. He couldn't erase what he'd allowed to happen. V understood that very well.

The chief's screams were growing louder. V glanced over her shoulder as she felt the cold chill of death emanating from inside the tower. It made her skin crawl even more, thinking of the chief writhing in agony.

The wound on her arm began to ache with a stinging sensation. V could see it was closing, but it felt as if it were infected. She wondered if she should be concerned. Once everything was over, maybe she could ask Odessa about it.

The wolves began to sniff the air and move about restlessly. When V noticed this, she quickly glanced over at Woeton. His expression turned grim as he walked over to where he had placed his spear earlier.

V began to listen more carefully to the sounds around her. How had she not noticed it before? Perhaps the chief's screaming had masked everything else. The wolves began to howl loudly. V still didn't feel fully recovered from the earlier fight.

This didn't bode well—especially since an exorcism was underway.

She began marching toward the gate.

"Go inside, Woeton," she ordered.

"Danger is revealed by the wolves' howls. 'Tis a guardian's duty to guard against the wicked."

"Do it inside the tower."

V removed the large metal bar from the doors, then pulled the chain to open the gate. The large doors swung open, and she was greeted by the field of greenery and the trees beyond. She then looked up at Yama on the wall.

"Close the gate behind me."

"But—"

Yama started to protest but stopped. She nodded and came down from the wall. She marched over to the chain and began pulling the doors shut.

Unlike the Wescreans, these unknown figures were coming from the south.

V's eyes allowed her to see clearly in the dark. She saw them hiding in the trees and the shadows. Her only guess was that they were Hiorians. They had finally come to avenge their lost comrades.

V began to wonder what exactly they had been doing over the past few days. Likely, they had been building their forces and planning the attack. It seemed logical—but now, the chevaliers who once occupied the tower were gone.

In the darkness, V saw traces of spiritual energy. Suddenly, a volley of arrows shot from the forest. They were coated with spiritual energy, which meant they would be far more dangerous. V swayed from side to side and began to levitate.

This ability had taken time to get used to, but she was getting the hang of it. She assumed she could levitate because she was like a ghost. Her body had been burned to ashes, and yet she returned in a form capable of incredible things.

Unlike revenants—and possibly Odessa—V walked a thinner

line between the living and the dead. As she evaded the arrows, she became lost in thought. She spun gracefully as she waltzed through the field of greenery.

The movements of approaching warriors broke her trance.

Emerging from the forest were the Hiorians. What surprised her was that they wore armor. It wasn't as refined as the Wescreans' or the Crimson Sentinels of Vostaylia, but it showed progress. They were choosing to advance their society.

The Hiorians surrounded V with spears, swords, and bows. She raised her hands to show she surrendered. The number surrounding her had to be at least fifty. Men and women alike stood ready—trained warriors, every one of them.

"A cursed spirit oversees dis tower?" a voice asked from deep in the crowd.

V looked around to see a woman pushing her way through the warriors. The woman who now stood before her had long, thick, curly hair. Her lithe frame was clothed in dark garments. A look of frustration and sorrow covered her face.

In her hands, she wielded a spear. As V examined the woman, she couldn't help but notice the resemblance.

Could it be that this was Odessa's mother?

If so, it was the worst possible time for her to arrive. Seeing her daughter turned into a cursed spirit doomed to roam the night could push her into madness. V assumed the woman had already learned of her family's fate. She had come here for revenge.

"The Wescreans that were here have already been dealt with," V said softly.

The Hiorian woman looked perplexed. Some of her people began whispering among themselves.

"Your tongue is of the Vostaylian people. Why are you in da land of Wescreas?"

"I have business with their proclaimed new king."

The woman scoffed and raised her spear, preparing to strike. V had no desire to fight. She felt fatigued, and dawn would be breaking soon. Still, she didn't expect the Hiorians to show mercy. They had spent generations learning how to rid the world of monsters like her.

"I do not wish to fight, so please lower thy weapons," V requested.

"You expect us to let a cursed spirit continue to haunt the living?" a male Hiorian asked.

"I did not ask to become this. 'Tis now my soul's purpose to punish the ones who made me. My soul shall not be soothed until my vengeance is quenched."

"Who made you dis way, then?" the woman with the spear asked.

"The Acolytes—at the request of Sorin Dracul and Jiya Ashspell."

Several of the Hiorians gasped. They hadn't expected her to say Jiya's name. But now they had a common enemy. She hoped this revelation would help her cause.

"Enough of dis! Everyone, attack!" a booming voice commanded.

"No, wait!" the woman with the daggers shouted.

But it was too late.

The Hiorians surged forward. V leapt into the air just as a blade grazed her arm. Her skin burned, and the flesh throbbed. The weapon had to be silver.

Hiorians always came prepared to face creatures of the night.

V relocated herself to a position where she wouldn't be easily surrounded. As she watched the Hiorians rushing toward her, she heard screaming in the distance. She looked toward the tower and saw a giant wave of spiritual energy erupting into the air. Whatever was happening inside had gotten intense.

As V prepared to be attacked again, she wondered who had called for the assault. She'd thought the woman she believed to be Odessa's mother was the leader. It surprised her that they acted without her command.

As the Hiorians closed in, V noticed a small group breaking

off and rushing toward the gate. She couldn't let them reach it. She lunged forward, cutting through the crowd. She evaded many of their attacks, though some struck true. Her body was covered in deep cuts that weren't healing fast enough.

She intercepted the group nearing the wall and held up her hands, trying to stop them—but they kept coming. She had no choice.

She fought.

As she engaged them, her mind filled with memories of the past—of her lover teaching her how to fight. He had shown her how to combat enemies without killing them. As she moved, she saw flashes of him demonstrating techniques.

With little effort, she disarmed the Hiorians one by one, striking in ways that incapacitated without causing permanent harm. Those with high spiritual power were more difficult—she avoided them, recognizing they were on Leon's level or stronger.

Then a voice rang out—loud and sharp.

The woman V believed to be Odessa's mother shouted, her voice cutting through the chaos. A strong gust of wind followed, silencing the crowd. The Hiorians stopped and looked toward her as she pushed her way to the front.

"I was not certain before, because of da corruption I sensed—but my child is near. What did you do to her?" she asked, angered.

V stood silently, lowering her head with great remorse. She regretted what she'd done. It had been selfish. She wouldn't deny it—but she wouldn't let Odessa's mother kill her daughter. Even if they believed cursed spirits should be destroyed.

"She lay dying and said she wanted revenge on Jiya, so I..." V trailed off.

The woman's face twisted into a mask of disbelief and disgust. Tears welled in her eyes as she hunched forward, trembling. Another woman wrapped an arm around her to comfort her. As she wept, a tall Hiorian man stepped forward.

He had brown hair braided into two ponytails, a thick curly

beard, and deep-set eyes. Compared to V, he stood at least six foot four, his body toned and scarred.

"Neliah is broken by the loss of her family. What you have done has made it harder for her to grieve. For now, we must slay her daughta—so that her soul may rest," he said in a deep, gruff voice.

"When Jiya is defeated, I will oversee putting Odessa to rest."

"You have done enough! We will deal with you both here and now!" he exclaimed.

He raised his sword—but the sound of the gate doors opening filled the air.

Everyone turned.

Emerging from the stronghold was Yama, her battle hammer in hand. The Hiorians readied themselves again.

"What are you doing, Yama?" V shouted.

"I would be befallen with shame if they struck ye down before me," Yama said.

"Why have you chosen to protect an evil ting such as she?" the Hiorian man asked.

"Forgive me, but I must ask for ye to lay down thy weapons against V. I must request this—for she helps me with grace."

"How does one who feasts on da essence of life help you?"

"A sacrifice I would be—if not for her. My chief be benighted by something."

The Hiorians glanced at each other, uncertain. V listened to their murmurs. She had no idea what they would decide—but some clearly still wanted to kill her.

"Da screaming dat we hear—is it thy chief?" one of them asked.

"Yes," Yama answered.

The tall Hiorian stared at the sky with a look of concern. He lowered his head and sighed. Slowly, he raised his hand.

The Hiorians lowered their weapons.

V assumed he was one of their commanders. This was unexpected, but a relief.

"From what I can sense, 'tis a specter dat hath grown quite

strong. Is someone trying to cleanse him?" he asked.

"Yes—Odessa," Yama replied.

He looked over at Neliah, who had gone quiet. "Come with me, Neliah," he said gently.

"What are you plannin', brudda?"

Neliah wiped her tears and stepped forward. She followed her brother as he approached Yama. She stood firmly in his path, a statue guarding the tower.

He stared at her with intensity. She didn't move.

"Let them help, Yama."

She continued staring, then finally stepped aside. The Hiorian commander marched into the tower. The others followed. V waited a moment before going inside with Yama.

What she saw made her breath catch.

Black ooze poured from the chief's mouth. His body twisted in unnatural ways as he fought the restraints. Odessa stood within the ring of salt, pouring her spiritual energy into the circle. Dirt covered the chief's feet, grounding him to the living world.

The specter began seeping out of him, taking shape as a shadowy creature. Something felt wrong. Neliah noticed it instantly. She pushed Odessa aside and took over, her brother by her side.

Odessa stood back, stunned. V and Yama moved beside her. A look of guilt crossed her face.

How long would this take? Would it even work?

The chief continued to convulse. Then a voice spoke through him—mocking, hateful. It laughed maniacally. It wasn't his voice.

V scratched her head, overwhelmed. This spirit wasn't subtle.

Woeton and his people stared in shock. Even the Hiorians were silent, watching Neliah and her brother work. They pulled their life force into glowing spiritual energy, casting it around the circle. Unlike Odessa's, theirs carried no corruption.

Everything began to shake.

The specter burst from the chief's body, spiraling into the air. V saw a glimpse of a face—twisted, deformed, obscured by shadows. It was drawn into the urn. A loud howl echoed from the specter as it vanished into the vessel.

Neliah sealed it.

She breathed heavily, sweat dripping from her brow. She handed the urn to her brother. The Hiorians cheered.

Neliah silenced them with a wave.

V realized something wasn't right. The chief sat slumped, motionless. But she could hear his heartbeat—faint, but present.

They waited.

Hours passed in silence until sunrise. V and Odessa moved into the shadows to avoid the sun. Eventually, the chief stirred.

His eyes opened slowly. He looked at the chains binding him, then around the room.

Did he remember anything?

He said it felt like being stuck in a long dream.

Neliah and her brother waited, then removed his restraints. They helped him stand. Woeton stepped forward and handed him his staff.

The chief's eyes found Yama.

"Shame has befallen our village because of me. No penance will grace me with forgiveness," he said, voice heavy with guilt.

"Ye were benighted," Woeton said.

The chief raised a hand to silence him. Woeton bowed and stepped back. Yama remained quiet, her eyes filled with emotion.

"I was benighted—but my sins were my own," the chief said.

V hadn't expected that. He was owning his actions. It meant that part of him did blame Yama's father for what happened to his daughter.

These spirits—parasites—were dangerous. Hard to remove, harder still to forget.

"V, I thank ye for protecting Yama," the chief said.

"I merely did what I thought was right," V replied.

"All ye shall be welcomed in our village. Feast with my people as thanks."

"Our rations?" Yonten blurted.

Woeton smacked him on the back of the head. Yonten winced, rubbing it as the others chuckled.

"Forgive us," said Neliah's brother. "But we must prepare for battle. Winter is upon us."

"Gamba, we need not rush into another fight," Neliah said.

Gamba looked at her seriously, placing his hands on her shoulders. "Jiya must be dealt with—before da dark forces he plays with destroy us all."

"Does thy people have a plan to defeat him?" V asked.

The siblings looked at each other.

"Oba came this way to meet wit da prince's men. Seems dis tower be taken from them," Gamba said, uncertainty in his voice.

V frowned. Fifty warriors wouldn't be enough—not against the Wescrean army and their revenants.

"We have a group scoutin' another stone wall," Neliah added.

"Do you believe they can take the fortress?" V asked.

"The Runehelm family is with da Dawnspells. Some of our finest warriors," Gamba said.

"How many can fight?" V pressed.

"More than us."

"Enough to defeat a thousand Wescreans?"

Gamba said nothing. His silence was the answer.

V sighed. War might mean extinction for the Hiorians. Their population had already been devastated.

"Going to war with Wescreas could spell the end of your people. I don't think it's wise," she warned.

"We barely have a home. We've been betrayed over and over. Now one of our own has become a traitor!" Gamba said, voice rising.

"We shall not meet our end so easily, Vostaylian," Neliah

declared.

V hadn't expected her to refer to her homeland. Clearly, they had been to Vostaylia once. Another mystery.

"We should leave the tower soon. It will likely be besieged again. If we move before they arrive, it will confuse them," V advised.

She thought of Leon. He said he would return.

It was time to move.

"Where would we go?" Neliah asked.

Before V could speak, the chief stepped forward.

"I wish to extend my offer once more."

Gamba and Neliah turned to him.

V wanted to see their village. She'd never been up the Scarstone Mountains. This was her chance.

"Fine. We accept this offer with grace," Gamba said.

He and Neliah bowed their heads. The chief smiled faintly.

V didn't know if they would win the coming war—but she was glad these two races were beginning to unite.

"At dusk, we shall journey through the mountains," the chief said.

Everyone nodded. V glanced at Odessa, who was deep in thought—biting her nails.

V gently took her hand to stop her. She saw the worry in her fledgling's eyes.

CHAPTER 10

Odessa's Isolation Pt. 4

Another night had befallen the land, and Odessa set out on another journey with her people. They were following the gray-skins into mountainous terrain to see a place she had never seen before. Slight specks of white were slowly falling upon the land. The gray-skins told her the trip would take a few days.

The air quality in the high terrain felt so pure. It didn't feel as tainted as it did in Wescreas. Odessa didn't see many strange sights due to the fog clouding the area. The coming dawn was something that concerned her.

Because she and V couldn't travel during the day, it raised concerns for both of them. When V spoke up, Odessa's mother gave them clothing that covered them from head to toe. It was made from thick fur belonging to creatures known as prowlers.

They had thick black fur with blue stripes that sometimes glowed. She never knew how or why their stripes glowed, but it fascinated her. The clothing could potentially protect them from the sun, but she wasn't certain.

The higher they went into the mountainous valley, the thicker the fog became. Her supernatural eyes still allowed her to see clearly. Although, V had told her the chief once said it was easy to get lost while venturing to their home.

Which was why most of them now carried torches—to help keep track of one another and not get lost. Odessa could hear things lurking as they marched. She assumed none of the hostile creatures attacked because of their large numbers.

As she marched alongside V and Yama, she glanced over

her shoulder. Her people marched silently behind her, but she caught some of their gazes. Once again, she saw expressions of disgust and disdain. It caused her to grab at the arm that had been branded with scars.

Her mother hadn't made any effort to speak with her. That saddened her greatly. When she tried to approach her, the woman walked right past. It gave her even more reason to try and end this journey as quickly as possible.

She didn't want to be overcome by the madness that came with the thirst for blood. Nor did she want to become even more hated by her family. As she looked over her shoulder again, her eyes searched for her cousin.

It didn't take long to spot him. He walked behind his father, Gamba. His name was Jawara, which meant "lover of peace." The name fit him perfectly because his very presence was peaceful. A gentle soul, he was, and everyone took to him like moths to a flame.

Jawara preferred to plant flowers and make potions to heal others. A natural-born herbalist who was quite exceptional. Despite his father always taking him on hunting trips, he enjoyed tending to the people and the land. If anyone would still accept her, she hoped dearly it would be him.

As she stared at him, trying to get a sense of how he felt, his eyes finally caught her gaze. He looked a bit surprised. Odessa's eyes widened, and she quickly turned away. Maybe it was best if she didn't know how he felt.

The hope of having at least one family member still accepting her was better than knowing all of them had disowned her. She couldn't face Jawara if he felt the same way as his father.

"What troubles you?" a soft voice asked in a whisper.

Odessa lifted her head and looked to see those sapphire blue eyes staring at her. V looked deeply concerned, slowing her pace to walk directly beside her.

"I... it is nothin'," Odessa muttered.

She had no desire to burden V more than she already had. V seemed to have a great deal on her mind. Odessa felt that adding to it would be selfish. She wanted to do her best not to be a burden.

One thing she desired was to end this curse of hers. The faster they got to Jiya, the better. Although, she still had to learn more about what she could do. Not only that, but she had to improve her self-control over the thirst.

Not long ago, they drank the blood of a deer. It gave her a bit of strength and slightly rejuvenated her. But after the fight to protect the tower, she now felt a little drained. The thirst was slowly beginning to return.

Having her hands covered in human blood had been nerve-wracking. The desperate urge to taste it had slowly overtaken her. Had V not rushed over to stop her, she might have done it. What would have become of her if she had?

Would she really lose herself and become a full-fledged monster? She didn't know anything about the world anymore. Too many new mysteries were being discovered every night.

One thing she had noticed lately were the crows. A few times, she heard them flying overhead. Even now, as they walked through this thick veil of fog, she heard the croaking of the birds.

It was peculiar to her, but she didn't think much of it. Especially since V didn't seem to notice or care. The calls made the thoughts in her mind louder. The more she tried to ignore them—even with her supernatural hearing—the more they surfaced.

"It would appearth that the one stuck in thought is you," a voice teased.

She looked up to see V staring at her once more. A faint smile formed on Odessa's face. "You might be rubbin' off on me."

A warm smile appeared on V's face. Odessa was grateful to her—she clearly knew something was wrong. But instead of prying, V seemed to opt for easing her thoughts.

"In a time past, I had been told thy people often go on fishing trips before and after the winter," V mumbled.

"Aye. I am sure a family got tasked with dat duty while da

others are here fightin'."

"I always wanted to go fishing..." V said in a saddened tone.

Odessa looked over at her curiously. "You never went fishin'?"

V shook her head with a disappointed look. Odessa thought for a moment, then decided something. She nudged V in the arm, wearing a serious expression.

"After dis is over, maybe I shall take you fishin'—before I am ready to leave da world?"

V's eyes lit up with excitement. "I think I would like that."

Odessa smiled and nodded. She figured maybe out on the sea would be a good place to meet her end. Even though she never learned to swim, she loved the sea. The wondrous waves that swayed in rhythmic motion always soothed her when she stared at the horizon.

For now, she had to calm her mind and focus on the task at hand. War was the priority. From what she understood, her people had never experienced war—until now. Sometimes it saddened her that it had to become a thing in her lifetime.

*

After hours of walking, everyone stopped to rest. The sun had lightened the foggy sky. Odessa and V found a place in the shade to sit. The gray-skins had taken a trail that led into a valley below. They went hunting for food, with a handful of Hiorians tagging along.

Odessa saw Gamba and her mother talking with the chief. With her supernatural hearing, she could hear them well. From what she gathered, the chief was telling them about what had happened to him. They all seemed to be enjoying each other's company. That was a good sign—it meant they were trying to learn each other's social norms.

With humans, it clearly hadn't been so easy. If it had, maybe none of this would've happened.

Odessa wouldn't have become this creature that thirsted for blood. Her brother and father would likely still be alive. Maybe her sister would still be with them. She let out a deep sigh of frustration.

"The sun robs us of our strength, but we can endure," V muttered.

Odessa said nothing as she stared up at the gray sky. Her eyes winced at the faint glow of sunlight piercing through the thick veil of fog. She began to think about how, somewhere in Wescreas, people were being slaughtered mercilessly.

It was a thought that made her antsy. This journey was interesting—but it felt like their time was being wasted. She believed she could end the war. Then again, she knew Jiya held a power she couldn't yet comprehend. Not with the book in his possession.

"Do you think there are more strange tings like us out there?" Odessa asked.

It had been a sudden thought. She didn't know much about what they were, besides being cursed. V described them as something akin to revenants—but also like the vampyr creatures.

"Are you asking if there are more people with our affliction, or just other supernatural entities?"

"Aye!"

V furrowed her brow as she stared at Odessa for a moment. Odessa worried her question might've been too vague—or too complicated. No. That couldn't be it, could it?

"I do not see myself as special, so I will assume there are more things out there."

Odessa sat in silence, mulling over the response. She didn't know if she could accept that. If there were others like them— thirsting for blood—her people were in danger.

Then again, she hadn't seen signs of others like them. Only the vampyrs had been an issue, and they hadn't been as active lately. She found that strange, and began to wonder why.

"Try not to worry about such things for now. Enjoy the company of your people," V said.

Odessa looked around at the Hiorians nearby. She didn't feel like she fit in with them anymore. They probably wanted to put an end to her. It wouldn't surprise her if they were just waiting for the right moment.

Still, as she listened, their conversations weren't about her. Most of them were discussing tactics—ways to defeat the revenants and take the book from Jiya.

As much as she wanted to rush to Fodmery, she realized she needed rest. Her body felt weak from the sun—and from resisting the thirst. Until she could control that, battle might be the last thing she needed.

She leaned her head back against the large rock and closed her eyes.

She assumed they would continue their journey soon.

CHAPTER 11

The journey to the Scarstone tribe's village took about a week. By then, the greenery they had seen was blanketed with a sheet of white. Despite that, V and Odessa still had to wear the special coats given to them by the Hiorians. From what she had been told, the material was made from the fur of creatures known as prowlers.

These coats covered their exposed skin, allowing them to travel during daylight. The problem was that the sun still made them weak. Traveling proved difficult for them. When they rested, they would talk about many things.

V could sense Odessa was bothered by something. Clearly, her nerves were getting to her. As much as V wanted to pry, she knew better than to force her to open up. In time, Odessa would likely express what was on her mind.

At least, that's what V hoped for. She didn't like seeing Odessa down in spirit. V knew it had mostly been her fault— since she had turned her into something her people shunned. The plausibility of Odessa feeling like an outcast was apparent.

This journey they were on didn't help either. She saw the stares Odessa's people gave her. Both of them endured as best they could while trekking up the mountain trail.

Along the way, Odessa had noticed the wound V had sustained during her fight with Leon. She tended to it quickly once she realized how bad it was. Odessa told her that if she had ignored it any longer, there would've been dire consequences.

As they continued traveling, V spoke with Gamba. She showed him the map she had found in the tower. With it, they could plan their attacks accordingly. As they talked, she began to feel a sense of excitement. The odds of winning were slim, but they had a fighting chance.

The cards were slowly shifting in her favor. Although, the biggest issue remained the path she would need to take. Leon had proven to be a powerful foe—and he was just a revenant. She didn't yet have the spiritual power to defeat him.

At the moment, the biggest mystery seemed to be Judith. What kind of person would she be? Would she be some spoiled brat who claimed the throne by name alone? V couldn't be sure, but she truly hoped it would be a woman with wisdom.

She had no desire to help a fool reclaim the throne. Another concern was whether the Hiorians would receive any support from this so-called princess. From what she understood, Odessa's father had trusted the prince and his men.

As V continued to drift in her thoughts, she saw the village. It sat perched beside a cliff. V could see down into the valley, though from this height she could hardly make out the land below. Even with her strong eyes, the mist remained a veil that separated the village from the lower lands.

The smell of something delectable filled her nostrils. Unfortunately, as good as it smelled, she knew she couldn't eat it. The only thing her body seemed capable of ingesting now was blood. She longed to be alive again—but that would never happen. Now, she could only hope to see the one she loved again.

Upon reaching the village, she saw more gray-skins. They gawked at the Hiorians with curiosity. V hoped dearly that these two races would come together. Humans were innately destructive. That was something V had quickly come to learn.

The chief led the Hiorians to the center of the village. Along the way, V saw many buildings made from stone and wood. She assumed they went into the valley and cut down trees. Another fascinating thing she noticed were the plants—many of them she had never seen before.

Earlier, she saw strange flowers that the chief told her only bloomed during a full moon. It made her want to wait for the next one, just to witness them. Unfortunately, she had a mission to complete.

They arrived at the village center where a large stone rested. It had a painting of a figure on it. Once V got close enough, she saw it more clearly. The figure appeared to be a giant woman tending to the land.

This painting fascinated V—and it seemed to catch the attention of some of the Hiorians as well. As the chief waved his people over, a faint tension filled the air. This came as no surprise, given that a race of foreigners had just entered their home.

"Everyone, please welcome these Hiorians! For twelve cycles I hath been adrift against our ways. I am beholden to them— for they have freed me from the clutches of what benighted me!" the chief exclaimed.

The gray-skins stayed silent, exchanging looks. V had a bad feeling about this. A small group of gray-skins stepped forward. They wore clothing with bright blue patterns. V assumed this meant they were important figures, like the chief himself.

A woman with hair unlike anyone else's stepped forward. Her skin was also a lighter shade of gray.

"We hath come to an agreement—that thy leadership must be challenged, Tenzin."

V's eyes widened. This did not bode well. The Hiorians likely wouldn't be welcomed here. Neither would she, since they would likely see her presence as a problem for the land. She looked to the chief, waiting for his response.

"Despite my affliction... I cannot excuse my past. Thus, my role as chief can be no longer." The chief bowed his head toward the strange group.

V looked for Yama and saw her standing near a stone surrounded by strange plants. Behind her were more stones with paintings. As V walked over, she noticed the stones seemed to tell a story.

She tugged at Yama's clothing to get her attention. Yama hunched down so she could hear. V pressed her lips to Yama's ear.

"Who are those people?"

"'Tis the council. Now it is all for naught, for they failed to be of council," Yama replied.

As V considered this, she wondered if it was similar to her father's court. They were people he trusted to help rule the land and oversee aspects of the kingdom.

"Why did they allow those sacrifices?"

"Grief bestricken Thora." Yama pointed to the woman with white hair. "As for the others... they be nothing more than cravens."

"Why bring lowlanders here?" someone asked.

V turned to see a tall male gray-skin push the woman aside. His rough exterior made him look like a leader. He towered over the chief.

"Ye must hath forgotten what betided the last time lowlanders came here," he said in a gruff tone.

His voice gave V the impression that he was quite old. The gray-skin had steel blue eyes and a grimace across his face. He clearly didn't approve of the Hiorians in the least—which caused V to notice Gamba pushing his way forward.

"It would appear we are not welcome, and we apologize for our unwelcomed arrival. We shall leave at once," Gamba said with a bow.

He turned and raised his hand high in the air, making a gesture that caused all the Hiorians to begin turning back.

V remained, waiting and hoping someone would ask them to stay.

The female gray-skin seemed to hesitate. "Wait!" she shouted.

All the Hiorians stopped and turned around again. Gamba stared at her, brow furrowed, arms folded.

"Ye cometh all this way—so I am sure you are tired. Yama hath returned to us because of thee." The woman, Thora, waved in Yama's direction.

V saw Yama standing with a conflicted expression. It

seemed she didn't know whether she should feel welcome. The young gray-skin had run away, after all. But V understood the reason—her way of life had been twisted by an evil spirit, and she'd lost her family because of it.

V hoped that now that the chief had been freed, Yama would be safe. That she could live among her people again. Ending the sacrifices seemed like the logical first step toward healing.

As V moved through the village, she overheard some of the villagers talking. Some complained about the chief's return and bringing Hiorians. Others questioned whether he should be forgiven.

Despite that, a few villagers seemed to enjoy the Hiorians' presence. V didn't expect all the gray-skins to be accepting—but she hoped they would be open-minded. Unfortunately, she couldn't say the same for herself.

She could feel their stares as she tried to remain hidden. Every effort she made to stay out of the way seemed futile. They all noticed her—and stared with distrust. She even saw some gripping their weapons that were nearby.

*

As the night went on V watched as the Hiorians and gray skins seemed to get along fairly well. They dined and laughed together. V watched as Yama appeared to grow quite familiar with a Hiorian. This made V happy that these people were getting along.

"It would seem my cousin has taken a liking to Yama," a voice said.

V turned to see Odessa walking over to her. She looked toward Yama and the young Hiorian. She quickly noticed the striking resemblance he shared with Gamba. This brought her to the conclusion that this Hiorian might be his son.

"I hope that your people have gained a genuine ally in this world."

"I do not know what da future holds," Odessa said coldly, "but I do not plan to be around long enough to see it."

V merely stared at her in silence. The bells of guilt rang

loudly. She had taken away any chance for Odessa to be with her siblings. Not only that, but her morality had begun to shift. The others might not notice, but V saw the dark shadow looming over her friend.

"I am sorry."

Odessa looked at V, her face twisted in confusion. "Why do you apologize?"

"'Tis my fault you hath become this. Something you never wished for. But due to a selfish need, I..."

"I said I wanted to punish Jiya, and I still plan to do dat."

"Yes... but after much thought, I realize my true intentions."

"What do you mean?"

"Aforetime, there once was a princess without a crown. She fell for a man from another world. Not long after their union, they began expecting. Unfortunately, tragedy struck—leading to his death, and her being abducted."

Odessa seemed unsure where this was going. V hoped she would simply indulge the tale and listen. Instead of speaking, Odessa gestured for her to continue.

"The princess was captured by people who worshiped something baleful. They wanted to use her to bring that thing into the world. She died with her child still in her womb. Not long after, she returned... from the other side."

"Where are you going wit dis?"

V looked at Odessa with a deep gaze. "She realized everything about her had changed. What had been done to her filled her with rage. Then, suddenly, she was beset by pain in her stomach." V sniffled.

She gently pressed her hand against her stomach, memories of the past rushing back. Her body trembled as she recalled the excruciating pain.

"It maddened her... causing her to slit open her own womb. Two small, lifeless bodies fell out of her."

She began to have flashbacks of that night—one that changed her world forever. Every dream she had faded into ash. Slowly, V stared up at the sky and sighed.

"Dis story makes no sense."

"The little ones were so pale and cold. It filled the princess with more rage... but also despair. As she wept with them in her arms, she heard a faint sound."

V placed a hand on Odessa's shoulder, gently pulling her close. She pressed her palm to Odessa's chest. Odessa stared at her, confused.

"The sound of a beating heart. The princess looked and saw their pale complexions grow warm. Life flowed into them as their eyes opened."

"So somehow they lived. Dat should be a good ting, right?"

'Tis life that should not come from something that is dead. And the princess knew... she could not care for them. What she had become would only bring danger."

"So what did da princess do?"

"A friend found her and took them away. Gone. The princess was alone. And she would remain alone... for a long time."

V turned away, folding her arms across her chest. She finally acknowledged her mistakes—and her feelings. The end of her journey couldn't come fast enough. The thought of reuniting with her lover gave her hope she wouldn't be alone forever.

"I think I understand now," Odessa said softly.

V remained silent as she watched the Hiorians and gray-skins mingling. They genuinely seemed to enjoy each other's company. For now, she hoped to clear her head and rest. She needed to find a place for herself and Odessa to hide from the sun.

She left Odessa and made her way to the chief, who sat on a stone beside members of his council. Their conversation seemed heated. V debated whether she should interrupt.

As she stood watching, she heard footsteps approaching. She turned her head to see Woeton, wearing a nervous expression and holding two mugs. He glanced at one, then offered it to her.

She hesitated. She couldn't drink it. But not wanting to be rude, she took it with a faint smile. "Thanks."

"Ye hath done something extraordinary," he said, gesturing to the village around them.

"I did not do anything. Alas, I hope thy people and the Hiorians can build a relationship."

"There is uncertainty in the land, but these people are caretakers of it too."

V wasn't sure what he meant, exactly. She assumed he meant the Hiorians didn't harm the land as humans did—cutting down forests, burning fields.

"Hiorians are much better companions than humans," V said, venom in her voice.

"Why do ye speak of thy people with such disdain?"

"It's my people who made me the monster I am." V snarled. "Anywise, do you hath a place where Odessa and I can rest? The sunlight is not our friend."

Woeton stared at her for a moment, then looked around and nodded. He gestured for her to follow. A flicker of hesitation passed through her, but then she followed.

As she passed a crowd of people chatting, she wondered what her life could have been. Had Jiya not brought the Acolytes and the new king of Vostaylia to Silverkeep... would she have had a happy life? Would she have met the gray-skins?

Not a day went by without her wondering what could have been. A curse came with being brought back from the spiritual world. To be honest, she couldn't even remember what that place was like. All she remembered was fire—then darkness—then drowning.

When she could finally see again, she found herself near the place where she died. She had never understood how the supernatural world worked. Its mysteries both fascinated and terrified her.

She followed Woeton as they climbed higher. He led her up a steep hill. Though she wanted to ask where they were going, she stayed quiet. After five minutes, he came to a halt.

"There is a cave just up ahead."

His voice was uneasy. V could hear his heart beating fast.

She didn't like it."You seem aghast. Why?"

Woeton looked at her, then toward the cave. "'Tis believed a changed one is sealed in there."

"Then why show me this? I want to rest—not fret over fighting," V frowned.

"Tis only a legend. I'm sure you'll be fine."

V looked around, taking in the view of the other mountains in the distance. Fog obscured the world. High in the mountains, the wind blew fierce. This place felt peaceful—and she understood why the gray-skins never left it.

"Well, thanks," she muttered, still gazing into the fog.

"What sort of danger do thy people face up here?"

"There are quite a few creatures we struggle against."

"Like what?"

Woeton glanced at the sky. Then he raised a hand above his head. "During storms, we face a great threat from above." He pointed upward. "When lightning strikes, ye must graith thyself."

V looked up, following his gaze. "What are you babbling about?"

"We call them Licron. Large, winged beasts with dark blue plumage."

V stared at him, intrigued. She wanted to know more. But for now, she turned and began heading back to the village. She had secured a resting place. Now, she wanted to learn more about the tribe—and ensure Odessa kept her thirst under control.

When V returned, she found Odessa standing alone, staring off the cliff. V walked over and peered down. Even with her supernatural vision, she couldn't see anything past the thick veil of mist.

"We need to plan our next move."

"I know. We shall venture to the keep soon," V said softly.

"My people's population is small. We cannot fight a country like dis. And we should not expect any help from da gray-skins."

"Odessa, we'll figure it out in time. Wars are never easy—and they can last a long time."

"I know you don't want to... but we could get to Jiya and end everything wit ease. All you have to do is—"

"No. If I go down that path again, I might hurt the likes of them." V pointed to the people not far from them. "I'm fond of these people."

"You said you wanted revenge. Jiya robbed you of da life you should have lived."

"Why do you keep talking like this?"

Odessa stared into the distance. V couldn't understand why her dear friend seemed off. She looked down and noticed Odessa was biting her nails again. The thirst was getting worse.

"It's getting harder to control myself. I can't even be around my own people."

"I know it's not easy. But you're strong. That much I know. Please... just bear it a little longer."

V gently placed her hand on Odessa's shoulder. She hoped to comfort her, but the tension in Odessa's body was clear. The young Hiorian trembled, and V's worry deepened.

"Come with me. It's time for us to rest—sunrise will be here soon."

The two of them made their way toward the path Woeton had shown earlier. As they moved through the village, they said their goodbyes. Before they could reach the path, Gamba approached. V noticed Odessa trying to avoid his gaze.

"You cannot avoid me forever, child," Gamba said softly.

"I'm not avoiding you," Odessa mumbled.

"You cannot even look at me?"

A silence settled between them. Even the breeze and nearby chatter couldn't fill the gap. V thought to speak—but didn't. This wasn't her moment.

"What do you want me to say, Uncle?"

"Have you talked to your mama?"

"She does not want anything to do wit me," Odessa said

coldly.

She began to march ahead, but Gamba gently grabbed her. Odessa turned toward him abruptly with a fierce glare. V quickly placed her hand on Gamba's shoulder. He looked at her before gently letting Odessa go.

"She worried about you and your brudda. She and I searched for all of you. We found your papa, and I believe da grave I assume you made for Omari. When we could not find you, we feared da worst."

Gamba grew silent for a moment before glancing over at V. She didn't like the look he gave her one bit. He didn't have to say anything—she knew what he thought.

"Neliah has no idea whether your sistah lives. Your eldest brudda died while huntin'. Now her mate and youngest son are gone too."

Odessa kept her head low, a look of unhappiness growing. She grabbed at her arm and seemed to shrink. "I know, uncle."

"So how do you expect any of us to react when we arrive at da tower and discover what you have become? You have been cursed!" Gamba exclaimed.

"Alright, you made thy point," V muttered.

"You be silent!" Gamba snapped.

V stared at him, astonished. "I counsel you to mind your tongue when you speak to me."

"I need not be advised by a cursed spirit dat I will slay when da time comes."

Gamba turned away from Odessa and stepped closer to V. He towered over her, like most of the Hiorians and gray-skins now surrounding them. Despite that, V felt no fear. Her powers made her former human self look pathetic.

"Again, it would be wise to mind your tongue. I have great respect for your people, but I will not continue to tolerate your disrespect," V said menacingly.

"You are like those vampyrs—which makes you a danger to da livin'. My family have spent years learnin' to kill da likes of them. Do you truly believe I can be an ally wit such a ting?"

"I didn't choose to become what I am. Not only that, but you hath no idea of the torment of having to live like this. Every night I try so hard not to be like those things out there!"

V noticed people beginning to turn and listen to the argument. She had no desire to draw attention. Now she felt their unwelcoming, distrusting gazes. For years she'd been alone to avoid this very thing. When she finally thought she could form bonds again, it was all slipping away.

"If you despise what you are... then die," Gamba whispered.

V stiffened and stared at him blankly. Emotions boiled over inside her. Another curse of her kind—her emotions were far more intense than when she was alive. Rage, especially, could become a world-ending storm.

"What is the meaning of this?" a booming voice questioned.

V looked up to see the chief marching over with the female gray-skin he had been speaking with earlier. Concern shadowed his face. V instantly felt a heavy wave of guilt.

"I think it would be wise for me to take my leave."

"This cannot be! Ye just got here, and I had asked for thy help in finding my daughter—if she still lives."

"I will look for her... or find out what became of her. I just think 'tis time I go back to being on my own."

V turned and, instead of heading for the mountains, decided to return to the tower. It would be dangerous—but she had nowhere else to go. She wasn't surprised when Odessa rushed to her side. Neither said a word. They walked together in silence.

"I shall follow!"

V glanced over her shoulder and saw the chief. He handed his staff and decorated coat to the woman from the council. She looked just as perplexed. It made no sense why he'd choose to come.

"Tenzin? Why?" Thora asked.

The chief turned toward her with a look of longing and regret. "Thora, my core. 'Tis my fault our little girl hath been taken. The path of atonement is a wary path I must follow."

"Thy people are in need of you, Chief Tenzin," V said as she walked back over to him.

"They have wonderful leaders amongst the council. Thora, Palden, Norzin, and Lhamo are great leaders."

"If you come with me, you might die. I cannot protect you from the Wescreans or the revenants. I am not strong enough."

"The loss of a child leaves an emptiness in the chest that can never be filled. 'Tis an emptiness that makes death no longer something to fear."

V stared at him, then glanced at Odessa. She stood alone, waiting. She didn't protest. V considered how Odessa would struggle with temptation—but despite that, she believed Odessa could endure.

"Fine. I wish to find a person named Judith."

"Do ye know where to go?" the chief asked.

"We came north to reach your village. If I'm not mistaken, it would be further north—near the mountains."

The chief thought for a moment, then turned in the opposite direction and gestured for her to follow. V looked at Odessa, signaling her to come. She made this decision because she knew Odessa wanted to make progress. The longer they waited, the stronger the thirst became.

V and Odessa followed the chief through the village. The gray-skins lined up on either side of the path, chanting something as he passed. Along the way, a gray-skin handed him a battle axe. V wondered why they had such weapons if they didn't go to war.

These weapons weren't for hunting—at least not any animal she knew. But Woeton had described powerful mountain beasts before. A gray-skin blew into a large horn, its low hum echoing across the mountains.

V knew she'd have to write this down in her journal. Her scholarly mind was still fascinated by the mysteries of the gray-skins. She had much to learn about the Hiorians, too.

Before they could leave the village, Yama caught up with them. She carried her battle hammer and a large bag slung over her shoulder. What surprised V more was seeing Yonten,

Woeton, and Dharma.

Dharma was the scarred woman who had joined them days ago. V had spoken with her and liked her. She was Yonten's older sister and had raised him after their parents died. She also practiced archery—something rare and valuable in their village.

She would be a useful asset, especially since Odessa had brought the bow she found at the tower. Now they had two skilled archers.

Three azure wolves joined them. One padded over to Odessa. V still found the bond between them strange—but maybe it was what helped keep Odessa sane.

"What are ye doing?" the chief asked.

"To follow the chief into the unknown, for we have sworn to protect thee."

"Tis a journey where there may be no return. Ye must live. Especially you, Yama."

"My life is beholden to V, whom I wish to follow," Yama said with conviction.

"You said you won't take life—but I must to achieve my goal," V said, stepping forward.

She appreciated their support, but they needed to understand her path. If they wanted to survive, they would have to kill. And if they didn't fight for their survival, she would leave them behind.

"A path must be crossed... but I shan't cross it until it stands before me."

V stared at all of them. She didn't know what to say. Then she turned to the chief and poked his arm.

"If you allow them to follow, they are your burdens."

The chief nodded slowly. He looked at his people, deep in thought. Then he exhaled and gave in.

"None shall fall!" he declared.

They all nodded in agreement. The matter was settled. The chief took the lead, and everyone followed in silence.

The journey would be difficult for Odessa and V. Roaming by

day would be a challenge.

Once they left the village, V felt her nerves calm. The argument with Gamba had snapped her back to reality. No matter how much she loved the Hiorians, they would never truly accept her.

"Mayhaps I know what behooves you to leave?" the chief asked suddenly.

"I do not belong." V's words were dull and straightforward.

CHAPTER 12

Act 2: Yama's venture from home pt. 1

The chill of the night air was ever-present. White flakes continued to fall and cover the land. It was still early in the winter, but it was fast approaching. Treading this path toward an unknown destination, Yama marched in silence. She had no clue where they were going, but she didn't care. Anything to get away from the place she no longer saw as home.

Yama tugged at the thick coat made of fur she had on. It had been made by her elder sister—something she had come to cherish dearly since her death. It had been three years since she was sacrificed by the chief.

The pain of losing her still lingered. The fear she felt from her sister on that day still haunted her. Despite having lived up in the mountains for years, her body was accustomed to the cold. Although, for some reason, on this night, she felt the cold.

Up in the mountains, the wind blew quite violently during this time. In a few more days, the greenery would be covered in white. After managing to escape being sacrificed, it relieved her that she would get to see another season of the frost.

Alas, she feared that she couldn't spend another night among her people. Even though they discovered their chief had been bewitched, she could no longer face them. Whenever she looked at them, she only saw the people who stood by as her family had been killed—the few years where they made her suffer. For the last few years, she spent every waking night dreading the moment she would be sacrificed. At first, she had been prepared to accept her fate, but something urged her to run. This hadn't been the first time she fled.

Yonten had called her a coward, but it mattered not to her.

All she wanted was to live so her family could still live on in the world. Woeton and Yonten had caught up to her after a few nights of running. Thankfully, the woman known as V had appeared. Yama glanced over her shoulder to see V and Odessa following behind her. Their eyes were both filled with what she felt to be either regret or grief. Despite the short time with them, she had experienced something she hadn't in a long while. With them, she felt safe—and at times, they acted like a family.

Despite not getting to talk to Odessa much, she sometimes felt a sisterly feeling from her. She enjoyed her company, but sometimes she could tell she was struggling with something. It made her want to help, but she couldn't get the courage to speak. This frustrated her because she knew there was a connection, but they felt so far apart. Odessa had a fierce personality that made Yama shy away from speaking to her. Not only that, but she also admired that fierceness. If she had it herself, maybe her people wouldn't have gotten away with so much over the years.

As for V, Yama took note of the motherly nature she possessed. She recalled when V woke up after passing out from her fight with the masked warrior. When she saw Odessa covered in blood, she rushed to clean her up. Yama understood their curse caused them to act strangely at the sight of blood. It frightened her—but she didn't care. For her, being by their side felt safer than living among her own people.

She stared at the chief up ahead. He walked a few feet ahead of everyone, holding up a torch. Woeton and Yonten followed behind him with torches as well. The wind made the flames flicker. The faint chirping of crickets filled her ears, pulling her out of her thoughts. She began to look around into the foggy night. Her eyes couldn't make out much in the dark, but walking barefoot allowed her to connect with the land. She could feel the vibrations of the earth—it reminded her of a heartbeat.

Having left her village and descended into the lowlands seemed to connect her more deeply with the natural world.

Seeing so many new things made her want to leave home even more. If she stayed in the village, there were countless wonders she'd never get to see. From what V had told her, there were vast bodies of water west of Wescreas. In the mountains, there were springs and a river down below. The river was beautiful—it rolled off a cliff and poured into another body of water.

That was the largest body of water she had ever seen. Her people called it Scarstone Falls. What V described made it seem like nothing to gawk at. As she followed behind Yonten, she recalled how the two of them used to go to the falls and swim. Growing up, she'd seen him as a friend—especially since their families had been close.

Which made it hurt more that he was so willing to have her sacrificed. No—it angered her beyond words. Woeton had become the leader of the village guardians. They were the main hunters and fighters. She remembered him following her father around constantly, always claiming to look up to him. Yet he stood by and let him die.

And to make matters worse, Woeton allowed Yama's mother and sister to be taken. She gritted her teeth and clenched her fists in frustration, thinking about his cowardice. How could she ever return to the village with so much resentment in her heart? The anger inside her was suffocating. Truthfully, if she hadn't met V and Odessa, she would've died in the lowlands.

Now she was leaving the village again. V had implied the chief's daughter might still be alive. Yama had no idea how that could be true—it had been over thirteen years. Who could've taken care of her all this time? There were so many mysteries she wanted answers to. One of them was whether the chief truly harbored a grudge against her father. She knew he'd been bewitched, but he had implied his hidden feelings played a part in his actions.

Knowing this, she knew she could never forgive him. Even so, she felt compelled to accompany him—to learn the fate of his daughter. Uncertain of what the truth would bring, she still had to know.

As she looked ahead, she heard Odessa's voice. It had a somber tone. Yama had noticed her tone was often like this. Sometimes it was soft and calm. Other times it sounded just like this—or completely flat. Yama looked over her shoulder to see Odessa and V had stopped. Odessa was pointing toward the sky and had unsheathed one of her daggers. Yama looked up into the sky curiously. With the fog and darkness, she couldn't see anything.

Back in the village, she had spoken with Odessa's cousin. Talking with him made her feel something she hadn't felt in a long time. He even tried teaching her about different remedies. It was clearly something he was passionate about, and it amused her. The idea that the land could help heal them gave her a sense of kinship with him.

Yama began to wonder again what Odessa had seen in the sky. She tried to listen—hoping to hear something—but all she caught were crickets and rocks falling down the trail. She returned her attention to V, who merely shrugged and turned back around. When V's gaze met hers, Yama startled at those sapphire eyes and quickly turned forward again.

Yama thought V had a kind, loving heart. She was the shortest among them, but also the deadliest. Whenever Yama looked at her, she could feel the land warning her to run.

It frightened her to her very core—but she didn't think V would hurt her. At least she hoped not. She understood little about V's desires, but she sensed a fragment of honor in her. Even if it was only a sliver, Yama believed it was enough to trust her.

"You be afraid?" a voice asked.

Yama tensed as she looked to her left. V stared at her, brow furrowed, concern on her face. That concern was something Yama had come to appreciate. Even when V was deep in her own thoughts, she always checked on Yama and Odessa.

"I am but a traveler once again being whisked away from me home," Yama frowned.

It wasn't a complete lie. She truly feared leaving home. The world below was strange and full of dangers. Men clad in metal rising from the earth terrified her. No matter how many times they fell, they rose again.

Still, she knew there was more to see in the world below. Things she'd never witness in the mountains.

"You did not hath to leave."

"'Tis grief and suffering that awaits me there."

V seemed to consider this. Whatever she thought remained a mystery to Yama. All she knew was that she couldn't go back.

"I understand the ailment that plagues thee. Although... the world outside that home of yours is filled with woe," V said, her voice uneasy.

It made Yama wonder what truly led to V's transformation. She hesitated—but had to ask.

"What led to your ailment?"

Yama paused as soon as the words left her lips. Had that been rude? V suddenly stopped walking, and Odessa bumped into her.

Now Yama had two sapphire-eyed women staring at her.

"'Tis the vile acts of my own blood that turned me into this... heathen that I am."

V's eyes were full of disgust—as she stared at her hands. It was an unsettling sight. Odessa looked just as confused as Yama. But Yama knew—Odessa had no idea what was going on.

As silence settled over them, a voice called out in the distance. They turned and saw a flickering flame. Three figures stood in the distance.

"Onward we must march," V sighed.

Yama nodded and followed. Odessa walked in silence beside her. Yama wanted to speak to her—but hesitated. Why?

She let out a disappointed sigh as her shoulders slouched. Then she simply followed closely behind V and Odessa.

It would be a long journey. Filled with horrors. But it was still better than staying in that village.

CHAPTER 13

The group had traveled for a few hours before the sun began to peek over the horizon. Luckily, they found a cave where they chose to rest. After investigating it thoroughly, they concluded that nothing would come to cause trouble.

Since the sun had risen, V and Odessa rested deep inside the cave. The azure wolf creature that had grown fond of Odessa lay beside her. She sat silently, stroking the fur on the creature's head.

The others were out searching for food. V had no idea when they'd be back, but she felt relieved to have some silence. The thirst had begun to stir in her. Although, after years of discipline, she could manage a while longer.

The problem was that Odessa still struggled. It had only been a little over a week or two since she had been turned. V suspected her senses and emotions were stronger than her own—likely due to being a Hiorian.

While the others were out hunting, V sat taking notes in her journal. Everything she had recently learned, she jotted down. As she flipped through some of the parchments she had written on, she saw her sketches. She had drawn portraits of Odessa and Yama.

Out of all of them, the one of her lover was the most important. She stopped and stared at it, longing to see him again. Not a day passed that she didn't miss his voice or his laughter. The thought of seeing him smile again saddened her.

Her mind wandered, remembering how they met. A scout had been sent to search for the Acolytes and their lair. For some reason, he hadn't returned for nearly two years. When he finally did, he brought with him a large group of people.

V recalled that the scout had stumbled upon them defeating the vampyrs. Then he spent time among them, learning their language while teaching them his. By the time they arrived at her home, they spoke almost fluently.

They were highly intelligent people who caught on quickly. V had been fascinated. When her father met with the Hiorian leaders, that was when she first crossed paths with her lover. She didn't speak to him much then, but she couldn't hide her attraction to him.

After several months spent teaching her people how to fight the vampyrs, some of the Hiorians left—returning to an area outside the Wescrean and Vostaylian countries.

Fortunately, the Craft family remained, which allowed her to spend more time with her lover. She got to know much about him and the adventures that led to his arrival in her country.

Her relationship with him grew complicated when her father began considering marrying her off to the Wescrean prince. Her father hoped it would form an alliance between the two countries. That had been his belief—up until the betrayal that forced her to flee her home.

"Who is dat?"

V snapped out of her deep train of thought and looked up to see Odessa staring at the sketch. She had been lying down not long ago. V hadn't even noticed she'd woken up. As she stared at Odessa, she tried to recall her lover's name.

"'Tis my beloved, Jorah."

Odessa examined the sketch with intrigue. V stared at it, realizing how much her art had improved. When she'd been human, she often struggled with drawing. Now it seemed like a simple task. Jorah had taught her how to sketch, and now it felt like his hands were guiding hers.

"He appears to be a Hiorian. So dis is da person who had your heart when you were still human?"

"Yes."

A faint smile formed on V's face as she once again recalled

the past. She could hardly remember how his voice sounded, though she knew it was a voice you could listen to without ever tiring.

"Again, I am sorry dat you had him taken from you."

"'Tis not your fault he's gone, dear," V said softly.

"It was Jiya dat killed him, no?"

"Yes... but he was already practically dead. Anyway, I have been wanting to know if you knew Jiya personally."

"No, but someone I knew believed in his cause. They left to follow him."

Odessa's expression darkened with regret and anger. The look reminded V of her own betrayal—when she learned her uncle had played a part in her suffering. V assumed this person Odessa referred to had been someone she loved or trusted.

"Love can be cruel like that," V said, watching Odessa's reaction.

"What?"

Odessa looked up at her with wide eyes. V smiled, seeing the young Hiorian's embarrassment bloom.

"I assumed you loved and trusted this person."

"I would not go so far as saying I loved them," Odessa muttered.

"What will you do if we stumble upon this person?" V asked.

Odessa didn't reply. She reached into her bag and pulled out one of her daggers. Without a word, she mimicked a hacking motion with it.

V shook her head in disbelief. She didn't want Odessa to be forced to kill someone she once cared for. It seemed too cruel a destiny.

"My people live much longer than humans, but since our population is declining, da elders wanted da youth to have children. My father had me paired wit a young warrior from da Silvercloud family."

"Okay, but how did he get involved with Jiya?"

"Jiya and his revenants attacked da settlement we built near da Dark Sea. He told everyone he planned to build a kingdom for our people."

"If he seized Wescreas to build a kingdom, why not follow him?" V asked.

"After hearin' about his attack on da Grimm and da Caskthorne family eleven years ago, no one wanted to follow him. Not only dat, but years earlier he nearly wiped out your lover's family."

"The begrudgery he had toward the Craft family still eludes me. His mate had been part of their family—yet he killed them. And I saw no remorse."

V recalled the attack Jiya orchestrated on Jorah's family. There had been many causes: conflict with Jorah's father, his mate Malika leaving him, and the suicide of his daughter. He blamed the Craft family for it all. Another reason V despised him—he blamed everyone but himself.

"Whether it had been personal or not, he has made himself an enemy to us."

"So how did your mate end up showin' fealty to him?"

Odessa tensed at the question. She instinctively grabbed the arm with the strange scars. V noticed this and grew more curious but refrained from prying.

"He never believed humans would ever accept us. Not if we tried bein' friendly. He believed that showin' them our strength would teach them we are not to be trifled wit. Dat was how he saw tings."

Odessa's eyes stared off into the distance. V assumed she was reflecting on the past. It made her wonder what Jiya had done while she lived in solitude. So many years spent away from society—she had no idea what Odessa and her people had been forced to endure.

V stared up at the cave ceiling, wondering if it would all be worth it in the end. What exactly would she accomplish by killing the people who took her lover and family away? Would it do anything for the Hiorians? She didn't even know if she would find real satisfaction.

"I must confess that your lover had a point. Humans always

destroy what they fear and cannot understand."

"We are not like da humans!"

"Your people never went to war with each other?"

"I grew up here, where my own people have attacked me..."

V took a second to process this. She recalled Jorah telling her about fights that happened between families, but no one ever died. As she thought more, she remembered Jiya and A'Jorah getting into a fight. Jiya had been beaten bloody, but A'Jorah hadn't taken it further. Unlike humans, she had believed that Hiorians showed more restraint in their emotions. Jiya had changed all that by becoming the enemy of his own people.

"Do you have misgivings about taking lives?"

"Before you turned me, it always bothered me. Havin' to kill humans dat attacked us bothered me a great deal. Now dat I have changed, it feels easy."

Once again, V had to consider the choice she made. She couldn't take back what she had done. As she thought more on the matter, she wondered: would she be punished once she passed on? Odessa had spoken of guides to the Spirit World. It made V wonder if they also determined what happened to one's soul.

"I do not know what happens on the other side, but there's no turning back now," V mumbled to herself.

"I do not know if da soulseers will punish me, but I will accept whatever fate dat awaits me," Odessa agreed.

There were still things V felt she needed to know. Soulseers intrigued her. Every time Odessa mentioned them, V thought about the night she had been chained to the stake. The figure watching from a distance had a strange presence.

"Do you think defeating Jiya will make a difference?" Odessa suddenly asked.

"A difference in what regard?"

"If he is defeated, will my people have a better life?"

"It depends on whether the other countries begin to see your people as a threat."

"Then dat means we will be at war until we are wiped out,"

Odessa muttered, frustrated.

"I will ensure that everyone has a common enemy," V said with utmost conviction.

"What do you intend to do and gain from dis quest? A few times, you mentioned regret and seem to waver wit your convictions."

V sat there and thought long and hard about Odessa's question. Revenge had been what brought her back, but she had never acted. She'd even heard stories of the things Jiya had done. Not only that, but she'd heard of what the king of Vostaylia had been up to for years.

The only one she knew little about was the woman from the Acolytes. She had heard rumors of their movements but nothing definitive. Even if she had known more, would she have done something?

Instead, she remained hidden, trying to control her powers. Why hadn't she gone berserk and burned everything down? Why had she only started traveling again a few weeks ago? These were questions she thought about often. Still, she didn't have a definitive answer.

And then there were the horrible things she had done. Before trying to wean herself off blood, she had killed innocent people. Some of those people were Hiorians. Unfortunately, she couldn't tell Odessa that.

"My regret comes from the horrible things I did in the beginning."

"I suppose you will not speak on dem."

V looked at Odessa with a regretful expression. "You'd despise me if I told you, so please don't ask."

Odessa's face showed she was thinking deeply. A flicker of suspicion crossed her eyes before she closed them. "Fine."

"I assume this war has been going on for quite some time?"

"Aye. We haven't made any progress against Jiya's forces. And those men dat killed my papa and brudda... they implied dat da prince is dead."

"Are you sure this person named Judith will be on our side?"

"No. But if she is a threat to us, then we shall kill her."

Odessa clearly wanted to get things over with quickly. Unlike V, she still had the fire of vengeance burning bright. V had begun to question whether that flame still burned in her at all.

Had Odessa been without V, she might've started drinking blood and gone on a frenzy. Odessa likely wanted to end it all so she wouldn't have to constantly resist. Even if they decided to go to Fodmery, they were still far from it.

They would have to travel a great distance. Gamba had likely already sent his people to battle. Another thing—V didn't know how much ground she could cover at supernatural speed. She had never tried it before.

"If we go to Fodmery, we'll likely encounter more revenants. We don't know how strong they are. Leon was quite the threat for me."

"Then we should consume more blood to raise our strength. Once we have dat strength, we can tear through dem wit ease," Odessa explained.

"My fear is that if you drink too much, you'll become besotted—and go on a killing spree."

"Once Jiya and Zahur are dead, then you can end my sufferin'."

Odessa leaned closer to V, a brooding look on her face. This young woman seemed like she had something to prove. It made V wonder. Even though she felt she knew so much about her, in reality, she knew very little.

"Tell me—what drives you to be so impatient?"

"When Jiya came to our settlement a few years ago, he killed my friends dat refused his offer."

"Okay. And what of this man you refer to as Zahur?"

Once again, Odessa grabbed at the scarred arm. "I got close enough to Jiya to kill him, but Zahur stopped me. He even disrespected my family!"

Odessa's nails dug into her arm as she shuddered with anger. V sensed there had to be more to this story. Did Zahur do something else? V wanted to know everything.

"I'm sure there's more to it than that."

"What do you mean?"

"I get the feeling he said or did something to you that's haunted you since. I believe whatever it was is the reason you're so unyielding about going to Fodmery."

Odessa sat quietly, clearly reflecting. Whatever happened was the root of her rage. If V understood it, maybe it would help her plan.

"My papa and his had us paired together. For my family's sake, I tried to love him. In a way, I think I did... but he was cruel to me."

Odessa fell silent. Her expression darkened. V could feel the hatred in her. Now she understood the significance of the scars. Zahur had been abusive. The thought made V dig her nails into her palms, dark ooze seeping out.

A woman scorned could be truly dangerous. Zahur had hurt Odessa emotionally and physically. He broke her trust—and disrespected the family she had loved more than her own life.

"What happened, Odessa?"

Odessa stared off into a corner, her eyes full of rage and confusion. V had already concluded Zahur caused the scars, but she needed Odessa to say it.

The silence irked her. She could see the weight Odessa carried. She just wanted to help her lift it.

"He told me he's da reason my older brudda is dead." She shuddered, then slowly gestured toward her arm. "He also confessed dat havin' to be around me disgusted him."

V stared at her, dumbfounded. She had no words. How could she ease Odessa's pain? It didn't seem possible. But now she understood everything.

Odessa had lost all her siblings. One had been taken by the man she was paired with. A man who also abused her.

A stream of dark red tears began to pour down Odessa's cheeks. V watched as something inside her stirred. A flash of memory returned: a burning hamlet, dead Hiorians, a young woman weeping while holding two small bodies. The only thing left of her twin brother.

V's face trembled. She clenched her fists, black ooze dripping from her palms. The dying flame inside her reignited into a wildfire.

Seeing Odessa cry awakened it once more.

"After we go to Judith's keep, we shall go straight to Fodmery."

Odessa's distraught expression turned to confusion. "What?"

"I will do what I must to end this," V said, filled with new conviction.

"What made you decide so suddenly?"

"I don't know if I've earned the right to say this, but... you've become the only family I have. With that in mind, I want to punish the person who brought you to tears."

Odessa stared at her, stunned. Then she looked around, as if trying to find the right words—or decide if she'd heard V correctly.

To V's surprise, Odessa leaned in and hugged her tightly.

"Thank you."

CHAPTER 14

Yama's Venture from home pt. 2

The sky was a dreary gray as the clouds covered the scene. Glimpses of sun rays peeked through and illuminated the mountain landscape. A blanket of white had begun to fully cover the land. The fog that usually obscured the scenery wasn't as thick in the lower area where Yama now found herself roaming.

There was a soft breeze in the air. It relieved Yama a bit because the harsh winds of the night had been troublesome. Having a moment of calmness in the air felt good.

She, along with Dharma and Yonten, had ventured off to hunt for food. The chief had gone elsewhere to speak with Woeton in private. Yama had kept her distance from Dharma and Yonten.

As they tracked the footprints of what Yama assumed to be from a silvermane, she found herself mostly looking around. Silvermanes were large feline creatures that stalked the Scarstone Mountains.

While they were busy tracking, all she could do was marvel at the scenery she hadn't seen in a long while. The Scarstone Mountains formed a valley of rugged peaks, a verdant tapestry surrounding a large stream. At the moment, the lush greenery was blanketed in white.

Below, she could see where the stream cascaded off a cliff into a larger body of water. She could make out beautiful meadows that surrounded the stream. It had been a long time since she had ventured this far outside the village. She had been very young, but she still remembered.

"Do ye remember we would swim together here?" a voice

asked, startling Yama.

She looked over to see Yonten's steel blue eyes staring at her. He wore a plastered fake smile. Yama rolled her eyes and looked away. There wasn't much she wanted to say to him. Her anger toward him still burned, and now he had the audacity to act friendly.

"How could I recollect something from whence I was so young..." she muttered.

She folded her arms across her chest and brushed past him. Dharma was up ahead, kneeling, examining something on the ground.

"Ye must be maddened for what I said," Yonten called after her.

She stopped and stood motionless. For once, he had the wherewithal to acknowledge his foolishness. Yama bit her lip and took a deep breath. Taking a step back, she turned to face him.

"For once ye are able to use that mind instead of that foul mouth," Yama retorted with an annoyed grin.

Yonten's lips trembled, his expression darkening. Yama could see he was trying to be nice, but her lack of kindness likely frustrated him. She knew him too well to believe his apology was genuine—it likely came at Dharma's urging. It had always been like this. Dharma and Yama's sister had remained close friends even after the tribe sacrificed Yama's father.

Yama had tried to keep her friendships, but the betrayal had taken root. When the chief ordered her mother to be sacrificed, only a few had spoken up. Dharma's mother had been one of them—and she had been killed. After that, no one opposed the chief again. Eventually, Yama lost her sister too.

"Why do ye hath to be so... headstrong?" Yonten stepped toward her. "I try to show you kindness to atone for my past transgressions toward thee!"

"Ye chased me from my home! Named me a coward and even tried to slay me!" Yama shouted with rage, lunging at Yonten and pushing him.

He was caught off guard and stumbled, tumbling down the side of the trail. Yama's eyes widened in horror as panic gripped her. Yonten's spear had fallen to the ground at her feet.

Dharma came running, screaming. Without thinking, Yama picked up the spear and leapt after Yonten. She used the weapon to slow her descent, careful not to injure herself.

Her heart pounded as she raced down the steep slope. Yonten had landed in a level area below. As she reached him, she saw something she hadn't expected—two large figures emerged from a place she couldn't see from above.

Large beasts with thick manes of silver.

Yonten lay on the ground, writhing in pain, clutching his shoulder. Yama landed hard beside him. The sudden movement startled the creatures. When Yama got a good look, she realized they had stumbled upon the den of two silvermanes.

Their yellow feline eyes stared menacingly. Yama gripped the spear tightly, bending her knees. Silvermanes were muscular and agile. Though taller than the average human, Yama was small for a grey skin. Facing a silvermane was terrifying.

Only once had she faced one before—when she accompanied her father on a hunt. He had told her how strong their jaws were. A bite could tear off a limb effortlessly. Their claws, too, could cut through flesh with ease. Even a graze could cause severe blood loss.

Yama tried to calm herself. The earth beneath her whispered: run. But she couldn't—not with Yonten injured. Despite all he'd said and done, she cared. Besides, this was her fault. If she hadn't acted in anger, he wouldn't be here.

"Are ye mad? Run!" Yonten groaned.

She ignored him, keeping her eyes locked on the pacing beasts. Which one would attack first? Maybe she could handle one—if she was fast and precise.

She began to wonder why she had thrown herself into danger. She didn't want to die—not yet. There was so much she hadn't experienced. If she died here, her family's legacy would end.

The larger silvermane snarled and stopped pacing. Yama guessed this one was the male. He was bigger, but the female was likely the more dangerous.

Her father had once told her—if you back away slowly, the male might back off. But the female... she was always ready to hunt.

"Back away slowly if ye can," Yama said.

"What?" Yonten whined.

"Back... away," she repeated.

She felt him behind her, his weight leaning on her for support. His breath tickled the back of her neck. He was in the way. The female silvermane still paced, and Yama only glanced at him briefly.

Then the male lunged.

Yama shouted and raised the spear. Her body trembled as she pushed Yonten back slightly. Her breaths came fast. Beads of sweat dripped down her forehead.

She couldn't panic.

She had to keep them at bay—just long enough. She hoped Dharma would come back with help. It was the only plan she had.

If both beasts attacked at once, they would die. Being mauled by a silvermane was not the death she wanted.

The wind picked up. Snow fell heavier. Her bare feet crunched in the snow as she inched back. Her people were trained to endure the cold—but this wasn't just cold. This was survival.

"'Tis my fault it hath come to this," Yonten whispered.

"What?" Yama asked, eyes still locked on the beasts.

"We wouldn't be here if I'd been a better friend. I was the craven."

She didn't expect that. And for once, his words sounded sincere.

"I pushed ye because I became blinded with madness. When we escape this fate, I shall atone for this," she said nervously.

He laughed—a breathy, pained laugh. He was badly hurt.

"Ye owe me nothing. I should've stood by thy side when the chief ordered the sacrifice of thy family. Ye says my words are foul—but my heart is pure. My love for thee hath depths I cannot express."

Yama froze. Love?

Was he serious?

Had he hit his head that hard?

She didn't understand any of this.

Before she could react, the male silvermane lunged again. Yama yelped and aimed the spear—but something pushed her aside.

Yonten.

He collided with the beast as it bit into his neck. He screamed in agony, staggering but staying on his feet. They grappled. Grunting. Bleeding.

Yama stood frozen. Her limbs trembled. Her mouth opened to scream, but no sound came.

Move.

She had to move.

He was going to die.

Red poured down Yonten's body, staining the snow and stone beneath them.

"Find it in thy heart to forgive an ole fool!" he shouted.

Then he and the creature fell from the cliff.

"No!" Yama screamed.

Her chest ached as she gasped. Warm tears spilled down her face. She gripped the spear.

Then the female silvermane attacked.

She turned just in time, jamming the spear into its chest. Blood gushed. She screamed and forced it onto its back. Rage consumed her. She yanked the spear out and drove it in again.

And again.

And again.

She didn't know how long she did it—until someone grabbed her.

She struggled—until a voice reached her.

Dharma.

Slowly, the fury ebbed. She looked up and met Dharma's worried eyes. Yama shoved her away and looked out over the cliff.

She couldn't look at her.

She couldn't believe it.

Why?

Why did he do something so foolish?

For her?

How could she ever face Dharma now?

"Where is Yonten?" Dharma croaked.

Yama curled into herself, knees to her chest. She rested her head there, tears cascading.

"Forgive me," she whispered—then wept even harder.

It was her fault.

She let her emotions get the best of her.

Now someone was dead.

Would they even find his body?

Footsteps approached.

"Where be Yonten?" a voice called.

Yama looked up to see Woeton rushing over. The chief followed, face heavy with concern.

"Ye pushed him down here. 'Tis thy fault he's gone!" Dharma screamed.

Yama shivered.

Yonten had died for her.

And he... confessed his love?

She couldn't process it.

Just pain.

Deep, stabbing pain in her chest.

She clutched it, trying to breathe.

Would she ever be forgiven?

CHAPTER 15

The sound of waves gently hitting the surface of something stirred V from her slumber. She groaned as she groggily opened her eyes. The first thing she noticed was that she was staring up at the sky. From what she could tell, the sun was beginning to set.

That had been the first thing she saw, but then something else caught her attention. It made her gasp as her heart skipped a beat. When she placed a hand over her chest, she became even more shocked. How could this be?

Sitting up and staring into the distance was a familiar face. His warm brown skin and long brown hair brought tears to her eyes. Realizing she was lying in his lap, she reached up to touch his face. He felt real, and his skin was warm.

His silvery eyes looked down at her curiously. Then his pearly whites appeared as he leaned over her. V let out a laugh as she struggled not to cry. She didn't understand what this meant, but it made her happy.

"Did I wake you?" he asked in his deep voice.

"No." V smiled. "Where are we?"

She sat up slightly and saw that they were on a boat, not far from the coast. From what she could tell, they were in the Gray Sea. How had they gotten here?

"You said you wanted to go fishin', remember?" he asked.

V thought for a moment, wondering what was happening. She sighed, then let out another laugh. "Whatever dream I just had felt so real I must have forgotten about this."

The wind picked up, whipping V's hair wildly across her face. It obscured her vision, and she had to push it aside to see properly. When she turned back toward her lover, to her dismay he was gone. Instead, someone else stood there.

"Forgive the intrusion upon your dream," the figure said softly.

He wore dark-colored clothes with a purple cloak. His coarse gray hair hung in wild locks that blew with the wind. His glowing eyes stared at V with such intensity that she trembled.

These eyes were nothing like a revenant's dull green shade. In those deep spirals of purple and teal gems, she saw vastness. His sclera were pitch-black, like the night sky.

"You..."

"So back then you did see me. Good."

The figure turned his head and looked out at the sea. V followed his gaze and noticed the sky was beginning to darken. Nothing made sense, and confusion pressed in on her.

"What is the meaning of all this?"

"You're asleep, which you haven't done in a while. I reckon this dream of yours is what you imagined your future with Jorah Craft to be. Sadly, this dream will never come to pass."

"Well, I shall go fishing with Odessa before—" V stopped, falling silent. Why was she thinking of that now? "How are you in my dream, and what do you want?"

"The world of dreams is merely a gateway to the Spirit World," the figure said, his face somber.

"Then perhaps he was an illusion?"

The figure sat silently, expressionless, making it impossible for V to know what he thought. Everything about him felt otherworldly.

"He found a way to leave a part of his soul tethered to you, so he's always near. I don't think you realized it, but I believe it's what made you hesitant to seek revenge."

V sat silently, taking in his words. She placed her hands over her heart, wondering if Jorah had reached a safe place in the Spirit World. She didn't want him to be suffering.

"He is at peace with his people, by the way."

"Who are you?"

"His people called me... a soulseer."

"Are you here to guide my soul to the afterlife, then?"

"No."

"Then..."

"I am merely going to observe the events to come."

"For what reason?"

"Another like me broke a rule long ago. They escaped their confinement and wreaked havoc here in the living world. I thought they had been destroyed, but I fear they still exist."

"What does that have to do with me?"

"Everything happening now is due to the meddling of that traitor."

"So what I have become is because of them?"

"Among other things, yes."

"What else are they involved in?"

"The *Tome of Eneida*, in particular... and the madness of that Hiorian."

V sat in silence, her thoughts heavy. She didn't know how to respond to this new information. Still, it wouldn't stop her from seeking revenge. Dreaming of Jorah, knowing it would never come true, only fueled her fury.

"Will you hinder me from claiming my revenge?"

"I would much rather see how things play out."

"I've done a great deal of harm over the years."

"Indeed. And you will certainly do more unforgivable things as you continue on your path."

V frowned in confusion. His expression never changed, his gaze fixed on the horizon.

"You're okay with me slaying more people?"

"I only guide the dead to the Spirit World and slay spirits too dangerous to remain among the living."

"Am I not a dangerous spirit?"

At last, the figure turned his head and looked directly at her. "The spirits I speak of are ancient and far worse than you. Although... I will ensure a just ending to your story."

V stared blankly at the soulseer. She didn't understand anything he had just told her. This first encounter with such a powerful spirit didn't fascinate her—it infuriated her. His words were more puzzling than enlightening.

Then the soulseer stood, rocking the boat. He looked down at V once more and placed his foot on the side.

"Once you fully take the plunge into darkness, you will fall into madness. The path you must walk for revenge will make you unrecognizable."

His words fell like a warning as he leaned forward, pressing his weight down. The boat tilted, and V was thrown into the water. Panic surged through her as darkness swallowed her whole.

*

V's eyes shot open and she sat up in a panic. She looked around, wild-eyed, trying to figure out where she was. It didn't take long for her to realize her surroundings. Next to her sat Odessa, who watched her worriedly.

"Are you alright?" Odessa asked.

"Forgive me. I was lost in a dream."

"Dis is da first time I've seen you actually sleep. You seemed at peace for a moment, but then you grew restless."

"Sorry I caused you concern." V tried to plaster on a fake smile.

"Do you wish to talk about it?"

"'Tis not important," V said reassuringly.

Odessa nodded and leaned back against the cave wall. She returned to working on the bow she had brought from Skyreach Tower. While the image of her dream lingered, V reached for her journal. She picked it up along with her quill so she could begin writing and sketching what she had seen.

Her thoughts drifted back to the soulseer's words. There were so many questions she wished she had asked. Who was the being orchestrating everything? The book Jiya used to control revenants was clearly a concern to the soulseer. But what else—besides her—did this traitor have their hand in?

There were too many questions, and she didn't expect answers anytime soon. She had no idea how long this journey would take. Even after finishing here, she would still have to return to Vostaylia—and she would have to do that without those who now traveled with her. That journey would be much more personal.

As she sat there, a loud commotion erupted near the cave's entrance. She looked up to see the gray-skins shuffling in, dragging the corpse of a large creature. Woeton dropped the silver-furred beast onto the ground, and immediately V noticed the shift in the atmosphere.

Tension weighed heavily in the air. Something was wrong. One of the gray-skins was missing. Then she spotted Yama, who marched to a corner and sat down.

V could hear her sniffling, as if she had been crying. What had happened? The chief tried to calm Dharma, but she only shouted, cursing at both Yama and the chief.

"What has happened?" V called out.

The sudden silence was eerie. Everyone froze. V didn't understand what was going on, but she noticed Yonten had not returned. Had he gone back to the village? No. This was something far worse.

"None of this should hath happened!" Dharma cried.

Woeton stepped forward and wrapped his large arms around her. She collapsed against him, weeping. The chief watched for a moment before approaching V and Odessa. His grim expression showed deep regret. He leaned against the wall and slid down to sit. V stared at him, waiting.

"Yonten and Yama appeareth to hath argued. He fell near a den belonging to silvermanes." The chief choked on his words, struggling to hold back tears.

"Silvermanes? Is that what that creature is?" V asked.

"We hunt them for food, alas, they be dangerous." He sniffled.

V looked at the massive feline-like corpse. Even Woeton had struggled carrying it, despite his size and strength.

"Yama will not speak of what happened. She only pleads for forgiveness."

"Do not force her to explain. In time she will speak her truth," V said firmly.

The chief nodded, then stared at her. "What is thy plan?" he asked, suddenly changing the subject.

V had no real plan yet. All she knew was that Judith was the daughter of the fallen king. If she could reach her and offer help, perhaps she could gain an ally. It would be easier to approach Fodmery with an army at her side. While they fought the chevaliers and revenants, she could focus on killing Jiya.

Still, something about Judith felt odd. From what V knew, most women in Wescreas had little battle prowess. They were rarely enlisted in the military. It had been the same in Vostaylia as well.

"I hope to gain an ally from this quest," V answered.

The chief regarded her a long moment, then lowered his head, lost in thought. Too many troubles weighed on them all. V noticed Odessa had moved beside Yama, wrapping an arm around the grieving young grey skin.

V's mind wandered back to the soulseer's words. If a higher power had been pulling the strings all along, then they were nothing more than pawns in a greater scheme. The thought frustrated her, but at this point, all she cared about was revenge. The soulseer had said the traitor was her problem—so why dwell on it further?

She needed to see this through. Otherwise, her soul might never know peace. But what would Jorah think of what she had become? Would he still love her? Insecurity tightened around her chest. Running her fingers through her hair, she imagined the disgusted look on his face.

If he had been an exorcist, he would have killed her without hesitation. Odessa once told her that her people saw only two paths when it came to spirits. That raised more questions about Jorah. What kind of man had he truly been? From what she knew, he had always tried to keep an open mind.

"Do ye foresee the Hiorians victorious in their battle?"

V snapped out of her thoughts. The chief was staring at

her, and she had nearly forgotten he was there. Clicking her tongue, she took a moment to consider. The Hiorians were strong—but not merciless. And mercy would almost certainly be their downfall.

"I am uncertain."

"I pray that Sifadi is in their favor. My mind would hath been forever benighted by the baleful thing that took me."

V nodded, reflecting. "That spirit had been latched onto you for many years. 'Tis amazing you still remain."

"There hath been moments where I lost time..." The chief looked lost, scratching the palm of his hand. Clearly this troubled him—how much had he done without memory?

"Mayhaps the thing corrupting you had taken over."

"Perhaps," he muttered. "It doth not erase the shame of all that was done. I cannot erase the suffering I hath caused."

"One day, thy people may find it in their hearts to forgive."

"What of Yama?"

V glanced at the girl, who still wept in Odessa's arms. "What about her?"

"Because of me, she hath no family. And today hath wounded her even more."

The look of regret on his face was unbearable. V doubted he would ever free himself of it.

"Much of her family left the village because of the changed one long ago."

That phrase again—the changed one. V had heard it before, but never explained. Now she might finally learn.

"The one sealed in that cave?" she asked.

"Yes... She fled to the lowlands, like Yama. The humans defiled her and slew her. Then, on a night such as this, she returned to our village, benighted, with eyes of blood."

The chief's voice shook with fear as he recalled the story. To her surprise, it made V shiver as well. She had thought nothing could frighten her anymore.

"My father watched her feast on the blood of our people before she was subdued. We knew not how to slay her, so that cave is where she has remained."

V sat in silence, wondering whether the existence of the changed one had cursed the land itself.

"What made most of Yama's family leave if you were able to stop her?"

The chief's face darkened. "Mayhaps the shame of being kin to a monster."

His words sent chills through V. Was he implying the changed one was related to Yama? She longed to know more, but feared pressing him might drag him back into despair— and despair made him vulnerable to corruption.

"Alas, that specter fed on my darkest thoughts. I brought greater shame upon my family than the changed one did upon hers. That is why I shall not return to the village after this journey."

"You should let thy people decide thy fate if you truly wish to atone. And remember, they are guilty as well—for failing to stand up for Yama's family."

The chief remained silent, reflecting on her words.

"Well, I am going to set out at dusk. I cannot linger in this sadness for too long."

The chief nodded and took a deep breath. V glanced at Woeton, still trying to console Dharma. The grief was heavy, suffocating.

But V felt nothing for Yonten. She had never liked him.

Yama was her only concern and at the moment she had no idea how she would approach her. Odessa was comforting her, but she couldn't talk to her. She did not know how, so V would have to sooner or later.

*

Nightfall came after a few hours of rest. V trudged through the rubble, following closely behind the chief. Beside her walked Odessa and Yama, while Dharma and Woeton trailed behind. They descended the mountain trail, returning to the lowlands.

The fog still covered most of the area, obscuring their vision. V could see well in the dark, unlike the others. The chief carried another torch to illuminate the path for them.

V listened carefully to the sounds around them, alert for predators. At the moment she heard only the wind howling, along with the faint noises of bugs and small animals—nothing alarming.

As she walked silently behind the chief, her thoughts deepened. She knew Jiya likely remained in Fodmery, but she wondered about Roxana. Over the last few years she had heard very little about the acolytes.

That was no surprise; they preferred to remain in the shadows. Still, she found it strange that no one else had emerged with an affliction like hers. Yet the number of vampyrs had grown significantly in recent years.

How did they make more of them? She had always wondered. For Odessa, she had to drink V's blood. In turn, V had drunk hers, which seemed to forge a strange bond between them.

V glanced up at the sky, wondering if she could truly accomplish her goal. She needed to make progress before the Hiorians and rebel army were crushed by Jiya's forces. If they engaged the enemy now, they would surely lose. After her talk with Odessa, she had accepted the path she must take.

A part of her didn't want to kill Jiya right away. She considered capturing him—making him suffer. Torturing him endlessly until he begged for death. She shook her head violently, forcing herself out of the dark corner of her mind.

The vengeful flame inside her had reignited, fiercer than she expected. She needed that fire, because she could not afford to waver anymore. No matter what happened, she would find her way to Jiya—and she would end him.

*

V and her group traveled on until they came upon a tower in ruin. Had it still been whole, it would have risen tall enough to touch the sky—or so V believed as she stood marveling at it. The gray stone tower's top half looked as though it had caved in on itself.

The massive wall that once surrounded it—built of some unfamiliar material—had long decayed and collapsed. Across the land, ruins such as these could be found, remnants of old wars. V had been fortunate to be born in a time when no great war raged.

But during her teen years, conflict between her homeland and Wescreas had begun. Once she was turned into this unfamiliar thing, she stopped keeping track of battles between Vostaylia and Wescreas altogether.

She no longer knew whether war had erupted again between them. Still, since Jiya had seized Wescreas, it was likely the Vostaylians had kept their distance. With the undead at his command, Jiya was a threat none could ignore.

V intended to eliminate him so he could no longer endanger anyone. In truth, she didn't care what became of Wescreas after she killed him. The country would need years to recover from the devastation she planned to bring.

As her thoughts churned, she followed Odessa across the fortress grounds toward the tower. V craned her neck, trying to glimpse the top, but being so close made it harder to see its height as she had earlier.

After a few minutes, Odessa emerged from the tower. She quickly found a shaded place inside where they could rest until nightfall. From where V stood, she could just make out in the distance what she assumed was Judith's keep.

She had no desire to rush forward until she had a proper plan. What would be the best way to approach a princess likely burdened by the weight of her throne?

Thoughts ran rampant in V's mind once again. Would Jiya prove a powerful foe? Did she have the strength to defeat him? Surely he had the tools to kill her if she shared weaknesses with vampyrs. Sunlight, silver, and beheading could all bring them down.

But when it came to the sun, she only suffered painful burns. For vampyrs, exposure meant bursting into flame. Did that mean she could never truly die from sunlight? She didn't know —she had only dared stand in it a few times, each time excruciating, her skin blistering before healing.

"You are brooding again," a voice said.

V turned to see Odessa watching her, leaning against a moss-covered wall, her cloak draped over her shoulders. Weeds sprouted from the cracks in the stone. A faint smile touched V's lips as she thought about how much her life had changed.

Once, she had lived in a great castle. Now she lurked among ruins and caves, unable to watch the sunrise, unable to enjoy the delicacies of her homeland. All of it stolen by those who sought power—or fought for some trivial cause they believed in.

"Tonight will be the beginning of my crusade for vengeance," V muttered.

She glanced at Odessa and found determination in her face. V cared deeply for this young woman. A part of her regretted turning such a beautiful soul, yet Odessa was also the reason her conviction for revenge had reignited. She had become the closest thing V had to a daughter.

Her gaze shifted to Yama, sitting alone. V wanted better for her too. These young women were the purest she had met in years, and now their lives had been tainted by her and her family.

"Yama, dear," V called.

The girl looked up, surprised and confused, as V gestured for her to come closer. Though she and Odessa had to stay in the shadows, she didn't want Yama to sit by herself.

Yama came and sat a few inches away, her expression downcast. V knew it was guilt—guilt over whatever had happened with Yonten. She didn't want Yama to keep holding that weight alone.

V worried for her. She wanted Yama to live, to build a family, to have a story greater than tragedy.

"I wish to confess something," V finally said.

For a moment, she considered speaking of the changed one. But she doubted the chief or anyone had told Yama she might be related to that cursed figure. Perhaps the punishment of her family came not only because of the chief's grief for his daughter, but also because of that connection. Still, V thought better of it.

Yama's brow furrowed. "What do ye mean?"

"Whether it be by fate's hand or mere chance... I am glad that we met."

The words left Yama taken aback. She stared at V, confused. V decided her suspicions about the chief's dark secrets would remain unspoken. Yama had suffered enough—she didn't need another reason to feel cursed.

"You delivered me from an ill fate... my life is yours," Yama whispered, her eyes filling with tears.

V bit her lip, wishing she could say something more to comfort her, to keep her from growing distant from her people.

"Then you must know," V said gently, "that whatever happened upon the trail is not thy burden to bear."

She looked at Yama with deep concern, seeing the pain behind her soft eyes. If she had the power, she would erase every hurt Yama had endured. She would do the same for Odessa.

"I pushed him into a pit of silvermanes." Yama's voice cracked, her lips trembling, her eyes wet with tears. She was on the verge of breaking down again.

"By mischance," V murmured.

"No! I was maddened by his pathetic attempt at forgiveness!" she cried. "Had my emotions been steadier, he would still be here."

V wrapped an arm around Yama and pulled her close. She had no words for that. All she could do was wish she had been there. It wasn't as if Yama had done it on purpose.

"I tried to redress my fool-hearted mess by giving him aid. Alas, he pushed me out of the way to face the beast alone." Yama sniffled.

"Mayhaps I judged him too harshly. Never had I foreseen

him doing such a thing."

Yama fell silent, resting her head against V's chest. As V held her, she breathed in the scent of Yama's hair. It reminded her of mountain air—pleasant and calming. Fitting, she thought, as she tightened her embrace.

"I fear he exposed his heart to me, but I cannot take heed of his words."

V was startled by this remark. Yonten had done something she had never expected—he sacrificed himself, just as Jorah once had for her. The thought struck a nerve deep within her cold persona.

It had only been a few weeks, but their time together had meant much to V. These young women had eased her loneliness. Yet she knew that after this journey, she would be alone again. Returning to Vostaylia was a quest she had to face without them—nor did she wish for them to share in it.

The waiting for nightfall gnawed at her mind. After her meeting with Judith, she would set out on a path of destruction. Nothing would be off limits anymore. The plunge into darkness could no longer be delayed. Her determination burned like a blazing flame, making her nostrils flare as she imagined the bloodshed to come.

"Tonight you must stay at this tower. Do not leave here, do you understand?" V glanced at Yama.

She was uncertain how Judith would respond, and feared she might need to force an audience. She didn't want Yama anywhere near that danger. Whatever happened tonight, Yama must be kept safe.

"I will help as best I can. Please allow me to stand by thee."

"No. I only wish to speak with the princess, but I cannot be certain she will welcome me."

"V—"

"Please respect my wishes."

Yama sat in silence, her expression full of defeat. V knew how hard this was for her—Yama felt indebted. But for V, there was no debt to repay. If anything, Yama's only duty was to live on. That was all that mattered.

"I kept a promise that I wish to keep."

V turned to her. A promise? To whom? "What do you mean?"

"Odessa's kin, Jawara, asked me to look after her. And I intend to honor that."

"Jawara asked that of you?"

V turned to see Odessa staring at them in confusion. She had been resting, but clearly had been listening.

"He did…"

Odessa's face showed disbelief. The evidence of not being sure of how to respond appeared plastered on her face. V didn't know how to respond to this matter either. In spite of that, hearing that her cousin wanted her to be safe seemed to give Odessa a sense of joy. As for V it gave her a sense of hope that Odessa still had a connection with some of her family. Even if Gamba and Odessa's mother shunned her, at least someone in her family still cared.

"I wish I had gotten to talk wit him but instead I avoided him"

A look of regret began to form on Odessa's face. V knew Odessa would never want to live as a creature of the night forever. She had chosen this path only for revenge. Once that was won, she would long for death.

"Maybe when we reach Fodmery, our paths will cross before the end," V murmured.

"Maybe."

Odessa leaned back against the wall and closed her eyes, withdrawing into her own thoughts. She needed rest, for the battle ahead would be long.

"Are you good with a bow?"

V returned her attention to Yama, who looked briefly confused, then nodded. Her face grew thoughtful.

"If I must be, then yes," Yama answered.

"If you see us in dire straits when I speak with the princess… then shoot."

Yama stared, her mouth slightly open, searching for words.

In the end, she only nodded. V gave a faint smile, leaned against the wall, and closed her eyes. She would need the rest.

CHAPTER 16

Yama's venture from home pt. 3

Yama watched as Odessa leaned back and closed her eyes. Then V asked an unexpected question.

"Are you good with a bow?"

Yama was still surprised at how easily V could shift her manner of speaking to match those around her, no matter their culture. It amazed Yama. V had a way of pulling people together, as if she were the thread binding them to one another.

V turned her attention back to her. Yama blinked at the sudden question, confused, before nodding. She fell into thought for a moment.

"If I must, then yes," she answered.

"If ye see that we are in a dire situation when speaking to the princess... then shoot."

Yama stared, mouth slightly open, searching for words. In the end, she only nodded. A faint smile spread across V's face as she leaned back against the wall and closed her eyes to rest.

While they rested, Yama sat in silence, thinking about everything that had happened. She had never expected to meet these two strange individuals—but if she hadn't, Woeton and Yonten would have captured or killed her.

Her feelings were a mess. Anger had been festering in her heart for so long, but now other emotions had surfaced—emotions she didn't understand. When she thought about Odessa's cousin, a strange flutter rose in her chest, quickening her heartbeat.

And then there was Yonten. His words haunted her. Why did he have to speak such nonsense? V thought it had been a confession of love, but Yama had never seen him that way. So why did his death leave her so conflicted?

The guilt weighed heavily. If she hadn't let her emotions spiral, she wouldn't have pushed him. She could have ignored him as she always had. A few times, on their way back to the village, he had tried to talk to her. She had only turned him away.

Slowly, Yama rose to her feet, needing air. A part of her wanted to talk to Dharma, but she knew it wasn't wise. The last time she tried, Dharma had given her nothing but a cold stare.

She wandered through the ruins of the tower she saw Dharma resting in a run down room. The door was slightly ajar which had been what prompted Yama to peak inside. She bit her lip as she gripped her hand on the rugged door.

Before she decided what she should do, she felt a large hand rest upon her shoulder. Her head whipped to the left to see Woeton towering over her. He had a grave look on his face as he shook his head. Yama lowered her head as she began to pout.

What could she do to rectify her mistake? Her foolish actions cost the life of Dharma's beloved little brother. She knew there was likely nothing that could fix that. All she wanted was for Dhamra to forgive her. Despite how she felt about the situation of being a sacrifice she still admired Dharma.

As she reflected on the past briefly, Woeton urged her to follow him outside. A bit of reluctance overcame her as she watched as his figure headed down the hall.

The sky greeted her with its heavy gray-blue canvas. Snow fell more thickly than in the mountains, and for the first time in a while, there was no fog to obscure her view. The air smelled of coming rain.

"Tis a troublesome time for us all. Ye must let her mourn for now," Woeton said, his voice gruff.

"I wish to redress the damage I caused her."

"There is nothing to fix, young one. We all carry burdens."

His words told her everything—he carried his own guilt. For all his strength, he had failed her family too. He hadn't stood up for her father when it mattered, though he had always claimed to look up to him. He had become chief of the guardians after his death, but that only deepened Yama's pain.

She wanted to be angry with him. She also felt sorrow. And now, regret for what had happened to Yonten burned in her chest.

"I could have protected him," she whispered.

Dharma now clung to Yonten's spear, their grandfather's heirloom. It was all she had left of her family. Yama clenched her fists until her nails dug into her skin. She didn't know what to feel anymore. Part of her thought no one should blame her, after all she had lost. Another part believed Dharma never deserved to lose her brother, no matter how irritating he had been.

"Silvermanes be dangerous creatures, and ye be but a frail pup," Woeton said with a weak grin.

Was he joking? At a time like this? Yama frowned at him. A second later, his eyes widened in embarrassment.

"'Tis but a jest! I meant not to sully the mood."

A short laugh slipped from Yama's lips despite herself. She looked away, scanning the clearing. Not far off, the chief sat alone with his staff, staring at the sky.

She had noticed him doing that often of late. Seeking guidance from Sifadi, perhaps. Unlike V, Yama could not see spirits, but she could feel them. For now, the chief seemed free of corruption—but she still felt something off about him. Something she could not forgive.

He had haunted her childhood. She had lived in fear of him taking another from her family. When her sister died three years ago, her dreams had been filled with dread that he would come for her. That had been quite a few times she had ran or hid but they always found her. Not only that but there were times when they even imprisoned her.

When the day for her to be sacrificed finally came she knew she had to run and was going to give up. The fact she made it to where V had been seemed to be a gift from Sifadi. Her salvation that saved her life.

"I will not fey ignorance to thy fondness to the one known as V." Woeton began. Yama raised an eyebrow as she stared at him with curiosity. "I do not deem it wise for ye to grow affixed to her."

Yama stayed quiet, weighing his words. The time she had spent with V and Odessa had shown her the darkness they carried. She knew they thought of themselves as monsters. But she had seen a true monster—and it was not them.

Why should she heed him?

"The path she takes leads only to death," Woeton said at last. "Be wise not to follow her shadow, lest ye meet the same fate."

"I shall heed thy words," Yama replied, "but hear me well—the village is no longer my home."

Woeton's mouth fell open, and he coughed awkwardly into his hand. Yama held her ground. Her decision was final.

She could not return to that place, not with its memories and its ghosts. Not with the weight of Yonten's death pressing down on her.

"Do reconsider…"

Yama glanced at him, seeing not the stern guardian but an older brother worried for her.

"Dusk shall mark the end of our paths together," she said quietly.

She turned and walked back into the tower. Woeton's hand brushed her shoulder as she passed, but she didn't slow. There was nothing more to say.

CHAPTER 17

The night came as a silent whisper, and V sprang from her slumber. The sound of crickets stirred her awake. Once again, snow had begun to fall upon the land.

She readied herself and picked up her sword. The blade she had found in Skyreach Tower was hers now. She would have preferred a weapon forged specifically for this crusade, but it no longer mattered.

V marched down the long corridor. The doors of the tower stood open, and the gray-skins were gathered there, staring outside. Dharma was the first to notice her approach.

She said nothing, only leaned against the wall in silence, her eyes dark with anger. V didn't see Yama or Odessa anywhere. She had no idea where they were. Without a way to communicate, if they had gone off on their own, how could they possibly work together?

"Where is she?"

Dharma pointed outside. "I forbade her to go, but ye hath procured her fealty."

V raised a brow at Dharma, studied her for a moment, then nodded. "You would be wise to forgive her."

When V glanced back, Dharma's expression was blank. V shook her head in disappointment and continued toward the door—only to find Woeton blocking the way.

"Allow me to accompany ye," he said.

"Woeton!" Dharma exclaimed.

The request caught V off guard. They had hardly spoken, and now he wanted to follow her? Absurd. Perhaps he thought protecting Yama was his duty.

"You are a man... they often do as they please. Just know I

am not responsible for ye."

With that, V shoved him aside and marched into the snowy terrain. Her hair was quickly dusted white by the steady downpour. She scanned the darkness, listening for Yama's heartbeat.

It wasn't far. She quickened her pace. She didn't want them to act before she was ready. A plan had to be made—Yama couldn't yet handle flaming arrows.

The fog was thick, unsurprising in the shadow of the mountains. It only made the keep's location seem more peculiar. Still, it worked to her advantage. Judith had likely chosen this stronghold for its distance from the capital.

V spotted Yama and Odessa lying low on a hill, overlooking the keep. From there, they had a clear view of its walls. V thought getting closer would be better. She needed to know how many men were posted.

She crouched and crept up beside them. Yama held something pressed to her eye. At first, it looked like a wooden rod, but V quickly recognized the designs—an ornate spyglass. A tool of the Hiorians, used at sea.

"Where did ye get that?" V whispered.

Yama startled, nearly dropping it, but Odessa caught it in time. V almost laughed but covered her mouth to stifle the sound.

"I had not noticed ye. Forgive me." Yama quickly composed herself. "Jawara gave it to me." A flush colored her cheeks.

V smiled faintly. So Yama had taken a liking to Odessa's cousin. If that was true, then V all the more wanted Yama to survive. If love was possible for her, it deserved a chance to blossom.

From what Yama had said earlier, Yonten had confessed feelings for her. V was relieved she hadn't returned them. His death was unfortunate, but she still disliked him.

"What do ye see?"

"Men on horseback approach."

V's eyes widened, and her hand tightened on her sword. The time had come. She nodded, already planning to move closer.

Her hearing caught only muffled voices at this distance. Thirty more feet, and she could make out every word.

"Let us move a little closer, Odessa," V ordered. "Yama, hang back."

Without checking for Yama's response, she moved forward. Woeton appeared at her side, spear in hand, trudging silently through the snow. It annoyed her—she hadn't asked for his help. Whatever drove him was his own enigma, and she forced herself to ignore him.

Closer now, she caught the first clear shout.

"Open the gate, princess! King Jiya demands ye show your fealty to him!"

The words sent a chill through her.

She looked to her side and realized Odessa was gone. Her shadowy figure was already advancing. V clicked her tongue in frustration and dashed after her.

Why had Odessa broken off? Then V heard another voice— one she recognized instantly. The very voice from that night. Rage exploded inside her. Now she understood why Odessa had run ahead.

This night, perhaps, they could end the Hiorians' troubles once and for all. Jiya Ashspell was here. At last, V would face him. After all these years, the chance had come. This night would change everything.

She crept closer to the chevaliers massed at the gate. Among them she saw revenants—easy to spot, with their glowing green eyes and dust-like aura. They had no scent, no life about them.

The chevaliers were too focused on the gate to notice her. Like a shadow, she fell upon the first group, tearing through them. The air filled red.

The battle at Judith's Keep had begun.

*

The cries of battle rang loudly throughout the area. Crimson red flooded the ground, bodies scattered everywhere as the sound of metal against metal echoed through the mountains.

Arrows were being fired from the wall down upon the chevaliers battling the two assailants. Cries of death filled the air. A mist blanketed the field, obscuring vision slightly.

V and Odessa fought against the chevaliers that rushed them with great effort. Some even attacked from horseback. She cut down the horses as well as the men without mercy.

As she tore through them with her sword, blood splattered across her face, some even reaching her lips. She tasted it, and a rush of power flowed through her. Frenzy began to take hold as she let loose.

The revenants all wore dark armor compared to the Wescreans. Without hesitation V rushed them, letting out a battle cry. They swung their weapons, but she evaded, moving around them as if she were dancing. A wave of ghostly flames trailed from her hand, engulfing them.

Their souls cried out as their undead bodies withered. V pressed forward, eyes locked on the man she wanted most. Sitting atop a black horse was the man she had set out to kill.

His eyes fixed on hers, wide with disbelief. Two chevaliers in dark armor stepped in front of him, standing their ground. V didn't care about them, though she could sense the great spiritual power they carried.

As she advanced, more chevaliers rushed at her. Their armor was dark like those protecting Jiya, but she could smell them. Their scent was Hiorian. She felt their spiritual power radiating—stronger than most, and a problem for her.

Her hands trembled on the hilt of her sword. Why now? Was it because they were Hiorian? In their faces she thought she saw Jorah and his sister.

"You shall not reach the king, accursed spirit!" one of them shouted.

He rushed forward, sword ready to strike. V froze—she could not bring herself to kill him. But then, to her horror, a blur appeared. A glint of silver flashed into his neck.

The ground was painted red as he gasped and fell to his

knees. Dropping his sword, he clutched his throat before being kicked down by his attacker. V looked and saw Odessa standing over him, a fierce look in her eyes.

This woman was changed—her wrath fully unleashed. Nothing would stop her now.

"Odessa?"

"They betrayed their kin. They are not my people. That makes them my enemies—show no mercy."

Her words dripped with venom. The other three Hiorians hesitated; one even lowered her weapon.

"Is that you, Odessa? What have you done to yourself?" the female Hiorian asked.

Odessa didn't answer. She moved, vanishing from sight to anyone without supernatural senses. A heartbeat later she was behind the woman. With a cleaving strike she tore through her armor.

The woman's arm hit the ground, blood spilling from her shoulder as she screamed. Odessa kicked her down and turned to the others.

V meant to watch, but chevaliers rushed her. She fought without hesitation, blocking and parrying as arrows rained down. The shafts pierced gaps in the chevaliers' armor.

A surge of energy erupted from the two Hiorians fighting Odessa, the clash sending waves of wind across the field. The pressure was immense. V cut her way forward, her eyes fixed on Jiya.

He was the only Hiorian she would never hesitate to kill. She marched on, blood soaking her skin and clothes. Raising her hand, she touched her lips to the blood there—its tainted taste told her what she already knew. Corrupt. Worthless. Still, it gave her energy, a whirlwind of power spiraling around her and making the chevaliers hesitate.

Arrows still rained from above, yet strangely they seemed to brush past her, as if she were shielded. The keep's defenders remained behind the gate, only the archers offering resistance.

V glanced at the gate—Jiya's men battered at it with a ram,

shields raised to protect their own. The rest fought her and Odessa. Only the revenants and Hiorians posed a true threat.

Three revenants stepped before her, glowing eyes empty. The tallest rushed her, sword swinging. Their blades clashed with such force the ground cracked, chevaliers thrown back. V roared and shoved him off balance, only for him to block again. Another revenant rushed from the side—

A spear tore through its neck. No blood spilled, but the revenant stumbled. Woeton appeared, heaving it from the ground and slamming it down.

"This is a sea of balefulness! Ye be a fool to fight alone!" he shouted.

V engulfed her foe in ghostly flame, his screams ending as his eyes went white. She glared at Woeton.

"I have nothing to lose. You are the fool to risk thy life for one you do not know."

Still, she pressed forward, cleaving through chevaliers. Jiya remained atop his horse, watching. Her pace quickened, her feet lifting from the ground.

Odessa appeared beside her, cleaving through men like a storm. Together they were unstoppable.

One of Jiya's chevaliers stepped forward, daggers glowing with green energy. His spiritual power was immense— stronger even than Leon's.

"Zahur!" Odessa shouted.

Her aura rippled as she and Zahur struck, their blows cutting the air itself. Chevaliers collapsed, bodies painting the stony terrain like a blank canvas.

They stood there both unwavering and merely grunting as one tried to overpower the other. Odessa no longer was a normal Hiorian so she used pure strength to push him back. The only reason he managed to hold his ground was because he expelled a great deal of spiritual force to combat her.

A smile started to be etched on V's face as she realized this would be their chance to end this for sure. Then she noticed the other chevalier take a step forward with her battle axes.

She felt a strange power emanating from the weapons this warrior wielded.

The power she felt made her slightly cautious. She also took note of the person's scent which smelled neither human or Hiorian. V rushed over to protect Odessa from an attack.

Fortunately, V got there in time and blocked the attack of the large chevalier's axe. The chevalier had steel blue eyes. Not only that but V could see part of their face. They had stony gray skin.

Then V noticed the chevalier's snowy colored hair hanging out of the helmet. By the chevalier's grunts of frustration, V could tell this person to be female. They were without a doubt a female grey skin.

Disbelief struck V as Zahur's voice carried across the field.

"What did you do to yourself, little mouse?" he asked Odessa.

"Stop calling me dat!" she roared.

Odessa shoved him back, causing him to fall to the ground. A few arrows landed right where he had fallen. He looked surprised—so did V. She glanced over her shoulder, scanning the area. It didn't take long to see who had fired.

Yama knelt a short distance away from the battle. It seemed she had intentionally aimed at the ground, perhaps as a signal that she was nearby to support. Then V turned her attention back to the grey skin.

"I had wondered what happened to you, Princess Vlatka." Jiya's voice caught her attention.

She pushed the gray-skin chevalier away and leveled her sword at him. "Your day of reckoning hath come!"

Jiya scoffed, a smile curling on his lips. "I see dat you have gained mysterious powers. Roxana claimed you had not returned, yet here you are. And still, you are not the vampyr I expected."

"Tonight I will slay you!" V cried.

She lunged forward, but before she could reach Jiya, the gray-skin chevalier stepped in front of him again, her axes raised.

"If you wish to reach me, you must first cut down my royal guard," Jiya chided.

"Why did you take her away from her people?"

Confusion flickered across Jiya's face. "I took her from the acolytes. Her people are unknown to me, but she is special nonetheless."

"What is thy name, young one?" V asked.

The female chevalier stayed silent. V looked at Jiya, puzzled. Perhaps her accent confused the girl. The gray-skin whispered something in the Hiorian tongue, and Jiya replied in kind.

"I am Raisa Ashspell!" she exclaimed.

"Stand aside, child," V urged.

"No."

V could sense she was young—barely a teenager. It made her think of her own children, who would have been around that age if they had lived.

Rage flared in her chest. Jiya had turned a child into a warrior. She couldn't bring herself to raise her blade against her, but vengeance did not care about age.

"This man has slaughtered his own people! He killed the love of my life!" V snapped.

Her nostrils flared as she fought to contain her rage. Raisa was only a pawn, manipulated her whole life. V was certain she was the chief's daughter. Fate, it seemed, had woven their lives together.

Jorah had once believed in fate, in powers that guided its flow. V had always rejected the idea—until now.

"He fights for da greater good of his people, and I will not let you hinder dat!" Raisa shouted.

"What greater good? He slays his own because they will not enslave humans! Tell me, does he enslave his people as well?"

V stepped forward, and Raisa faltered. Her heartbeat thundered in V's ears—fear and doubt, impossible to hide. Jiya had not trained her well enough.

"Wescreas can be a place where my people have a home," Jiya

said coldly. "Those who stand in the way are my enemies. The former princess is my enemy, for she will not bend da knee."

At last, V understood. They sought to erase the last trace of the former king's bloodline. Jiya had learned well from humans—usurpers must destroy all who oppose their crown.

"Why curse this child to bloody her hands?" V's eyes locked on Raisa.

"I trust her wit my life above anyone here," Jiya replied.

"You swore your people would not be like humans, yet you've become exactly like them!"

Jiya said nothing, but his eyes betrayed him. She saw a man who had lost his way. He would not waver now.

"Face your fate and fight me! Do not hide behind her like a coward!"

V glanced left—Odessa was still locked in combat with Zahur. His helmet was gone, a scar bleeding at his temple, his hair matted by rain.

Raisa kept stealing glances at him, concern etched on her face. She seemed torn, caught between loyalties.

"I do not need your fondness for Zahur distractin you, child. go aid him," Jiya commanded.

"But I—"

"Go!"

V didn't stop her. She only gestured for Raisa to move. Odessa fought like a woman possessed, her bloody rage unyielding. V couldn't prevent what would come between Raisa and Odessa.

Her focus was Jiya. If she ended him quickly, perhaps she could stop the others from tearing each other apart.

Jiya drew his sword, unlike any V had seen before. Narrow at the base, widening toward the tip, with a strange curve at the end. Its surface gleamed black, etched with carvings that ran red like veins. A sinister aura radiated from it, ominous and heavy.

"You are as beautiful as da day you were lost," Jiya mused. "I have never complimented a human besides you—so be grateful, for it will be da last."

He darted forward with such speed that V had to step back. She barely blocked the strike. As their blades locked, she heard whispers from his sword. Her undead body shuddered, and she pulled away.

Jiya only smiled, pressing his attack with relentless aggression. V backpedaled, parrying desperately. He had the upper hand—years of skill and training she did not. Strength alone could not make up for that.

But she was not alone. Arrows flew past her, forcing him to break his pursuit. V seized the moment, striking back with ferocity. Her blows rattled him, driving his heels into the earth under her strength.

A sense of excitement slightly overtook V. She began rushing at him with incredible speed, even levitating in the air as she attacked him. He countered everything, but the look on his face showed worry. As V continued to pounce around, slashing at her enemy, she noticed the blood on the ground moving.

She didn't pay it any attention at first, but when Jiya's sword started to glow, she knew something was wrong. He gained distance and stuck the sword into the ground. The blade appeared to drink the blood of the dead chevaliers scattered around them.

A surge of power erupted, and V could hear the howls of something ominous from the sword. Jiya began to smile as the ground shook and split apart. He moved toward her, and the spiritual force she felt from him seemed suffocating.

It made her hesitate to attack, for she had no idea what this sword could actually do. The weapon seemed to have a spirit living within it, something V had never heard of before. Asking Odessa about it once they got out of this situation felt important.

"I have held my position of power because da *Tome of Eneida* has helped me craft da tools to change da world!"

Jiya swung his sword, and a dark miasma washed over the area. V leapt into the air and looked down to see some chevaliers cut down by the attack—even those twenty feet away. Then he swung the sword downward. It cut through the air with a whooshing sound.

V evaded again and saw a long gash carved into the ground. The power fascinated her but also frightened her. Despite that, she needed to press forward. Victory awaited once she defeated him. She would taste revenge and find some solace in her soul.

Her sword stayed close as she lunged forward. She swung slow and steady, each stroke like a brush on canvas. Jiya blocked every strike with ease, but she managed to draw closer.

"Why do you not use those blue flames against me?" Jiya taunted.

"I want to cut off your head, not burn your soul," V retorted.

Jiya laughed, swinging his sword at an angle. V blocked, but he suddenly shoved her with his shoulder, knocking her backward. She hit the ground, rolling quickly out of the way.

Back on her feet, she rushed him again. His sword whispered as it cut through the air. Their blades met once more—but this time, something different happened. His blood-soaked sword sliced through hers effortlessly.

V's eyes widened in horror as the top half of her blade clattered to the ground. A wicked grin spread across Jiya's face. Now defeat loomed while victory seemed certain. He leveled his sword at her as she stood frozen in disbelief.

"Is dis da depths of your conviction to slay me? Even though your eyes and soul have changed into something anew, you still are human," he said with disappointment.

With a swift motion, Jiya raised his blade. V lowered her broken weapon, ready to accept a shameful death. She only hoped Odessa could forgive her lack of conviction. But before he could strike, she heard something whistle past her.

Jiya cried out in pain as an arrow pierced his shoulder. V turned to see his wound, then felt a hand grab her and pull her aside. A towering figure charged at Jiya—Woeton, bloodied and cut, had come to her aid.

"Begone from here!" he roared.

Woeton pressed forward, spear thrusting in precise strikes, quick and sharp. Jiya parried, countering blow for blow. V noticed black spreading from some of Woeton's wounds—signs of revenant corruption. Without aid, he would die from the spiritual poisoning.

V forced away her shame and charged with her broken sword. She had to fight close now, dangerously close. Jiya needed only one clean strike to kill her.

She attacked wildly, her blade slashing with reckless force. Concern flickered across Jiya's face as he struggled to fend them both off. Forced back, he stumbled. Woeton lunged, spear aimed for a fatal blow—

But suddenly he cried out, knocked forward by a strike from behind. He collapsed, a battle axe buried in his back.

V turned, expecting the gray-skin chevalier—but instead saw Zahur, his face twisted in shock.

Time seemed to slow. Odessa lay on the ground. The gray-skin chevalier too.

Rage.

An explosion of spiritual power burst from V as she screamed. She rushed forward before Zahur could react. His eyes went wide, a gasp tearing from him.

A heartbeat thundered in V's ears. Blood sprayed from his mouth. He looked down to see her hand buried in his chest. V's lips trembled, her fangs bared. With her free hand she ripped away the metal covering his neck.

The monster she had feared within herself was unleashed at last. Blood poured into her mouth like water from a well. Power surged, and the world faded to darkness.

CHAPTER 18

Yama's venture from home pt. 4

The downpour of snow continued on as the battle raged. The clashing of metal sounded like a low rumble of thunder. Shouts and grunts filled the air. A sea of red painted the white sheet that blanketed the land as Yama watched in horror from a distance.

"So this be war..." she muttered to herself.

Yama fired her arrows from the safety of the large rocks not too far from the keep. The warriors were swarming around Odessa and V. She moved in closer so she could keep sight of both of them.

There were so many warriors that she felt as if she was shooting into a river, hoping to catch a fish. Her feet marched through the snow as she moved around. She maintained her distance but needed to ensure she had good shots to provide support.

At the moment, from what she could see, V and Odessa had no need of her aid. They were single-handedly wiping out a whole army. She couldn't believe her eyes. As she watched, her body trembled uncontrollably. Was it fear or excitement that she felt? She had no way of knowing for sure.

While standing with her bow, she felt footsteps moving about in the snowy terrain. She turned to see Woeton approaching. His face bore determination, and in his hand he gripped his spear tightly.

"Ye will not take heed to my counsel, so I shall no longer stand in thy way," Woeton said as he stood beside Yama.

"Why do ye carry thy spear?"

"If she be the one ye choose to follow, then I feel only to pay my debt to her."

His words were final as he began to march forward onto the battlefield. Yama wanted to stop him but didn't know what to say. She merely stood in silence as his large frame grew smaller and smaller, plunging into the sea of warriors.

Woeton sprang right into action, charging through enemies, striking them down with his spear. His blows were fast and steady. Yama saw no hesitation in his movements. For a large man, he had great agility. It was clear to her why he had become the lead guardian of their village.

She watched as he managed to reach where V was. Yama used her spyglass to get a better look. From what she could see, they had a brief exchange of words. It lasted only a second before they returned to fighting.

Yama continued to use her spyglass to spot Odessa. She saw her rush past V, moving like a blur. It was almost difficult to make out Odessa's movements. Within a second she saw Odessa strike a warrior who also carried daggers.

They exchanged blows that seemed to cause debris to rise into the air. Whatever they were doing appeared supernatural to her. How could they alter the land with such little effort? She couldn't help but wonder as she returned her attention to V.

Yama quickly spotted her standing in front of a warrior that towered over her. Behind him was a man resting atop a horse. He had thick, long hair and pointed ears. Yama quickly realized he was a Hiorian. A scar ran across his face.

She assumed this was the man V wanted to slay. Yama felt something unsettling as she gazed at him through the spyglass. She quickly looked away and returned her focus to V, who appeared fixated on the warrior before her.

She couldn't clearly see the warrior's face, but she did see long white hair streaked with black. Yama froze. This couldn't be possible, could it? She wondered for a moment before brushing off the far-fetched thought.

As she watched, the man on his mount gestured to the warrior. The warrior stepped aside, and he climbed down from his mount. Wasting no time, he drew his sword as a smile formed on his face. Yama couldn't tell what was happening.

There was a brief exchange before V made the first move. A blur of motion, then swords clashed. She still couldn't understand what she was seeing as the two fought. Her spyglass revealed the strange weapon the Hiorian wielded.

A sword coated in black, with what looked like red veins running through the blade. He swung the weapon with great force, each strike shaking the ground. A strange miasma flowed from it.

It moved unnaturally, and the people around him collapsed, blood erupting from wounds Yama hadn't seen inflicted. The sight jarred her, and she lowered the spyglass, readying her bow. She needed to support V.

Yama had no choice but to move in closer as she readied her bow. She set an arrow and pushed forward to get a clearer shot at the Hiorian. It felt wrong to aim at Odessa's people, but this one was different.

As she got closer, she saw the Hiorian gaining the upper hand. Quickly, she drew the string back and aimed. Her breath steadied, her muscles tight.

Through the spyglass she saw V clash with the Hiorian again —her sword broke in half, and she faltered. Yama knew she couldn't miss this shot or V would die. The Hiorian closed in, his blade ready to strike.

Yama released her breath—and the string.

The arrow whizzed through the air into the sea of warriors. Just as the Hiorian raised his sword, it struck his shoulder, halting his advance. Yama froze, motionless, and caught V glancing back at her.

Then Woeton appeared, plunging into the fray. He stepped forward, spear in hand, striking at the Hiorian without hesitation. Yama raised her spyglass again for a better look.

Excitement overtook her as she watched Woeton fight. Had he been in a war before? She wondered, watching the way he struck and evaded with precision. Through the spyglass, she saw his body badly wounded, yet somehow he pushed on, ignoring his scars.

Everything seemed to be turning in their favor as Woeton lunged for a final blow—until something cut through the air and struck him in the back. Yama dropped her bow and covered her mouth in horror. She moved the spyglass and saw a Hiorian warrior standing with his hand extended.

She quickly looked back—something protruded from Woeton's back. Her heart raced as she watched him collapse to his knees. A bloodcurdling scream tore through the air. V was standing over him in fury—then vanished.

Yama searched desperately, only to see her suddenly before the Hiorian who had struck Woeton. What happened next sent chills crawling across her body. V ripped at the man's armor, then sank her fangs into his neck.

The sound of a horn echoed in the distance. Shouts rang out as the tide of battle shifted. Yama watched the scarred Hiorian give orders and rush toward V. He picked someone up from the ground—stone-colored skin, a mane of long hair. Yama's lips trembled. Her earlier fear was true.

The Hiorian rushed off with her as warriors withdrew from the battlefield.

What wickedness had she just witnessed? She lowered the spyglass and wiped her eyes. Rain soaked her clothes and hair, weighing her down. She had to leave. Yet as much as she wanted to run, she couldn't abandon her friends.

V's screams tore through the air as she descended into madness. Blue fire blazed, engulfing warriors who collapsed in agony. More red stained the snow as the land itself seemed to writhe in disgust.

Her connection to the earth made her feel every cry. Still, Yama moved forward without thinking. As V rampaged, Yama sought Woeton and Odessa. She felt responsible for Woeton stepping onto the battlefield.

Had he come to prove a point—or to make up for the past?

She didn't know, but she needed answers. If he lived, she needed to hear them.

Closer to the field, the sight of scattered bodies made her sick. How could anyone fight on while their comrades were slaughtered? This was the way of humans, something she couldn't understand.

Her body stiffened as she forced herself through the carnage V had wrought. Finally, she found Odessa lying motionless. Kneeling beside her, she checked for a pulse. Nothing—panic seized her.

Then Odessa groaned, and Yama stumbled back. Relief and fear flooded her. She scrambled to her feet and looked around. She had to calm V, had to get them out.

Arrows rained from the sky, aimed at V, but none struck her. She rampaged on, unstoppable. The woman who had once fought her inner darkness was gone—consumed entirely.

Yama could not lose more people she loved. Sprinting, she chased after V, ignoring the land's desperate cries to flee. Like always, she ignored the warnings.

CHAPTER 19

The area was illuminated by the bright blue flames that V had created. Instead of burning, they caused things to wither away, destroying the life essence within. Chevaliers were being killed left and right as she went on a frenzy.

Some of the horses ran about in a panic. V tore through them with her bare hands, her fangs bared as she bit into their thick necks. They struggled as she slaughtered them. Her eyes darted left and right, locking onto her next prey.

Jiya had managed to get away and had succeeded in taking Raisa with him. A few of the chevaliers had also fled, and Woeton's body had disappeared. This angered her even more, and she cried out in frustration.

She yelled again as fury erupted from her chest, prompting her to pounce on the chevaliers in front of her. Her fingers tore through their armor like claws. She screamed in wild rage as they continued to attack her. Others pushed their way through the gate to fight men in dark green cloaks—likely chevaliers following the orders of the one known as the princess.

"Slay the monster!" a chevalier cried out.

He rushed toward V with his sword overhead, swinging it downward to cut through her chest. She caught the blade with her bare hand. The sudden stop of his momentum left him staring at her in shock.

Archers fired their arrows at her, and some pierced her flesh. Unfortunately for them, she felt nothing but a slight sting. She knew of very few weaknesses besides the sun. Although, weapons of silver left wounds that lasted longer.

She swung her hand and cut through the chevalier's neck. Her fingertips were drenched in red. As she marched forward, she tasted the blood, and the intoxication took over. While pulling the arrows from her chest, more chevaliers rushed her.

She dashed forward and grabbed one by the throat before he could lift his sword. With brute strength she lifted him off the ground and slammed him onto his back. The force broke the ground apart and sent debris flying.

A sharp jolt of pain made her look down. The tip of a sword had pierced through her belly. Someone had managed to get behind her. She hissed in pain, grabbed the sword's tip with her bare hand, and snapped it off. Then she turned to face her assailant, who stood in disbelief.

V stared at him briefly before striking his chest. His eyes widened as a strange sound filled V's ears. The chevalier flew back, rolling across the ground. She stared at his motionless body for a moment.

His heartbeat faded into silence. Then she turned away and resumed fighting. There were fewer chevaliers than before—most were dead or had fled with Jiya. None of their deaths could sate her rage.

She needed Jiya's head for what had happened to Odessa and Woeton. Her conviction for revenge boiled over. All she saw now was red—and she needed more of it.

"V!"

She kept fighting, tearing through her enemies. Their numbers dwindled quickly. No longer could they take the keep. Nor could they escape her wrath. Since she had let Jiya slip away, his men had to pay for his cowardice.

"V!"

A hand gripped her wrist firmly. She whirled around, ready to kill the one who dared touch her. But when she raised her free hand to strike, she froze. The sky-blue eyes staring at her with fear and worry snapped her out of her rage.

V blinked a few times, realizing Yama had rushed over to stop her. She glanced over her shoulder and saw the chevaliers had backed away. None were trying to attack her anymore.

She then looked down at her hands. They were stained in

deep red. She tried to wipe the blood onto her clothes, but they too were soaked.

"Ye have done enough. Let us get to Odessa and leave," Yama pleaded.

"But, the keep..."

V glanced over her shoulder. The chevaliers attacking the keep were being forced back. On the wall, she spotted a young woman with curly red hair that stopped at her neck. No more than eighteen, yet determination blazed in her eyes.

Judith had successfully fended off the invaders. If V had continued her rampage, an innocent girl and her people might have died. Lowering her head, V gazed across the battlefield.

Odessa still lay motionless on the ground. But with her mind clear, V could see spiritual energy still flowing in her. She rushed to her friend's side and knelt. Odessa had been stabbed in the stomach with Zahur's dagger.

A faint smoke rose from the wound. V grasped the dagger but hesitated. Finally, she pulled it free as Yama lifted Odessa slightly. Odessa's eyes shot open as she cried out in pain.

She spat up a black substance, writhing in agony. V sniffed the dagger and realized it had been coated with something— likely the reason the wound wouldn't heal. She threw it aside and bent over Odessa, cradling her face and pressing their foreheads together. Even though Odessa longed to be free after her revenge, V could not bear to lose her.

Their journey would end one day, but V still had much to learn from her—and she longed to spend more time together. They had promised a fishing trip as a send-off.

After all, Odessa had become like a daughter to her. To lose her here would plunge V back into unbearable loneliness. Her soul ached at the thought. She needed Odessa to survive.

"I could not kill dat young one, forgive me," Odessa sputtered.

"No, 'tis fine. Now let us get you out of here."

V didn't know if it would work, but she had to try. She opened her mouth, her fangs elongating, and bit into her wrist. When she pulled away, black substance bled out. She pressed her wrist to Odessa's lips.

Odessa hesitated, then opened her mouth, revealing her fangs. She bit down and drank. V caught the terrified look on Yama's face as it happened. There was no joy in this, but it had to be done.

"Forgive me. I do not wish to show ye this," V said softly.

Yama shook her head. "Ye never asked to be cursed."

V remained silent as she waited for Odessa to finish drinking. Once she let go, Yama picked her up off the ground. This had been the result of her first encounter with Jiya after years. She would have lost had it not been for Woeton.

Despite giving Woeton the cold shoulder, she couldn't ignore the fact that seeing him struck down hurt her soul—especially when she still didn't understand why he had come to fight alongside her.

Now his body had been taken somewhere for who knows what. V gritted her teeth in frustration. She had to go after him, but for now she needed to rest and get cleaned up. As they walked across the field of the dead, V heard something overhead.

She looked up to see a murder of crows flying above. When had they arrived? V couldn't believe the number of crows spiraling in a circle. There had to be at least a thousand of them.

Madness had overtaken the area as her flames still raged. The bodies of chevaliers lay everywhere as she marched through their remains. All of this, and she had failed to defeat Jiya. Everything had to end soon—especially if the Hiorians were to survive this war.

She felt that her failure here would enrage Jiya, which meant he would likely be twice as violent toward his people when they attacked Fodmery. V had others she wanted revenge on, but right now Jiya felt the most important.

Deep down, she felt something telling her he had to be stopped soon. Ever since she had been put through that ritual, he had been disrupting the natural order. By bringing about these revenants, he had to be creating irreparable consequences. V felt it all came at some cost, but she didn't yet know what price the world was paying for his actions.

She only knew that her failure to defeat him here meant more revenants would likely join the war. Whatever Jiya had set out to do in the beginning seemed to have changed. Maybe he had lost his way, like V once did.

"I failed, and now I fear a reckoning be on its way," V confessed.

Yama glanced over her shoulder, sadness in her eyes. "My dad had watched many wars between humans. I hath never expected it to be this brutal."

"'Tis because more than just humans be a part of this war now."

Wars were never pretty and always brought casualties. Her father had fought in many before she was born. Now she was part of one herself. If her father had still been alive, he might have fought in this war too.

V hated wars because they didn't always change things for the better. Sometimes things became worse. With that in mind, she began to wonder if the Hiorians and people of Wescreas could ever rebuild.

"Do ye know why Woeton chose to follow us?" V asked.

Yama stopped in her tracks and remained silent for a moment.

"Maybe he wanted to atone for his past mistakes."

"How would taking part in a battle that has nothing to do with him atone for the past?"

V couldn't begin to understand what had been going through his mind. All she knew was that he had sacrificed himself for her. He didn't have to—but he did. A sadness she hadn't expected began to stir.

"He gave counsel to not follow ye. To follow your shadow means death. 'Tis what he said, and I told him I shan't return to the village." Yama sniffled.

V moved closer to Yama and saw tears trickling down her cheeks. Her lips trembled as she tried to say something more, but only sighed in frustration. Yama started walking again, still holding tightly onto Odessa.

As she walked away, V stood in place, staring at the sky. The crows were still swirling above. So many things about this strange world she still didn't understand. As she raised her hand toward the sky, she felt a breeze. The blood and battle she had tasted today seemed bittersweet. Still, she had much to do and couldn't afford to give up as she had tonight.

*

The return to the ruined tower had proven to be dreadful. V didn't know how to prepare herself to break the news of Woeton's demise. The chief sat silently outside, appearing to meditate.

Yama walked past him as she carried Odessa inside. V stalked over to the chief and stood by him. He remained silent, his eyes closed for a moment. The sound of bugs was the only thing filling the air.

"I sense two... no, three of ye hath returned."

He finally opened his eyes, revealing steel blue irises. The chief examined V, looking her up and down. His expression didn't change, which struck V as odd. Her clothes were soaked in blood, yet he didn't seem the least bit concerned.

"Who failed to return?"

V stayed silent. When she finally parted her lips to speak, Dharma came marching out of the tower, tears streaming down her face. Her eyes were red, filled with anger and confusion.

"I see now," the chief muttered.

"'Tis why I did not wish for any of ye to come along."

"I must get his body!" Dharma cried.

She started toward Judith's keep, but V moved swiftly to block her path. Dharma looked down at her, then tried to shove her aside. But V wouldn't budge, standing firm like a statue despite her smaller frame.

"Move!" Dharma yelled.

"Dharma, ye must calm down," the chief cautioned.

She glanced at him with frustration, then looked back at V and stepped away. V didn't know Dharma's relationship with Woeton, but clearly, there had been fondness between them.

"I fear his body hath been taken, so it would be pointless to go after it," V finally confessed.

Dharma stared in disbelief. She clenched her fists, looking around as if desperate to strike something. V understood—she felt the same urge.

"Can we go inside? There is much to discuss."

"Why did he follow ye out to battle?" Dharma sniffled.

"I never asked... which may be another thing I come to regret."

V marched toward the tower's entrance, glancing back to ensure Dharma wouldn't run off like a fool to recover Woeton's body. Instead, she saw the chief consoling her, like a father with his daughter.

Turning away from the scene, she headed inside. A few seconds later, she found Odessa resting against the wall with her wolf companion curled beside her. Yama sat across, watching over her like a protector. V knelt next to Odessa.

Slowly, Odessa opened her eyes, shame clouding them. "I failed to get revenge."

"Zahur is gone, so you have no reason to fight anymore."

"Jiya must die before I can rest."

V bit her lip, unwilling to accept that she had failed to kill him. She had no desire to see Odessa endure the torment of trying to cling to morality. Tonight, V had indulged fully in the monster lurking inside her.

"Also, I heard him call you Vlatka. Is dat your name?"

V stared at her before replying. "She and I are two different people now."

Odessa fell silent, lost in thought. V no longer recognized the person called Vlatka. She had even begun to forget what that woman had looked like.

"I had the chance to kill dat gray-skin, but I hesitated..."

Odessa stared off, silent. V placed a hand on her to coax her into continuing. She wanted to know what troubled her underling.

"When I looked at her, I saw Yama. It felt like I was about to kill someone I saw as a sistah."

V's eyes widened, then softened with relief. Odessa hadn't allowed her wrath to consume her entirely—she still held onto some moral compass. V glanced at Yama, who sat silently, unaware of the words spoken in a tongue she didn't understand.

With that in mind, V wondered if she should tell the others about Raisa. If she did, the chief would surely insist on continuing to follow her. But Woeton had already suffered a tragic fate, and V had no desire to see more of them die.

The Hiorians were already locked in battle, and V feared the worst. She had to reach Jiya quickly. This time she would not let him break her will. Even without a sword, she would defeat him.

The blade he carried unsettled her—it felt strange, frightening. Yet with her powers, she had no reason to fear. She hadn't even unleashed everything at her disposal. She had to do better, for the sake of those who might fall because of her failures tonight.

"I am glad you did not slay her, Odessa. She may be on Jiya's side, but I think she can be reasoned with. I don't know how, but I feel there is a way to separate her from him."

Odessa studied V for a moment before nodding and closing her eyes. Her wounds would heal, but her mind needed rest. So did V.

"Yama, I think 'tis time ye and the others return home."

"I hath made up my mind—I shan't return. I saw whom I believe is Tora on that battlefield," she said firmly.

Shock spread across V's face. She hadn't planned to reveal anything, but Yama had seen her.

"None of ye were supposed to die. 'Tis my fault, and I wish not to see more of ye fall," V stammered.

"I will not abandon Odessa or ye," Yama retorted. "And if Tora lives, I must press onward."

A faint, broken smile touched V's lips. Part of her longed to spend more time with Yama. But another part knew Yama would die if she continued.

"I will not allow ye to follow me," V declared.

"I helped ye in battle, and I wish to do it again."

"The next battlefield will not be one ye can hide and aid me from a distance. Enemies will be everywhere," V warned.

"I take heed of thy words, but I will not change my path," Yama said with confidence.

V clicked her tongue, deciding to leave the matter for later. She needed rest—the road ahead would be long. Fodmery would be her next destination with Odessa.

As V pondered her next move, Dharma and the chief appeared at the entrance. Dharma's fists were clenched, her face set with determination.

"I want to retrieve Woeton's body so we can bury him with his family," she demanded. Then she glanced at Yama before looking back at V. "I cannot bury me brother, but... maybe I can lay Woeton to rest."

V sat silently, unsure how to respond. Clearly, Dharma wouldn't take no for an answer.

"None of you will listen, so do as you wish. Except ye, Yama. For thy family's sake, ye must live," V cautioned.

"If ye are going out there, then I am too. Forgive me for being headstrong," Yama said sincerely.

There was nothing left to say to change their minds. The chief remained silent, but V assumed he, too, would continue. They were choosing to be part of a war unlike anything the land had ever seen.

The supernatural forces at play both excited and frightened V. She lay back and stared up at the old ceiling, already beginning to crumble.

CHAPTER 20

Act 3: Jiya's treachery Pt. 3

A few hours had passed since leaving the keep. A mist had fallen upon the land as the snow fell. Jiya and his men had fled a great distance. Many of his men had remained at the keep while others were with him. He had not foreseen the arrival of Vlatka. To see her again had surprised him.

She possessed otherworldly power that frightened and amused him. He knew that if the ritual years ago was successful, she would return from the Spirit world. Although, he had not expected her to come back the way she did.

As he rode in silence along a trail, he raised the *Tome of Eneida*. It was made of old leather and had strange symbols etched into its surface. A lock kept the book closed.

This ancient book possessed spiritual power beyond Jiya's imagination. He used it to make fallen warriors revenants. It also allowed him to craft weapons with supernatural attributes. Of course, something like this came at a cost.

"Was she not what you expected?" a voice asked.

Jiya's head jerked as he looked around nervously. He had ordered his men to ride ahead so he could be alone. Their lanterns illuminated the path as he followed. His mount's hooves crunched through the trail of white that lay before him.

He felt himself trembling and grabbed his arm. "Maybe I'm hearin' tings again," he muttered.

"Da end is comin', my dear friend."

Jiya felt chills creeping over his body. He turned his head to see the shadow of a horse moving beside him. Mounted on the shade was a man cloaked in black. He held a lantern with a teal flame inside.

Seeing this apparition made Jiya reach for his sword.

"Dat's no way to greet an old friend, is it?" the stranger asked.

Jiya pulled the reins on his horse, causing her to neigh loudly. His eyes widened, his mouth hung open. The man before him looked like a Hiorian—but not just any Hiorian. This man bore the face of one Jiya had killed many years ago, around this very time of year.

"Why do you wear dat accursed face?" Jiya shuddered.

The stranger pushed back his locks, revealing spirals of purple and teal-colored eyes. "I am not strong enough to take my real form. How you see me is beyond my control."

Jiya glared at the figure, fuming with rage. He didn't like this at all, especially after having just encountered the woman who once loved the man before him. No. Jiya touched the scar on his face. This wasn't the man who had left him with that scar.

Before him now was the one who had given him the book—the soulseer who granted him the power to make all this happen. He hadn't seen them in a long time and wondered what had happened. Could this be a sign of the end?

He couldn't accept it. He still had much to do. Losing now would ruin everything. Wouldn't it? Had he accomplished his goal? Forcing his people to cast aside their prideful notion that killing was beneath them?

Ever since they came to this land, pacifism had only brought them death and enslavement. It infuriated him to no end to see his brethren die. This soulseer had come to him years ago, appearing as an apparition in the shadows.

Back then, the shade had a feminine voice—sweet as honey, yet laced with bitterness. Jiya had been on the brink of death after his family was attacked by assassins.

The same way he had attacked the Craft family's hamlet years ago was the same way his family had been killed. He had lost everything then. His daughter committed suicide, and his mate had long left him.

Many times he wondered if she still lived. Would she ever forgive him for the horrendous things he had done? He had searched among the surviving members of the Craft family but never found her. He assumed she either died or went her own way. Did it even matter anymore?

Jiya recalled that after being given the book and taught how to use it, he plotted to kill Sorin. He knew Sorin had sent the assassins that killed his family. As much as he hated to admit it, he had respect for Vlatka's father.

Sorin, however, had always been treacherous. The only reason Jiya wavered in killing him was because Sorin's daughter had confronted him. Strange, how that young girl foresaw his plot.

She reminded him of his own daughter, which made him weak. He knew he had to break that weakness, and so he walked the dark path—one that stained his hands with sins that could never be washed away. Under his armored gloves, his hands were stained black.

No matter how much he scrubbed, the ink-like residue never came off. It frustrated him, but he continued his quest to force his people to fight. By becoming their enemy, he knew they would have no choice but to take up arms.

Had he not offered aid to Sorin, many families would already have been wiped out. Being the one to cut down his own people filled him with guilt. Yet he would rather it be by his hand than by a pathetic human like Sorin.

"Jiya..."

Jiya pulled himself from his thoughts and looked at the apparition beside him. "Why have you come? Why now?"

"Because da two of you have at long last crossed paths. I gave you power and told you to do wit it as you pleased. Now I wish to know if you accomplished what you set out to do."

Jiya hadn't expected this question. For years he had wondered if every choice he made was worth it—slaughtering children to harden his heart, killing people he once called friends, butchering their families.

The end of his journey would be to return to Vostaylia and kill Sorin. That had always been his true desire. But for now, he needed his people to change. Had he accomplished that yet? He couldn't be certain until the newly chosen elders of his people stood before him.

"You gifted me wit power dat gave me a chance to change da world. Giving humans da knowledge to learn spiritual arts is a double-edged sword. It will endanger my people, but maybe it will allow dem to wake up!"

"You believe da power I gave you to be a gift?" the apparition whispered.

Jiya furrowed his brow. The apparition had a faint smile as they brushed their locks aside.

"I have watched you from da shadows, and it appears to be more of a burden than anythin'."

"A burden in what way?"

"Maybe you thought it a gift in da beginnin', but da more you slay your people, I can see dat you are finally facin' da truth."

Jiya narrowed his eyes. "What is dis truth you speak of?"

"You have become isolated from your people. Da Hiorians dat chose to follow you are drawn to dat power out of fear or envy. No one here truly loves you."

"Silence..."

"They all hate you. You even hate yourself."

"I said to be silent!" Jiya snapped.

The stranger scoffed and shook his head slowly. Jiya huffed, trying to regain his composure. He didn't appreciate this apparition's ability to get under his skin so easily.

"Be mindful of how dat power affects da land and da living..."

The apparition spoke with a glance. Jiya eyed them and sneered, unsure of what they meant.

"Papa!" a voice called out in the distance.

Jiya looked ahead to see a silhouette in the mist, a lantern flickering as the figure drew closer. When they came near enough, he saw who it was—Raisa, disheveled and weary.

"Good, you are awake."

"Aye! Forgive me for being so... weak."

Jiya's face twisted into a frown. He didn't want to hear such words from any of his children. Even though they weren't related by blood, he loved her dearly.

"You are not weak, child."

Raisa turned her mount to face the proper direction. They rode side by side in silence for a few seconds. Jiya glanced around and saw the apparition had disappeared. It had always been this way.

"I cannot find Zahur..." Raisa muttered, her voice raspy.

"I do not approve of your fondness for him. He is a man, and you are but a child!"

"Papa... he is but a mentor. I have no such interests for anyone." Raisa glared at Jiya, her stone-colored cheeks flushing slightly.

"Your blushin' tells me otherwise," he taunted.

"Dat Hiorian killed him?"

Jiya was surprised by the sudden question, though he had expected it to come. Despite taking Zahur under his wing, he had never trusted him. He knew the kind of man he was and wanted him far from his daughters.

The young Hiorian woman Vlatka had taken under her wing had been one of Zahur's victims. Jiya only knew this because of how Zahur treated her when he went to recruit followers.

"No, she didn't... she hesitated."

"She did da same when she had a chance to kill me..." Raisa said, pressing her finger to her chin.

"Her soul is a gentle one..."

That made Raisa fall into deep thought. "How do you know dis? Her eyes were bloodlusted... if I had not gotten in da way then—"

"Zahur was not a good man. It does not change what I saw when I first met her," Jiya barked.

Raisa stayed silent as they rode on, trailing behind the rest of the group. Jiya needed everyone to keep moving—he had no way of knowing whether Vlatka pursued them.

"May I ask you somethin', Papa?"

"You can ask me anythin', my child."

Raisa was quiet for several seconds, whatever troubled her weighing heavily. "When will you be able to stop usin' dat book?"

The question unsettled him. He didn't even want to think about the book after speaking with the soulseer. "Why do you ask me dis?"

He raised his lantern toward Raisa's face, forcing her to squint and shield her eyes.

"I can feel dat it changes you... I do not want to lose you to dat ting, Papa..."

Her words made his heart tremble. Reflexively, he clutched his chest with his free hand. He never wanted her involved in this. Truthfully, he never had. But he couldn't let the acolytes experiment on her again.

He didn't know their intentions, only that when he saw her, the image of his daughter rushed into his mind. Without thinking, he had whisked her away from the shelter the acolytes kept her in.

"Do not fret about me, my child," Jiya said softly.

"Dat not an easy task..."

Jiya let out a husky laugh and glanced toward the sky. "Do you know of da current state of dat giant?"

He changed the subject. He had no desire to think of the book or the soulseer who had given it to him. Instead, he wanted to learn more about the man who nearly killed him— one who bore a resemblance to Raisa.

"He still breathes, I heard..." Raisa quickly fell silent.

"By da look on your face, I know what you're thinkin'. You are like him."

"What am I then? How did I end up wit da acolytes you saved me from?"

Raisa's questions were ones he couldn't answer. He knew she felt out of place. No matter how much he tried to keep his children close, she likely still felt alone. She had no maternal figure in her life.

"Maybe we can ask him," Jiya suggested.

"Maybe..."

"Then it is settled. If he survives until we reach camp, we can ask him at first light," Jiya concluded.

The two continued onward, picking up their pace to catch the others. With snow falling heavier, the air grew colder. Jiya had never been fond of cold weather, though his homeland winters were much harsher. With that in mind, he pressed on.

CHAPTER 21

The sound of waves gently hitting the surface of something stirred V from her slumber. She groaned as she groggily opened her eyes. The first thing she noticed was that she was staring up at the sky. From what she could tell, the sun was beginning to set.

She saw a murder of crows flying above. It took her a moment to realize where she was. She sat up to see the strange figure staring off into the distance. The wind began to blow, causing V's hair to whip wildly across her face. It obscured her vision, forcing her to adjust it so she could see him properly.

"You again?" she complained.

His glowing otherwordly eyes stared at her with an empty gaze. "You could have ended things, but you accepted defeat once your sword broke."

Shame fell over her as she listened to his cold words. His statement rang true—she had faltered in doubt when her sword shattered. His weapon had felt alive, throwing her completely off her focus.

"That sword he had... do you know anything about it?"

"Likely something crafted using that tome. The tome was made with the power of a soulseer, and in the wrong hands it can weaken the veil."

"What happens if the veil is weakened?"

"It distorts the balance of things that were set in place. The living will grow sick, while spirits grow stronger and more physical."

"That... is a bit frightening."

"You best be careful when you face him again," the soulseer warned.

V remained silent as she pondered the origins of the strange book Jiya had come across. Where had it come from, and how could it make such a dangerous weapon? Too many unexpected things were surfacing in her quest for revenge.

"There is so much I don't know about the Spirit World. How hath the Hiorians been able to learn so much?" V asked aloud.

"I believe it has been roughly thirty years since their land was wiped out," the soulseer began.

"I am well aware of that, but that doth not explain—"

"Many years ago, a conflict between two elders happened, and one was believed to have been slain by the other—something the Hiorians often looked down upon," the soulseer explained.

V stared at him in disbelief. She had never heard of this. Jorah hadn't told her everything about his homeland. Sometimes she assumed it was because of the trauma from what he had witnessed.

"Well, that Hiorian came back from the dead thanks to the traitor. He learned how to awaken spiritual awareness and also told his people about the spirits that sometimes slipped through the veil." The soulseer turned toward V and leaned closer.

His glowing eyes seemed to look deep into her soul. It unsettled her, her body trembling. Why did this entity have to be so eerie? His stare made her skin crawl.

"This Hiorian's name was Juma Ashspell. It is my understanding that, like his father, Jiya is a mere pawn. He is but a man so broken that his mind has become twisted."

V stared off in disbelief. Some of what the Hiorians had learned came from Jiya's family. Did he start slaughtering other families because they took what they had learned and cast him aside? To turn against his people for something like that seemed questionable.

She wanted to stop guessing intentions—Jiya would be the only one who could truly give her answers. Yet she felt it wouldn't matter. Nothing he said could stop her from killing him. He had done too much harm to his people and the land. Nothing could redeem him.

"The knowledge of dealing with vampyrs... did that also come from Jiya's father?"

"No. That came simply from trial and error. Most of the creatures they faced in their homeland were ones this land has never seen before. When it came to vampyrs, they tried everything until they figured them out."

This explanation made sense. As she reflected on the past, she remembered how often they experimented with herbs and other things. They were a people always seeking knowledge, endlessly creative.

"I have watched in the shadows for a while and have come to understand that Sorin would have killed every single Hiorian," the soulseer muttered.

V tensed at the name, her heart skipping a beat. It felt strange to feel it again after so many years. Alas, this was only a dream—or something beyond her understanding. All she knew was that her uncle also had to die. His time would come, but first she needed to stop Jiya.

"Jiya has slain two Hiorian families, not Sorin," V chided.

The soulseer remained silent. V scoffed. Maybe he wanted her to shift the blame away from Jiya and onto Sorin. But it wouldn't work. She had seen and heard enough to know everything happening here stemmed from Jiya's madness.

She would still have her revenge. Killing Jiya would further damage his people's reputation with the humans. And raising the dead had to come at a cost—one too great for him to pay alone.

"I am seen as a monster, but that dastardly fool has done far worse than me," V scoffed.

"Someone needs to put him out of his misery. The power he wields does not belong in this world. That means you cannot accept defeat so easily again. I pray you do not allow another to sacrifice themselves for you to realize that."

The soulseer stood, causing the boat to rock. Crows swooped

down, swarming around him. Their loud cries pierced V's ears, forcing her to cover them. As she watched the soulseer vanish, the boat rocked violently as waves began to rise.

V looked around—the atmosphere had changed. The sky above darkened. Slowly, she turned her head to see a massive wave forming. Her eyes widened in horror as it crashed down, swallowing the boat whole.

*

V's eyes shot open as she sat up in an unnatural way. She looked around the area to see that Odessa remained in her sleeping position. As she continued to look around, she saw that Yama had disappeared.

V staggered to her feet and listened. She didn't hear anyone in the tower. Their heartbeats were a bit farther away, which meant they were outside. Unfortunately, she couldn't use the clothing that protected her from the sun—it had been cut to pieces.

She stared at her cloak unhappily. A ray of light acted as a wall, keeping her trapped in the dark. Slowly, V approached it and hesitated. Then she gradually held out her hand. As it bathed in the dull sunlight, she felt a tingling sensation.

She winced and pulled her hand back. It didn't burn, but it felt uncomfortable. The longer she stayed in the light, the more she assumed her skin would begin to burn. The curse upon her kept her from ever enjoying sunlight again. A part of her wondered if that would be how she would one day meet her end. To watch the sunrise one last time would be blissful.

As she stood silently, Yama came into view. What took V by surprise were the three figures following behind her. A woman with reddish hair and green eyes stared at V. Standing behind her were two men dressed in armor.

"I take it ya are the person known as V," she said in a soft voice.

A chuckle almost escaped V's lips. The young woman tried to sound threatening, but her voice was far too gentle for it to be taken seriously.

Not only that, but it caught V off guard that this woman spoke Vostaylian. Likely she did so to convince the gray-skins to let her inside. Without that, the language barrier would have caused a fight. V bowed, her face close to the wall of sunlight that separated them.

"You must be Judith Jacquard."

The woman referred to as Judith looked perplexed. She glanced at one of the men beside her. "Ja, I am."

"Now, pray tell, how tis you found us?"

"Despite the snow, my scouts were able to track the footprints that led here," Judith explained.

"Fine. So what do you want?"

"It is a wee bit hard to see ya. Would ya mind coming out of the dark?"

Judith squinted as she tried to peer into the shadows. V hated the fact that she was confined. She couldn't step out without being burned by the light.

"You doth not need to see me to tell me why you are here."

"Ya forced the Hiorian known as Jiya to flee. This allowed us to keep from being captured—or worse."

Judith bowed her head, gratitude flickering in her expression. V couldn't yet tell this woman's true motives, but something compelled her to listen. A part of her saw herself in this young lady.

"I had come to seek an alliance, but—"

"Well, that brings me to why I am here. I would like to ask for ya help in aiding my quest to retake my father's throne."

"To seek the aid of a monster amuses me..." V trailed off. "Let's say I were to aid you. What would become of the Hiorians not on Jiya's side? The ones who have been helping you reclaim the throne?"

Judith's eyes widened and she stiffened. She fell silent, her gaze shifting as she searched for the right words.

"These people possess power I cannot begin to understand. My people would only see them as dangerous..."

"If you choose to harm those who came to these lands with the intent to aid us, then you are my enemy!" V exclaimed.

"I have no intent to harm anyone who has shown kindness and generosity to me. Besides, my brother has been working with them to reclaim parts of our kingdom's territory," Judith explained.

V remained silent. She felt uncertain about Judith. Part of her thought she could trust her, but she also knew people's feelings were fickle and ever-changing.

"All they wanted was a home—and as far as I know, Vostaylians and Wescreans alike met them with the blade," V said coldly.

"I am quite aware—and gutted—when I think of the things my father did. Just because I had been a child does not mean I had been naive."

"Jiya took over this country in hopes of building a place for his people to live after their home was destroyed. When this war is over, thy people will cast down their rage upon the innocent."

V stepped forward toward the light, careful not to expose her skin. Her intense gaze made Judith take a step back.

"In the beginning, I understood Jiya's reason for attacking humans. We did it to his kind all the time, raiding the small villages they built outside the country. Now he just seems intent on wiping us out—or enslaving us for his amusement."

"That is what happens when a foolish man becomes entranced by power. If I help you defeat him, then I expect you to try to rebuild the relationship between humans and Hiorians here," V demanded.

"They are foreigners who walked onto our land expecting us to give them a home without anything in return. That was a foolish choice they made."

"They taught your people how to kill those prowlers that plagued Wescreas, did they not?"

Judith stiffened again, eyes wide. She lowered her head, clearly troubled.

"Oh, and they made medicines that saved people from illnesses once thought to be a death sentence. I know this because they saved my mother," V chided.

"I see your point, but ya can't expect my people to care about any of that after what Jiya has done! Besides... do ya know he has taken my people as sacrifices?"

Now it was V who stiffened, shocked. She hadn't known he was doing such a thing. But why? What purpose could it serve?

"Why would he do such a thing?"

"Sir Nabil believes it has something to do with that tome," one of the chevaliers blurted.

The other chevalier punched him in the arm. Judith cast him a displeased look. V raised her brow in suspicion. The name *Nabil* didn't sound Wescrean. He had to be Hiorian—meaning Judith had Hiorians with her at the keep.

This made V question why Judith would speak so harshly if she had Hiorians aiding her. Slowly, V began to dislike the young woman.

"Who is Nabil?"

"He is... a Hiorian who has been aiding in keeping me safe."

Judith lowered her head, but V saw her beige skin flush red. Was she blushing at the mention of this man's name?

"Then why would you come in here declaiming such nonsense about them? You take their kindness and return it with disrespect!"

Judith raised her finger. "The things I have said are what I believe my people will feel when this is over. My feelings toward them are not negative."

"You will be queen, so you hath the power to make thy people accept the Hiorians!"

"My heart is open to them, but I will not force my people to accept them. That would simply make me a tyrant and cause my own people to despise me."

"Yet, you say they aided your brother in his plight to reclaim your homeland."

Judith remained silent as a look of guilt formed on her face.

V saw that this brought everything to a crossroads. Even if she were to defeat Jiya, the damage had already been done. The Hiorians would have to find another place to live. Even if they settled in lands claimed by no kingdom, the likelihood of safety seemed slim.

"This Nabil person... I take it he has won thy heart."

Judith's face once again turned red. One of her chevaliers coughed as he tried to conceal his snickering. The other struck him to silence him.

"It is complicated, and with everything happening, I doubt it will be a long-lived affair." Judith wore a wistful look on her face.

"So I assume you're choosing thy people over love. I must admit I had been incapable of doing that."

V had to accept that Judith was the complete opposite of her. It made clear why V would never have been a good ruler, even if her uncle had not betrayed everyone. Judith accepted her duty as queen.

"Will ya help me defeat Jiya?" Judith asked.

"If I don't?"

"Then my people will likely die. It's been hard to feed six hundred people in that keep."

V thought about this for a bit. She didn't know how to respond to this at all. She also wondered how many of those people were actually warriors. Jiya still had the superior forces.

V stood there in silence, considering the request. Her biggest concern was the aftermath. What would be the Hiorians' fate? Would they be able to make it out of Wescreas and return to their hamlet by the coast?

"If you die, then what?"

Judith seemed taken aback by the question. "Then the Jacquard dynasty ends."

"So to make a deal with the wicked is your only way to prevail?" V laughed.

"Amongst those dead warriors you slaughtered, we found one of them to be alive," Judith suddenly blurted out.

"What of it?"

"He is one of Jiya's sons."

V's eyes widened in disbelief. She couldn't believe what she had just heard. Then she realized Jiya likely wanted to revive his family. All of his siblings and cousins had been killed. Reviving the Ashspell family did not come as a surprise.

What bothered her was the fact that this son of his could have been nothing more than a child. How had she not noticed him? Why would Jiya allow him on a battlefield like that? Too many questions spiraled in her mind.

"I am hoping that I can use him as leverage. So if ya choose not to help me, this will be my next option to get things sorted," Judith explained.

"I care about the Hiorians that stand against Jiya. Thy people will likely turn their focus on them once Jiya is defeated. That is where I have my misgivings about aiding you," V explained.

"Ya have my word that I will try to build a better relationship between my people and the Hiorians."

V listened to the woman's words—and her heartbeat. From what she could gather, she seemed genuine. Either way, V would be going after Jiya to end the terror he had brought upon this country.

"I will come to the keep tonight. I want to meet this son of Jiya's. After that, we will talk more."

"Fine."

Judith bowed her head and turned away. Her protectors followed her out. Yama stood silently, watching them leave. V let out a deep sigh as she realized she had much thinking to do.

*

After Judith had left, everyone came in to where V and Odessa were resting. They all sat down in silence, each with much on their minds. The gray-skins had lost another one of their own. V and Odessa carried the weight of failure heavy upon them.

Dharma had been the angriest about Woeton's death. It made V curious to know more about their relationship. When she met him and Yonten, it had seemed as if Woeton had been his mentor.

"What was thy relationship with Woeton, Dharma?" V blurted before she could stop herself.

Dharma looked at her in confusion. Her expression shifted to annoyance, then softened into a regretful look. "He looked out for me and my brother since our parents died."

As V thought about this, she wondered how old Woeton had been. She had the feeling he was older than them but younger than her—no more than thirty-something, she assumed, while Dharma looked to be in her late twenties.

"The tears I saw yesterday felt as if there were more to it than that."

"So what? He's gone because of ye!" she snapped.

V merely stared at her in silence. She had no rebuttal, because Dharma was right. Had she not frozen in defeat, maybe he wouldn't have been killed.

"'Tis my fault," Yama muttered.

Dharma's attention snapped toward her. "What?"

"It had nothing to do with her!" Yama said louder.

Everyone stared, surprised. Dharma's face twisted into rage as she glared at Yama. "Ever since we met her, he's been trying desperately to win her approval! He got killed because she benighted him!"

"She saved my life while ye stood by as my family got killed! Woeton and Yonten chased me to take me back to die! All of ye were benighted!" Yama spat.

Finally, Yama had let her frustrations spill out. V felt a flicker of relief—she didn't want the girl to keep her feelings buried. That would only rot her from within.

This argument had been inevitable. V had foreseen such a dire confrontation, though she hadn't expected it to come now.

"So ye chose to push my brother for revenge?"

The question cut through the air like a blade. Everyone stared at Dharma in disbelief. Yama sat silently, struggling for words that would not come. At last, she rose and left.

V wanted to follow, but the sun still shone overhead. She could not pursue her. As V sat in silence, she heard a whistle. She glanced over her shoulder to see Odessa commanding the wolf creature.

It bolted after Yama, which filled V with relief. Even though Odessa couldn't understand the words, she could sense the tension.

"Ye hath no shame?" V asked, her glare sharp.

Dharma met her gaze blankly before slouching, lowering her head.

"I am a craven, scorned by my weakness to protect those I love," Dharma mumbled.

V could sense her regret, and in that moment, respected her more. "I know ye blame me for Woeton going out to battle but... I think it was to prove himself somehow to her." V sighed.

The silence in the room was deafening. To V, however, the heartbeats of those around her and the distant chirping of birds filled the quiet. She also heard the wolves skulking nearby.

She glanced at the chief, who hadn't said a word. He simply sat and watched the ordeal unfold. V wondered why. In some way, he must have felt guilt. But she didn't need his words to sense his pain.

At last, he rose, drawing Dharma's gaze upward. Without a word, he walked away, likely to go outside and find Yama.

"I will give heed one last time," V said firmly. "This is not thy fight. Ye all can go home. The whereabouts of the chief's daughter can be obtained by me alone."

"I must bring Woeton home, so I will not turn back without him."

V shook her head in disbelief. The woman was foolish, but V understood. When Jorah had died, she too had been unable to think clearly. And when she returned, he had been all she searched for.

CHAPTER 22

Jiya's treachery Pt. 2

The wind howled loudly at first light. With the dreary gray sky overhead, the sun's vibrance was hardly noticeable. It made Jiya wonder if Vlatka could move about at a time like this. The sun illuminated the land, but the rays were dull.

As Jiya marched through the camp, he could finally feel the winter's embrace. Every breath he took was visible. He huffed and puffed as his body shivered. Despite this, he had to pretend it didn't bother him. Unfortunately, something felt off in his body, though he couldn't explain why.

They had set up this camp before heading to the keep the night before. He looked around at his warriors. The revenants didn't need to sleep, so they were always on watch. The humans huddled near their tents around a fire.

His Hiorian warriors kept to their own area. He cared very little about their separation. In the end, he wanted his people to fight for a place to call home. No longer did he believe they should beg for it or try to appease the humans by adjusting to their customs.

He would take Wescreas and build a home for his people. Some had scattered across the land, but once he cemented his position, he would send for them. A home where they would no longer suffer persecution from humans.

As he continued toward the area where they kept the giant, a commotion broke out. He turned to see some of his men fighting with weapons drawn. Unsure of what had happened, he hesitated.

Then he saw a hysterical Hiorian woman screaming as she swung her sword at a human warrior. Her long braids were pulled into a ponytail. As Jiya marched over, he noticed tears streaming down her face. He had no idea what the situation was, but he had to stop it.

"What is da meanin' of dis here commotion?" Jiya shouted in a booming voice.

The Hiorian woman ignored him and tried to cut the human warrior down. Jiya rushed in front of her and caught the edge of her blade. Blood dripped to the ground, staining the white snow. Her eyes were dazed, her breaths short and rapid.

She wielded a short sickle-shaped sword that had proven many times how well it could chop through armor. Jiya had been lucky she had eased up on her swing. Otherwise, she would have cut through his hand.

"Makena... what is da cause of your rage?" Jiya asked in a gentle tone.

Makena's eyes blazed with fury, but she slowly began to relax as she backed away. She tried to speak, but her distress choked her words. A Hiorian male stepped forward and bowed his head, drawing Jiya's attention.

"Lord Jiya... it would appear dat Sir Lahaye snuck your son Badru into our ranks," the Hiorian said nervously.

Jiya froze. A glance at his hand revealed a gash in his palm. His heart pounded as a storm of emotions overtook him. How had he not sensed his own son's presence? Slowly, he turned to face the human warrior, Sir Lahaye.

"Is what Ashur say true?"

The warrior trembled as Jiya's eyes locked on him. "Forgive me, my lord... he begged me to help him. He felt unseen by ya and wanted to prove himself as a capable warrior."

The warrior's rambling only fueled Jiya's fury. He turned to Makena, who was bawling, comforted by Ashur's hand on her shoulder. Jiya seized him.

"How did dis happen? Hm?"

"I... there were many of us, so—"

Jiya shoved him aside before he could finish. He then grabbed Makena, who looked up at him in shock, her eyes clouded with tears.

"You are his mama and you did not realize he was wit us?"

"You blame me for dis?" she demanded angrily. "I was here while you went to battle!"

"Of course I blame you!" Jiya snapped. "You were to ensure he stayed at da castle!"

Makena's eyes widened. Before Jiya could react, she slapped him across the face. The cold air made the sting sharper. He held his cheek, glancing around to see his people staring in disbelief.

He had to make an example of her. Mother of his child or not, she couldn't go unpunished for such disrespect. Jiya glared, balling his fist.

"Do it! I have endured worse from you anyway!" she shouted.

Jiya's chest heaved as rage overtook him. He let out a roar and struck her, knocking her into the snow. She cried out in pain as blood poured from her nose.

"Da next time you strike me will be da last time you breathe!"

"If you had been more attentive to him, maybe dis would not have happened!"

"What?"

"You show more interest in da children you have wit da queen and dat other human!"

Jiya stared down at her, frustration twisting his features. Of all the women who bore his children, she was the most irksome. He loathed her defiance, yet admired her fierce spirit. She had always been a fighter.

She had lost many of her relatives when he attacked her family. Things hadn't gone as planned, and he suspected they had all died. He had only meant to kill a few, but they had been ready to fight to the death. He took no pride in it, but he wanted to restore his bloodline. She had become the second concubine to bear him a child.

"I understand your anger toward me for all dat I have done to you, but I know dat you are glad he is gone."

Makena stared at him in disbelief. "How could you say such a ting? Dat is my baby you speak of!"

"He is but a reminder of all da horrible tings I did to you," Jiya said coldly.

Makena's eyes widened, then dropped away in shame. Her anger faded into despair. Jiya took no pride in breaking her spirit, but it was the only way he knew to keep her loyalty.

"We will honor him by winnin' da war. I am certain they will be on their way to Fodmery soon."

Jiya turned from Makena and faced Sir Lahaye. His actions, too, could not go unpunished. Slowly, Jiya reached out his hand toward the warrior.

"The sword, boy," Jiya ordered.

"My lord... please forgive me. I only wanted to help him win ya approval," Sir Lahaye pleaded.

"Sword!" Jiya repeated.

Sir Lahaye trembled as he reached for his blade. From what Jiya could tell, the warrior was no more than in his early twenties. He had youth and a long life ahead of him.

"I understand your efforts, but you allowed him to fall. If you helped him sneak into da ranks of dis army, then he was in your charge. Dat means you were responsible for him, correct?" Jiya asked.

"Ja!" Sir Lahaye agreed. "I should have kept a closer eye on him. Please, grant me mercy," he begged.

Sir Lahaye hesitantly handed over his sword. Jiya examined it, weighed it in his hands, then stepped closer. Lunging forward, he plunged the tip of the sword into Sir Lahaye's chest. The young man gasped as blood spewed from his mouth.

"Da mercy I grant you is to let your soul rest in peace!"

Jiya pulled the blade free and let him collapse. He stared down at the lifeless corpse for a moment before tossing the sword aside.

"Dispose of him!" Jiya ordered, turning away.

He marched on toward the area he had been headed earlier. As he walked through the camp, he saw Raisa nearby with a displeased look on her face. Shame forced him to avert his eyes.

He knew that when his time came, he would not be forgiven by his people. All he could hope for was that his children would still see the good in him. But as he thought, he began to wonder if there had ever been any good in him at all.

The revenants stood guard over the wounded giant. Woeton lay on a gurney they had built, heavy chains binding him so he could not escape. He was positioned on his stomach so the healers could tend his wounds.

A female Hiorian worked carefully, spreading a paste she had concocted to keep the wound from infection. Jiya knelt to meet the giant's gaze. If he remembered correctly, he had heard him speak to Vlatka in the Vostaylian tongue—though it sounded strange compared to what Jiya had been taught.

"What are ye?" Jiya asked, adjusting his speech so the giant might understand.

The giant only stared. His silence irritated Jiya. If he would not speak, Jiya would finish him off. He had no intention of allowing him to recover anyway.

"Me name be Woeton of the Scarstone tribe. Humans call us gray-skins," he finally answered.

"'Tis a pleasure to meet you, Woeton. You may call me Jiya."

Woeton took in a raspy breath. "So ye be the one who hath defiled the land."

The words struck a nerve, almost provoking Jiya to strike the wounded man. He forced a deep breath to calm himself. "Why have you taken up arms with Vlatka?"

Woeton furrowed his brow. "I know not of a Vlatka."

"Da monster of a woman you protected last night..."

Realization flickered across Woeton's face. "So that be her true name..."

"She goes by something else?"

"We call her... V. She heard our chief's daughter could yet live."

Jiya stared in silence. Then the truth struck him. Slowly, he turned his head in search of Raisa. If she learned this, she might no longer feel so alone—she could be reunited with her true family.

But he couldn't allow Woeton to tell her; she didn't know the Vostaylian tongue. Jiya had only taught her the Hiorian tongue and a little Wescrean. The language barrier served his purpose.

Still, if he were to fall in battle, she would be alone. He thought of how she and her siblings got along. The youngest ones adored her. His eldest biological daughter had a strong bond with her. The problem was with Badru and the other four —who often mocked her for not being a true Hiorian, for not having a mother.

It angered him, but he didn't want her to pull away. Losing her would feel like losing his first daughter all over again.

As he debated what to say, another female Hiorian seized his hand, snapping him out of thought. She began tending the gash on his palm—he had nearly forgotten he was bleeding.

"Well, you should give up on the matter. You will not live for long."

Jiya's words were cold as he looked back at Woeton. He could not allow this man to live. Turning to the healers, he declared:

"You wish for us to leave him for dead?" one asked cautiously.

"I may make him a revenant when we return to da city. So continue to tend to him."

"As you wish."

Jiya straightened and turned toward Raisa. She sat sharpening her axes. Luckily, they had retrieved the one Zahur had thrown at Woeton. The pair were special, carrying spiritual power. Jiya knew he had to speak with her—she would be upset with him.

"You are upset wit me?"

"You did not have to treat Lady Makena like dat."

"She disrespected me in front of my men. Not only dat, but she allowed Badru to slip past her and end up on dat accursed battlefield," Jiya explained.

"You are his papa. You should be responsible too..." Raisa

muttered.

Jiya chewed his lip, nearly shouting. He couldn't believe she would say such a thing. Hearing the disappointment in her voice stung.

"Perhaps you are right..." Jiya admitted.

He looked around at the camp—warriors chatting, tending to the wounded they had retrieved. He had half a mind to order them to leave the fallen behind, but he worried that would kill their morale.

"What did dat other gray-skin say?"

Jiya turned to her, surprised by the question. "How did you know dat is what he is called?"

"People in da city call me dat, and he looks like me, so..."

Jiya pursed his lips. He had to decide how much to tell her. If she knew someone who might be her true father was out there, would she leave him?

"He says his name is Woeton, and he belongs to somethin' called the Scarstone tribe. Which means there are more of them somewhere in the Scarstone Mountains."

Raisa sat in silence, then returned to sharpening her axe. Jiya twiddled his thumbs. Keeping this from her would be selfish... wouldn't it?

"You have family out there. A mama... a papa who may be lookin' for you," Jiya said, rubbing his arms.

The cold felt sharper now. His armor and cloak did little to warm him. Raisa, though, loved the cold. She sharpened her axe bare-handed.

"You are my papa," Raisa mumbled. "Knowin' what I am, and that there is more of my kind, is enough for me."

Her words relieved him. He had feared she would long to find them. Instead, she seemed not to care.

"So you do not wish to find out about your real parents?"

"No."

The response came quicker than he expected, without hesitation. A quizzical smile spread across his face before he looked into the distance.

"You won't hurt him, will you?"

The question surprised Jiya into silence. He had planned to turn Woeton into a revenant. The man's survival after being struck by one of the weapons crafted with the *Tome of Eneida* intrigued him.

"He may not survive his wounds. Your axes are quite powerful," Jiya said carefully.

"Oh."

Jiya watched her as she continued sharpening. He wished he could read her thoughts. Would she despise him if he made Woeton a revenant? If he didn't, the man might recover. But forcing Vlatka to kill him again could benefit Jiya.

A choice had to be made—and soon.

CHAPTER 23

The night crept its way into the sky as V finally emerged from the tower. The snow had stopped for the moment, but the land was covered with what appeared to be six inches of it. A slight breeze had begun to form in the area. Tonight would be a night to prepare for battle. Everything had to end soon, for there was no longer any reason to procrastinate.

Her talk with Judith had gone unfinished. Not only that, but many pieces of this future battle still felt unaccounted for. She had no way of knowing how the Hiorians were faring.

She hoped and prayed that they were safe. If they were to encounter Leon and his men, that battle would be a troublesome one. Leon had been strong—but only because she had refrained from drinking blood.

Now things had changed, for she had tasted a great deal of blood last night. She felt powerful, her body no longer sluggish. As she marched across the field toward the keep, she began to wonder if she could find a proper sword.

Odessa and the others followed in silence. The chief carried a torch he had fashioned to illuminate the area. For V and Odessa, the torch was unnecessary—they could see clearly in the darkness.

The smell of ash lingered in the air outside the keep. V assumed Judith had ordered the bodies of the dead burned. Ever since revenants became a consistent occurrence, it had become common practice.

After walking a good distance, they finally stood outside the keep. V waited in silence, staring at the heavy gates. It took over two minutes for the guards on the wall to fetch someone to open them.

This annoyed V somewhat, but she let it go. When the doors finally opened, they were greeted by a group of chevaliers without helmets. This allowed V to see the various shades of red hair. All of the men stared at her in awe.

As she marched through the gate with Yama and Odessa at her side, she sensed their eyes drifting to Odessa and Yama. Likely, these people had never seen Yama's kind before. Perhaps they had only encountered Raisa.

V noticed a group of men sitting under a tent, a small fire burning nearby. To her left was a modest horse stable. To her right stood a few small buildings, which she assumed to be homes.

The keep itself was larger than the fortress that surrounded Skyreach Tower. Walking within its walls, V almost convinced herself this place was a small village.

Up ahead rose a larger structure resembling a small castle. Clearly, this had been their stronghold for some time. V wondered how long they had been here. Had they been moving forces to protect Judith while Jiya pursued her?

From Odessa, she had learned that Jiya had taken control five years ago. That meant Judith and her brother had been fighting him for that long.

If they had remained here the whole time, V felt impressed. They had endured for years while feeding the many people now gathered here. Clearly, the war was reaching its climax. Jiya had raised his forces to end it completely.

As V continued forward, someone approached. To her surprise, he was not human. His pointed ears and silvery eyes gave that away. Unlike the armored men around him, he wore garments more fitting for a hunter or scout.

"Da aura of your spirit is strange," he said, his eyes lingering on Odessa. He spoke in the Hiorian tongue. V began to wonder if more Hiorians were here.

"Who are you?" V asked.

He looked at her briefly, surprised. "My name is Nabil Grimm."

A despondent look crossed his face. From what V remembered from Odessa, his family had been attacked by Jiya. She wouldn't be surprised if they had all been slaughtered.

"'Tis a pleasure to meet you. Might I ask where Princess Judith is?" V asked with a polite smile.

"She will be here soon. May I ask your names?"

V glanced back at the gray-skins, who shifted nervously. Their wolves growled lowly at the gawking men, clearly distrustful. They had likely never been around so many humans —or strayed so far from their home.

"You may call me V."

She bowed her head respectfully, then glanced at Odessa, wondering if she would reply. Instead, the girl remained silent, staring into the distance. V felt something had broken inside her young comrade—a sea of emotions barely contained behind her eyes.

"This is Odessa Hollow. These people... humans call them gray-skins. 'Tis a Vostaylian tongue they mostly speak."

V wasn't sure if Nabil knew any language besides his own and Wescrean, but she tested anyway. To her surprise, he stepped closer to Yama.

Yama stiffened and took a step back, glancing at Odessa and then her own people. "Do ye know Odessa?"

Nabil blinked, then glanced at Odessa. "I have heard of her family, but I am not familiar wit her specifically."

"Oh," Yama replied.

"May I know your name?" Nabil asked in his soft accent.

"Yama."

"It is a pleasure to meet you," he said with a bow.

V leaned closer to Nabil. "I summarize you've spent a great deal of time here."

Nabil blushed, scratching his head and chuckling nervously. Clearly, something troubled him.

As V studied him, the sound of chains drew her attention. Judith appeared with a group of warriors, escorting what looked like a prisoner. To V's shock, it was a boy—no more than thirteen.

He had almond skin and pointed ears. Clearly, a Hiorian. But why was he in chains? Then she recalled Judith's words: a survivor had been found among the dead.

Closer now, she saw the bruises and wounds covering him. Stripped of most of his garments, he shivered in the cold.

Why had they dragged him onto the battlefield? If he was truly Jiya's son, how could Jiya have allowed it? Worse, how could he have left him behind?

Too many questions spiraled in V's mind.

"Who is this child?" V asked in an eerie tone.

The boy appeared frightened out of his mind. His eyes were transfixed on V, his shivering body trembling at the sight of her. V stared at the chains that confined him. They didn't appear to be made from any material she was familiar with.

"This is Badru, Jiya's son," Nabil answered.

"How can you be certain that he is Jiya's son?"

"...he told me."

Nabil looked over at the boy, who stood in silence, shivering. The fear in his eyes disheartened V. She sensed nothing but innocence in him.

"My people will not survive here forever. The winter brings the fever, and with little provisions this conflict must end. I don't want to, but I must do what I have to for the sake of my people," Judith said in her Wescrean accent.

Her speech sounded more elegant than Leon's. The way Leon spoke gave her the impression he had been of lower nobility, though his armor and rank had suggested otherwise.

V looked at Nabil. "You are fine with this?"

"She fights for her home. Da boy's father has soiled it and robbed her of many loved ones. If Jiya can be reached at all, it will be through his son."

Nabil's words carried doubt and shame. V heard it, and his heartbeat told her he was clearly uncomfortable. She shook her head in disappointment.

"Jiya has become a monster and brought shame upon our

people. We may have dealt with attacks from time to time from da humans, but he has gone too far," Nabil explained.

"You do realize you will not be able to stand by her side in the end, don't you?" V asked.

Nabil tensed at her words. He snuck a glance at Judith. Her expression revealed her confliction. V concluded that if Judith succeeded in reclaiming the kingdom, she would either execute or exile the Hiorians from her country.

To think that this eighteen-year-old girl could already have the mindset to use people for personal gain and then cast them aside sickened her. She had no desire to truly help Judith. But she did want Jiya dead.

The greater the numbers outside the castle, the better. Yet V now felt conflicted—she had no idea what she truly wanted to do. Once it all ended, she would have to find a way to keep the Wescreans from turning on the Hiorians.

"The Hiorians, I believe, are working their way to Fodmery to take down Jiya. I believe they will be of great help in your cause. That is—if you don't intend to betray them in the end," V proposed.

Judith stood silent for a moment, pondering. "I haven't heard from my brother, so I fear he has fallen… with this in mind, what they do is not of my concern—just yet. Anyway, ya are not Hiorian, so why is their fate so important to ya?"

"'Tis simple. They saved my mother, and they aided my country when we were on the verge of being wiped out by vampyrs," V explained.

Judith stood quietly for a second before glancing at Odessa and then back at V. "I have seen the sorcery ya can do. Ya are no human."

"No, I am not. At least not anymore, for humans are cruel creatures. Also, what I do is not sorcery," V chided.

"I watched ya conjure blue flames. I have seen Hiorians cut through people without being close to them, but I have never seen blue flames. Jiya's sword created something that cut through some of his own men. Ya mean to tell me that is not sorcery?"

"What the Hiorians are able to do is something known as spiritual arts. At least, that is what she calls it."

V gestured toward Odessa, who still seemed detached from the conversation. V grew concerned—her fledgling looked lost. She longed to help her but had no idea how.

"She appears to be like ya, based on the color of her eyes," Judith concluded.

"I... turned her into what she is in order to save her life." V lowered her head as guilt stirred inside her. "Whatever we are is akin to the vampyrs, but also the revenants."

Judith's eyes widened as she stepped back. Her chevaliers reached for their weapons in fear. Odessa, at last, snapped to her surroundings.

She quickly drew her daggers, fangs bared, hissing at them. V slowly raised her hands and approached Odessa. She had no intent to fight these people—so long as they did not harm the Hiorians once Jiya was gone.

V sneaked a glance at Odessa again. She thought of Zahur. Drinking his blood had given her a glimpse of what she assumed were his memories. Brutal killings of children, of his people, and of the way he treated Odessa.

It had been fleeting, but enough. She understood the significance of Odessa's scars now. Her anger washed away by the knowledge that she had ended his life for what he had done.

V returned her attention to Judith. "You came seeking my help, so I assumed you were prepared to make a deal with a monster."

Judith ordered her men to stand down. The tension eased as they withdrew their hands from their weapons. Nabil stood perplexed, his eyes darting.

"Now that I think on it, the fact you sought my help instead of the Hiorians tells me all I need to know."

V looked around at the chevaliers, reading the doubt in their eyes. She didn't trust them and no longer desired to help in their crusade. At first she thought Judith might be a good ally—

but no longer.

"Forgive me for saying this, Nabil, but if you follow thy heart, it will lead to thy doom."

She made no effort to watch his reaction. Instead, her eyes fixed on the chained boy. She could drag him to Fodmery and kill him in front of Jiya. The thought made her realize she was falling into the path the soulseer had warned her of.

"If you are truly Jiya's son, and you survive all this, then I hope you choose a better path than he did."

With that, V turned away, deciding she would head to Fodmery now. But she would need a way to travel without exposure to the sun. She scanned the area for something of use.

"What are we going to do now?" Yama asked.

"I am going to continue to Fodmery. If you insist on coming, then I shan't hinder you. The lot of you are so headstrong."

A small giggle escaped Yama's lips. It gave V a measure of relief to know she still had laughter within her. V loved the girl's smile, though it carried deep sorrow.

The chief stepped closer to V. He hadn't spoken much to anyone in some time. Yama had been the only one he spoke to —back when she stormed from the tower.

"Forgive me, but will you still look into what happened to my daughter?"

V stared at him in shock. She had wanted to tell him about Raisa. She couldn't be certain, but who else could the girl be? She had to be his daughter.

This complicated everything, and V had neglected to tell him for that reason. She feared it would hinder her quest for revenge. Now she needed to decide what to say.

After a moment of reflection, she decided truth was the only way forward. She had nothing to lose by telling him. But he would be more determined than ever to reach Fodmery.

"I believe she still lives—and has been raised by Jiya," V confessed.

The chief stood motionless for a second. His chest expanded as he drew in a deep breath through his nostrils. He sighed and placed a hand on his head.

"So she still lives... I am glad."

V considered saying more but found no words that seemed right. Dharma placed a hand gently on the chief's arm, comforting him as he closed his eyes. They stood in silence while chevaliers around them muttered.

"Judith!" V called out, breaking the silence. "By any chance, would you have a carriage with no windows?"

Judith turned to her in disbelief. "Do you think I'd just give you something after you insulted me and refused to help?"

V turned fully toward her, her menacing aura rising. It caused everyone to reach for their weapons. As she approached, the chevaliers stepped in front of Judith.

"I could slay all of you here and think nothing of it. My request does you no harm," V said darkly.

She no longer cared to feign peace. After last night, she needed to end this war. Another would surely follow between the Wescreans and the Hiorians. But first, she would put an end to this one—and then deal with Jiya.

"Fine. There is a carriage near the stables. General Mathias here will make the proper accommodations."

Judith gestured to an older man with short, curly strawberry-blonde hair. He looked surprised, at first ready to argue, but quickly thought better of it.

"I will get right to it, my lady!" he exclaimed with a bow.

General Mathias marched toward the stables. As he passed V, Yama, and Odessa, he muttered under his breath. Thanks to her supernatural senses, V heard him clearly.

"Abominations, are we?" V called out.

He stopped mid-stride, armor rattling as he turned slightly. Fear was written across his face. V heard his heartbeat quicken.

"Calm yourself, general. I wouldn't want you to die of something trivial, like an attack of the heart," V taunted.

The man grabbed at his chest, then hurried his pace. V scoffed, noting the wary side glances from the other men.

"Ye are taking this character seriously," the chief whispered.

A brief smile tugged at V's lips, but it faded as she turned away. "The end is nigh. Once this is over, we will part ways—and I am afraid you will grow to hate me."

"I am with ye till the end," Yama muttered, following close behind.

CHAPTER 24

Jiya's treachery pt. 4

It was a long journey back to Fodmery. The travel had taken approximately six or seven long nights. Jiya had only allowed his people to rest during the day. They moved at night.

Judith would not have been the problem, but if Vlatka and Odessa had been with her, then he would have real trouble on his hands. Now he had found himself back in the city he had conquered five years ago.

Here, he held the greatest advantage.

If Vlatka came here with Judith, she would surely lose. He felt certain of it. The number of warriors at his disposal, as well as the revenants, was triple what he had taken with him to the keep.

As he trotted along the trail through the city, he looked over at Raisa riding on his right. Then he turned to his left to see Makena riding in silence, with Ashur a bit behind her.

When he returned his attention to Makena, he noticed the bags under her eyes. He grimaced, deciding he should speak to her. They had likely lost a son after all. Part of him still believed there could be a chance his son Badru survived.

Despite being only twelve years old, Badru had always displayed an incredible sense of survival. Jiya realized he had not spent much time with him. The only memory he could recall clearly had been about three years ago, when he took him hunting. Badru had gotten cornered by a prowler.

Jiya merely watched to see if he could handle himself. Badru managed to escape, but he did not kill the creature. That failure had slightly disappointed Jiya, but he had been intrigued by the way Badru tricked the beast into losing track of him.

"Badru still lives..." Jiya muttered.

He noticed Makena slowly turn her head toward him. She wore the look of someone who had already lost hope. He began to feel cruel for saying such a thing, but he needed her focused.

"Did da *Tome of Eneida* tell you dat?" she asked, sass in her tone.

Jiya's lips trembled as he fought the urge to say something cruel. He understood she needed to grieve, but he couldn't tolerate her disrespect much longer.

"My child is a survivor, so I know dat he would not have fallen so easily."

Makena huffed, her breath visible in the cold, then turned away. "If my boy lives, then he is out alone in dat cold valley— or he is their prisoner."

"Badru is smart, and I am certain he may still be alive..."

"*May* still be alive?" Makena questioned. "You just declared dat he still lives! Which is it?"

"Makena..."

She quickly fell silent and lowered her gaze, turning her head back toward the road. The horses huffed as they trekked along. As they passed buildings, Jiya saw citizens rushing about, carrying wood and food to their homes.

He had ensured that many people invested in preparing for the winter. Unlike the other places in Wescreas, Fodmery was ready. Lanterns illuminated the streets as people moved about.

"If there is a chance he lives... may I go and search for him?" Makena asked suddenly.

"No."

"Why not?"

"We need to ensure dat da people here are protected. A battle will likely be brought to us soon," Jiya emphasized.

"Could we at least ask Alora to see if she could track his soul wit her dowsin' practice?"

"Now is not da time for dat."

As they continued on, he saw a rider approaching on a black horse. The sound of a battle horn in the distance startled Jiya, and he looked around as citizens scattered in panic.

The rider drew near, revealing himself. Leon the vile sat on his mount, staring at Jiya with pale green eyes. His dull copper hair whipped in the wind, dusted with snow.

"Lord Jiya... it appears we are under attack. Seeing dat ya have returned from a long battle, I request ya rest and let me take care of this," Leon proposed.

Jiya looked at him in confusion. Leon was a revenant he had taken extra steps to create, specifically so he would be an exceptional warrior to lead the army protecting one of their strongholds. Jiya wondered why he was here, in the city.

"It has been a fortnight since I left. I suppose since you are here, I can entrust dis task to you. Although, I must know why you left your post."

Leon rubbed the back of his neck, an awkward grin spreading. "I received a summons to the capital while ya were away. It was about sightings of the rebel army."

Jiya stared at him suspiciously, sensing a lie. But why would anyone send for him when Jiya already had forces in the city capable of wiping out the rebels without Leon's help?

As the horn continued to echo, he dismissed the thought.

"See to it dat you bring me one of da elders—alive!"

Leon nodded and pulled his reins. "How will I know an elder?"

"Elders will have black or blue ink on their face when in battle."

Leon nodded again and moved aside to let Jiya's forces pass. Then he spurred his horse into the night, galloping until he disappeared around a corner.

"Ashur!"

"My lord?"

"Follow him. Keep a close eye on him. Do not engage in battle —just pay attention."

"As you wish..."

Ashur turned his horse and rode off the way they had come. Jiya looked over his shoulder, watching until he vanished around a corner.

"Leon likely paid a visit to da queen..." Makena muttered.

Jiya glanced at her with suspicion. Had he overlooked something? As quickly as the thought came, he forced it away. He continued on to the castle.

They were under attack, but he felt Leon could handle it—so long as the attacker wasn't Vlatka. Just in case, he needed to make preparations. The cold chill he had begun to feel since facing her returned.

A part of him felt excited to face her again. She had displayed incredible powers, ones that would truly challenge him. He wanted to grow stronger, to be ready in case other human countries learned of his actions in Wescreas.

It surprised him that the prince had not sought aid from neighboring nations. But now, the boy was no longer a problem. His sister, while no immediate threat, still had to be eliminated.

His council had advised him that removing the former king's heirs would be wise. With them gone, his children would hold the claim.

As he rode in silence, a faint smile crept across his face. He placed a hand on his head, almost laughing at himself.

When had he started thinking like these humans? It disgusted him. Heirs meant nothing. Kingship meant nothing.

Restoring his family—and forcing his people to fight for their right to live—was all that mattered.

*

Jiya finally arrived at the castle. Many of the Hiorian warriors were there. Before him stood a towering structure, its walls built from the finest stone, with archer posts on all sides. As he rode through the large gates, he saw some of the Hiorians working.

He assumed they were preparing for battle in case it reached the castle. Thankfully, he felt certain it wouldn't. They would be safe from any danger.

He dismounted, his boots landing on the crunchy snow. One

of the Hiorian warriors rushed over and took the reins of his horse.

With Raisa and Makena behind him, he marched toward the entrance of the large building—made of dark ore and constructed with imposing walls. He gently placed his hands on the stone doors and pushed them open. A whisk of warmth greeted him once the doors parted. Still, he felt the chill he couldn't shake.

It had become a chill like the substance that covered his hands. No matter how much he tried to rid himself of it, it remained. As he marched through the large hall with Raisa and Makena at his side, beautiful smiles greeted him.

His heart fluttered as a group of youth rushed toward him. Before him stood five of his children, clinging to him for dear life. A warm laugh erupted from him as their giggles soothed him.

Their ages ranged from fourteen down to two years old. The two-year-old, however, was nowhere to be seen, and he glanced around. She was a mischievous little girl he was always chasing after.

"Papa... Badru ran away," one of his daughters blurted suddenly.

Her teal-colored eyes looked up at him with shame. Jiya's laughter quickly faded. He straightened as he looked down at his children. The little girl before him had pointed ears and dark brown hair that nearly appeared black.

"I am aware of dat, Camelia," Jiya sighed.

"I tried to make him stay, Papa, but he would not listen," Camelia pouted.

As she crossed her arms, another of Jiya's daughters embraced her. Her name was Ramona, his eldest after Raisa. Her silvery eyes flicked with sadness toward Makena.

Jiya looked and saw Makena walking away. He moved to stop her but felt a hand grip him. He turned to see Raisa, disapproval in her gaze. Jiya bit his lip and let Makena go.

"Papa..."

"What is da matter, Camelia?"

As he looked down, he noticed her eyes were transfixed elsewhere—staring past him. A chill prickled his shoulder, making him shiver.

"What is dat... shadow?"

Jiya's eyes widened. He turned to see that unwanted face again—standing behind him, amused. Why were they here, and how could his daughter see them?

"What shadow, my child?" Jiya lied.

"She is probably tired, Papa... I will see to it dat she gets to bed," Raisa offered.

"No!" Camelia snapped.

The sudden response shocked Jiya, and he saw Raisa step back, hurt flashing in her eyes. By now it should have been normal. The only siblings she had a good relationship with were Roxana and his second daughter, Asha. Even his two-year-old often liked to follow Raisa.

"Why are you so mean to our sistah, Camelia?" Ramona complained as she moved away from her.

Camelia said nothing, only pouting. Jiya rested his hand on her head. "Stop bein' so childish and mean to her. She is family whether you like it or not."

Raisa walked down the hall. Jiya felt disheartened, though Ramona and Asha chased after her. Only three of his children remained before him: Camelia, his son Jira, and his youngest, Radhi.

Jira and Asha were twins, their mother from the Craft family, known for birthing twins often. As he looked at his son, Jiya thought of the man he killed years ago—if he remembered correctly, he too had been a twin.

His eyes then turned to his youngest boy, Radhi. His mother had been from the Caskthorne family—stubborn folk, which explained Radhi's behavior.

"Da three of you are such lil brats." Jiya bent closer to them.

He stuck his tongue out playfully. They mimicked him, and his laughter rang again. These were his salvation if he were to fall. As he laughed, holding his children, he glanced over his shoulder.

The apparition remained, turned away, walking down the hall. Another conversation with the soulseer was the last thing on his mind, but he suspected it had to be important.

"Camelia..."

"What is it, Papa?"

Her big green eyes gazed up at him. He cupped her brown cheeks in his hands. A smile formed on her face, showing the gap of a missing tooth.

"Find your mama and have her meet me in my study."

"Okay! Come on, Jira and Radhi."

Camelia grabbed her brothers and hurried off. A Hiorian guard watched them vanish around a corner. Jiya stood motionless for a moment before turning away in search of the apparition.

As he marched down the hall, he pulled off his cloak. A passing maid took it. Keeping it on only made him feel colder. Now, inside the castle, he felt slightly better.

The halls were crowded with revenants marching about. In the forge, the gray-skin Woeton awaited him. There, he would turn him into a revenant. For now, he had to discover why the apparition had returned.

He entered his study to find them by a bookshelf, their black cloak dissolving into smoke. The chill returned as Jiya shut the door. The air felt thin, and he tugged at his collar.

"How can she see you?" Jiya demanded.

"Did you forget dat you coerced one of your concubines to be my vessel?"

Jiya shuddered at the realization of what he had done. If he fell, he didn't want the soulseer near his children. Everything he had done needed to die with him. If the soulseer lingered with his family, it would ruin them.

"Dat woman needed no coercion to do anythin'. Now stay away from my children," Jiya warned.

Silence stretched. The apparition tilted their head. "Da one wit da eyes of a soulseer is just as much my child as yours."

Jiya's eyes widened in horror. What did this mean for Camelia? Would the soulseer control her for their bidding? Trembling, Jiya worried for his little girl.

"A full moon is comin'..."

Jiya eyed the soulseer warily as he crossed to his desk. He looked out the glass doors leading to the balcony. The sky was dark with a purple hue. Clouds hung thick, but a faint light glowed beyond them. Snow poured onto the city, stirring nostalgia. A full moon would soon rise.

"What of it?"

"It would seem symbolic, does it not?"

"What are you talkin' about?"

"Upon a night like dis, you created your enemy—the one you have finally come across. She now sets out to destroy dis city."

Jiya huffed through his nostrils. "If she makes it here, then I will kill her... again."

"Full moons are when da veil between dis world and da Spirit world be da weakest."

Jiya looked over at the apparition, who stared at him with their otherworldly eyes. "What does dat mean?"

"Spirits in dis world are stronger during a full moon. And spirits clawing at da veil from da other side have a better chance to slip through da cracks."

Their words unsettled him, and he didn't like what they were implying. Did they think Vlatka would beat him? That was impossible—he had an army of revenants and the tome that created weapons capable of vanquishing something like her.

"I do not care if she is stronger tomorrow night... I will defeat her."

"Whether you win or lose, da consequences dat will come are already far too great to prevent."

Jiya bit his lip as he wondered what would happen. The number of his people who had taken refuge in the settlement he was building had dwindled over the years. He understood he had to take the blame for that, but he felt the end would justify everything.

"There will be more war, but wit da sacred eight and my revenants I can make da humans submit and show respect to my people."

"Da weapons you call da sacred eight will lead everythin' to ruin. Your misguided actions will lead your people to ruin."

Jiya slammed his hand on the desk in frustration. "Why do you care? You are in dis world hidin' from somethin'! Not only dat, da tome feeds da souls to you!"

The apparition merely stared at the ancient book Jiya now held in his hand. They shook their head and looked toward the door. A knock startled Jiya, forcing him to recompose himself.

"Come in!" he ordered.

The handle turned, and the door creaked open to reveal a woman clad in black. Her long, luscious dark brown hair bounced as she stepped into the room.

Her eyes almost resembled those of the apparition—teal-colored, with sclera black as night. A veil of shadow seemed to cling to her. Jiya held his breath as he moved from around the table.

"Roxana..."

"You summoned me, my lord?" She bowed with a smile.

She looked at the apparition, and her smile faded. Jiya understood—she could see them because she was their vessel. The consequence of being the soulseer's vessel was that they used her to regain power. In return, they prolonged her life and allowed her to wield the power they drew by living within her.

Jiya examined her as he approached, his eyes on her high cheekbones. He gently caressed her face, rubbing his thumb against her heart-shaped lips. Her skin was soft and warm.

"I must portend dat da end is nigh," Jiya said with a nervous smile.

"Mayhaps you care to explain?"

"I bear da tidins of Vlatka Dracul's return from da other side."

Roxana's eyes gleamed with excitement. "She thirsts for vengeance!"

"She did not come back as a vampyr..."

"'Tis to be expected..."

"What?"

"Stefan Constantin created the acolytes. He caroused on the blood of bats and bathed in it. No one truly knows how he became what he did. 'Tis believed to be a curse."

Jiya stared at Roxana, confused, then glanced at the apparition. "How have more vampyrs appeared over the years?"

"Stefan's bite is said to be a curse. Anyone who survives da bite is benighted and becomes like him."

Jiya stroked his chin in thought. Then what had been the ritual Roxana made those people undergo? It had led to her and the rest being punished by their higher command. Had he not intervened, she would have been executed.

"I am lost—for I do not understand what you did to Vlatka..."

Roxana's eyes shifted away. "A voice called to me..."

Jiya stared at her in disbelief before slowly turning his gaze on the apparition. "You are a snake..." he hissed.

"It amuses me dat you think I am to blame."

"Who else would it be but you? I have not encountered any other soulseers! And from what you told me, soulseers are da only beings dat can change da form of a soul."

"There are ancient and vile spirits—beasts dat feed on other spirits and da souls of da living. Though a few are capable of a higher form of thinkin'."

"You are a liar..."

"I may not tell da whole truth, but I am far from a liar."

Jiya clicked his tongue and looked away. He didn't know what to believe. Clearly, higher forces had been at play, leading Roxana to attempt an unknown ritual. She had no idea what it would do and foolishly followed a voice. A voice that made her a fool.

"I displeased you... forgive me."

Roxana knelt before Jiya. He stared down at her in silence.

Unlike his other concubines, she had proven the most loyal. Yet he didn't know if she was loyal because she loved him—or because he offered her power.

"You did nothin' to vex me, but we must prepare. Vlatka's wrath will be upon us."

Jiya turned away and looked out the window. The chill gripped him once more, making him shiver as he wondered what the coming nights would bring.

CHAPTER 25

Almost a week had passed since leaving Judith's keep. V expected Judith to be on the move by now. Her reasoning for going on ahead had been to cross paths with the Hiorians. Currently, V and her group were resting on a hill. From here they could see the city of Fodmery.

The city had been built by a large river that led out toward the Dark Sea. It was surrounded by hills and trees, now covered in a sheet of white. Overhead, the purple sky cast down specks of white, with a full moon looming over the city.

A marvelous sight—but also a disheartening one. The irony was that everything had come full circle. Her heartbreak and anger had begun on a winter's full moon. Now she would claim vengeance on a night similar to that. Then again, if she failed here, it would only mean she had died again on a night much like the one when she lost everything.

V continued to look on at the sight before her. Trails led in many different directions. Two watchtowers were erected to spot enemies. The rooftops of the buildings were covered in ice, and faint fog filled the air. It felt like the perfect time to gain revenge—almost a poetic reminder of what happened years ago.

V stood in the moonlight, staring down at the city. White flakes showered her as she took a moment to bask in it. Not far from one of the watchtowers she saw what looked like a battlefield. Instead of white, the ground was covered in splotches of red.

Bodies were scattered everywhere. From what she could tell, it was a mixture of chevaliers and Hiorians. Among them she noticed chevaliers in the attire of Judith's men. V assumed this had been a group her brother commanded. They had already reached Fodmery—and had lost a great many warriors.

As V stared silently, Odessa stepped beside her and looked up at the moon. "Dis will be da final voyage, I suppose."

V glanced at her with adoration, pulled her close, and gently hugged her. Tonight would be the night to end things—and the night Odessa could finally rest.

"I hath enjoyed every minute with you," V said sincerely.

She looked at the sword she had taken from Judith's keep. It was well made, but she feared it would not hold up against Jiya's supernatural weapon. For now, all she could do was hope to get close before he could swing it.

She turned toward the gray-skins, who were resting under a large tree. The three wolves that had followed them since the village lay asleep.

The tree itself drew V's attention. Its placement seemed odd —no other trees grew nearby, and it stood alone, tall and large.

V walked toward them with a serious look on her face. She could feel something off. She sensed powerful things lurking in the city, and she didn't want the gray-skins near when they came after her. Still, she knew they were stubborn. No matter what she said, they would not leave.

"I fear henceforth shall be where we must part ways."

Dharma stood and stepped in front of V. Her towering frame was not intimidating in the least. "I will find Woeton's body and bring him home."

V stared up at her for a second, then placed her palm against her chest. With a gentle thrust, Dharma was knocked back and slid across the ground.

"You would die with ease if I were thy enemy. Now imagine an enemy with an army of people with power like that. The Hiorians are not present—you will not hath any help in battle."

Dharma remained on the ground, breathing heavily, staring at V in disbelief. The chief stood to his feet, determination radiating from him.

"Dharma... go home, please. Tell Thora that I am sorry," the chief ordered.

Dharma looked at him in disbelief. Then she shook her head and stepped closer. "I chose to follow ye, so I will do it until the end."

"Ye will die—and maybe end up like Woeton," the chief chided.

Dharma was silent for a moment. "Yama."

Yama had been staring into the distance, hugging herself to keep warm. She turned her head toward Dharma. V wondered what she would say, as the two hadn't spoken much since their argument.

"Mayhaps I have been unfair to ye..." Dharma began. Slowly, she walked toward her, holding her brother's spear and her own weapon. "I grew angry with ye for the loss of my brother, but I know ye never meant him harm."

Dharma held out the spear. Yama looked at it in confusion. V felt relief—perhaps their relationship could mend.

"Why do ye give me this?"

"He loved ye—as strange as it may sound. I also love ye, for we are family. Forgive me for not acting as such." Dharma's raspy voice cracked as tears welled in her eyes.

V stood in silence, relieved. All she wanted was for Yama to live. For that to happen, her people needed to atone for their past mistakes. This was only a beginning, but it was a start.

"Yama, ye know well that everyone honors what the chief says. I am to blame for thy suffering. Forgive Dharma and the others, please."

Yama stepped closer, fire in her eyes. "I was imprisoned at times so I could not run. 'Tis hard to forgive."

V stiffened at the words. She had never heard this before. The idea that they had imprisoned her so she could not escape enraged her. No wonder Yama carried such frustration.

This wound would linger. Yama still bore the pain of losing her family—and the trauma of being made a prisoner.

The chief, once possessed by a spirit, had his mind clouded. Even so, he accepted his faults and sought atonement. But no atonement could erase unjust deaths—or the imprisonment of an innocent child.

"I understand thy frustrations. Still, I alone should carry the byrden of our people," the chief said.

His words would not reach Yama. Which meant she likely would not return to the village once this was over. V didn't want that for her, but she hoped Yama might change her mind in time.

Dharma still held the spear out. "I understand if ye doth not forgive me. I just want ye to know I doth not blame ye for Yonten."

Yama stood in silence, staring at the spear. Hesitantly, she took it, tears streaming down her face. Her teeth rattled— whether from the cold or her sobbing, V could not tell. The breeze felt colder now.

"If ye all are going down there to search for something, then get yourselves together," V ordered.

The gray-skins turned their attention back to her. She needed to get into the city, but it was heavily guarded. Fighting outside the walls would cost her too much time.

"We need to find out if the Hiorians are still around here," V explained.

The gray-skins exchanged glances, then looked back at her and nodded. Relief washed over V.

"Scout the area and see if you can pick up on a trail—but be careful," V ordered.

She turned away, looking for Odessa. Her comrade remained at the edge of the hill, gazing at the scene below. V joined her, peering down. The bodies of Hiorians lay scattered once more.

She heard voices. A small fleet of horsemen and chevaliers moved across the battlefield, stabbing fallen Hiorians to ensure they were dead.

At the rear, a chevalier on a black horse followed. V recognized his spiritual aura—Leon again. This time, his face was visible. From what she could tell, he was handsome, though a scar marred his features.

His long mane of copper hair flowed in the wind. His dead green eyes scanned the battlefield, searching. As V watched, she noticed Odessa inching forward.

Glancing back, she saw the gray-skins had moved, likely tracking the Hiorians. If they fought now, the city would be alerted. Still, she felt confident she could cause great damage alone.

Before she could speak, Odessa leapt. She soared through the air, a fall that would kill a normal person. V watched as the Hiorian landed gracefully near a horseman. In a blur, she cut him down and vanished before the others noticed.

The horse bolted in panic, sending the men into confusion. Odessa cloaked herself in shadows. The chevaliers waved their torches, unable to spot her.

"Arm ya'selves, for we have visitors!" Leon ordered.

V scoffed as she descended, the breeze caressing her skin. Instead of landing, she hovered in the air. The warriors and their horses startled. Her eyes locked on Leon.

A huge smile spread across his face as he unsheathed his sword—a finer blade than those of his men. V admired it, already thinking to claim it as a trophy.

"So, we meet again, mon cher!" Leon shouted.

As V floated toward him, the sound of a horn cut through the air. The rest of the forces had been alerted for battle. In that moment, V knew they would be in for a long night. She wanted to rid Jiya of the majority of his forces before sunrise.

The horsemen rushed toward her, but Odessa moved swiftly. Her blades cut through their armor with ease. Blood paved the ground as V continued toward Leon. He dismounted his horse, preparing for battle.

"I thought I'd never see ya again after not finding ya at Skyreach Tower!" he said with excitement.

V never got used to how fast Wescreans tended to speak. She always thought their language annoying—sometimes they said so much that if you didn't listen closely, you missed everything.

Leon marched toward V, excitement gleaming in his eyes. From what she could tell, he had been in his thirties when he died. She knew nothing of him but expected much from someone with the title he carried.

The cries of his men as they fell to Odessa filled the background. V stood before Leon, power flowing through her. She would not allow a repeat of the first time they met.

In the blink of an eye, she swung her sword. Leon parried but looked surprised. She struck again, bringing her blade down hard. Leon blocked, but the force behind her strike made the ground beneath him give way.

He gritted his teeth, eyes widening. V roared and swung again, and Leon met her rageful strike with his own. Their weapons clashed, spiritual energy surging. A gust of wind reverberated through the air.

"I am gobsmacked! Ya are much different from the last time we met!" Leon growled.

V pushed him back with great force. He stumbled but held his ground. Lunging forward, she evaded his blade and seized him by the neck. She knew he couldn't feel pain, but that didn't matter.

With a single bound, she carried him high into the air. For a brief moment, they hovered above the carnage below. Then they plummeted. V slammed Leon into the ground, debris and rubble scattering everywhere.

She stomped on his sword hand, keeping him from fighting back. He stared in disbelief as she raised her sword, spiritual energy channeling into the blade. Disappointment filled her gaze.

"I thought you'd be much more doughty than this."

He scoffed and jutted out his chin, exposing his neck further. This man had accepted defeat. She had hoped he would beg for mercy or at least put up more of a fight.

Before she could deliver the final blow, something whizzed through the air. A flaming arrow struck her, setting her clothes ablaze. She staggered back in surprise.

More arrows struck, making her wince, though the flames did not burn her flesh—only her garments. In the distraction, Leon scrambled to his feet.

He stared at her as her clothes burned. With a swing of his blade, a gust of wind blew away the flames—but also cut into her. Black blood seeped from the wound.

"Clearly, the flames don't burn ya. But I have no interest in fighting a naked woman."

V frowned, confused by his words. Why would he care if her clothes burned away? He'd have the advantage if she felt embarrassed.

"You are not living up to the title of being vile," she joked.

He laughed as he raised his sword. V steadied hers, prepared to end it. Arrows rained down, and Odessa moved through the battlefield with impossible speed, cutting down the fodder in their path.

V knew she had to finish Leon quickly. She remembered Jorah and his sister's lessons—battles didn't always last long. One wrong step or a faster blade could end it in an instant.

She lowered herself, preparing to strike. The sounds around her muffled. Time seemed to stand still as she gripped her hilt tight, feet digging into the ground before she lunged.

Excitement surged through her as she rushed Leon. He charged too, crying out. The clash of steel echoed as they dashed past one another. V froze as something wet trickled down her stomach.

She looked over her shoulder. Leon lay stiff on the ground—his head had rolled a few feet away. He was defeated, but she had not emerged unscathed.

V walked over and picked up his sword. Traces of his spirit still lingered. Blue flames ignited in her hand as she knelt beside him. Believing this would keep him from returning, she set the ground ablaze, engulfing Leon and the other corpses in supernatural fire.

When she looked around, no one was left standing. The warriors from the watchtowers were dead. Odessa stood alone, surrounded by bodies, drenched in blood, fury etched in her eyes.

More chevaliers—and revenants—surely waited deeper in the city. V longed to press on, but her wound throbbed. She remembered that revenant wounds were toxic to the spirit.

A bellow of laughter erupted from her as she collapsed, staring up at the sky. Blue fire filled the night, painting the sky. Her gaze locked on the moon as she pondered what would happen next. Part of her hoped Judith would bring her forces, so she and Odessa could focus on Jiya.

The crunch of boots on dirt reached her ears. Odessa stood over her, eyes filled with nothing but rage.

"You are hurt, yet you are laughin'. Why?"

V looked at her for a moment before smiling softly. "We are so close to ending this nightmare, dear."

Odessa glanced around before sitting beside her. Things would change after all this—V had no idea what the future held for the Hiorians or the gray-skins. She only knew the people of Wescreas would never welcome them.

"I guess we should rest for a moment before movin' forward," Odessa said.

"I agree. Taking the enemy head on would waste too much time."

V knew she needed to replenish her strength before doing anything else. The smell of blood was everywhere. She decided she would drink from the recently dead. It wouldn't be as good as the living, but freshly spilled blood would still do.

*

About an hour passed before the Hiorians' camp was found. The gray-skins were the first to greet them, while V and Odessa remained in the shadows. Among them were chevaliers wearing the cloaks sworn to Judith.

She saw many of them wounded, their spirits in the pits of despair. They had clearly been defeated—emotionally and physically. V watched as the chief spoke with Odessa's mother.

As she listened, she couldn't help but wonder where Nakia was.

She had been sitting in the shadows for twenty minutes, scanning the camp, but could not find him. Had he been killed in battle? She hadn't seen his body on the battlefield they had just crossed. The thought concerned her greatly.

V noticed Yama spending time with Jawara. She seemed happier when she spoke with him, which gave V some relief —at least Yama still had the heart to open up to someone. Dharma sat alone beneath a tree, crafting arrows for battle.

The chief, Neliah, and a chevalier made their way to the edge of the camp. V and Odessa waited patiently for them to approach. When they were close enough, V emerged from the shadows. Odessa, however, remained hidden, seemingly avoiding her mother.

"Neliah..." V greeted the Hiorian with a serious tone.

"I see you are still quite... cursed," Neliah taunted.

V scoffed, a faint smile tugging at her lips. "Where is your wondrous brother, Neliah?"

A look of despair crossed the Hiorian's face. She inhaled deeply as her eyes welled with tears. Before they could fall, she sniffled and wiped her face.

"He and a few others were taken captive when they infiltrated da castle. I fear they have been executed—or made into revenants."

V stood silently as she absorbed the information. She hadn't liked Gamba much, but he was a Hiorian with good intentions for his people. She respected him for that, so hearing this stung.

"What is your plan now?" V asked.

"We are not certain. Our numbers are diminished. We may go back to our settlement and hope he does not come to destroy it," Neliah confessed.

V felt disappointed they were giving up—but she couldn't deny she understood. They had lost many of their people, and if they continued fighting, they'd be wiped out completely.

"Do you think there is a faster way to the castle?" V asked.

Neliah considered. "If you can fly like da vampyrs, then maybe. We tried sneakin' through some secret passages, but failed."

V clicked her tongue, pondering the proper course of action. Without another word, she turned away.

The chevalier stepped forward and bowed. "Pardon my intrusion, but I am Captain Raynard. I served under Prince Jacques. I take it ya are the mysterious V Lady Neliah has spoken so much about."

He extended his hand toward V. She only stared at it silently until he lowered it. He looked about thirty years old. V sensed honor in him. His eyes did not show defeat, but what she thought to be hope.

"'Tis a pleasure to meet you, Captain. I reckon the prince has truly been slain?"

Captain Raynard fell silent, a grim look on his face. "He was wounded in battle and taken some time ago. Our scouts have been unable to learn his fate."

"That is unfortunate."

"Despite that, I know the princess still lives without a doubt. Which is why, if ya plan to attack Jiya at the castle, we will try to assist you."

V studied him in silence, a finger resting on her chin. She knew if they marched into the city without a plan, his men would die. They needed a way in with minimal loss. At last, she nodded and turned away.

"Gather thy men—but be forewarned: if you choose to follow me, stay out of my way."

"Understood!" Captain Raynard bowed before marching off, calling to what was left of his men.

"What are you goin' to do?" Neliah asked.

"I am going to slay Jiya," V said menacingly.

"Take care of my child."

V glanced back with disappointment. "She is right here, if you wish to speak with her."

Neliah stood frozen, silent. What did she have to consider?

This was her daughter, yet she acted as if she didn't want to speak. Instead, she bowed her head and turned away.

V watched her leave, then walked to where Odessa sat. The young Hiorian's sadness was plain, no matter how she tried to hide it. V knelt before her and cupped her face. Odessa looked at her, confused.

"Forgive me for placing this curse on you."

V leaned forward and pressed her lips to Odessa's forehead. She had adopted Odessa as her own. That meant she was responsible for her until the very end. Odessa, still confused, wrapped her arms around V and hugged her.

If Odessa's mother would not speak to her, then V would. She would not go into the final battle without saying what she needed to say.

As the two embraced, Yama and Jawara approached. V looked at them with approval. Jawara was tall and handsome, though he didn't resemble his father much. His braids were covered by a cloth wrapped around his head. His gentle eyes were fixed on his cousin.

"I feared I would not see you again."

Jawara knelt beside Odessa. She lowered her head in shame. V watched his face shift to confusion before he took her hand. Odessa looked at him nervously as they sat in silence for a moment.

"I know my pa has been hard on you for what you've become. But you are still my family, and I know dat you are a kind soul. I... want you to remember that."

Odessa placed her hand on his face, then glanced at Yama. V still didn't understand how Odessa couldn't understand Yama, but Jawara could. Perhaps his father had spent much time learning and teaching the Vostaylian tongue.

"Let's get going, Odessa. The night is still young, and I want to finish this."

V felt guilty breaking the moment, but they had no time to waste. She believed Judith would arrive soon, and she wanted to thin the enemy first.

It would also give her time to decide how to deal with Judith. A part of her feared that if Judith claimed the throne, she would order harm on the Hiorians. With this in mind, V considered making her another enemy.

"Yama, I want you to stay with Jawara and his people. Make sure they return home safely," V requested.

Yama looked conflicted. V understood—the girl wanted to continue with her, but her heart clearly leaned toward the young grey skin.

"Forgive me, but I wish to accompany you," Jawara interrupted.

Everyone looked at him in shock. None of them had expected this. Odessa jumped up and grabbed her cousin, shaking her head.

"We are goin' to do horrible tings, and I do not wish you to be part of dat!" she exclaimed. "Besides, you are a lover of peace, not violence. I could not live with myself if I exposed you to..."

"How could I continue to love peace when my people are sufferin' and my pa is gone?" Jawara asked.

Odessa stared, conflicted. She clearly didn't want him risking his life. V didn't want him to come either—she felt it would dishonor his father. Unlike Nakia, she had quickly grown to like Jawara.

"Keep your eyes on your destiny, and I will be behind you followin' mine," he said confidently.

"You may come with us, but I will not be responsible for you. Do not die!" V ordered.

Jawara nodded and bowed gratefully. As V turned to walk into the shadows, she froze. Memories surged—horrors from her past. Her hands trembled as she recalled the atrocities she had committed.

She turned to the ones about to follow her. How could she lead them while carrying such dark secrets? With the end near, she felt she had to confess.

"Before you follow me into what could be the end of us all, I must confess my past transgressions—all the horrible misdeeds I have done..."

Odessa grabbed V's arms, startling her. Their eyes locked, Odessa's filled with hope.

"Whatever you have done is not important."

"But you do not know what—"

"I do not care!" Odessa exclaimed. "None of us were there. You have shown regret and remorse. Why punish yourself more by tryin' to make us question our desire to follow you?"

V wanted Odessa to know what she had done when she was first turned. It wouldn't absolve her—it would only make the world hate her. And that, perhaps, would make it easier to accept what she had become.

"Now let us go and put an end to Jiya's madness."

Odessa's words rang with life. For days V had worried the spirited young Hiorian she met was gone. But a trace of her still remained.

V nodded, turned, and followed Odessa.

CHAPTER 26

Jiya's treachery pt. 4

The sound of water bubbling echoed through the air. Inside a large room, a furnace howled as coal burned within. In this room were tables with tools and materials collected from the wilderness. These items were used to create weapons for Jiya's army.

Things like silver, salt, and iron were all found on a table. Jiya stood silently with the *Tome of Eneida* floating in the air. Its pages flipped as ripples spiraled around him. Faint whispers of the souls the book had absorbed filled the room.

Before him stood a large container filled with water. At the bottom lay the corpse of a man. He didn't always have to create revenants this way, but he took these measures when he wanted to make one powerful. He had done this with Leon.

Leon had done well protecting the city from the rebel army that tried to infiltrate the castle and breach the walls. A part of Jiya felt shame because he had heard that many of his people had been slain.

Now he heard they were under attack again. That meant Vlatka or Judith had reached the city. With this in mind, he wanted to prepare in case the rebel army tried to use the secret passages to enter the castle again.

A part of him had considered letting the man in the container live—especially since he could have given Raisa answers about her identity and her origins. But it was too late to go back. Jiya had to press onward. A war needed to be won, and he needed all the support he could muster.

"I sense you are afraid..." a voice said from behind Jiya.

He looked over his shoulder to see that wretched face again.

The shade cloaked in black, wearing the face of a dead man, stared at him. Jiya loathed being reminded constantly of killing that poor soul. Truthfully, a part of him regretted it.

The man had been honorable, but the face Jiya now saw was that of the one who had driven his daughter to suicide. Jiya had tried to reach her on the other side. His people had learned the dangers of communing with the dead, but also the closure it could bring to speak with a loved one again.

For him, there was no closure. Every time he reached through the veil, his daughter never answered. He just wanted to know why she had taken her life. Could her silence have been her way of punishing him? Even now, every attempt went unanswered.

"I wish dat you could bear another face..." Jiya muttered.

"What you see is up to you, not me. I have no strength to take a true form yet," the apparition replied.

"How are you here if Roxana is your vessel?"

"My true self rests in her. What you see before you is a part of me dat I left behind in da tome you carry."

Jiya grumbled and turned back to his work. As he did, that same chill gripped him—the same one he had felt since leaving the keep. A week had passed, but the chills hadn't gone away. He then noticed his right hand trembling.

"It is alright to admit dat you are afraid."

"I cannot lose here. I must end tings here so dat I can finally face Sorin."

"You did all dis just to build the courage to face a human? I thought humans were beneath you—yet you fled his country despite havin' da chance to kill him," the apparition said condescendingly.

"His daughta discovered my plan and got in my way. I only allowed him to live for her sake," Jiya confessed.

"Ah... Anastasia Dracul. Curious, what happened to her..."

Jiya flinched at the chilling words. He didn't like humans, but that young girl had been good-hearted. It was the reason he had spared Sorin. He had also noticed how poorly Sorin treated his daughter. He neglected her, and there had been disgust in his eyes.

The fact she still chose to protect him had made Jiya hesitate in his revenge. Now this being implied something else—something that unsettled him. Did something happen to Anastasia? By now, she would be a young woman—if nothing had happened to her.

"What are you tryin' to say?"

"I presumed Roxana would have told you. You did have her keepin' watch in Vostaylia, no?"

"I have had enough of you tryin' to twist my mind!" Jiya barked.

The apparition raised their hands in mock surrender. "I only feel it wise dat you know da consequences dat may yet come."

Jiya blinked several times, troubled. What had Roxana done to Anastasia? Had she killed her to prevent her from interfering the next time he went after Sorin? The only way to know would be to ask her. It would gnaw at him otherwise.

He turned back to the large container. The water glowed green as Woeton's eyes opened. No longer light blue, they were now a dull greenish color. Woeton sat up, confusion on his face.

A twisted smile crept across Jiya's lips. "It is a pleasure to see dat you have returned to da world of da livin'."

Woeton stared at his hands, now covered in a dusty residue common to revenants. Their skin always turned paler too.

"I hath been benighted... ye will rue da day I get da chance to slay ye!"

His eyes burned with fury, which amused Jiya. He recalled how Leon had made a similar proclamation—yet Leon had returned to the dirt, his soul now at rest.

"Your yearning for vengeance shall go unfulfilled. I will not be slain by you," Jiya mocked, imitating Woeton's tongue.

He laughed and turned away, marching toward the forge doors. He needed to return to the castle to prepare for battle. As he neared, the doors suddenly swung open. He stepped back as cold air lashed his face.

Jiya shielded himself, squinting to see who entered. Roxana stood there, concern on her face. He gestured for her to shut the doors.

"Pardon me, but I hath come with terrible news..." Roxana's voice was nervous.

"What is it?"

"I have just received word that Leon has been slain in battle —along with a large portion of thy revenant forces."

"Da time for da final battle is upon us. Have da members of da Sacred Eight meet in the war room," Jiya ordered.

"Shall I summon Raisa?" Roxana asked.

"Aye! I must speak wit her as well. A plan to escort da children to safety must be made."

"'Tis safer for them to remain in the castle. Vlatka will not reach thee—or our family," Roxana said with confidence.

"I do not wish for da lil ones to be exposed to more of dis battle," Jiya commanded.

"What of the queen?"

"What about her?"

Roxana hesitated. "She is bedridden—she will likely conceive within the hour."

Jiya stared at her in silence. He had claimed the former king's queen, Genevieve. He knew she had only offered herself to protect her children and her life. She had insisted that marrying her after defeating the king would help legitimize his succession.

They shared a two-year-old daughter. Now she would bring another child into the Ashspell bloodline. His family was slowly being restored. But first, he had to ensure their safety.

"Fine. Ensure dat she is well guarded," Jiya finally said.

Roxana looked concerned but finally nodded her head. "What of the rest of thy concubines?"

Jiya raised an eyebrow as he stared at her. She lowered her head, hiding those accursed teal-colored eyes of hers. He valued her loyalty, but he often wondered if she stood by his side only because of the power he had gained. Did she truly believe in him and his cause?

He then looked at the apparition, who remained next to the container where Woeton sat. Jiya began to wonder if the soulseer had used Roxana as a pawn. The woman had been overtly loyal, doing everything he asked of her.

She had left her family to follow him, even becoming a vessel for the soulseer to regain power. If she hadn't agreed, then Jiya himself would have become the vessel in order to gain access to the *Tome of Eneida.* Her loyalty—or obsession with him —seemed to know no bounds.

"Da children still need to be nurtured, so Zahina and Ramla will leave the castle wit them. You, on da other hand, must remain at my side," Jiya said in a honeyed tone.

Roxana's cheeks flushed redder than they already were. Her eyes shifted away as she grew flustered. Jiya glimpsed the ring on her finger. It had been crafted from silver and iron, with a jade-colored gem embedded in it.

It was the first weapon he had created. The ring could manipulate the spiritual energy within the land. That meant its wielder could bend the land to their will—or drain the life force within it to heal wounds.

"I shall ascertain this... vampire that Vlatka Dracul hath become be vanquished," Roxana vowed.

Jiya stared at her, perplexed. He had never heard the word *vampire* before. As he thought it over, he decided he liked the name. Vlatka had a similar thirst for blood as the vampyrs, yet she was also something far different.

"What does dis word *vampire* mean?"

Roxana paused. "To be restored by the pyre."

Jiya smiled, amused, before his expression darkened. "I like dis name. Now, before I send you away... I must ask you somethin'."

Roxana's eyes widened, what he assumed to be excitement flickering in them. But what weighed on his mind would erase it quickly. If he didn't like her answer, he would likely kill her where she stood.

"What happened to Ana?"

Roxana's excitement faded. She tilted her head slightly, confused. "Forgive me, for I doth not know anyone by that name."

"Anastasia Dracul... da daughta of Sorin."

A look of horror spread across her face as realization dawned. She quickly dropped to her knees, bowing her head at Jiya's feet.

"Forgive me! You conspired to slay Sorin, so I whisked her away. I had hoped to harbor her from the bloodshed." Roxana began to cry.

"So she is alive and well..."

"I doth not know!" Roxana cried.

"What?" Jiya roared, his voice rising.

"When I returned to the place I had taken her, she had disappeared." Roxana's voice trembled as she remained bowed on the ground.

Jiya grew furious and kicked her down. She cried out in pain as she scrambled away. "Da fact you hid dis from me disappoints me and angers me!"

"Forgive me, my love!" she sobbed.

"You do not love me!" he shouted.

Roxana remained on the floor, eyes wide, tears streaming, her mouth ajar. She was speechless. Jiya noticed the apparition now standing behind her. When had they moved there? That chill crawled up his body again.

"We will discuss dis at another time. For now, gather da Sacred Eight and station them at their posts in da city."

Roxana staggered to her feet and dusted herself off. "As you wish."

"Do not worry about Raisa. I will speak wit her myself. Now leave my sight." Jiya waved her away.

She looked conflicted as she backed toward the door, her eyes fixed on him. Finally, she turned, pulled the doors open, and once again the cold wind rushed in. She strode out into the snow, back toward the castle.

Jiya stood silently, alone, watching the doors close. The apparition remained by the door, staring at him. Then Woeton's tall frame appeared beside him.

"I declaim what I said earlier. Ye will be slain by thine own people. 'Tis a more fitting end for the likes of thee," Woeton said coldly.

Jiya scoffed and turned away. He had no reason to heed the words of a man who had become his slave. He slowly raised his hand, and the *Tome of Eneida* appeared before him. Pages flipped as ripples of green light flowed around him and Woeton.

"Maybe it would have been wise to sew your mouth shut," Jiya retorted.

He waved Woeton off and walked away. Preparing for battle and ensuring his family's safety were now his priorities. He could not lose to Vlatka. She, and Judith as well, had to be defeated.

Once he destroyed the kingdom of Wescreas, he would finally set out to kill Sorin. His people would claim the land of Wescreas for themselves. Then he would leave—and at last claim his revenge on the man who had slaughtered his family.

*

It took a few minutes to reach the war room within the castle. On his way there he spoke with some of the chevaliers roaming about, ordering them to prepare for battle. Some of the Hiorians were sent to the different passageway entry points in preparation for an attack from within the castle.

The revenants he had left were stationed to guard the wall as well as the courtyard. He had to fortify the castle to ensure that he didn't lose. As he walked down the long and wide hall, he began to think. The queen's current condition concerned him.

She had gone into labor, and he wanted to be present for the birth of his child. He had failed to do this a few times before. He had no desire to risk losing any of his children—they were meant to ensure his family lived on. The Ashspell family had been the ones to spend time understanding the Spirit World thanks to his late father.

Jiya now stood outside a large set of doors trimmed in gold. The handles bore the likeness of a feline creature carved from the same metal. He took a deep breath and pushed the doors open.

Inside, he was greeted by a large room. On either side stood statues of humans he didn't care to know. Along the walls hung paintings of what he assumed were members of the Jacquard family's royal line.

In the middle of the room stood a large table. Around it were a group of people with weapons in hand. Two were bickering until they noticed his arrival. They stood at attention, then kneeled as he approached.

Among this group were Raisa and Roxana. The other four had their faces covered, their cloaks concealing their features. Roxana had helped him choose these individuals.

Two of them were Hiorians, one was Vostaylian, and the other had been a foreigner Roxana had taken under her wing. That made him question whether the foreigner was loyal to him or to Roxana—something that often concerned him about them holding such dangerous power. But he had known the risks when selecting who could inherit such powerful tools.

"Da war has been brought to us, so now we must fight!" Jiya exclaimed.

The four warriors before him cheered with determination. Raisa and Roxana, however, were silent. Jiya had no plans of sending Raisa to the front lines. He would give everyone a specific task.

"I summoned all of you because we must divide and conquer! I forged the weapons with the blood and bones of the fallen. Their strength is yours!"

"What are our orders, Lord Jiya?" one of the masked warriors asked.

Jiya looked at her and examined the weapon in her hand. The shaft was iron, wrapped in cloth, and the blade was made from silver. He called this weapon *Fulgur.*

He believed that if she went to face Vlatka, she could win with it. The javelin carried destructive power, resembling a lightning bolt when thrown. Few knew this, but the weapon's power came from a spirit bird. If V were struck, she'd die instantly—of this he felt certain.

"There is somethin' dat Roxana calls a vampire on her way to slay me. Her name is Vlatka Dracul, and I want you and..." Jiya paused.

His gaze rested on a tall masked man wearing silver gauntlets. A devious smile spread across Jiya's face as he raised his hand and pointed at him. "You will accompany her as support. Da two of you will slay Vlatka for me," Jiya ordered.

The two glanced at each other before nodding in agreement. They bowed toward Jiya, concluding his orders. Now he had to consider where else protection was most needed.

There were many warriors patrolling the city. Anyone coming through the gates would surely be defeated. With this in mind, he knew not all of them were needed here.

His attention shifted to the other masked woman standing beside Raisa. She held a sword crafted to resemble the blades of her homeland. It possessed spiritual power that could both burn and heal.

"I want you to lead our warriors in da fight to keep da enemy out of da castle!" Jiya ordered.

The masked woman bowed silently. She rarely spoke, and Jiya knew little about her. He had seen her face a few times— behind the mask was a foreigner. Wescreans and Vostaylians were the only groups he was truly familiar with. All he knew was that Roxana had saved her.

Then he turned to the spearman. The weapon radiated spiritual energy that carried the touch of death. Anyone struck would freeze.

"Retrieve Zahina and Ramla. Take them and da children to Slyburn Stronghold."

The spearman bowed, hand over his chest. It may have been

wiser to keep him within the castle walls to aid in the defense, but Jiya knew his bloodline had to be safeguarded above all else.

"Raisa..." Jiya said, turning to his adopted daughter.

Raisa straightened, eyes fixed ahead. "What would you like for me to do, Papa?"

He wanted to send her away, but something told him she should stay. Not to fight, but because most of the other children wouldn't want her near them. At his side she seemed happiest, and he wanted to acknowledge her feelings.

"You will lead the men within the castle in case these walls are breached."

Relief spread across Raisa's face. "Thank you for not sending me away, Papa."

Jiya nodded approvingly. Then Roxana stepped forward. Their gazes met briefly before she knelt before him. As she did, Jiya noticed the mischievous soulseer lurking again.

"What will I do?" Roxana asked nervously.

Jiya stroked his chin in thought. "Take those two to find Vlatka. Once they begin to fight her, you will return to me."

"Thy wish is my command," she said, though her tone carried weak determination.

"Good. Now I must go and tend to da queen—she is about to bear another Ashspell."

Jiya turned and marched back the way he had come. That cold chill once again crept over him, tugging at the collar of his cloak. No matter how warm the maids kept the castle, it never left him.

CHAPTER 27

The moonlight's gaze shined bright in the night sky. Snow fell harder now as the wind picked up. The moon illuminated the land in a way that made the sight beautiful. Unfortunately, the beauty was tarnished by the smell of blood nearby.

The gory scene covering the land outside the city walls only conveyed the future to come. Once inside the city, only bloodshed would follow. V knew that no matter what path she took, it would lead to destruction. Her desire for revenge could not be satiated through peaceful means.

It took about thirty minutes riding in the carriage to return to the hill with the tall tree. When she emerged from the carriage, to her surprise, she saw a fleet of chevaliers mounted on horses. A few held lanterns, and one carried the flag of the Jacquard family.

V glanced over her shoulder at the small fleet that had followed her. From what she could tell, Captain Raynard had close to seventy men under his command. She had worried the number would be smaller, but this small fleet could still prove useful.

The chevaliers ahead of them turned to face V and her group. Without hesitation, they raised their weapons, prepared to fight. V ignored them and moved swiftly between them, standing before Judith, who waited outside her carriage with Nabil and Badru at her side.

The chevaliers chattered and gasped when they realized V had slipped past them. She had to show them once again they were no match for her. Judith stared at V in silence for a moment as the wind howled and the cold air caressed her skin. V noted the men around her shivering, their teeth chattering, while she remained unaffected.

She could feel the cold, but her body no longer shivered. Perhaps because her human body had been destroyed years ago. As she looked at her hands, she thought about all the things that now made her different from her former self.

"I had expected ya would already be at the castle with ya power. Maybe I was wrong to think ya alone could handle all of this," Judith taunted.

A scowl formed on V's face. This young woman had become quite vexing with her constant attempts to taunt her. Were all Wescreans like this? V had thought the girl would be different when they first met. Truthfully, Judith had proven to be quite the disappointment.

"Do you think it wise to mock me? I could easily kill you and these blokes in their rubbish armor. Besides, if I defeat Jiya, then you will have no right to claim your throne. It would be mine to claim, for I would have been the one to liberate the people of Fodmery," V chided.

Judith's cheeks were already red from the cold, but they flushed darker. Her teeth chattered as she clutched the thick fur coat likely given to her by Nabil. The Hiorian stood silent by her side. He did not appear to be shivering, though his brown cheeks carried a faint red tinge. Slowly, he stepped forward.

"No reason to be fightin' amongst each other..." Nabil shuddered.

V looked at him, acknowledging the seriousness in his eyes. He was right—they had a common enemy. Nothing else mattered but Jiya. V nodded in agreement. Wasting time bickering with a brat served no purpose.

She could likely reach the castle, but her concern was for the rest of her group. They had no way of getting there as quickly as she and Odessa. Avoiding needless fights would be impossible for them. Still, they had each agreed to focus on their own goals.

Dharma wanted to retrieve Woeton's body, which meant she might have to kill him again if he had been turned into a revenant. The chief wanted to find his daughter Tora, now known as Raisa. Everyone's goals diverged, but thankfully none would interfere with the others.

Unlike before, V saw that Judith could be an ally, since they had similar goals. But where their paths coincided was in the means of achieving them. Judith likely had no intention of truly fighting Jiya—because she would lose. That meant she needed to use Badru. For V, all that mattered was finding and killing Jiya.

Judith and her men could draw Jiya's forces, but how long could they hold? Their numbers were small, and V had no idea what other things lurked in the city besides revenants. She could already sense powerful forces nearby.

"The castle is in the middle of the city, a bit of a distance from here," V muttered.

As she stared into the distance, she heard someone approach from behind. She turned to see Captain Raynard. He exhaled deeply, his cold breath misting in the air. When he reached her, he knelt in the snow, his armor rattling with the movement.

"Princess Judith Jacquard... I, Captain Antoine Raynard, ask that ya accept me and my men into ya fold. We wish to march with ya into the city and help ya reclaim ya family's throne."

Judith stood in silence, staring at him. V grew impatient, wondering what she could possibly be thinking. Then it occurred to her that perhaps she did not know what had become of her brother.

"Where is my brother Jacques?"

"I am gutted to bring the news that he may have been taken after being gravely wounded," Captain Raynard answered.

Judith drew in a deep breath as her expression darkened. She had to be furious and struggling to accept the heartbreaking news. V pitied her, but war always meant loss. The longer she journeyed, the more people she met who had lost dearly because of Jiya.

Had this been Jiya's true intent? Destroying families, sowing more tension between people—even his own. What sort of outcome had he envisioned that would make things better? V wondered if his goal had grown larger than he ever desired.

"That is a shame, but I have no time to grieve. We are still gravely outnumbered," Judith concluded. "Where are the Hiorians?"

Captain Raynard paused, shame flickering across his face. The glimmer of hope V once saw in his eyes had dimmed. "We tried to attack the city the other night, but we suffered great loss against Leon Astier, who is now a powerful revenant."

Disgust twisted Judith's expression. V became instantly curious about her reaction. What was her connection to Leon the Vile? Had she once been betrothed to him? If so, it would amuse V to learn—but it hardly mattered now, since he had been killed twice.

"That bloke had already been a problem when he still lived..."

"Nothing to fret about!" V exclaimed, holding up the sword she had taken from defeating Leon. "I have already slain him and nicked his sword!"

Surprise spread across Judith's face before relief softened her expression. Whatever Leon meant to her, she would never face him again. Nabil glanced at Judith, who still bore a trace of disgust.

"We still need to figure out how to handle this," Nabil interjected.

"Odessa and I can easily reach the castle," V confessed.

"The castle likely has the strongest of his forces waiting—including the Sacred Eight," Captain Raynard sighed.

V looked at him as he stood from his kneeling position. She hadn't heard of the Sacred Eight before. Were they supposed to be Jiya's strongest warriors? If so, it explained the eerie presence she felt nearby.

"What is this Sacred Eight you speak of?"

"Prince Jacques would often go off on his own to gather intel. Some time ago, he returned to our camp with news that Jiya had created eight powerful weapons. Jiya himself has one, but we never learned about the others."

"How did your prince retrieve this information?" V prodded.

"Someone in the castle was trying to help us. But they stopped sending word after we lost the prince. I suspect it was the queen trying to aid us."

"I do not accept that dodgy excuse for my mother would aid us. She abandoned us like a coward when Father had been slain in the throne room!" Judith blurted out angrily.

Everyone looked at her in surprise. V didn't know any of the dynamics about what had happened to her family. She only knew that her father had been killed and Jiya had taken the throne. Now they had to worry about sacred weapons—unknowns in this battle. V had power, but how would she fare against weapons Jiya had likely crafted with the help of the *Tome of Eneida*?

"If you didn't have enough information on the weapons, why would you attack the city?"

"Gamba had spotted Jiya leaving with a large amount of revenants and chevaliers. We planned our attacks, and last night I thought we could finally overtake the city. After our few attacks hadn't drawn out anyone who might wield a sacred weapon, I ordered an attack."

Captain Raynard bore a look of shame and regret. He had likely begun blaming himself for the loss of so many Hiorians and his own men. V felt sorry for him—it reminded her of the times her father lost men in battle with the vampyrs. He had often worn the same look that Captain Raynard now possessed.

"I, along with a few others, made it to the castle using the secret passages. We encountered four of the Sacred Eight there. Gamba managed to defeat one while helping us escape, but..." Captain Raynard fell silent.

No one spoke for several seconds.

"I am going on ahead."

V didn't want to hear anything else. If she was going to get her revenge, it had to be now. Jiya, now within her reach, needed to die. Her years of anguish had to end—she wanted, one day, to be reunited with Jorah.

As V started to push past everyone, Badru rushed toward her. Some of the chevaliers drew their weapons. Without thinking, V moved closer to the boy. He bumped into her, stumbling back and falling into the snow.

"Are you brave, or just plain foolish?" V stared down at him with an emotionless gaze.

His silver eyes filled with tears. Shackles bound his ankles and wrists as he shivered.

"Don't hurt my mama or my siblings, please!" he pleaded.

V's gaze softened. She looked at Judith, then at Nabil.

"Why not give this boy something to keep him warm?" V frowned. "If you plan to keep him as a hostage, then at least take care of him!" she demanded.

"He is the son of my enemy..." Judith said coldly.

"He is a child!" V retorted.

Nabil sighed, removed his coat, and knelt beside the boy. He wrapped it around him; it nearly swallowed him whole. Badru looked frail—the fact he hadn't died of hypothermia amazed V.

"What is your mama's name, child?" V asked softly.

Badru sniffled as Nabil helped him to his feet. "Makena... Grimm."

Nabil's eyes widened as he stared at the boy. V watched as he grabbed Badru's face, looking into his eyes. His lips trembled as he collapsed to his knees. Clearly, this had been something he never expected. Judith hadn't either—she froze as Nabil broke down, bawling.

"What is the meaning of this, Nabil?" Judith demanded.

"Makena is my elder sister... when my family was massacred, Jiya took her and left me for dead," Nabil sobbed.

"Well, this is quite the turn of events..." V muttered in disbelief. "Maybe we should try to locate Makena and see if she can help us defeat Jiya."

"If she is on his side, then she is my enemy. Forgive me, Nabil."

V watched as Nabil pressed his forehead to the boy's. He

gritted his teeth as he rose slowly to his feet. "Makena and dis boy are all da family I have left. I will not risk losing either of them."

"We could try to request a parley," Captain Raynard suggested.

Now they were all at odds. How things would play out had become a mystery. V didn't like it, but she understood it had come to this. She had warned Nabil at the keep, but she hadn't thought it would be like this. The option for a parley might have been the best action—but V had no intention of going about it that way.

"Do not do this, Nabil. I need ya at my side if I am to succeed. If Jiya can be reasoned with, then Makena will not have to be harmed."

"You have no intent to work tings out wit my people if we win dis war. Once you've gotten what you wanted, you will no longer need me," Nabil said, his voice trembling.

A silence fell as the two of them locked eyes. Clearly, there would be no moving forward until this was resolved. While they stood in tension, V noticed something—the carriage she had ridden in was leaving.

Her eyes darted from side to side. The grey skins had taken off. Why had they chosen to leave now? Then she saw Odessa standing beside Badru. The chevaliers drew their weapons. Odessa unsheathed her daggers and cut through Badru's shackles.

"I will meet you at da castle."

V stared at her, confused. "What are you planning to do?"

"We will not get anywhere wit da two of them arguin'."

Without another word, Odessa grabbed Badru and Nabil. The chevaliers rushed her, but she leapt high into the air. V watched her glide toward a building. The chevaliers turned their attention on V, but she struck them down with ease.

She rushed to the edge of the hill. In the distance, she saw Odessa land gracefully on a rooftop with Badru and Nabil.

"What is she doing?" Judith panicked.

"Focusing on the task at hand. Jiya must be defeated, and quarreling with your lover won't accomplish that."

"Captain Raynard!"

From behind, V heard the rattling of armor. She turned to see Captain Raynard approaching.

"Ya called for me?"

"You should make haste—and maybe send a few into the secret passages. By the time I reach the castle, you should be able to slip in with ease."

V leapt into the air, her body gliding like a feather. She couldn't truly fly, but she could cross great distances before landing on the stone rooftops.

If she continued like this, she would reach the castle in minutes. Her eyes locked on it as the cold air kissed her skin. Anticipation for the final battle gnawed at her.

As she moved, the smell of burning reached her nose. Below, buildings had been set ablaze. Shouts of panic filled the air. Hooves pounded against the city streets like war drums.

Odessa had clearly begun to cause a ruckus. V only hoped her fledgling could slip away and reach the castle safely—and that whatever plan Odessa had devised, taking Nabil and Badru with her, would work.

CHAPTER 28

Jiya's treachery pt. 5

Jiya had waited patiently as he watched the queen give birth to their newborn son. He now held the child in his arms as he cried. He had missed the birth of most of his children besides Ramona and Camellia. This would be the first time in a long while he was present.

He stared at the silver-eyed babe in his arms. The curly reddish-brown hair was expected, since his mother was human. As Jiya held him, one of the midwives approached with a bowl of herbs mixed into a paste.

Jiya looked at her, then placed a finger into the greenish substance. He drew a spiral on the babe's stomach. Many Hiorian families had traditions—some similar, others unique.

The Dawnspell family had been the family his great-grandfather came from. After a falling out with his brother, he created the Ashspell family. Ever since then, every newborn Ashspell had this done upon birth.

The spiral represented growth and good health. With this blessing, Jiya hoped this newborn would live a long life—one that didn't lead him down a path like his foolish father. Jiya wanted the world for his children.

Over in the bed, the queen rested, exhausted from pushing the child out. Two Hiorian women served as her midwives.

Jiya began to think of his other concubines. Were they preparing to leave as he had requested? He also thought of Makena —likely roaming the castle with Ashur. Jiya respected Ashur for his trustworthiness, unlike his brother Zahur. Although, he didn't like the fondness Ashur seemed to have for Makena. Jiya didn't love any of these women, but no one else could have them.

"What shall we name you, lil one?" Jiya asked aloud.

The baby cooed, his little eyes gazing up at his father. That strange chill crept over Jiya again. As he stared at his newborn, he realized he had fulfilled everything he had set out to do—or so he hoped. The Hiorians now despised the humans even more, no doubt. He had no illusions—they would march here to slay him for all he had done.

That meant they would have to bloody their hands with the blood of the humans who stood in their way. His only true obstacle was Vlatka. He had to eliminate her so he could finish here and head to Vostaylia.

"Can we name him Leo?" a weak voice called out.

Jiya turned to see the queen's soft green eyes fixed on him. Her fair skin had grown pale from the loss of blood. As he considered her words, anger overtook him. Did she take him for a fool?

"I shall not name a child of mine after your lover Leon!" Jiya snapped.

The queen's eyes widened, her cheeks flushing red. "Ya think I... no, ya are mistaken, my king!" she cried.

"Silence! You take me for a fool? Now I see why you were so quick to throw yourself at me after I slew your king! Not for da sake of your children, but to still be able to see dat scoundrel of a warrior!"

The queen's face twisted with shame and horror. She shook her head repeatedly, her mouth agape. Jiya scoffed, staring at her in disgust. Before he could say more, a hurried knock came at the door.

One of the midwives hurried from the queen's bedside to answer. When she opened it, Ashur and Makena stood in the doorway. Seeing them together sparked Jiya's temper, though he chose to let it pass. He wanted to enjoy the birth of his son.

"Forgive us, but... Gamba has asked to see you," Ashur bowed.

"Ah... so Gamba has finally decided to consider my offer?"

Jiya asked with intrigue.

"I am uncertain, but if you have da time, I will gladly take you to him," Ashur replied.

Jiya reluctantly turned to one of the midwives and handed her his son. He looked at his little boy once more, their eyes meeting. In them, Jiya envisioned the future he wanted: a life filled with love, surrounded by Hiorians, in a kingdom they had built.

Finally, he turned away and approached Ashur and Makena, who waited patiently at the door. As he exited the room, he began to wonder about their relationship. They were around the same age.

"You two are always together. I do not like dat," Jiya admitted.

Ashur rubbed the back of his neck nervously. Makena lowered her head, scratching her hand. Jiya scoffed at how obvious they were.

"You served your purpose, Makena. Wit dat said, I will not stand in da way of your happiness."

Jiya glanced at them briefly before marching down the hall. Once Judith and Vlatka were defeated, he could give this city to his people. They could rebuild with its abundant resources. His goal seemed so close—but he had to ensure Vlatka didn't get in the way.

*

It took a bit of time to get to the west wing. A great deal of activity filled the halls, with many of the Hiorians standing guard at known secret passages. These passages weren't only for escaping the castle—they were also used to move through it faster.

He arrived at the room where Gamba was kept. Two guards stood on either side of the doors. Both bowed as Jiya approached. He knocked, waited a second, then opened the door. Inside, he saw Gamba out on the balcony. His chains rattled as he turned to face Jiya.

The tall Hiorian wore a serious expression. Jiya smiled as he approached, but Gamba shuffled back into the room, his gaze grim, still fixed on Jiya.

"So you finally wish to speak wit me," Jiya jested.

"Da city looks to be gettin' burned to da ground," Gamba replied.

Jiya started to respond but felt a lump in his throat. He quickly covered his mouth and coughed. When he lowered his hand, he realized his palms were moist. Then came the chill —the same that had plagued him since his encounter with Vlatka. What did it mean?

"It would seem our people are truly angry wit me," Jiya tried to joke.

Gamba's stare remained blank. "You are no longer one of us. And what is happenin' out there has nothin' to do wit my people."

"Why did you call for me?"

Gamba stayed tight-lipped, shuffling toward a chair placed beside a wooden desk. Jiya watched as the brooding Hiorian sat down, still saying nothing as he stared blankly at him.

"So many of these revenants protect you. Behind them are humans, and then our people. I finally understand what you were tryin' to do."

Jiya furrowed his brow, intrigued by the conclusion Gamba had come to. "Tryin' to do what?"

"You are tryin' to force us to change so we can survive in dis new world. Back home, we never killed each other—da creatures in da forests, da sea, or up in da mountains did dat." Gamba sighed.

"Aye! It is not da same here..."

"Dat I am aware! In these lands, people are driven by greed and fear of one another. They kill out of jealousy or for sport..." Gamba's face twisted in disgust.

Jiya's heart raced—finally, someone seemed to understand him. If he could get one elder on his side, the others might follow.

"Aye! Dat means we cannot just let them do as they please to us! When we arrived here, we traded wit them, gave them knowledge of many tings. And how did they repay us?"

Gamba said nothing for a moment. "Wit death and chains..."

"Aye!" Jiya smiled, stepping closer. He knelt before the man, lowering his head.

"You knew we would not change, so you forced us to." Gamba glared at him with anger.

Jiya's gaze softened as he reflected on all he had done. "Aye..."

"Your soul is blacker than da wretched woman who cursed my niece."

"You speak of Vlatka Dracul... she will be dealt wit. After I slay her and her uncle back in Vostaylia, I shall accept my fate," Jiya said sincerely.

He knew he couldn't live among his people after all he had done. His children would restore the Ashspell bloodline. Perhaps he'd have a few more before the end of his journey. Jiya stroked his chin as he considered it.

"I may somewhat understand your reasons, but you have doomed us regardless. Even if you succeed here, word of what happened will spread across dis land."

"Dat is da point! They will know not to trifle wit us."

"No... war will come in many ways—whether from humans or spirits you have likely angered."

Jiya stared at him in disbelief. He had hoped for a different outcome. Persuading Gamba to fight alongside him would have been ideal. Convincing him could sway the other elders.

"Wit da Sacred Eight, our people will be unstoppable."

"I managed to best one of da wielders of da Sacred Eight!" Gamba exclaimed.

Jiya pressed his lips together, lacking a rebuttal. Gamba had indeed killed the Wescrean warrior Fabien Lussier—an obnoxious man Jiya had loathed. Losing him felt more relief than loss.

"Aye! You did—but he was human. Imagine if you wielded dat weapon."

Jiya leaned in close, eyes wide. He longed to win Gamba over, to ensure his own victory. If Vlatka survived fighting two of the Sacred Eight, she would be weakened but furious.

"I do not wish to take part in da destruction of our people. Dat is the only outcome of your current actions," Gamba said coldly.

Jiya stared in disbelief. Gamba wouldn't budge. Even though Jiya had given him good living conditions—better than rotting in the dungeon below, infested with vermin—he refused.

Jiya slowly stood upright, disappointment in his eyes. "What if more tings like Vlatka Dracul begin to come out of da shadows?"

"Then it would be your fault. Her existence is a consequence of dat book you used to twist da world," Gamba replied.

Jiya opened his mouth, then shut it. He turned away, stroking his beard. In the silence, the apparition emerged from the shadows. Jiya realized he had been a pawn in their greater scheme. They were planning something that would change the world.

Like a fool, he had played into their hands, moving their pieces for them. Rage boiled in him as he covered his face in disbelief. He had lost his way, blinded by fear and anger.

"All dat I have done... it is far too late to fix tings. I can only hope dat whatever fate awaits me... my children may live, and perhaps rectify my errors," Jiya sighed.

He didn't know if he spoke to Gamba or the apparition. Either way, he could accept whatever outcome came tonight. If victorious, he would continue his quest for vengeance. If he fell, at least he would die knowing he had sparked change.

"Placin' such a burden on children is cruel," Gamba said behind him.

"My papa is da one who taught us of da Spirit World. If I am da reason our people fall into danger, then it must be my children who save us."

Jiya turned back to Gamba. He saw disbelief in his eyes. They would never see eye to eye. That much was clear. An idea struck him. He reached into his bag.

Slowly, he drew out the tome. It whispered as pages flipped, ripples of green light spiraling around him. The whispers grew louder as bubbles formed in the air. Jiya watched as something surfaced.

At last, a sword floated before him. The blade was long and slender, needle-like, with a perfect point for piercing armor. Jiya grasped it, feeling its power surge through him.

He placed it on the table near Gamba. No words were spoken as Gamba stared in confusion. Jiya then withdrew a key from his pocket, placing it beside the sword before turning away.

"You can take dat weapon wit you as you leave. If you choose to stay, I hope it is to aid me."

Jiya didn't look back as he approached the door. He stopped when he heard Gamba's chains rattle. For a moment he waited, but nothing followed. Sighing, he gripped the handle and turned the knob.

CHAPTER 29

As V landed on another building, she sensed movement nearby. What she heard sounded like paws faintly moving about in the snow, stalking something.

She went to the edge of the roof and looked down. In the dark, she saw four large feline creatures. Their thick black fur and blue stripes gave away their identity. These were prowlers, creatures that had terrorized Wescreas for years.

As she continued to peer down at them, she heard something behind her. She turned to see three people in dark cloaks. One of them faced another direction, allowing her to see a symbol on the back of the cloak. It was a strange symbol with what appeared to be a black bird in the middle.

The tallest of the group stepped closer to her. She quickly drew the sword she had taken from Leon. The power surging from it coursed through her as she readied for battle. She didn't know who these people were, but they were living beings.

All of them were breathing and had heartbeats. Although, she could see something like a black veil surrounding the one facing away. This made her wary, for she could sense they had spiritual power.

The tall cloaked figure wore gauntlets that seemed to be made of silver. By his scent, he had to be a Hiorian. She truly had no desire to harm Hiorians, but she had come too close to her goal now. Mercy would not be in the enemy's favor this time.

V knew to be cautious with this one. Another figure carried a spear and had a feminine frame. She too smelled like a Hiorian, which meant both were strong. V took a step back; she had no idea what to expect. What sort of power did these weapons possess?

Then she began to wonder if they were among the Sacred Eight. If that were the case, these weapons would prove dangerous. She had to be careful. If Jiya created them, she had no doubt he crafted them to defeat powerful enemies.

"Who are you?"

When V asked this, the hooded figure who had been facing away turned around. For some reason, V couldn't shake the sense that she knew this person. Then the figure pulled back her hood. The face that greeted her made the rage inside V boil to the surface.

The woman's dark brown hair and beautiful face matched the one V yearned to kill. She realized this woman hadn't aged a day. Not only that, but the woman's eyes were strange—when V gazed upon them, she saw only the eyes of the soulseer she had spoken with.

"Roxana?" V blurted out in disbelief.

"Tis good to see you, Princess Vlatka. When the ritual was completed and you did not return within the next few nights, I feared something had gone amiss," Roxana replied.

"How hath you not aged?" V demanded.

A strange, twisted smile formed on Roxana's face. "Have you taken a gander at yourself lately? You look exactly the same as well."

V gritted her teeth, seething with anger and confusion. "Because you did this to me!" she hissed.

Her fangs bared as she stepped toward her enemies. She wanted to cut them down instantly, but something in the back of her mind warned her to stop. Her hesitation came from the strange veil of black she saw around Roxana.

"And every acolyte at that ceremony has been punished," Roxana said.

A look of regret flickered across her face. V didn't understand what she meant. Why would they be punished if they were meant to summon the spirit they worshipped?

"Punished for what?"

"I performed an unsanctioned ritual."

V's eyes widened in disbelief. "Then why did you do it?" she snapped.

Roxana stood silently, seeming to search for the best answer. "I... did it for Jiya."

V stared at her in disbelief. Hearing this almost made her hunch over with laughter. What she sensed on Roxana's face seemed to be love. She had fallen for that traitorous Hiorian. Now killing him would be all the more fulfilling.

"I have yearned for years to slay thee. Now I can relish thy demise when I present thy head before him!"

V lunged forward, sword raised to strike Roxana down. Before she could reach her, a ripple surged between them, and the large cloaked figure with the gauntlets appeared. Instinctively, V braced herself, raising her sword.

The strike carried immense power. It sent a ripple through the air and made V's hand tremble as she held her blade. Her feet slid back, pushing her to the edge of the roof. She had to make sure not to be struck by those gauntlets—they seemed to be coated in silver. Had Jiya discovered silver could harm her? She had no way of knowing. Another thing she noticed was the immense spiritual energy surging from them.

He pressed forward as sparks jolted around his gauntlets. When he swung his arm, a sharp sound tore through the air. V leapt back as the force from his strike ripped through the wind.

She went flailing across the rooftops, taking a moment to recompose herself—but it didn't last. The other cloaked figure bounded across buildings, carrying a javelin wrapped in cloth and etched with strange symbols. A ripple of energy manifested around the weapon as the woman raised it to throw.

V continued moving toward the castle but glanced back. The javelin flew with all her might. A spark of bright blue blinded V as something whistled through the air. She shifted barely an inch.

A sharp pain jolted from her side through her whole body. She cried out as her body stiffened. Not only that, but she saw lightning strike the building in front of her. Her body fell forward, paralyzed from the graze.

She crashed onto the street. Glancing up, she saw a giant hole in the building across from her. What in the world were these weapons? Could spiritual energy truly be harnessed with such destructive force?

Questions flooded her mind as she staggered to her feet. Immediately, she noticed prowlers stalking from the shadows. She looked down at her side to see a deep gash left behind.

Her black blood dripped onto the ground. The smell of smoke grew stronger, obscuring much of the area. Screams and panic echoed through the city. Odessa had caused chaos, but V now wondered if Roxana had more people with her.

The prowlers edged closer. Five of them, the stripes on their backs beginning to glow. A low growl rumbled from their throats in unison. V's eyes darted left and right, waiting to see which would strike first.

She bared her fangs and hissed. With a swing of her sword, a gust of wind tore through the air. V wanted to show dominance. The prowlers slowly backed away, still growling, their eyes fixed on her.

Her relief didn't last long. The man with gauntlets stepped onto the street. She raised her sword, ready. To get to Roxana, she would have to kill him.

"How could you betray your own people?" V demanded.

The man stood silent for a moment. "We did not betray our people. We sacrifice ourselves so dey can change to survive in dis new world."

V's face twisted in confusion. Jiya had brainwashed them into believing this madness.

"I do not wish to slay you, but if you stay in my way, I will have no choice," V warned.

"I knew dat da path I chose would be treacherous. I accept whatever be da outcome!"

The man rushed forward with startling speed, pulling back his arm to strike. Ripples shimmered in the air around his gauntlets, surging with spiritual power.

V leapt over him as he swung. The impact tore through the space she had just left, the concussive force blasting debris everywhere.

When V landed behind him, she instantly swung her sword. But he leaned left, avoiding the cut. How had he reacted without even looking back?

The enemy twisted around to strike again. V leapt high into the air—but as she rose, something swiftly approached. She jerked her head just in time to evade a deadly blow. A jolt of electricity still caught her, striking her down.

Her body plummeted to the ground a little distance away from the hooded figure with the gauntlets. She groaned in pain as she struggled to get up. The footsteps of the enemy slowly approached her. Frustration welled up inside her again.

Why were there more needless obstacles? All she wanted was to kill the man who had killed the one she loved. These Hiorians created turmoil within her. A part of her hesitated every time because she did not want to cause their people harm. Humans had hurt them enough, and she didn't want to be another enemy to them. But constantly standing in her way made it hard for her to keep the monster inside her from breaking free.

"When Jiya spoke of you, we expected a much mightier foe," the man said in a gruff voice.

"He must have mistook you for someone else!" a feminine voice exclaimed from behind V.

V glanced over her shoulder when she heard a static sound. She looked to see the masked woman holding her javelin, blue sparks visible at its tip. Somehow, these people had managed to tap into spiritual powers V herself hadn't been aware of.

The weapons they carried brimmed with what seemed like spiritual energy. A part of her wondered if their weapons somehow had spirits of their own. V had become fascinated by them.

Unfortunately, they were a hindrance, and they needed to

be dealt with. V channeled her spiritual energy into her sword until she managed to ignite it with blue flames. Then she moved, using the shadows around her.

It was as if the shadows enveloped her, concealing her from her enemies. They looked around in confusion for a moment as V slipped away. She needed power—and that meant she needed blood.

A few streets over, she found a small group of chevaliers running to put out some of the fires. She licked her lips in delight and sprung into action. Some she cut down with her sword. She grabbed one chevalier and tore off his armor.

She plunged her fangs into his neck and let the crimson blood fill her mouth. Memories always affected the taste, and she could taste the wicked things this one had done in life.

As she drained the poor warrior, one of his comrades rushed to help him. V pulled away from the now-dead man and threw his body at the other. A faint chuckle escaped her lips as she went on a frenzy, swinging her sword wildly.

It only took a minute for her to paint the street in blood. She cut down about thirty men before the masked warriors with Roxana appeared. Roxana herself walked into view, her eyes wide in disbelief.

"In Vostaylia there were whispers of a beautiful malefactor who pillaged villages of Hiorians and peasants alike. I had my doubts, but seeing this vampire you have become tells me everything," Roxana sighed.

The words made V go stiff as memories she had tried to bury resurfaced. She remembered losing control when she tried to refrain from drinking blood—the thirst had grown unbearable, and she had attacked a village.

It had been a place where Hiorians were hiding. She had killed them herself. Her list of regrets already bore many shameful acts. V gritted her teeth, clenching her sword.

"So it's a vampire I've become?"

"One restored by the pyre," Roxana said coldly.

V stood silently, absorbing the information. Then she

thought of what she had done as a vampire, and self-loathing filled her. "After I get my revenge, I will atone for those sins."

Roxana scoffed, shaking her head. "Tis been fifteen years! You vowed to set everything asunder—yet thy uncle still lives!"

V's nostrils flared as she snarled. Roxana spoke no lies, and V couldn't accept it. She could have taken revenge, but instead she had cowered in the shadows. After her atrocities, she had run away and hidden.

"You could have prevented so much, but you did nothing!" Roxana laughed.

V roared and lunged forward, sword raised to strike. The man with the gauntlets stepped in front of Roxana. V had predicted this and quickly prepared.

All the blood she had spilled was drawn to her. When she got close enough, she let him strike her—but pressed her blood-covered hand into his chest. Her fingers dug through his light armor and into his flesh.

She cried out in pain as thunder tore through the air. Her body flailed backward, slamming into the ground and rolling until a building stopped her. Her chest burned; when she looked down, she saw her bosom slightly exposed and the imprint of his fist embedded in her flesh.

Black blood spewed from her lips as she struggled to rise. She held out her hand and clenched it into a fist. In the distance, she heard the man cry out in pain. The blood she had driven into him hardened, piercing his chest and reaching his heart.

Her skin burned, but it had been worth it if he was dead. She staggered, drained of strength. Wincing, teeth gritted, she stumbled down the street.

Roxana had disappeared again. The masked man had collapsed, while the woman with the javelin stood over him, motionless. V could hear the woman's heartbeat racing, her breath heavy with stress as she stared down at her companion.

The woman turned to V and slowly removed her mask. She had beautiful chestnut skin, dark brown braids, and silver eyes filled with rage and despair. Tears welled as she threw the mask to the ground. V didn't know her relationship to the man, but she saw the same despair she once felt losing Jorah. But she had no remorse for killing him.

"You will pay for what you did to him!" the woman roared.

She sprinted forward, raising the javelin to throw. Sparks formed around it as she closed the distance. V knew this would be a dangerous gamble, but she wanted to test her power. Channeling her spiritual energy into her sword, she took a stance.

A strike that could split a building in half—that was what she envisioned. The woman let go, and the javelin shrieked toward V. Her eyes widened as she swung her blade downward.

A bright blue light blinded her as a massive explosion shook the area.

*

Debris filled the air as buildings crumbled. The sound of electricity jolted all through the area. In the middle of the street, a large tear in the ground was visible. Such catastrophic damage on this scale was unimaginable.

Unfortunately, the world had begun to change, for the balance between the living and the dead had altered the rules of reality. Smoke and flames now plagued the city. The cries of the citizens echoed all around.

Barely standing in the middle of the road was V. She had a huge hole in the right side of her chest, her body frozen as pain sparked throughout her. The javelin had torn through her like she was nothing. Had she been human, she would have been dead.

V struggled to move forward as her vision blurred. She looked up toward the sky to see a murder of crows spiraling above. The soulseer was somewhere nearby. Did this mean she had failed and was on the brink of death?

No. She rebuked that thought because she couldn't accept death just yet. Her revenge hadn't come to fruition. As she willed herself forward, she smelled blood. The sweet aroma pulled her along as she stumbled down the street.

On the side of the road lay the woman who had thrown the javelin. She still lived, but her arm had been severed. Blood spewed from the wound like a river. Her face had gone pale as she lay there helplessly.

V collapsed in front of the woman, her face landing in the pool of blood. She lapped it up with her tongue, trying to regain her strength. As she lay there, she felt the wound slowly begin to heal. The sweet blood that touched her lips soothed her pain.

"You truly are a monster if you survived dat," the woman choked.

V struggled to lift her head to meet the woman's gaze. Defeat was etched into her face—she clearly had no more strength to fight or move. Death would likely come to her soon.

"My desire for revenge is too strong for me to be slain by the likes of thee," V coughed as she tried to get up.

She crawled over to the woman and tore off a piece of her cloak. Her body felt stiff as she moved to cover the wound. This act clearly confused the woman, who stared at her with suspicion. Once V had finished binding the bleeding, she fell onto her bottom.

"Why are you tryin to help me?" the Hiorian woman asked.

"I never wanted to harm you. Jiya is my enemy because he betrayed his own people and slew the man I loved."

The Hiorian winced as V tightened the cloth around her arm. "Nyack had been my mate... but now he's gone."

V stared silently, then glanced at the dead body lying a few feet away. A sense of regret swelled within her. She had done to another what Jiya had done to her. No—she reminded herself—they had intended to kill her.

"Forgive me. Alas, the two of ye sought to slay me. Jiya hunted down my lover's family. I feel sorry it had to be this way, but I do not regret protecting myself." V's words were stern but sincere.

"Which family did your mate belong to?" the Hiorian asked

weakly.

"The Craft family."

The woman's eyes went wide before she lowered her gaze, shaking her head in disbelief. "Dat is my family."

V stared at her in shock. How could she willingly join Jiya if he had killed her family? It made no sense—unless it was fear. Even then, there was no excuse for slaughtering other families of her own race.

"Why would you join him if he slew your family?" V asked angrily.

The Hiorian looked up at V with a flicker of fear. When V saw it, she finally understood. She didn't see a woman before her anymore but a scared little girl—and it softened her gaze.

"I had been sixteen when he came! Slaughtered my mama and papa, then took my twin sistah to be his mate. Out of fear, and wantin to stay wit my sistah, what choice did I have?" the Hiorian exclaimed.

"I am sorry you had to endure that, but you no longer hath to be afraid of him. Tis my sole mission to slay him," V said, placing her hand on her chest.

"You are dis Vlatka Dracul dat he fears... now I see why," she said nervously.

A faint smile formed on V's face. "What be your name?"

The Hiorian hesitated. "Zalika..."

V stared at the woman she now knew as Zalika, then struggled to her feet. She towered over the helpless Hiorian. She had the power to end her life—to punish her for daring to try to kill her.

"Do you know where thy sister be?"

Zalika remained silent, staring at V with worry. She placed her trembling hand over her wound. "Likely bein kept in da east wing of da castle."

"Can you stand?"

V's words carried on the wind. With it came the smoke and the smell of fire. The chaos in the city had grown tremendously. She had to hurry to the castle to end it all.

Slowly, Zalika staggered to her feet. V held out her hand, looking around for the javelin. She focused her spiritual energy to reach for it. After a moment, a ripple of green resembling a hand wrapped around the weapon where it had pierced a wall.

It took effort to pry it free, but it began to move. V watched in awe as it flew through the air toward her. A faint whisper followed it. When it finally hovered before her, she urged Zalika to take it.

Zalika hesitated before slowly wrapping her fingers around it. "Why?"

"I am giving you a chance to choose to use this weapon to protect thy people."

Regret darkened Zalika's face. "He said dat da humans would have wiped us out if he did not do it himself. Those dat survived would then rise up to protect da rest of us from bein massacred by humans."

"In order to save thy people... he must first destroy them."

Zalika's eyes widened, then slowly nodded. "Dat is what he said... when he took me from Silverkeep."

V looked up at the murder of crows overhead. She didn't fully understand Jiya's reasoning, but she could glimpse it. Perhaps his intentions had once been honorable—but they were tainted by his lack of accountability for his own sins.

"I had been so caught up tryin to keep my sistah safe I did not see da consequence my actions would cause to da veil between us and da Spirit World," Zalika muttered.

V nearly asked her to explain but decided she would learn soon enough. She staggered down the road, her body aching and twitching from the javelin's jolts. She glanced back to see Zalika limping after her.

CHAPTER 30

Jiya's treachery pt. 6

Jiya sat silently alone in the throne room. He stared at the green banners hanging on the walls, the long green carpet that stretched all the way to the double doors at the end of the hall, and the pillars of stone that lined the path. Such a place didn't feel right for a Hiorian.

He wanted his people to adjust to the new world, but in doing so he had cast aside their ideals. He had betrayed everyone in his attempt to force change. His treachery had tarnished the name of his family even more.

As he sat in silence, thinking over everything that had happened in the past few years, the apparition appeared. Jiya took in a deep breath as he gripped the tome tightly on his lap.

"Did you accomplish what you set out to do?" the apparition asked.

"I sowed da seeds of change into my people. It is up to them whether my dream is fulfilled. As for da Ashspell name, it has been restored so long as my children survive all of dis," Jiya confessed.

"Makena has fled with Ashur..."

Jiya stiffened at this. He breathed deeply as he pondered his feelings, then shrugged, deciding it didn't matter. His son Badru had been lost anyway.

"Hopefully, they can make it out of da city."

The apparition moved slowly toward the steps that led to the throne. "Ramla managed to get your children out of da castle."

Jiya furrowed his brow, tilting his head in confusion. "What about Zahina?"

The apparition's face went still for a moment. Then a faint smile seemed to creep onto that accursed face. Jiya's nostrils flared as suspicion clouded him.

"Zahina and her twins chose to remain here until da return of Zahina's sistah."

Jiya's heart began to race. He didn't want the children to be present. It would be bad enough for the queen to remain, but the twins as well? As he stared at the apparition, it felt more and more like they were playing a twisted game.

Were they enacting divine punishment upon him? Everything had begun when he slaughtered most of the Craft family. If the children remained here, they would bear scars from his sins before they were even born.

Jiya slowly stood with the Tome of Eneida in his left hand. "Is dis what you wanted?"

With his right, he grabbed the sword resting at his side. He descended the altar steps until he was face to face with the apparition.

"You have salted da land of Wescreas by meddling wit da dead. Now we shall see what becomes of da land after dis great battle," the apparition smiled.

"Will da other soulseers hunt you down?"

"I had nothin to do wit dis. You did dis. And since you are still alive, I am sure da queen will not punish you—at least not until after you die."

The apparition turned away. Once again, that chill crawled over Jiya's body. He didn't feel cold, so what was it?

"You vile trickster... I will destroy you!" Jiya shouted.

He lunged with his sword. With a swift stroke, he tried to cut through the apparition, but it merely shifted to the side. As it moved, parts of its cloak broke into smoke.

"Trickster? I never tricked you—I warned you about da dangers of da tome."

Jiya sneered. "These twisted games you play is da reason your queen imprisoned you! Now look at you—powerless!"

A ripple of green surged from the apparition, washing over

the hall. A powerful gust of wind slammed Jiya across the chamber. His body struck the cold stone wall, the tome clattering to the ground.

He winced, struggling to rise, but the atmosphere had changed. The air grew thin. His skin crawled. His gut screamed for him to flee. He looked up to see the apparition's otherworldly eyes fixed on him.

"Do not let da lil power you gained from da book make you more foolish than you already are!"

Jiya gritted his teeth as he staggered to his feet. "Da real you is within Roxana, right?"

The apparition tensed. Jiya smirked, realizing he may have struck a nerve.

"If I destroy da tome and kill her, then you will be no more. Am I correct?"

"You would be wise not to try either of those tings," the apparition warned.

Jiya straightened, regaining his composure. They had made him feel weak, but only for a second. He refused to let it fester.

"You would be wise not to try your mind games wit me," Jiya retorted.

The apparition smirked faintly, then turned away. Without another word, it disappeared, leaving Jiya alone.

The throne room doors swung open and Roxana marched in. Jiya made his way back to the throne. The look of concern on her face told him he would not like the news she carried.

"What troubles you?" Jiya asked.

Roxana knelt at the altar, her head bowed. "Forgive me, but the enemy has infiltrated the castle."

Jiya sank into the throne, taking deep breaths. He stroked his temple with a finger. The battle had begun within the castle—expected, of course, since the secret passages would be used. But what troubled him was that the enemy had made it through the traps and guards.

"Judith will not succeed in reclaiming her family's throne."

He swiftly stood and marched down the steps. Roxana lifted

her head as he extended his hand to her. She hesitated, then took it, and he pulled her close.

"Find Judith and bring her to me."

"As you wish... my king."

Her eyes lingered on his, her breath sharp and quick. He could feel her heart racing. The control he had over her had proven useful over the years. It made him wish all his concubines had been this easy to bend.

"Do not lose track of her like they did wit her brudda."

"I shall not fail you."

Jiya held her close a moment longer. He was beginning to enjoy the power of a king over his subjects. What had once felt foreign was now something he craved.

Finally, he released her and watched her back away, cheeks red, eyes still locked on him. Then she turned and marched out the way she had come.

*

The minutes that Jiya sat waiting for someone to enter the throne room once again felt like hours. Finally, the doors swung open with Roxana dragging someone with her whip. Jiya furrowed his brow as he sat up, curiosity overtaking him.

"Dat does not appear to be da princess!"

Roxana pulled the whip one more time before stopping at the altar. Jiya eyed the person struggling to breathe. She had gray skin with long black hair. Her blue eyes were watery as she stared up at Jiya with fear.

"Another grey skin... of da Scarstone tribe, I presume."

"Forgive me, my king. I chose to take her as bait. This one here was closer to reach. Alas, I am certain the princess will come."

Before Jiya could respond, someone rushed into the throne room. Raisa had panic and worry in her eyes. She breathed heavily as she tried to catch her breath. Behind her stood Woeton, covered head to toe in blood.

"Let her go, Lady Roxana!" Raisa exclaimed.

"She comes to slay thy father. I too am troubled, for she appears to be of thy kind. Alas, we must protect our king," Roxana explained.

"Roxana..."

Jiya slowly rose from his seat. Roxana quickly turned to face him with an unsettled look. Her actions made Jiya angry—he wanted the princess, not some other bait. He hardly cared about anyone else.

Now Roxana would have executed someone who resembled his daughter Raisa. He couldn't allow such an irreparable error to go unpunished. Slowly, he drew his sword as he approached where Roxana stood.

"Did I not ask for da princess?"

Roxana lowered her gaze, shoulders slumping. "I... yes, you did."

"Then why is she not here, and instead you have brought me one of those savages?" Jiya snapped.

"Forgive me, my king. I shall retrieve the princess at once."

Roxana started to turn, but Jiya quickly grabbed her shoulder. He swung her around and drove his sword into her stomach. Raisa's scream echoed through the throne room.

The sword glowed as it drank the blood pouring from Roxana's wound. She stumbled back, clutching her stomach as blood flowed freely.

"As da vessel of dat wretched soulseer, you have been nothin but a hinderance!"

"What is da meanin of dis, papa?"

Raisa rushed to Roxana and caught her as she fell. Jiya stood silently, watching the ring on Roxana's finger glow. She pressed her hand over the wound as spiritual energy poured into it. Slowly, her wound began to heal. Jiya scoffed, concluding she had prepared for this.

He turned to the grey skin still lying on the ground. She had just managed to unwrap the whip from her throat. Jiya saw the burns the weapon left on her neck. He reached down, grabbed her by the hair, and began to pull her up—only to notice Woeton moving from his blind side, spear in hand.

But before Woeton could strike, he collapsed. Jiya erupted in hysterical laughter. As the giant lay struggling to rise, tears rolled down Jiya's face from laughing so hard.

"You cannot kill your master, sadly," Jiya sneered.

He returned his attention to the young grey skin glaring at him with rage. Her eyes mirrored the fury he once saw in Vlatka's. That chilling rage... he would not allow another Vlatka to come into being.

Jiya raised his sword to deliver a swift, clean death. Torture had no place here. She deserved a quick end.

But as he struck, his blade met metal instead of flesh. He turned his head to see Raisa, one of her axes braced between his sword and the grey skin.

"What is da meanin of dis, child?"

"I see now dat you have become lost behind dat book. Da look in your eyes shows me you take delight in dis. No longer can I stand for dis!" Raisa exclaimed.

Jiya tossed the grey skin aside and stared at his daughter in disappointment. He snapped his fingers and the Tome of Eneida floated to his side, its pages flipping as waves of green rippled out.

"You chose to stay when I wanted to protect you from da monstrous tings I planned to do to end all of dis!" Jiya roared.

Raisa stepped back as a large gust of wind exploded from around him. Debris floated into the air as an ominous force surged from the tome. A howling sound echoed through the chamber.

The doors burst open again. A young Hiorian with two more grey skins entered. The Hiorian was wounded, but he quickly raised his bow and drew an arrow. He fired at Jiya's head, but a bubble of green waves deflected it. A smirk spread across Jiya's face as the castle began to rumble.

"Dis is where it ends for da Wescrean kingdom!" he declared triumphantly.

A large number of warriors poured in. The princess marched

behind the front line, determination burning in her eyes. Jiya glanced toward a door in the far corner of the throne room. It burst open, releasing a unit of revenant warriors.

He had prepared for this moment. Either the princess would be defeated, or he would die. It no longer mattered. The only thing he desired was to make it clear to the humans that his people were not to be trifled with.

"Jiya Ashspell! Ya must stop your madness, now!" the princess shouted.

"Dis will end when you kneel—or strike me down!" Jiya bellowed.

He looked down at the gathering below. Hatred, disbelief, anger—all etched on their faces. None of it mattered anymore. His hands were already stained, and all he could do now was play the part he had chosen.

CHAPTER 31

It took a bit of time for V to manage to get to the castle gates. The trek through the city showed her the carnage left behind by Odessa. She couldn't believe she had done all this on her own.

Citizens had lost their homes and were fleeing the city. Many of the chevaliers were dead or busy trying to put out fires.

V began to wonder how Odessa managed to do all this while keeping Badru and Nabil at her side. Why had she even taken off with them in the first place? There were too many things V felt uncertain about at the moment.

When she got to the gate, she saw flames bright as the sun. Her eyes winced from the blaze as she marched forward. Captain Raynard and a few of his men were fighting the enemy chevaliers and revenants. They struggled, but still managed to push them back.

Odessa, on the other hand, was locked in battle with someone wielding a strange curved sword. It was single-edged, long enough for two hands, with a wavy pattern that added to its appeal. The spiritual energy oozing off the weapon produced what appeared to be flaming feathers with every strike.

As V walked slowly through the gate she could see the wounds on Odessa.

"Dat is Emiko, wielding one of da sacred eight," Zalika gestured with her javelin.

"Emiko? Tis a foreign name, no?" V asked curiously.

"Aye! She comes from a place known as Shey Dria."

V stood in silence for a few seconds watching all the battles before her. Then she lunged forward on instinct and got in between them. She swiftly swung her broadsword and cut a revenant's hand off. He merely watched as his hand and weapon fell to the ground.

Unlike her, they didn't feel pain. She also believed that they could roam freely during the day. Leon was an abnormal revenant, possessing power the others seemed to lack.

It would be something V could study after she finished what she needed to do here. She raised her hand, and blue flames ignited around the revenants. Some of them began to scream as they fell to the ground. V watched as their bodies withered and their spirits seemed to incinerate.

She observed this blazing spectacle briefly before setting her eyes on Odessa's fight. She had to help her before she got herself killed.

As she stood there, motionless, the sounds of swords and shouting ceased.

"You are truly powerful... and frightening," Zalika's voice called out.

V turned to see Zalika walking over. Clearly, her wound would make it hard for her to be of any use. If she wanted to find her sister, she had no strength to fight.

"You best hurry and find thy sister. I fear this castle will not remain standing much longer."

Zalika's eyes went wide before she nodded and quickly made her way toward the tall building looming over them like a giant shadow.

"Captain Raynard!" V called.

A second later, Captain Raynard rushed over. His forest-green eyes held a look of amazement. "Ya called for me?"

"Did you not use the secret passageways to get into the castle?"

"No. Princess Judith and her men took that route. Losing Badru left her with no choice but to take the castle by force," Captain Raynard replied.

"I see... can I entrust you with an important endeavor?"

"Ja! What will ya have me do?"

"Zalika must get to the east wing to find her sister and then be escorted safely out of the castle."

Captain Raynard's lips parted as his eyes darted from V to Zalika. Then he closed his mouth, took a deep breath, and nodded. Without another word, he waved to Zalika to follow him.

V watched briefly as they left, then turned her focus back to Odessa. With great haste, she reached her in a second, managing to block an oncoming attack from Emiko. V winced as she felt the flames sparking off the blade. Fire affecting her surprised her—but these flames were made from spiritual energy.

Now only inches away, V got a good look at Emiko's face. She had beige-colored skin and long black hair that reminded V of crows as it flowed freely in the wind.

"You are wounded..."

V glanced at Odessa, who stood with determination in her eyes. Her fangs were visible as she kept her gaze locked on the enemy.

"I am fine..."

"Where are Badru and Nabil?"

"I found his mama while we were movin through da city, fleeing with Zahur's brudda. I let them go wit her."

V raised an eyebrow. "Zahur's brother?"

"Aye! A much kinder man than dat wicked one you killed for my sake."

Odessa's eyes shifted briefly toward V, then she rushed at Emiko again. Their weapons clashed, sending a large gust of wind that pushed V back a step.

"Find Jiya! I will be right behind you soon!" Odessa shouted.

V stood in place, unwilling to leave Odessa behind. She worried for her but also understood she needed to grow. Odessa had to be able to fight her own battles.

"Do not dawdle—or I shall defeat him alone," V ordered.

Without another word, she turned and began walking toward the castle. At long last, revenge felt within her grasp. It was so close she could almost taste the bittersweet warmth of killing Jiya.

Killing him wouldn't just satisfy her thirst for vengeance

but would also benefit his own people. They would no longer feel threatened by one of their own. Although, what he had done would surely create future conflicts for them.

Alas, those were problems for the future. For now, he needed to be stopped. When she fought him before, she had seen how lost he seemed. He shouted so many things as if he had it all together—but truthfully, he had fallen astray. She too had fallen astray from the person she once was.

As she marched up the steps, flashes of a future she would never see crossed her mind. Thanks to Jiya, she had become a monster that thirsted for blood, weakened by the sun—and perhaps doomed to die from it.

"I knew you would come," a familiar voice said.

V looked up to see Gamba standing at the top of the steps. In his hand he held a strange sword: long, straight, and thin like a needle. Jewels adorned the guard, and a small chain hung from the hilt. Spiritual energy rippled off it.

"So you hath joined him..."

V couldn't hide her disappointment. As she waited for him to respond, she began to wonder where Jawara was. She doubted he had already encountered his father. That meant he was still searching somewhere in the castle.

"He chose da harsher path to remove da blinds dat cover my people's eyes."

V looked at Gamba with great disappointment. She believed he had more wisdom than his mouth conveyed. Sadly, she had been mistaken. Misjudging people had become a flaw of hers, it seemed.

"A path that makes thy people feared. If you hath not noticed, humans often seek to slay what they fear." V cautioned.

Gamba bit his lip and lowered his gaze. Clearly, he agreed with V's sentiments. For once he didn't seem to want to argue. It gave her a little delight seeing he had no rebuttal.

"I agree wit you. Dat book has corrupted him and da land. It has created tings like you—and I fear more shall follow."

"Then I must make haste to end him."

V took a step forward up the stairs, but Gamba impeded her advance. She glared with a menacing gaze. Wasting time with him would be a hindrance, especially if Jiya was trying to escape. She needed to find him and end this once and for all.

"We must get everyone out of dis city." Gamba cautioned.

"Why?"

"Da princess and her warriors got into da castle and cornered him in da throne room."

V stared at him blankly. Why did this require evacuating the city? It made no sense and hardly mattered to her. She only came to kill him—then leave.

"Then do that, but do not stand in my way."

She took another step, but Gamba once again blocked her. Her eyes ignited with rage as she aimed her sword at his throat. She had no more patience after nearly being killed a little while ago.

"I saw him open da tome and ominous tings seeped out of it. Da throne room became infested with black roots, and some of da princess' warriors dat touched it had their life drained. Even he has started to change."

Gamba trembled as he spoke, and the fear in his eyes finally made V understand the importance of his words. She lowered her sword and stared off into the distance.

"You must find your son. I fear he is in here somewhere."

Gamba's eyes widened in horror as he finally stepped aside. He rushed up the steps toward a large set of double doors. V sighed with relief as she started ascending after him, though worry about Yama lingered in her chest.

As much as she wanted to find her, dealing with Jiya now had to be her priority. If he had done something that could cause irreparable damage, he needed to be stopped. No more people needed to die because of his foolish actions.

Once inside, she found herself in a large hall. Corpses littered the floor. Black roots twisted in the corners, pulsing with green waves. As she stood motionless, she felt a suffocating sensation in the air.

Gamba rushed straight ahead, throwing caution to the wind. V followed after him, hoping he would lead her to the throne room. This would be where it all ended. He ran quickly, but she hardly needed effort to keep up.

After a minute, she stood in a long corridor. More bodies lay scattered, wrapped in roots. Green waves glowed brighter here. At the end of the hall stood a massive set of doors. Screaming and the clash of blades echoed from within.

"The throne room..." V shuddered.

Gamba continued onward with the strange needle-sword in hand. V clicked her tongue as she realized it would all end here. She rushed after him into the unknown. The doors swung open, revealing a horrific sight.

Jiya stood locked in battle with the chief, Jawara, and the princess. Many chevaliers who came with her had fallen. Roxana lay lifeless in a corner, and Raisa seemed to be trying to shake Yama awake.

Dharma stood in front of the two young grey skins, protecting them from a revenant. V's eyes widened in horror—it was Woeton attacking Dharma. The Tome of Eneida floated in the air, rippling with green light. The sound of whispers disoriented V as she stepped into the throne room.

Gamba marched down the green carpet with haste. "Stop dis madness, Jiya! Close da book before it consumes us all!"

Jiya ignored him, swinging his sword to unleash a strange miasma toward the princess. As she stumbled back, a chevalier rushed to her aid and shoved her aside. Blood splattered everywhere as the miasma engulfed him.

V watched the man collapse in a pool of blood. She couldn't believe the chaos before her. Revenants, Hiorians, humans—all mixed together in death.

Jiya advanced toward the princess. The chief blocked his path but was struck down with ease. V froze, wide-eyed, as Jiya ran his sword through Judith.

A chill ran down V's body as a burst of energy erupted from Judith. Jiya cackled with excitement as the shadow beneath him grew. Judith stumbled back and collapsed to the ground.

Quickly, V rushed to Yama's side. She knelt beside Raisa to check on her. Relief overtook her—Yama still breathed. Yet her condition filled V with fury.

"What path hath you chosen to follow? He has already slain the princess."

Raisa looked at V, wide-eyed, her mouth falling open. Her gaze darted from Yama to Jiya. Slowly, her eyes welled with tears. She lowered her head and sighed.

"He has been lost to da tome..."

V squeezed Raisa's hand. "Get her out of the city for me. Take care of her."

Raisa nodded, then grabbed Yama. V watched her carry her away. They both had to live—they were no longer needed here. This place would soon be a grave for the fallen.

Turning, V saw Dharma still struggling against Woeton. He overpowered her easily, about to strike her down—until V intervened. He froze and looked at her with a soft gaze.

"Ye hath to end my suffering, for I doth not want to slay her..."

V bit her lip. She didn't want to cut down a former ally. Annoying though he had been, she had grown fond of him. Dharma lay on the ground, tears in her eyes as she struggled to rise.

"Forgive me..."

V moved swiftly, shoving her hand into Woeton's chest. Her fingers wrapped around his heart. She felt no heartbeat, but ignited a small flame—just enough to put him down permanently.

His lips quivered as he sighed in relief. His body staggered and collapsed. Black vines crept toward him, but V burned them away with blue fire.

"Take him as far as you are capable, Dharma."

As she turned, her eyes caught the trail of blood where Roxana had lain. Her body was gone. Rage surged inside V—if Roxana had escaped, she would have to be hunted down again.

Finally, she marched toward the true battle. Jiya had already struck the chief down. Jawara tended to him while the princess fired arrows from afar—futile against Jiya.

Now Jiya and Gamba were locked in a duel. To V's surprise, Gamba showed great skill with his weapon. The needle-sword excelled at fencing and parrying. He looked a natural swordsman.

He pushed Jiya back on his heels, their weapons clashing as spiritual energy burst forth. Waves of force knocked debris across the hall. The sheer power amazed V.

Gamba leapt back for distance, landing near V. He glanced at her before turning back to Jiya. She did the same, noting Jiya's look of displeasure.

"Seein you here means those two failed to kill you." Jiya's cold words echoed through the room.

Standing before him, V finally saw the change overtaking him. His eyes glowed a pale green. A black shadow wrapped around him like a cloak.

A subtle grin formed on V's lips. "My thirst for revenge is far too strong for me to be slain so easily."

"I suppose it is better for me to be done wit you myself!"

Jiya lunged forward with bloodlust in his eyes. V charged at him, swinging the sword she had taken from Leon. They clashed with such force that the ground beneath their feet broke apart.

Whispers and howling roared from the tome floating in the air. Black roots tore through the ground like shadows, latching onto dead bodies. V caught glimpses of the roots draining the last remnants of life that remained in them.

As she and Jiya clashed again, he swung his sword differently, slipping past her blade to nick her wrist. She thought the wound small—but her black blood spewed out in torrents.

Jiya cackled as she stumbled back, trying to avoid his advance. Gamba intervened with a piercing strike, but Jiya easily countered, retreating to gain distance.

V grimaced, realizing the wound was much deeper than

she'd thought. How could such a small cut bleed so much? He had the advantage—better swordsmanship.

She pressed forward, swinging at his neck. Jiya struck down on her sword, knocking her off balance. As she fell forward, she saw his blade coming toward her, her eyes widening in horror.

Before it could reach her, a figure tackled her out of the way. Her body rolled, and when she stopped, she saw a familiar face. Kneeling on top of her, covered in blood, was Odessa.

"You hath made it back to me…" V smiled softly.

"You did not expect dat I would let you fight him without me, did you?" Odessa smiled weakly.

The clash of steel caught both their attention. Jiya and Gamba were locked in precise, brutal combat.

V stood and extended her hand. Spiritual energy flowed to her fingertips like a river. Blood in the room was drawn to her, forming into pellets. She flung them at Jiya, striking hard and knocking him off balance. He cried out as he raised a hand.

A massive black root burst from the ground, shielding him from the blood pellets. Gamba stood aside, watching in disbelief. Odessa flanked from the right.

They would end him here and now—together.

Odessa went in for the kill, but Jiya raised his hand, and a root sprouted from the shadow at his feet. V barely noticed it before it wrapped around Odessa, lifting her into the air. Her life force was being drained before V's eyes.

She leapt to aid her but was ensnared by roots herself. Helpless, she could only watch as Gamba fought desperately to evade.

Frustration boiled over. V channeled immense power, conjuring a large blue flame. A haze of light illuminated the chamber as the roots withered, shrieking and crumbling.

She rushed to free Odessa. Together they sprang into action, flanking Jiya while his back was turned. V aimed for his head as Odessa went for his side.

But Jiya leapt into the air, twisting his body. Black roots sprouted, carrying him upward. V struck at them with her sword, but the blade stuck fast. She grunted, struggling. Gazing up, she saw Jiya staring down at her.

"For someone so consumed by madness, he still proves to be a true warrior," Gamba groaned.

"Tis quite vexing, to say the least." V replied.

"We must destroy dat book!" Odessa exclaimed.

"We hath no idea what would happen if we do. It should be a last resort," V retorted.

With a hard tug, she freed her sword, then looked to see Judith's body entangled in black roots. Her life force had been completely drained.

"Tis over, Jiya! You hath slain the princess!" V shouted.

"It is over—but now I must slay you!"

He leapt from the giant root perch. V swung upward, knocking him aside. Gamba and Odessa rushed him, blades clashing as sparks flew. Desperation showed in Jiya's face.

V tried to aid them, but her wound still bled. She stumbled, black blood pooling at her feet. She felt lightheaded but pressed forward, gritting her teeth.

The three fought fiercely, cornering Jiya while dodging his sprouting roots. He targeted V, her sluggish movements giving the others openings. Through her pain, V smiled—he was faltering. His breath came ragged, his strikes slowing.

She lunged, grazing his chest with her blade. Blood spilled. Jiya roared, summoning massive roots that blocked her from her comrades.

When she broke through, she saw Odessa fighting Jiya alone. Gamba had been pinned by roots.

Odessa fought with a speed V had never seen before, pushing Jiya back. V rushed to help, but another root snared her. Her energy drained, her flames sputtered out. She struggled in vain.

Jiya swung at Odessa's head. She ducked, spinning forward, her daggers slashing his stomach. Blood sprayed. He swung wildly, but she pressed on, cutting his arms and legs until he stumbled.

Then a root snared her arm.

V's eyes widened. She hacked desperately, but too late. Jiya struck—a fatal blow to Odessa.

"No!"

Gamba broke free and charged, but Jiya kicked Odessa to the ground to free his blade. V tore loose and rushed to her side.

Odessa bled out, her wound refusing to heal. Her sapphire eyes stared up at V.

"I thought I could..." she choked.

"You must not leave me..."

"Forgive me..." she winced. "I want you to know—I am grateful you stood by me when my mama gave up on me."

V's eyes widened as Odessa wept. She held her tightly, then bit her own wrist, pressing it to Odessa's lips. Black blood trickled—but Odessa coughed it out. Her wound would not heal.

"Drink my blood... end his sufferin..." Odessa whispered, holding up her own wrist.

V trembled at the thought. But with no choice left, she bit and drank. Memories flooded into her—Odessa's pain, joy, sorrow, and secret love for her. For a fleeting moment, warmth filled V.

When she pulled away, Odessa's life was gone. V's lips quivered as rage consumed her.

She rose, powerful once more. Across the room, Jiya and Gamba fought, both gravely wounded. The Tome of Eneida floated nearby.

In an instant, V appeared beside Jiya. He swung, but she blocked with ease. She seized the tome in her bare hand. It burned, but she held firm, channeling her flames until it ignited. The book howled as it withered.

"No!" Jiya screamed, slashing wildly. V dodged, blocking every strike as the ground shook. The castle crumbled around them.

"Get Odessa out of here, Gamba!" V shouted.

But she kept her focus on Jiya, refusing to hesitate again.

He poured his life force into each attack, miasma waves lashing out. She darted through shadows, faster than his eye could follow.

Then, with one final surge, she drove her blade through his heart.

"So dis is how it ends..." Jiya gasped. "Does dis make you feel better?"

V stared silently at him as the roots consumed his body.

"I hope your soul is tormented for all that you hath done."

She tore his sword from his hand as he fell. The roots wrapped him fully, dragging him into the abyss he had unleashed.

Debris crashed all around as she stood amidst the ruin. Her revenge was hollow, unsatisfying—but at last, Jiya Ashspell was no more.

*

The city had completely been swallowed up by black roots. V had made it out of the castle as the roots overtook it entirely. A large wave of ripples appeared in the sky, giving V an ominous chill as she sat silently on the hill overlooking the city.

She still didn't fully understand all of Jiya's reasoning for the things he did. Although, she understood that this would force great change among his people. The Wescreans would be lost until they found another ruler. When that time came, the Hiorians would likely be in danger.

"Forgive me, for I failed to be with thee in the final battle," a singsong voice said.

V turned to see Yama standing with a look of regret on her face. Behind her were Jawara and Raisa. "I wanted to look out for Odessa but failed."

"No... it was not thy battle to take part in."

Yama stood silently as her eyes welled with tears. She quickly tried to wipe them away, but they had already begun to flow. V wanted to hug her, but she couldn't move. Now that she had plunged into darkness, she couldn't turn back. All she could do was cut the threads that still tied her to the little good that remained within her.

V looked around the area at the wounded people Captain Raynard had gathered. She saw Zalika with who she assumed to be her sister. The woman had two children huddled together by a fire.

Sitting alone with a baby was a woman with long red hair. Two servants tended to her. From what V could see, the woman reminded her of the princess. Could this have been her mother? Did it even matter, since the princess had died?

She continued to scan the camp and saw Dharma tending to the chief, who was wounded. Next to him was Woeton's body. V quickly looked away, feeling anger that Jiya had turned him into a revenant. She had no doubt he did it just to spite her.

Then V saw Gamba sitting in silence beside Odessa's body. He had covered her with a blanket he must have found somewhere. All this only made V question whether what Jiya had done was worth it. Was killing him worth all the lost lives?

She cursed the day she met Jiya and hoped his soul would never find rest. The crows that had circled the city all night were now steering clear. It felt like a foreboding sign, but V decided it was a concern for another time.

Now she needed to go while her blood still boiled—while her mind still felt dead set on killing. She turned to face Yama, for it would be the last time she saw her.

"Goodbye, Yama. Live for Odessa and my sake."

Yama looked at V with confusion on her face. She parted her lips to speak, but V turned away. Nothing she could say would change anything. V only hoped Yama knew how much she had grown to mean to her.

With no more words to say, she disappeared into the night. Revenge had tasted bitter, but she didn't plan to let it sour her thirst for more.

www.ingramcontent.com/pod-product-compliance
Lightning Source LLC
Chambersburg PA
CBHW070630260626
47161CB00007B/2650